THE TOWER OF SWALLOWS

By Andrzej Sapkowski

The Last Wish
Sword of Destiny
Blood of Elves
The Time of Contempt
Baptism of Fire
The Tower of Swallows

The Malady and Other Stories:
An Andrzej Sapkowski Sampler (e-only)

THE
TOWER OF SWALLOWS

ANDRZEJ SAPKOWSKI

Translated by David French

www.orbitbooks.net

Original text copyright © 1997 by Andrzej Sapkowski
English translation copyright © 2016 by David French
Excerpt from *Battlemage* copyright © 2015 by Stephen Aryan

Cover design by Lauren Panepinto
Cover illustration by Bartomiej Gawe, Pawe Mielniczuk, Marcin Baszczak, Arkadiusz Matyszewski, Marian Chomiak
Cover copyright © 2016 by Hachette Book Group, Inc.

Originally published in Polish as *Wieża Jaskółki*

Orbit
Hachette Book Group
1290 Avenue of the Americas
New York, NY 10104
orbitbooks.net

Published by arrangement with Literary Agency Agence de l'Est
Simultaneously published in Great Britain by Gollancz in 2016
First U.S. Edition: May 2016

Orbit is an imprint of Hachette Book Group.
The Orbit name and logo are trademarks of
Little, Brown Book Group Limited.

The publisher is not responsible for websites (or their content) that are not owned by the publisher.

The Hachette Speakers Bureau provides a wide range of authors for speaking events. To find out more, go to www.hachettespeakersbureau.com or call (866) 376-6591.

Library of Congress Control Number: 2016932537

ISBN: 978-0-316-27371-8

Printed in the United States of America

LSC-C

10 9

To Dun Dâre they came at dead of night
For to seek the witcher maid
They ringed the hamlet from all sides
And sealed it with a barricade

Seize her they would in perfidy
But their plans were all in vain
Ere the sun arose on the frozen road
Three dozen brigands lay slain

A beggar's song about the frightful massacre which took place in
Dun Dâre on Samhain Eve

'I can give you everything you desire,' said the fortune-teller. 'Riches, power and influence, fame and a long and happy life. Choose.'

'I wish for neither riches nor fame, neither power nor influence,' rejoined the witcher girl. 'I wish for a horse, as black and swift as a nightly gale. I wish for a sword, as bright and keen as a moonbeam. I wish to overstride the world on my black horse through the black night. I wish to smite the forces of Evil and Darkness with my luminous blade. This I would have.'

'I shall give you a horse, blacker than the night and fleeter than a nightly gale,' vowed the fortune-teller. 'I shall give you a sword, brighter and keener than a moonbeam. But you demand much, witcher girl, thus you must pay me dearly.'

'With what? For I have nothing.'

'With your blood.'

Flourens Delannoy, *Fairy Tales and Stories*

CHAPTER ONE

As is generally known, the Universe – like life – describes a wheel. A wheel on whose rim eight magical points are etched, making a complete turn; the annual cycle. These points, lying on the rim in pairs directly opposite each other, include Imbolc, or Budding; Lughnasadh, or Mellowing; Beltane, or Blooming; and Samhain, or Dying. Also marked on the wheel are the two Solstices, the winter one called Midinvaerne and Midaëte, for the summer. There are also the two Equinoxes – Birke, in spring, and Velen, in autumn. These dates divide the circle into eight parts – and so in the elven calendar the year is also divided up like that.

When they landed on the beaches in the vicinity of the Yaruga and the Pontar, people brought with them their own calendar, based on the moon, which divided the year into twelve months, giving the farmer's annual working cycle – from the beginning, with the markers in January, until the end, when the frost turns the sod into a hard lump. But although people divided up the year and reckoned dates differently, they accepted the elven wheel and the eight points around its rim. Adopted from the elven calendar, Imbolc and Lughnasadh, Samhain and Beltane, both Solstices and both Equinoxes became important holidays, sacred tides for human folk. They stood out from the other dates as a lone tree stands out in a meadow.

Those dates are also set apart by magic.

It was not – and is not – a secret that the eight dates are days and nights during which the enchanted aura is greatly intensified. No longer is anyone astonished by the magical phenomena and mysterious occurrences that accompany the eight dates, in particular the Equinoxes and Solstices. Everyone is now accustomed to such phenomena and they seldom evoke a great sensation.

But that year it was different.

That year people had, as usual, celebrated the autumnal Equinox with a solemn family meal, during which all the kinds of fruits from that year's harvest had to be arrayed on the table, even if only a little of each. Custom dictated it. Having eaten and given thanks to the goddess Melitele for the harvest, the people retired for the night. And then the nightmare began.

Just before midnight a frightful storm got up and a hellish gale blew, in which a ghastly howling, screaming and wailing were heard above the rustling of trees being bent almost to the ground, the creaking of rafters and the banging of shutters. The clouds driven across the sky assumed outlandish shapes, among which the most common were silhouettes of galloping horses and unicorns. The gale did not abate for a good hour, and in the sudden silence that followed it the night came alive with the trilling and whirring of the wings of hundreds of goatsucker nightjars, those mysterious fowl which – according to folk tales – gather together to sing a demonic death knell over a dying person. This time the chorus of nightjars was as mighty and loud as if the entire world were about to expire.

The nightjars sang their death knell in clamorous voices while the horizon became shrouded in clouds, quenching the remains of the moonlight. At that moment sounded the howl of the fell beann'shie, the harbinger of imminent and violent death, and across the black sky galloped the Wild Hunt – a procession of fiery-eyed phantoms on skeleton horses, their tattered cloaks and standards fluttering behind them. So it was every few years. The Wild Hunt gathered its harvest, but it had not been this terrible for decades – in Novigrad alone over two dozen people went missing without a trace.

After the Hunt had galloped by and the clouds had dispersed, people saw the moon – on the wane, as was customary during the Equinox. But that night the moon was the colour of blood.

Simple folk had many explanations for these equinoctial phenomena, which tended to differ considerably from each other according to the specifics of local demonology. Astrologers, druids and sorcerers also had their explanations, but they were in the main erroneous and cobbled together haphazardly. Few, very few, people were able to connect the phenomena to real facts.

On the Isles of Skellige, for example, a few very superstitious people saw in the curious events a harbinger of Tedd Deireadh, the end of the world, preceded by Ragh nar Roog, the last battle between Light and Darkness. The violent storm which rocked the Islands on the night of the Autumn Equinox was regarded by the superstitious as a wave pushed by the prow of the fearsome Naglfar of Morhögg, a longship with sides built of dead men's fingernails and toenails, bearing an army of spectres and demons of Chaos. More enlightened or better informed people, however, linked the turmoil of the heavens with the evil witch Yennefer, and her dreadful death. Others yet – who were even better informed – saw in the churned-up sea a sign that someone was dying, someone in whose veins flowed the blood of the kings of Skellige and Cintra.

The world over, the autumn Equinox was a night of spectres, nightmares and apparitions, a night of sudden, suffocating awakenings, fraught with menace, among sweat-soaked and rumpled sheets. Neither did the most illustrious escape the apparitions and awakenings; Emperor Emhyr var Emreis awoke with a cry in the Golden Towers in Nilfgaard. In the North, in Lan Exeter, King Esterad Thyssen leaped from his bed, waking his spouse, Queen Zuleyka. In Tretogor, the arch-spy Dijkstra leaped up and reached for his dagger, waking the wife of the state treasurer. In the huge castle of Montecalvo the sorceress Philippa Eilhart leaped from damask sheets, without waking the Comte de Noailles' wife. The dwarf Yarpen Zigrin in Mahakam, the old witcher Vesemir in the mountain stronghold of Kaer Morhen, the bank clerk Fabio Sachs in the city of Gors Velen and Yarl Crach an Craite on board the longboat *Ringhorn* all awoke more or less abruptly. The sorceress Fringilla Vigo came awake in Beauclair Castle, as did the priestess Sigrdrifa of the temple of the goddess Freyja on the island of Hindarsfjall. Daniel Etcheverry, Count of Garramone, awoke in the besieged fortress of Maribor. As did Zyvik, decurion of the Dun Banner, in Ban Gleann fort. And the merchant Dominik Bombastus Houvenaghel in the town of Claremont. And many, many others.

Few, though, were capable of connecting all those occurrences and phenomena with an actual, specific fact. Or a specific person. A stroke of luck meant that three such people were spending the night of the autumn Equinox under one roof. They were in the temple of the goddess Melitele in Ellander.

*

'Lich fowl . . .' groaned the scribe Jarre, staring into the darkness filling the temple grounds. 'There must be thousands of them, whole flocks. They're crying over someone's death. Over her death . . . She's dying . . .'

'Don't talk nonsense!' Triss Merigold spun around, raised a clenched fist, and, for a moment, looked as though she would shove the boy or strike him in the chest. 'Do you believe in foolish superstitions? September is coming to an end and the nightjars are gathering before taking flight! It's quite natural!'

'She's dying . . .'

'No one is dying!' screamed the sorceress, paling in fury. 'No one, do you understand? Stop talking nonsense!'

Several young female adepts appeared in the library corridor, aroused by the nocturnal alarm. Their countenances were grave and ashen.

'Jarre.' Triss had calmed down. She placed a hand on the boy's shoulder and squeezed hard. 'You're the only man in the temple. We're all watching you, looking for support and succour from you. You must not fear, you must not panic. Master yourself. Do not let us down.'

Jarre took a deep breath, trying to calm the trembling of his hands and lips.

'It is not fear . . .' he whispered, avoiding the sorceress's gaze. 'I'm not afraid, I'm troubled! About her. I saw her in a dream.'

'I saw her too.' Triss pursed her lips. 'We had the same dream, you, I and Nenneke. Not a word about it.'

'Blood on her face . . . So much blood—'

'Be silent, I say. Nenneke approaches.'

The high priestess joined them. She looked weary. She shook her head in answer to Triss's wordless question. Seeing that Jarre had opened his mouth, she forestalled him.

'Nothing, sadly. Almost all the girls awoke when the Wild Hunt flew over the temple, but none of them had a vision. Not

8

even one as hazy as ours. Go to bed, lad, you cannot help. Back to the dormitory, girls.'

She rubbed her face and eyes with both hands.

'Oh . . . The Equinox! This accursed night . . . Go to bed, Triss. We can do nothing.'

The sorceress clenched her fists. 'This helplessness is driving me to insanity. The thought that somewhere she is suffering, bleeding, that she's in peril . . . If I only knew what to do, dammit!'

Nenneke, high priestess of the temple of Melitele, turned around.

'Have you tried praying?'

*

In the South, far beyond the mountains of Amell, in Ebbing, in the land called Pereplut, on the vast marshes crisscrossed by the rivers Velda, Lete and Arete, in a place eight hundred miles as the crow flies from the city of Ellander and the temple of Melitele, a nightmare jerked the old hermit Vysogota from sleep. Once awake, Vysogota could not for the life of him recall his dream, but a weird unease prevented him from falling asleep again.

*

'It's cold, cold, cold,' said Vysogota to himself, as he tramped along a path among the reeds. 'It's cold, cold, brrr.'

Yet another trap was empty. Not a single muskrat. A most unsuccessful night. Vysogota cleaned sludge and duckweed from the trap, muttering curses and sniffing through his frozen nostrils.

'It's cold, brrr, hooeee!' he said, walking towards the edge of the swamp. 'And September not yet over! It's but four days after the Equinox! Ah, I don't recall such chills at the end of September, not for as long as I've lived. And I've lived a long time!'

The next – and penultimate – trap was also empty. Vysogota didn't even feel like cursing.

'There's no doubt,' he wittered on, as he walked, 'that the climate grows colder with every passing year. And now it looks as though the cooling will progress apace. Ha, the elves predicted that long since, but who believed in elven forecasts?'

Once again small wings whirred, and incredibly swift grey shapes flashed by above the old man's head. Once again the fog over the swamps echoed with the wild, intermittent churring of the goatsucker nightjars and the rapid slapping of their wings. Vysogota paid no attention to the birds. He was not superstitious, and there were always plenty of lich fowl on the bogs, particularly at dawn. The air was so thick with them he feared they would collide with him. No, perhaps there weren't always as many as there were today, perhaps they didn't always call quite so bloodcurdlingly . . . Ah well, he thought, latterly nature has been playing queer pranks, and it's been one oddity after another, each one queerer than the last.

He was just removing the last – empty – trap from the water when he heard the neighing of a horse. The nightjars suddenly all fell silent.

There were hummocks on the swamps of Pereplut: dry, raised places, with river birch, alder, dogwood and blackthorn growing on them. Most of the hummocks were surrounded so completely by the bogs that it was impossible for a horse or a rider who didn't know the paths to reach them. But the neighing – Vysogota heard it once again – was coming from one of them hillocks.

Curiosity got the better of caution.

Vysogota was no expert on horses and their breeds, but he was an aesthete, and was able to recognise and appreciate beauty. And the black horse he saw framed against the birch trunks, with its coat gleaming like anthracite, was extraordinarily beautiful. It was the sheer quintessence of beauty. It was so beautiful it seemed unreal.

But it *was* real. And quite really caught in a trap, its reins and bridle entangled in the blood-red, clinging branches of a dogwood bush. When Vysogota went closer, the horse put its ears back and stamped so hard the ground shuddered, jerking its shapely head and whirling around. Now it was clear it was a mare. There was something else. Something that made Vysogota's heart pound frantically, and invisible pincers of adrenaline tighten around his throat.

Behind the horse, in a shallow hollow, lay a body.

Vysogota dropped his sack on the ground. And was ashamed of his first thought; which was to turn tail and run. He went closer, exercising caution, because the black mare was stamping her hooves, flattening her ears, baring her teeth on the bit and just waiting for the opportunity to bite or kick him.

The corpse was that of a teenage boy. He was lying face down, with one arm pinned by his trunk, the other extended to one side with its fingers digging into the sand. The boy was wearing a short suede jacket, tight leather britches and soft knee-high elven boots with buckles.

Vysogota leaned over. And just then the corpse gave a loud groan. The black mare gave a long-drawn-out neigh and thumped its hooves against the ground.

The hermit knelt down and cautiously turned over the injured boy. He involuntarily drew back and hissed at the sight of the ghastly mask of dirt and congealed blood where the boy's face should have been. He delicately picked moss, leaves and sand from the spittle- and mucous-covered lips, and tried to pull away the matted hair stuck with blood to his cheek. The injured boy moaned softly and tensed up. And began to shake. Vysogota peeled the hair away from the boy's face.

'A girl,' he said aloud, unable to believe what was right in front of him. 'It's a girl.'

*

That day, had someone quietly crept up at dusk to the remote cottage in the midst of the swamp with its sunken, moss-grown thatched roof, had they peered through the slits in the shutters, in the weak glow of tallow candles, they would have seen a teenage girl with her head thickly bound in bandages, lying with almost corpse-like motionlessness, on a pallet covered in animal skins. They would also have seen an old man with a grey, wedge-shaped beard and long white hair, which fell down onto his shoulders and back from the edge of a broad bald patch that extended from his soiled forehead far beyond his crown. They would have noticed the old man lighting another tallow candle, placing an hourglass on the table, sharpening a quill and hunching over a leaf of parchment.

11

Seen him ponder and mumble something to himself, keeping a close watch on the girl lying on the pallet.

But it would not have been possible. No one could have seen it. The cottage of the hermit Vysogota was well concealed amidst the marshes, in a wilderness permanently shrouded in mist, where no one dared to venture.

*

'We shall note down as follows,' Vysogota dipped his quill in the ink, 'Third hour after my intervention. Diagnosis: *vulnus incisivum*, an open wound, dealt with great force using an unidentified sharp instrument, probably a curved blade. It encompasses the left part of the face, beginning in the infraorbital region, running across the cheek and extending as far as the parotid plexus and masseter muscle. The wound is deepest – reaching the periosteum – in the initial part beneath the orbit on the zygomatic bone. Probable length of time from when the wound was sustained to when it was first dressed: ten hours.'

The quill scratched on the parchment, but the scratching didn't last longer than a few moments. Or lines. Vysogota did not find everything he said to himself worthy of being written down.

'Returning to the dressing of the wound,' the old man began again, staring at the flickering and smoking candle flame, 'let us write as follows: I did not excise the edges of the cut, I limited myself to the removal of shreds of dead tissue and coagulated blood. I bathed the wound with willow bark extract. I removed dirt and foreign bodies. I put in sutures. Hemp sutures. Let it be written that I did not have any other kinds of thread at my disposal. I used a poultice of wolfsbane and applied a formed muslin dressing.'

A mouse scampered out into the middle of the chamber. Vysogota threw it a piece of bread. The girl on the pallet breathed restlessly and groaned in her sleep.

*

'Eighth hour following my intervention. Condition of the patient – unchanged. Condition of the doctor . . . I mean *my* condition . . .

has improved, since I have enjoyed a little sleep . . . I can continue my notes. It behoves me to commit onto these leaves some information about my patient. For posterity. Assuming that posterity reaches these swamps before everything decays and crumbles into dust.'

Vysogota sighed heavily, dipped his quill and wiped it on the edge of his inkwell.

'As far as the patient is concerned,' he muttered, 'let the following be noted down. Age, I would say, around sixteen. Tall, strikingly slim build, but by no means puny, no indication of undernourishment. Musculature and physical construction rather typical for a young elf-woman, but no mixed-blood traits found . . . Can't be more than one eighth elven. A smaller proportion of elven blood may, of course, not leave any traces.'

Vysogota only now seemed to have realised that he hadn't written a single word on the page. He put his quill to the parchment, but the ink had dried. The old man was not bothered in the slightest.

'May it be noted,' he continued, 'that the girl has had no children. I emphasise: I refer to old scars. No shortage of fresh wounds on her body. The girl has been beaten. Flogged, and by various means, probably at her father's hand. She has probably also been kicked.

'I also found on her body quite a strange distinguishing mark . . . Hmmm . . . Let's write this down, for the good of science . . . The girl has a red rose tattooed on her loins, right by the pubic mound.'

Vysogota stared at the sharpened quill point before dipping it into the inkwell. This time, though, he did not forget why he had done it – he quickly began to cover the page with even lines of sloping script. He wrote until the quill was dry.

'She was talking and shouting in befuddlement,' he said. 'Her accent and way of expressing herself – if I pass over frequent interjections in profane criminal cant – are quite confusing, difficult to place, but I would risk the assertion that they originate rather from the North than the South. Some of the words . . .'

Once again his quill scratched over the parchment, much too briefly to write down everything he had said a short while before.

And then he took up his monologue in exactly the place he had left it.

'Some of the words and names the girl mumbled in her delirium are worth remembering. And investigating. Everything suggests a very – I mean very – extraordinary person has found their way to old Vysogota's cottage . . .'

He said nothing for a while and listened.

'I just hope,' he muttered, 'that old Vysogota's cottage doesn't prove the end of her road.'

*

Vysogota bent over the parchment and even pressed his quill to it, but wrote nothing, not a single letter. He threw the quill onto the table. He breathed heavily for a while, muttered angrily and blew his nose. He looked at the pallet and listened to the sounds coming from it.

'It must be stated and noted,' he said in a weary voice, 'that things look very ill. All my endeavours may be insufficient, and my exertions in vain. My fears were well-founded. The wound is infected. The girl is most worryingly feverish. Three of the four cardinal symptoms of acute inflammation have appeared. *Rubor*, *calor* and *tumor* can easily be confirmed by eye and touch. When the post-treatment shock passes, the fourth symptom – *dolor* – will also appear. Let it be writ that almost half a century has passed since I have practiced medicine. I feel the years weighing on my memory and the dexterity of my fingers. I have little practical skill, and there is little I can do. I have painfully few resources or medicaments. The only hope lies in the young body's immune mechanisms . . .'

*

'Twelfth hour following my intervention. In accordance with expectations came the fourth cardinal symptom of inflammation: *dolor*. The patient is crying out in pain, the fever and shivers are growing stronger. I have nothing, not a single physic to give her. I have a small quantity of stink weed elixir, but the girl is too frail

14

to survive its effects. I also have monk's hood, but monk's hood would surely kill her.'

*

'Fifteenth hour following my intervention. Dawn. Patient unconscious. The fever advances rapidly, the shivers intensify. Moreover, powerful spasms of the facial muscles are occurring. If it is tetanus the girl is done for. Let us hope it is only the facial nerve . . . Or the trigeminal nerve. Or both of them . . . The girl would be left disfigured . . . But she would live . . .'

Vysogota glanced at the parchment, on which not a single word was written.

'On condition,' he said hollowly, 'that she survives the infection.'

*

'Twentieth hour following my intervention. The fever advances. The *rubor, calor, tumor* and *dolor* are reaching, I venture, critical limits. But the girl has no chance of survival, of even reaching those limits. Thus do I write . . . I, Vysogota of Corvo, do not believe in the existence of gods. But were they by any chance to exist, let them take this girl into their care. And may they forgive me what I have done . . . If what I did turns out to be in error.'

Vysogota put down his quill, rubbed his swollen and itchy eyelids, and pressed a fist against his temple.

'I have given her a mixture of stink weed and monk's hood,' he said hollowly. 'The next hours will determine everything.'

*

He was not sleeping, only dozing, when a knocking and a pounding accompanied by a groan wrenched him from his slumber. It was a groan more of fury than of pain.

Outside, the day was dawning. A faint light filtered through the slits in the shutters. The hourglass had run its course long before; as usual Vysogota had forgotten to turn it over. The oil lamp flickered, and the ruby glow of the hearth dimly lit the corner of the

15

chamber. The old man stood up and moved away the makeshift screen of blankets which separated the pallet from the rest of the room, in order to give the patient peace and quiet.

The patient had already picked herself up from the floor where she had fallen a moment earlier, and was sitting hunched on the edge of her pallet, trying to scratch her face under the dressing. Vysogota cleared his throat.

'I asked you not to rise. You are too feeble. If you need anything, call. I'm always at hand.'

'Well, I don't want you to be at hand,' she said softly, under her breath, but quite clearly. 'I need to pee.'

When he returned to remove the chamber pot, she was lying on her back on the pallet, fingering the dressing attached to her cheek by strips of bandage wrapped around her forehead and neck. When he went over to her again a moment later she was in the same position.

'Four days?' she asked, looking at the ceiling.

'Five. Almost a day has passed since our last conversation. You slept the whole day. That is good. You need sleep.'

'I feel better.'

'I'm gladdened to hear it. Let's remove the dressing. I'll help you sit up. Take my hand.'

The wound was healing well and cleanly. This time the removal of the bandages passed without the painful tearing of the dressing from the scab. The girl gingerly touched her cheek. She grimaced, but Vysogota knew it wasn't only from the pain. Every time she checked the extent of the disfigurement she appreciated the gravity of the wound. She made certain – with horror – that what she had touched before had not been a fevered nightmare.

'Do you have a looking glass?'

'I do not,' he lied.

She looked at him totally clear-headed, possibly for the first time.

'You mean it's that bad?' she asked, cautiously running her fingers over the stitches.

'It's a very long cut,' he mumbled, angry at himself that he was making excuses and justifying himself to a girl. 'Your face is still swollen. In a few days I shall remove the sutures. Until then I shall be applying wolfsbane and extract of willow. I shall no longer bandage your entire head. It's healing nicely. Very nicely.'

She did not reply. She moved her mouth and jaw, and wrinkled and contorted her face, testing what the wound permitted and what not.

'I've made pigeon broth. Will you eat some?'

'I will. But this time I'll try by myself. It's humiliating to be spoon-fed when I'm not paralysed.'

Eating took her a long time. She lifted the wooden spoon to her mouth cautiously, using as much effort as if it weighed two pounds. But she managed without the help of Vysogota, who was observing her with interest. Vysogota was inquisitive – and burning with curiosity. He knew that the girl's return to health would lead to conversations which could throw light on the whole mysterious matter. He knew it and couldn't wait for that moment. He had lived too long alone in the wilderness.

She finished eating and sank back onto her pillow. For a moment she gazed lifelessly at the ceiling and then turned her head. The extraordinarily large green eyes, Vysogota realised once again, gave her face an innocently childlike expression, now clashing violently with her hideously disfigured cheek. Vysogota knew those looks; a big-eyed, permanent child, were a physiognomy arousing an instinctive sympathetic reaction. A perennial girl, even when her twentieth, thirtieth, why, even fortieth birthday had long ago sunk into oblivion. Yes, Vysogota knew those looks well. His second wife had been like that. And his daughter, too.

'I must flee from here,' the girl suddenly said. 'Urgently. I'm being hunted. You know that, don't you?'

'I do,' he nodded. 'Those were your first words, which contrary to appearances were not ravings. To be more precise, they were among the first. First you asked about your horse and your sword. In that order. Once I had assured you that your horse and sword were in good hands, you became suspicious that I was the comrade of a certain Bonhart and wasn't treating you but inflicting the torture of hope. When, not without difficulty, I put you right, you introduced yourself as Falka and thanked me for saving you.'

'I'm glad.' She turned her head away on the pillow, as though wanting to avoid meeting his eyes. 'I'm glad I didn't forget to thank

17

you. I remember that vaguely. I didn't know what was reality and what was a dream. I was afraid I hadn't thanked you. My name's not Falka.'

'I learned that, too, although rather accidentally. You were talking in your fever.'

'I'm a runaway,' she said, without turning around. 'A fugitive. It's dangerous to give me shelter. It's dangerous to know what I'm really called. I must get on my horse and flee, before they catch up with me . . .'

'A moment ago,' he said kindly, 'you had difficulty sitting on a chamber pot. I don't really see you mounting a horse. But I assure you, you are safe. No one will track you here.'

'I'm certainly being pursued. They're on my trail, combing the area . . .'

'Calm down. It rains every day, no one will find your tracks. You are in a wilderness, in a hermitage. In the home of a hermit who has cut himself off from the world. To such an extent that it would also be difficult for the world to find him. If, however, you wish it, I can look for a way to send tidings about you to your family or friends.'

'You don't even know who I am—'

'You are a wounded girl,' he interrupted, 'running from somebody who does not flinch from injuring girls. Do you wish me to pass on some tidings?'

'There is no one,' she replied a moment later, and Vysogota's ear caught a change in her voice. 'My friends are dead. They were massacred.'

He made no comment.

'I am death,' she began again, in a strange-sounding voice. 'Everyone who encounters me dies.'

'Not everyone,' he contradicted, scrutinising her. 'Not Bonhart, the one whose name you screamed out in the fever, the one you are running from. Your encounter seems to have harmed *you* rather than him. Did he . . . did he cut your face?'

'No.' She pursed her lips, to stifle something which was either a groan or a curse. 'My face was cut by Tawny Owl. Stefan Skellen. But Bonhart . . . Bonhart hurt me much more gravely. More deeply. Did I talk about that in the fever?'

18

'Calm down. You're weak, you should avoid powerful emotions.'

'My name is Ciri.'

'I'll make you a compress of wolfsbane, Ciri.'

'Hold on . . . a moment. Give me a looking glass.'

'I told you—'

'Please!'

He did as she asked, judging that he had to, that he could delay it no longer. He even brought the oil lamp. So she could better see what had been done to her face.

'Well, yes,' she said in an altered, trembling voice. 'Well, yes. It's just as I thought. Almost as I thought.'

He went away, pulling the makeshift screen of blankets after him.

She tried hard to sob quietly, so he wouldn't hear.

*

The following day Vysogota removed half of the stitches. Ciri touched her cheek, hissed like a viper, and complained of an intense pain in her ear and heightened sensitivity in her neck near her jaw. Nonetheless, she got up, dressed, and went outside. Vysogota did not protest. He went out with her. He didn't have to help her or hold her up. The girl was healthy and much stronger than he had expected.

She only wobbled once outside, and held on to the door frame.

'Why . . .' she said, sucking in lungfuls of air. 'What a chill! Is it a frost or what? Winter already? How long have I been lying here? A few weeks?'

'Exactly six days. It's the fifth day of October. But it promises to be a very cold October.'

'The fifth of October?' She frowned and hissed in pain. 'How can it be? Two weeks . . .'

'What? What two weeks?'

'Never mind,' she shrugged. 'Perhaps I've got something wrong . . . But perhaps I haven't. Tell me, what is it that reeks around here?'

'Pelts. I hunt muskrat, beaver, coypu and otter, and cure their hides. Even hermits have to make a living.'

'Where's my horse?'

'In the barn.'

The black mare greeted them with loud neighing, joined by the bleating of Vysogota's goat, which was greatly displeased by having to share its lodgings with another resident. Ciri hugged the horse's neck, patted it and stroked its mane. The mare snorted and pawed the straw with a hoof.

'Where's my saddle? Saddlecloth? Harness?'

'Here.'

He did not protest, make any comments nor voice his opinion. He leaned on his stick and said nothing. He did not move when she grunted trying to lift the saddle, didn't budge when she staggered beneath the weight and flopped down heavily onto the straw-covered floor with a loud groan. He did not approach her or help her to stand. He watched intently.

'Very well,' she said through clenched teeth, pushing away the mare, which was trying to shove its nose down her collar. 'I get it. But I have to move on from here, dammit! I must!'

'Where would you go?' he asked coldly.

Still sitting on the straw next to her fallen saddle, she touched her face.

'As far away as possible.'

He nodded, as though her answer had satisfied him, made everything clear and didn't leave any room for speculation. Ciri struggled to her feet. She didn't even try to reach down to pick up the saddle or harness. She just checked that there was hay and oats in the manger, and began to rub the horse's back and sides with a wisp of straw. Vysogota stood in silence. He didn't have to wait long. The girl staggered against the post supporting the ceiling, now as white as a sheet. Without a word he handed her his stick.

'There's nothing wrong with me. It's just—'

'It's just you felt giddy, because you're sick and as weak as a kitten. Let's go back. You must lie down.'

*

Ciri went out again at sunset, after sleeping for a good few hours. Vysogota, returning from the river, happened upon her by the bramble hedge.

'Don't go too far from the cottage,' he said curtly. 'Firstly, you're too weak—'

'I'm feeling better.'

'Secondly, it's dangerous. There is a huge marsh all around us, endless tracts of reeds. You don't know the paths, you might get lost or drown in the bog.'

'And you,' she said, pointing at the sack he was dragging, 'know the paths, of course. And you don't walk that far, so the swamp can't be so huge at all. You tan hides to support yourself, I understand. Kelpie, my mare, has oats, but I don't see any fields around here. We ate chicken and groats. And bread. Real bread, not flatbread. You couldn't have got the bread from a trapper. So there's a village nearby.'

'Unerringly deduced,' he calmly agreed. 'Indeed, I get provisions from the nearest village. The nearest, which doesn't mean it's near. It lies on the edge of the swamp. The swamp adjoins the river. I exchange pelts for food, which they bring me by boat. Bread, kasha, flour, salt, cheese, sometimes a coney or a hen. Occasionally news.'

No question was forthcoming, so he continued.

'A band of horsemen on the hunt were in the village twice. The first time they warned people not to hide you, they threatened the peasants with fire and sword if you were seized in the village. The second time they promised a reward for finding your corpse. Your pursuers are convinced that you're lying dead in the forests, in a gorge or a ravine.'

'They won't rest,' she muttered, 'until they find a body. They have to have proof that I'm dead. They won't give up without that proof. They'll root around everywhere. Until they finally end up here . . .'

'It really matters to them,' he observed. 'I'd say it matters uncommonly to them . . .'

She pursed her lips.

'Don't be afraid. I'll leave before they find me here. I won't put you at risk . . . Don't be afraid.'

'Why do you think I'm afraid?' he shrugged. 'Is there a reason to be afraid? No one will find this place, no one will track you here.

If, however, you stick your nose out of the reeds, you'll fall straight into your pursuers' hands.'

'In other words,' she tossed her head proudly, 'I have to stay here? Is that what you mean?'

'You aren't a prisoner. You can leave when you want. More precisely: whenever you're able to. But you can stay with me and wait. Your pursuers will eventually become disheartened. They always get disheartened, sooner or later. Always. You can believe me. I know what I'm saying.'

Her green eyes flashed when she looked at him.

'And anyway,' he said quickly, shrugging and avoiding her gaze, 'you'll do as you please. I repeat, I'm not holding you a prisoner here.'

'I don't think I'll leave today,' she said. 'I'm too weak . . . And the sun will soon be setting . . . And anyway I don't know the paths. So let's go back to the cottage. I'm frozen.'

*

'You said I've was lying here for six days. Is that true?'

'Why would I lie?'

'Don't take on. I'm trying to count the days . . . I ran away . . . I was wounded . . . on the day of the Equinox. The twenty-third of September. If you prefer to count according to the elves, the last day of Lughnasadh.'

'That's impossible.'

'Why would I lie?' she screamed and then groaned, grabbing her face. Vysogota looked calmly at her.

'I don't know why,' he said coldly. 'But I was once a doctor, Ciri. Long ago, but I'm still capable of distinguishing between a wound inflicted ten hours ago and one inflicted four days ago. I found you on the twenty-seventh of September. So you were wounded on the twenty-sixth. The third day of Velen, if you prefer to count according to the elves. Three days after the Equinox.'

'I was wounded on the Equinox itself.'

'That's impossible, Ciri. You must have got the dates wrong.'

'I most certainly haven't. You've got some antiquated hermit calendar here.'

'Have it your way. Does the date carry such importance?'
'No. It doesn't.'

*

Vysogota removed the last stitches three days later. He had every reason to be pleased and proud of his work – the line was even and clean, there was no need to fear a tattoo of dirt embedded in the wound. However, the satisfaction of the surgeon was spoiled by the sight of Ciri, in sombre silence, contemplating the scar in the looking glass held at various angles and trying vainly to cover it by pulling her hair over her cheek. The scar disfigured her. It was simply a fact. Nothing could be done. Pretending that it was different could not help in any way. Still scarlet, bulging like a cord, surrounded by needle punctures and marked with the scars from the stitches, the scar looked truly horrifying. There was a chance of it undergoing gradual or even rapid improvement. Vysogota knew, though, that there was no chance of the disfiguring scar vanishing.

Ciri was feeling much better, and to Vysogota's astonishment and pleasure did not talk about leaving at all. She led her black mare, Kelpie, out of the barn. Vysogota knew that in the North the name kelpie was borne by a water spirit, a dangerous sea monster, according to superstition able to assume the form of a splendid steed, dolphin or even a comely woman, although in reality it always looked like a heap of seaweed. Ciri saddled her mare and trotted around the yard and cottage, after which Kelpie went back to the barn to keep the goat company, while Ciri went to the cottage to keep Vysogota company. She even helped him – probably out of boredom – as he worked with the pelts. While he was segregating the coypu according to their size and colouring, she divided the muskrats up into backs and bellies, slitting the skins along slats inserted into them. Her fingers were exceptionally nimble.

While they worked they had quite a strange conversation.

*

'You don't know who I am. You can't even imagine who I am.'
She repeated that banal statement several times and slightly

23

annoyed him with it. Of course, he did not betray his annoyance – he wouldn't betray his feelings before such a chit. No, he couldn't allow that, nor could he betray the curiosity that was consuming him.

Groundless curiosity, in truth, for he could have guessed who she was without any difficulty. Gangs of youths hadn't been rare in Vysogota's younger days, either. Nor could the years that had passed eliminate the magnetic power with which gangs lured whelps, hungry for adventure and thrills. Very often to their death. Whelps flaunting scars on their faces could count their luck; torture, the noose, the hook or the stake awaited the less fortunate of them.

Since Vysogota's younger days only one thing had changed – growing emancipation. Not only teenage boys, but also reckless girls, preferring a horse, a sword and adventures to lace-making, the spinning wheel and waiting for the matchmakers.

Vysogota did not say all that straight out. He said it in a round-about way, but so that she knew that he knew. To make her aware that if someone in the cottage was an enigma, it was certainly not her – a young thug from a band of underage thugs who had miraculously escaped a manhunt. A disfigured teenage girl trying to cloak herself in an aura of mystery . . .

'You don't know who I am. But don't worry. I'll be leaving shortly. I won't put you at risk.'

Vysogota had had enough.

'I'm not at risk,' he said dryly. 'For what peril would there be? Even if a search party were to show up here, which I doubt, what ill could befall me? Giving help to fugitive criminals is punishable, but not for a hermit, since a hermit is unaware of worldly matters. It is my privilege to give asylum to anyone who comes to my retreat. You said it correctly: I don't know who you are. How am I, a hermit, to know who you are, what mischief you've been up to and why the law is pursuing you? And which law? For I don't even know what law applies in this region, or what and whose jurisdiction I live in. And it does not concern me. I am a hermit.'

He had mentioned the hermit's life a few too many times; he sensed it. But he did not quit. Her furious green eyes pricked him like spurs.

24

'I am a penniless anchorite. Dead to the world and its concerns. I'm a simple, uneducated man, unaware of worldly matters . . .'

That was an exaggeration.

'Like hell you are!' she yelled, hurling a pelt and the knife to the floor. 'Do you take me for a fool? I'm not a fool, be sure of that. A hermit, a penniless anchorite? I had a look around when you weren't here. I looked in the corner, behind that rather filthy curtain. How did learned books get on those shelves, eh, my simple, ignorant man?'

Vysogota threw a coypu skin down on the pile.

'A tax collector once lived here,' he said light-heartedly. 'They are cadasters and bookkeeping ledgers.'

'You're lying,' Ciri grimaced, massaging her scar. 'You're lying through your teeth!'

He did not reply, pretending to be assessing the hue of another hide.

'Perhaps you think,' the girl began again, 'that if you have a white beard, wrinkles and you've lived a hundred years, you can easily hoodwink a naive young maid, eh? Let me tell you: maybe you would have tricked just any lass. But I'm not just any lass.'

He raised his eyebrows in a wordless, but provocative, question. He didn't have to wait long.

'I, my dear hermit, have studied in places where there were plenty of books, including the same titles you have on your shelves. I know plenty of them.'

Vysogota raised his eyebrows even higher. She looked him straight in the eye.

'This filthy sloven, this ragged orphan,' she drawled, 'is saying strange things. Must be a thief or bandit discovered in the bushes with her mush cut up. And yet you ought to know, hermit, that I have read *The History of Roderick de Novembre*. I've looked through the *Materia Medica* several times. I know the *Herbarius* you have on your shelf. I also know what the gules cross ermine blazon on the spines of those books means. It means the book was published by the University of Oxenfurt.'

She broke off, still observing him intently. Vysogota was silent, trying not to let his face betray anything.

'Which is why I think,' she said, making her habitual sharp, haughty toss of head, 'that you aren't a simple hermit at all. That you didn't die for the world, either, but fled from it. And you're hiding here, in the wilderness, disguised by appearances and a boundless reed bed.'

'If that is so,' Vysogota smiled, 'then our fates really have become uncannily entwined, my well-read young lady. This destiny has flung us together in a highly mysterious way. After all, you're also in hiding. You too, Ciri, are skilfully spinning a veil of deception around yourself. I am, however, an old man, full of suspicion and embittered senile mistrust . . .'

'Mistrust regarding me?'

'Regarding the world, Ciri. A world in which a deceptive appearance dons the mask of truth to pull the wool over the eyes of another truth – a false one, incidentally, which also tries to deceive. A world in which the arms of the University of Oxenfurt are painted on the doors of bordellos. A world in which wounded thugs pass themselves off as worldly, learned, and perhaps nobly born maidens, intellectuals and polymaths, reading Roderick de Novembre and familiar with the crest of the Academy. In spite of all appearances. In spite of the fact that they carry another mark. A bandit's tattoo. A red rose tattooed on the groin.'

'Indeed, you were right.' She bit her lip, and her face turned a crimson so intense that the line of the scar seemed black. 'You *are* an embittered old man. And a nosy old prick.'

'On my shelf, behind the curtain–' he nodded toward it '– is a copy of *Aen N'og Mab Taedh'morc*, a collection of elven fairy tales and rhyming parables. There is a story there of a venerable old raven and a youthful swallow, very fitting to our situation and conversation. Because I am a polymath like you, Ciri, let me quote an appropriate excerpt. The raven, as you certainly recall, accuses the swallow of flightiness and unseemly frivolity.

'Hen Cerbin dic'ss aen n'og Zireael
Aark, aark, caelm foile, te veloe, ell?
Zireael—'

He broke off, rested his elbows on the table, and his chin on his interlocked fingers. Ciri jerked her head, straightened up, and looked at him defiantly. And completed the verse.

'. . . *Zireael veloe que'ss aen en'ssan irch*
Mab og, Hen Cerbin, vean ni, quirk, quirk!'

'The embittered and mistrustful old man,' Vysogota said a moment later, without changing his position, 'apologises to the young polymath. The venerable old raven, sensing everywhere deceit and trickery, asks for forgiveness of the swallow, whose only crime is to be young and full of life. And very pretty.'

'Now you're talking drivel,' she said crossly, involuntarily covering the scar on her cheek. 'You can forget compliments like that. They won't correct those wonky stitches you tacked my skin with. Don't think, either, that you'll gain my trust by apologising. I still don't know who you really are. Why you lied to me about those dates and days. Or why you looked between my legs, when I'd been wounded in the face. And if looking was where it finished.'

This time she made him lose his temper.

'What are you saying, you brat?' he roared. 'I could be your father!'

'Grandfather,' she corrected him coldly. 'Or even great-grandfather. But you aren't. I don't know who you are. But you are certainly not who you pretend to be.'

'I am he who found you on the bog, almost frozen to the moss, with a black crust instead of a face, unconscious, and filthy. I am he who took you home, although I didn't know who you were, and was within my rights to expect the worst. Who bandaged you and put you to bed. Tended to you, when you were expiring with fever. Nursed you. Washed you. Thoroughly. In the tattoo region as well.'

She blushed again, but had no intention of changing her insolent, defiant expression.

'In this world,' she growled, 'deceptive appearances occasionally feign the truth; you said it yourself. I also know the world a little, if you can imagine it. You rescued me, tended my wounds, nursed me. Thank you for that. I'm grateful for your . . . your

27

kindness. Although I know that there is no such thing as kindness without—'

'Without calculation or the hope of some profit,' he finished with a smile. 'Yes, yes, I know, I'm a worldly man. Perhaps I know the world as well as you do, Ciri? Wounded girls, of course, are robbed of everything that has any value. If they're unconscious or too weak to defend themselves, free rein is normally given to one's urges and lust, often in immoral and unnatural ways. Isn't that so?'

'Nothing is as it seems,' answered Ciri, her cheeks reddening once more.

'How true a statement,' he said, throwing another pelt on one of the piles. 'And how mercilessly does it lead us to the conclusion that we, Ciri, know nothing about each other. We know only appearances, and appearances are deceptive.'

He waited a while, but Ciri wasn't hurrying to say anything.

'Although both of us have managed to carry out something of a provisional inquisition, we still know nothing about each other. I don't know who you are, you don't know who I am . . .'

This time he waited with calculation. She looked at him, and in her eyes there was the hint of the question he was expecting. Something strange flashed in her eyes when she posed the question.

'Who shall begin?'

*

Had someone had crept up after nightfall to the cottage with the sunken, moss-grown thatched roof, had peered inside, in the firelight and glow of the hearth they would have seen a grey-bearded old man hunched over a pile of pelts. They would have seen an ashen-haired girl with a hideous scar on her cheek, a scar which in no way suited her huge green childlike eyes.

But no one could have seen that. For the cottage stood among reeds in a swamp where no one dared to venture.

*

'My name is Vysogota of Corvo. I was once a doctor. A surgeon. I was an alchemist. I was a scholar, a historian, a philosopher and an

28

ethicist. I was a professor at the Academy of Oxenfurt. I had to flee after publishing a paper which was deemed godless. At that time, fifty years ago, it was punishable by death. I had to emigrate. My wife did not want to emigrate, so she left me. And I only ceased my flight when I reached the far South, in the Nilfgaardian Empire. Later I finally became a lecturer in ethics at the Imperial Academy in Castell Graupian, a position I held for almost ten years. But I had to run from there, too, after the publication of another treatise . . . Incidentally, the work dealt with totalitarian power and the criminal character of imperialist wars, but officially I and my work were accused of metaphysical mysticism and clerical schism. It was ruled I had been goaded into action by the expansive and revisionist groups of priests who were actually governing the kingdoms of the Nordlings. Quite amusing in the light of my death sentence for atheism twenty years previously! Indeed, it so happened that the expansive priests in the North had long since been forgotten by their people, but that had not been acknowledged in Nilfgaard. Combining mysticism and superstition with politics was a severely punishable offence.

'Today, looking back down the years, I think that had I humbled myself and shown remorse, perhaps the scandal would have blown over, and the emperor limited himself to disfavour, without using extreme measures. But I was bitter. I considered some of my arguments timeless, superior to this or that dominion or politics. I felt wronged, unjustly wronged. Tyrannously wronged. So I made active contact with the dissidents secretly fighting the tyrant. Before I knew it, I was in a dungeon with those dissidents, and some of them, when they were shown the torture instruments, pointed me out as the movement's chief ideologue.

'The emperor availed himself of his privilege to issue a pardon, though I was sentenced to exile, under the threat of immediate execution should I return to imperial territories.

'Thus I took offence against the entire world, against kingdoms, empires and universities, against dissidents, civil servants and lawyers. Against my colleagues and friends, who stopped being such at the touch of a magic wand. Against my second wife, who, like my first, thought her husband's difficulties a suitable reason for a divorce. Against my children, who disowned me. I became a hermit, here, in Ebbing, in the Pereplut Marshes. I inherited a dwelling from an anchorite I had once known. Unfortunately, Nilfgaard annexed Ebbing, and all of a sudden I found myself in the Empire again. Now I have neither the strength nor the inclination to continue wandering, so I must hide. Imperial sentences do not lapse, even in a situation when the emperor who issued it died long ago, and the present emperor has no cause to remember the previous one fondly or share his views. The death sentence remains in force. That is the law and custom in Nilfgaard. Sentences for high treason do not expire, and neither are they subject to the amnesties that every emperor proclaims after his coronation. After the accession to the throne of a new emperor, everybody who was sentenced by his predecessor is given an amnesty . . . except those guilty of high treason. It is unimportant who reigns in Nilfgaard: if news gets out that I'm alive and am breaking my sentence of exile, dwelling in imperial territory, my head is for the noose.

'So as you see, Ciri, we find ourselves in wholly similar situation.'

*

'What is ethics? I knew, but I've forgotten.'

'The study of morality. Of the precepts of conduct: of being decorous, noble, decent and honest. Of the heights of goodness, to which probity and morality carry up the human spirit. And of the chasms of evil, into which malice and immorality are flung . . .'

'The heights of goodness!' she snorted. 'Probity! Morality! Don't make me laugh, or the scar on my face will burst. You were lucky that you weren't hunted, that they didn't send bounty hunters after you, people like . . . Bonhart. You'd see what chasms of evil are. Ethics? Your ethics are worth shit, O Vysogota of Corvo. It isn't the evil and indecent who are flung down into the depths, no! Oh, no! The evil and decisive fling down those who are moral, honest and noble but maladroit, hesitant and full of scruples.'

'Thanks for the lesson,' he sneered. 'In truth, though one may have lived a century, it is never too late to learn something new. Indeed, it is always worth listening to mature, worldly and experienced people.'

'Mock. Go ahead and mock.' She tossed her head. 'While you

30

still can. For now it is my turn, now I shall entertain you with a tale. I'll tell you what happened to me. And when I'm done we'll see if you still feel like mocking me.'

*

Had someone crept up after nightfall to the cottage with the sunken, moss-grown thatched roof, had they peered inside, in the dimly lit interior they would have seen a grey-bearded old man listening raptly to a tale told by an ashen-haired girl sitting on a log by the fireplace. They would have noticed that the girl was speaking slowly, as though having difficulty finding the words; that she was nervously rubbing her cheek, which was disfigured by a hideous scar, and that she was interweaving her story with long silences. A tale about the lessons she had received, of which all, to the last one, turned out to be false and misleading. About the promises made to her which were not kept. A story about how the destiny she'd been ordered to believe in betrayed her disgracefully and deprived her of her inheritance. About how each time she began to believe in her destiny she was made to suffer misery, pain, injustice and humiliation. About how those she trusted and loved betrayed her, did not come to her aid when she was afflicted, when she was menaced by dishonour, agony and death. A tale about the ideals to which she was instructed to remain loyal, and which disappointed, betrayed and abandoned her when she needed them, proving of what little value they were. About how she finally found help, friendship – and love – with those among whom she should have sought neither help nor friendship. Not to mention love.

But no one could have seen that, much less heard it. For the cottage with the sunken, moss-grown thatched roof was well hidden among the fog, in a swamp where no one dared venture.

31

CHAPTER TWO

A west wind brought a storm that night.

The purple-black sky burst along the line of lightning, exploding in a long drawn-out clatter of thunder. The sudden rain struck the dust of the road with drops as viscous as oil, roared on the roofs, smeared the dirt on the skins covering the windows. But the powerful wind quickly chased off the downpour, drove the storm somewhere far, far away, beyond the horizon, which was blazing with lightning.

And then dogs began to bark. Hooves thudded and weapons clanged. A wild howling and whistling made the hair stand up on the heads of the peasants who had woken and now sprang up in panic, barring their doors and shutters. Hands, wet with sweat, tightened on the hafts of axes and the handles of pitchforks. Clenched them tightly. But helplessly.

Terror sped through the village. Were they the hunted or the hunters? Insane and cruel from ferocity or fear? Will they gallop through, without stopping? Or will the night soon be lit up by the glare of blazing thatch?

Quiet, quiet, children . . .

Mamma, are they demons? Is it the Wild Hunt? Phantoms from hell? Mamma, mamma!

Quiet, quiet, children. They are not demons, not devils . . .

Worse than that.

They are people.

The dogs barked. The gale blew. Horses neighed, horseshoes thudded. The gang raced through the village and the night.

*

Hotspurn rode up onto the hillock, reined in and turned his horse around. He was prudent and cautious, and did not like taking risks, particularly when vigilance cost nothing. He didn't hurry to ride down to the postal station by the small river. He preferred to have a good look first.

There were no horses or horse-drawn vehicles outside the station, only a single small wagon harnessed with a pair of mules. There was some writing on the tarpaulin which Hotspurn could not make out at a distance. But it did not look dangerous. Hotspurn was capable of sensing danger. He was a professional.

He rode down to the bank, which was covered in bushes and osiers, spurred his horse decisively into the river, crossed at a gallop among gouts of water, many splashing him above his saddle. Some ducks swimming by the bank flew away with a loud quacking.

Hotspurn urged his horse on and rode into the station courtyard through the open fence. Now he could read the writing on the tarpaulin, proclaiming 'Master Almavera, Tattoo Artist'. Each word was painted in a different colour and began with an excessively large, decoratively illuminated letter. And on the wagon's box, above the right front wheel, was a small split arrow rendered in purple paint.

'Dismount!' he heard behind him. 'On the ground, and fast! Hands away from your hilt!'

They approached and surrounded him noiselessly: Asse from the right in a silver-studded black leather jacket, Falka from the left in a short, green suede jerkin and beret with feathers. Hotspurn removed his hood and pulled the scarf from his face.

'Ha!' Asse lowered his sword. 'It's you, Hotspurn. I would have recognised you, but for that black horse!'

'What a gorgeous little mare,' said Falka with delight, sliding her beret over one ear. 'Black and gleaming like coal, not a light hair on her. And so well-shaped! Oh, she's a beauty!'

'Aye, came up for less than five-score florins,' smiled Hotspurn. 'Where's Giselher? Inside?'

Asse nodded. Falka, looking at the mare as though bewitched, patted her on the neck.

'When she ran through the water,' said Falka, raising her huge green eyes up to Hotspurn, 'she looked like a veritable kelpie! Had she emerged from the sea and not a river, I would have believed she was a real one.'

'Have you seen a real kelpie, Miss Falka?'

'Only in a painting.' The girl suddenly grew serious. 'But that would be a long story. Come inside. Giselher's waiting.'

*

There was a table by the window, which let in a little light. Mistle was half-lying on the table, resting on her elbows, almost naked from the waist down with nothing on but a pair of black stockings. Between her shamelessly spread legs knelt a skinny, long-haired individual in a brownish-grey smock. It could not have been anyone but Master Almavera, tattoo artist, busy tattooing a colourful picture on Mistle's thigh.

'Come closer, Hotspurn,' invited Giselher, drawing a stool away from the next table, where he was sitting with Iskra, Kayleigh and Reef. The latter two, like Asse, were also dressed in black calfskin covered in buckles, studs, chains and other elaborate silver accessories. Some craftsman must have made a fortune on them, thought Hotspurn. The Rats, when the whim to dress up seized them, would pay tailors, shoemakers and leatherworkers handsomely. Naturally, neither did they miss any opportunity to simply wrest any clothing or jewellery that took their fancy from anyone they assailed.

'I see you found our message in the ruins of the old station?' Giselher said, stretching. 'Ha, what am I saying, you wouldn't be here otherwise, would you? You rode here pretty quickly, I must say.'

'Because the mare is gorgeous,' Falka interjected. 'I'll bet she's fleet too!'

'I found your message.' Hotspurn did not take his eye off Giselher. 'What about mine? Did it reach you?'

'It did . . .' stammered the leader of the Rats. 'But . . . Well, to put it briefly . . . There wasn't time. And then we got drunk and were forced to rest a little. And later another path came up . . .'

Damned pups, thought Hotspurn.

'To put it briefly, you didn't do the job?'

'Well, no. Forgive me, Hotspurn. Couldn't be done . . . But next time, ho! Without fail!'

'Without fail!' repeated Kayleigh with emphasis, though no one had asked him to repeat it.

Damned, irresponsible pups. Got drunk. And then another path came up . . . To a tailor to get some fancy costumes, I'll be bound.

'Want a drink?'

'No, thank you.'

'Fancy some of this?' Giselher pointed at a small decorative lacquer casket among some demijohns and beakers. Now Hotspurn knew why a strange light was flashing in the Rats' eyes, why their movements were so nervous and quick.

'First-rate powder,' Giselher assured him. 'Won't you take a pinch?'

'No, thank you.' Hotspurn glanced knowingly at a red stain and a dwindling bloody streak on the sawdust of the chamber, clearly indicating which way a body had been dragged. Giselher noticed the look.

'One of the lackeys thought he'd play the hero,' he snorted. 'So Iskra had to scold him.'

Iskra laughed throatily. She clearly very aroused by the narcotic.

'I scolded him so much he choked on his blood,' she crowed. 'And the others were cowed at once. That's what you call terror!'

She was dripping in jewels as usual, and even had a diamond stud in her nose. She was not wearing leather, but a short cherry-red jacket with a fine brocade pattern. Her look was established enough to be all the rage among the gilded youth of Thurn. Like the silk scarf wrapped around Giselher's head. Hotspurn had even heard of girls asking for 'Mistle' haircuts.

'That's what you call terror,' he repeated pensively, still looking at the patch of blood on the floor. 'What about the station keeper? His wife? And son?'

'No, no,' Giselher scowled. 'Think we did for all of them? Not at all. We locked them in the pantry for a while. Now the station, as you see, is ours.'

Kayleigh swilled wine around his mouth, then spat it out on the floor. He took a small quantity of fisstech from the casket with a tiny spoon, meticulously sprinkled it on the spit-moistened tip of his index finger and rubbed the narcotic into his gums. He handed the casket to Falka, who repeated the ritual and passed the fisstech to Reef. The Nilfgaardian turned it down, busy looking at a catalogue of colourful tattoos, and handed the box to Iskra. The she-elf passed it to Giselher without taking any.

'Terror!' she growled, narrowing her flashing eyes and sniffing. 'We have the station in the grip of terror! Emperor Emhyr holds the entire world this way, and we only this hovel. But the principle's the same!'

'Owww, dammit!' yelled Mistle from the table. 'Be careful what you prick! Do that one more time and I'll prick you! Right through!'

The Rats – apart from Falka and Giselher – roared with laughter.

'If you want to be beautiful you have to suffer!' Iskra called.

'Prick her, master, prick her,' Kayleigh added. 'She's hardened between the legs!'

Falka swore copiously and threw a beaker at him. Kayleigh ducked and the Rats roared with laughter again.

'So.' Hotspurn decided to put an end to the gaiety. 'You hold the station in the grip of terror. But what for? Other than the satisfaction you derive from terrorising station keepers' families?'

'We,' Giselher answered, rubbing fisstech into his gums, 'are lying in wait. Should someone stop to change horses or rest, they'll be stripped clean. It's more comfortable here than on a crossroads or in the thicket by the highway. But, as Iskra has just said, the principle's the same.'

'But today, since daybreak, only this one's fallen into our grasp,' Reef interjected, pointing at Master Almavera, his head almost hidden between Mistle's parted thighs. 'A pauper, like every artist. Had nothing to rob, so we're robbing him of his art. Take a look at how ingeniously he draws.'

He bared his forearm and displayed a bloody tattoo: a naked woman who wiggled her buttocks when he clenched his fist. Kayleigh also showed off. A green snake with an open maw and a scarlet, forked tongue writhed around his arm, above a spiked bracelet.

'A tasteful piece,' Hotspurn said indifferently. 'And helpful when corpses are being identified. However, you failed with the robbery, my dear Rats. You'll have to pay the artist for his skill. There was no time to warn you; for seven days, from the first of

September, the sign has been a purple split arrow. He has one painted on his wagon.'

Reef swore under his breath and Kayleigh laughed. Giselher waved a hand indifferently.

'Too bad. If needs must we'll pay him for his needles and dye. A purple arrow, say you? We'll remember. If someone rides up with the sign of the arrow between now and tomorrow, he won't be harmed.'

'You plan to stay here till tomorrow?' Hotspurn said with slightly exaggerated astonishment. 'That's imprudent, Rats. It's risky and dangerous!'

'You what?'

'Risky and dangerous!'

Giselher shrugged, Iskra snorted and cleared her nose onto the floor. Reef, Kayleigh and Falka looked at Hotspurn as though he'd just declared that the sun had fallen into the river and must be fished out before the crayfish pinched it. Hotspurn understood that he had merely appealed to the reckless pups' good sense, of which they had little. That he had alerted these braggarts to risk and danger. Braggarts – all reckless bravado – for whom those concepts were utterly alien.

'They're coming for you, Rats.'

'What of it?'

Hotspurn sighed.

Mistle – without having taken the trouble to dress – came over to them and interrupted the discussion. She placed a foot on the bench and – twisting her hips – demonstrated to all and sundry the work of Master Almavera: a crimson rose on a green stem with two leaves, on her inner thigh, right by her groin.

'Well?' she asked, hands on hips. Her bracelets, which almost reached her elbows, flashed brilliantly. 'What do you say?'

'Exquisite!' Kayleigh snorted, brushing his hair aside. Hotspurn had noticed that the Rat had rings in his ears. There was no doubt that similar earrings – like studded leather or silk scarves – would soon be the latest thing among the gilded youth in Thurn and the whole of Geso.

'Your turn, Falka,' said Mistle. 'What will you have?'

Falka touched her friend's thigh, leaned over and examined the tattoo. From very close. Mistle ruffled Falka's ashen-grey hair tenderly. Falka giggled and, without further ado, began to undress.

'I want the same rose,' she said. 'In the same place as you, darling.'

*

'How many mice you have here, Vysogota!' Ciri said, breaking off her story and looking down at the floor, where a veritable mouse circus was taking place in the circle of light thrown by the oil lamp. One could only imagine what was happening in the gloom beyond the light.

'A cat would come in useful. Or, better still, two.'

'The rodents,' the hermit coughed, 'are coming inside because winter is drawing nigh. And I had a cat. But it wandered off somewhere, the good-for-nothing, and never came back.'

'It was probably taken by a fox or marten.'

'You never saw that cat, Ciri. If something took it, it would have had to be a dragon. Nothing smaller.'

'Was he that ferocious? Oh, that's a pity. He wouldn't have let these mice scamper all over my bed. Pity.'

'Yes, it is a pity. But I think he'll return. Cats always do.'

'I'll build up the fire. It's cold.'

'It is. The nights are perishingly cold now . . . And it's not even halfway through October yet . . . Go on, Ciri.'

For a while Ciri sat motionless, staring into the fireplace. The fire sprang to life with the new wood, crackled, roared, and threw golden light and flickering shadows onto the girl's scarred face.

'Go on.'

*

Master Almavera pricked, and Ciri felt the tears tingling in the corners of her eyes. Although she had prudently intoxicated herself before the operation with wine and white powder, the pain was almost unbearable. She clenched her teeth. She did not groan, naturally, but pretended not to pay attention to the needle and to scorn the pain. She tried blithely to take part in the conversation

38

the Rats were having with Hotspurn, an individual who wished to be thought of as a merchant, but who – apart from the fact that he lived off merchants – had nothing in common with trade.

'Dark clouds have gathered above your heads,' Hotspurn said, his dark eyes sweeping over the Rats' faces. 'Isn't it bad enough that the Prefect of Amarillo is hunting you, that the Varnhagens are pursuing you, that the Baron of Casadei—?'

'Him?' Giselher grimaced. 'I can understand the prefect and the Varnhagens, but what has that Casadei got against us?'

'The wolf is dressed in sheep's clothing,' Hotspurn said, smiling, 'and pitifully bleats *baa, baa, no one likes me, no one understands me. Wherever I appear they throw stones at me. They shout "Hallo". Why, oh why? Why such unfairness and injustice?* The daughter of the Baron of Casadei, my dear Rats, after her adventure by the River Wagtail, grows ever weaker and feverish . . .'

'Aaah,' Giselher recalled. 'That carriage with those four spotted horses! That maiden?'

'That one. Now, as I said, she ails, wakes up in the night screaming, recalling Mr Kayleigh . . . But especially Miss Falka. And the brooch, a keepsake of her departed mamma, which Miss Falka wrested from her dress. Various words are repeated all the while.'

'It wasn't like that at all!' Ciri yelled from the table, able to react to the pain by shouting. 'We showed the baron's daughter contempt and disrespect by letting her get away with it! The wench should have been ravaged!'

'Indeed.' Ciri sensed Hotspurn's gaze on her naked thighs. 'Verily a great dishonour not to have ravaged her. No wonder then, that the offended Casadei has assembled an armed squad and offered a reward. He has sworn publicly that you will all hang head down from the corbels on the walls of his castle. He also swore that for the brooch wrenched from his daughter he will flay Miss Falka. Alive.'

Ciri swore, and the Rats roared in wild laughter. Iskra sneezed and covered herself in snot; the fisstech was irritating her mucous membranes.

'We disdain our pursuers,' she declared, wiping her nose, mouth, chin and the table. 'The prefect, the baron, the Varnhagens! They can hunt us, but they won't catch us! We are the Rats!'

39

We zigzagged back and forth on the far side of the Velda and now those dolts are at sixes and sevens, going the wrong way along a cold trail. They will have gone too far to turn around by the time they catch on.'

'Let them turn around!' Asse said heatedly. He had returned some time before from sentry duty. No one had replaced him and no one seemed about to. 'We'll slaughter them and that's that!'

'Exactly!' Ciri screamed from the table, having already forgotten how they had fled from their pursuers through the villages beside the Velda and how terrified she had been.

'Very well.' Giselher slammed his open palm down on the table, abruptly putting an end to the noisy chatter. 'Speak, Hotspurn. For I can see you wish to tell us something else, something of greater note than the prefect, the Varnhagens, the Baron of Casadei and his sensitive daughter.'

'Bonhart is on your trail.'

A very long silence fell. Even Master Almavera stopped working for a moment.

'Bonhart,' Giselher repeated in a slow, drawling voice. 'That grey-haired old blackguard? We must have really annoyed someone.'

'Someone wealthy,' Mistle added. 'Not everyone can afford Bonhart.'

Ciri was about to ask who this Bonhart was, but Asse and Reef – speaking almost at once, in unison – were quicker.

'He's a bounty hunter,' Giselher explained grimly. 'Years ago he took the king's shilling, they say. Then he was a wandering merchant, and finally began killing people for the bounty. He's a whoreson like no other.'

'They say,' Kayleigh said quite carelessly, 'that if you wanted to bury everyone Bonhart has put to the sword in one graveyard, it would have to measure a good half-acre.'

Mistle poured a pinch of the white powder into the dimple between her thumb and forefinger, and sniffed it up vigorously.

'Bonhart broke up Big Lothar's gang,' she said. 'He carved up him and his brother, the one they called Muchomorek.'

'Stabbed them in the back, they say,' Kayleigh threw in.

'He killed Valdez, too,' Giselher added. 'And when Valdez

perished, his gang fell apart. One of the better ones. A solid, hard firm. Good scrappers. I thought about joining them at one time. Before we teamed up.'

'It's all true,' Hotspurn said. 'There's never been a gang like Valdez's and there never will be again. A merry air is sung about how they fought their way out of a trap at Sarda. Aye, bold they were, aye, daredevils they were! Few are their equal.'

The Rats suddenly fell silent and fixed their eyes on him, blazing and furious.

'The six of us,' Kayleigh drawled after a brief silence, 'once broke through a troop of Nilfgaardian horse!'

'We sprang Kayleigh from the Nissirs!' Asse snapped.

'Few are *our* equal!' Reef hissed.

'That is so, Hotspurn.' Giselher threw out his chest. 'The Rats are second to no other gang, not even Valdez's mob. Daredevils, you say? Well I'll tell you something about she-devils. Iskra, Mistle and Falka – the very three sitting here before you – rode in broad daylight down the high street in Druigh, and when they realised that the Varnhagens were in the tavern, they galloped right through it! Right through, I tell you! They rode in through the front and out into the courtyard. And the Varnhagens were left standing open-mouthed over broken beer mugs and spilled beer. Will you say that wasn't dashing?'

'He won't,' Mistle cut in before Hotspurn could reply, smiling nastily. 'He won't, because he knows who the Rats are. And his guild knows too.'

Master Almavera had finished the tattoo. Ciri thanked him with a haughty expression, dressed, and sat down with the company. She snorted, feeling the strange, appraising – and seemingly mocking – gaze of Hotspurn on her. She glowered at him, ostentatiously cuddling up to Mistle. She had already learned that such behaviour discomfited and cooled the zeal of gentlemen with flirtation in mind. In the case of Hotspurn she acted with a little more exaggeration, for the pretend merchant was not so intrusive in that way.

Hotspurn was an enigma to Ciri. She had only seen him once before and Mistle had told her the rest. Hotspurn and Giselher, she had explained, knew each other and had been comrades for ages, and had agreed signals, passwords and meeting places. During those rendezvous Hotspurn passed on information – and then they travelled to the road indicated and robbed the indicated merchant, convoy or caravan. Sometimes they killed a specific person. There was always also an agreed sign; they were not allowed to attack merchants with that sign on their wagons.

At first Ciri had been astonished and slightly disappointed; she looked up to Giselher, and considered the Rats a model of freedom and independence. She loved their freedom, their contempt for everything and everybody. And now they unexpectedly had to carry out contracts. Like hired thugs, they were being told who to beat up. But that was not all; someone was ordering them to beat someone up and they were sheepishly complying.

It's quid pro quo. Mistle had shrugged when Ciri bombarded her with questions. *Hotspurn gives us orders, but also information, thanks to which we survive. Freedom and contempt have their limits. Anyway, it's always like that. You're always somebody's tool.*

Such is life, Little Falcon.

Ciri was surprised and disappointed, but she got over it quickly. She was learning. She had also learned not to be too surprised or to expect too much – for then the disappointment was less acute.

'I, my dear Rats,' Hotspurn said in the meantime, 'might have a remedy for your difficulties. For the Nissirs, barons, prefects, and even Bonhart. Yes, yes. For even though the noose is tightening around your necks, I might have a way for you to slip out of it.'

Iskra snorted, Reef cackled. But Giselher silenced them with a gesture, allowing Hotspurn to continue. 'The word is out,' the merchant said a moment later, 'that an amnesty will be proclaimed any day now. That even if a sentence is hanging over someone, why, even if the noose is hanging over them, it will be waived if they simply present themselves to the authorities and confess their guilt. That applies to you too.'

'Bollocks!' Kayleigh cried, eyes watering a little because he had just inhaled a pinch of fisstech. 'It's a Nilfgaardian trick, a ruse! We old warhorses won't be taken in like that!'

'Hold hard,' Giselher halted him. 'Don't be hasty, Kayleigh. Hotspurn, as we know, doesn't usually dissemble nor break his

42

word. He usually knows what he's saying and why. So he surely knows and will tell us where this sudden Nilfgaardian generosity has come from.'

'Emperor Emhyr,' Hotspurn said calmly, 'is taking a wife. We shall soon have an empress in Nilfgaard. Which is why they're to proclaim an amnesty. The emperor is reportedly mighty content, so he wishes contentment on others too.'

'I don't give a shit about imperial contentment,' Mistle announced haughtily. 'And I won't be availing myself of the amnesty, because that Nilfgaardian kindness smells like fresh shavings. As though someone's been sharpening a stake. Ha!'

Hotspurn shrugged. 'I doubt that it's trickery. It's a political matter. And a great one. Greater than you, Rats, than all of the local mobs put together. It's politics.'

'You what?' Giselher frowned. 'I don't understand a damned thing you're saying.'

'Emhyr's marriage is political, and political issues are to be secured through that wedding. The emperor is forging a union through marriage, he wants to unify the empire more securely, put an end to border unrest, bring peace. For do you know who he's marrying? Cirilla, the heiress to the throne of Cintra.'

'Lies!' Ciri yelled. 'Hogwash!'

'By what right do you accuse me of lying, Miss Falka?' Hotspurn raised his eyes towards her. 'Perhaps you are better informed?'

'Certainly am!'

'Quiet, Falka.' Giselher grimaced. 'He pricked your tail on the table and you were quiet, and now you're bawling? What is this Cintra, Hotspurn? Who is this Cirilla? Why should it be so important?'

'Cintra,' Reef interjected, pouring fisstech on his finger, 'is a little state in the North over which the empire fought with the local rulers. About three or four years ago.'

'Agreed,' Hotspurn confirmed. 'The imperial forces conquered Cintra and even crossed the River Yarra, but had to withdraw later.'

'Because they took a beating at Sodden Hill,' snapped Ciri. 'They almost lost their breeches they retreated so fast!'

'Miss Falka, I see, is familiar with recent history. It's creditable,

creditable at such a young age. May one ask where Miss Falka attended school?'

'One may not!'

'Enough!' Giselher demanded quiet again. 'Talk about this Cintra, Hotspurn. And about the amnesty.'

'Imperator Emhyr,' the so-called merchant said, 'has decided to turn Cintra into a parasitic state . . .'

'A what?'

'Parasitic. Like ivy, which can't exist without a powerful tree trunk around which it wraps itself. And the tree trunk is, of course, Nilfgaard. There are other such states, such as Metinna, Maecht, Toussaint . . . Where local dynasties govern, or pretend to govern.'

'That's called a parent's antinomy,' Reef boasted. 'I've heard of it.'

'Nonetheless, the problem with Cintra was that the royal line died out . . .'

'Died out?' It was as though green sparks would shoot from Ciri's eyes at any moment. 'Died out, my hat! The Nilfgaardians murdered Queen Calanthe! Simply murdered her!'

'I do own–' with a gesture Hotspurn quieted Giselher, who was once again about to berate Ciri for interrupting '–that Miss Falka continues to dazzle us with her knowledge. The queen of Cintra did indeed fall during the war. It is believed that her granddaughter, Cirilla, the last of the royal blood, also fell. Thus Emhyr did not have much from which to create that apparent autonomy – as Mr Reef so wisely said. Until Cirilla suddenly showed up again, as if from nowhere.'

'Huh. Just fairy tales,' snorted Iskra, resting on Giselher's arm.

'Indeed.' Hotspurn nodded. 'A little like a fairy tale, it must be confessed. They say that this Cirilla was imprisoned by an evil witch somewhere in the far North, in a magical tower. But Cirilla managed to flee and beg for asylum in the empire.'

'That is one damn great load of false hogwash and balderdash!' yelled Ciri, reaching for the casket of fisstech with shaking hands.

'While Imperator Emhyr, so the rumour goes–' Hotspurn continued unperturbed '–fell madly in love with her when he saw her and wants to take her for his wife. So he offers an amnesty.'

'Little Falcon is right,' Mistle said firmly, emphasising her

44

words by banging her fist on the table. 'That's balderdash! I can't bloody under-bloody-stand what this is all about. One thing I know for certain: basing any hopes of Nilfgaardian benevolence on that balderdash would be even greater balderdash.'

'That's right!' Reef said, supporting her. 'There's nothing in the imperial marriage for us. No matter whom the emperor marries, another betrothed will always be waiting for us. One twisted out of hemp!'

'This isn't about your necks, my dear Rats,' Hotspurn reminded them. 'This is politics. There's no let-up to the endless rebellions, uprisings and disorder on the northern marches of the empire, particularly in Cintra and its surroundings. And if the imperator takes the heiress of Cintra for a wife, Cintra will calm down. There'll be a solemn amnesty, and the rebellious parties will come down from the mountains, stop besetting the imperial forces and making trouble. Why, if the Cintran ascends the imperial throne, perhaps the rebels will join the imperial army! And you know, after all, that in the North, on the far side of the River Yarra, there is war. And every soldier counts.'

'Aha.' Kayleigh grimaced. 'Now I get it! That's their amnesty! They'll give us a choice: here's a sharpened stake and there's the imperial livery. You can have a stake up your arse or the livery on your back. And off to war, to die for the empire!'

'Indeed,' Hotspurn said slowly, 'anything can happen in war. Nonetheless, not everyone must fight, my dear Rats. Of course, after fulfilling the terms of the amnesty, after disclosing and admitting one's guilt, a certain kind of . . . substitute service might be possible.'

'What?'

'I know what this is about.' Giselher's teeth flashed briefly in his weather-beaten face, blue from stubble. 'The merchant's guild, my little ones, would like to take us in. Caress and nurse us. Like a doting mother.'

'Whore mother, more like,' Iskra grunted under her breath. Hotspurn pretended not to hear.

'You are completely right, Giselher,' he said coldly. 'The guild may, if it so wishes, hire you. Officially, for a change. And take you in. Give you protection. Also officially and, also, for a change.'

Kayleigh was going to say something, Mistle too, but a swift glance from Giselher kept them both silent.

'Tell the guild, Hotspurn,' the leader of the Rats said icily, 'that we are grateful for the offer. We shall think it over, reflect on it and discuss it. And decide what to do.'

Hotspurn stood up.

'I ride.'

'Now, with darkness falling?'

'I shall overnight in the village. I feel awkward here. And tomorrow straight to the border with Metinna, then down the main highway to Forgeham, where I'll stay until the Equinox, and who knows? Maybe longer. For I shall wait there for anyone who has thought it through, and is ready to turn themselves in and wait for the amnesty under my protection. And I advise you not to dilly-dally, either, with your reflecting and your pondering. For Bonhart is liable to outpace the amnesty.'

'You keep frightening us with Bonhart,' Giselher said slowly, also standing up. 'Anyone would think he was just around the corner . . . When he's probably over the hills and far away . . . '

'. . . in Jealousy,' Hotspurn finished calmly. 'In the inn called *The Chimera's Head*. About thirty miles hence. If not for your zigzags by the Velda, you probably would have run into him yesterday. But that doesn't worry you, I know. Farewell, Giselher. Farewell, Rats. Master Almavera? I'm riding to Metinna, and I'm always happy to have company on the road . . . What did you say? Gladly? As I thought. Pack up your things then. Pay the master, Rats, for his artistic efforts.'

*

The postal station smelled of fried onions and potato soup. They had been cooked by the station keeper's wife, temporarily released from her imprisonment in the pantry. A candle on the table spat, pulsated, and swayed with a whisker of flame. The Rats leaned so tightly over the table that the flame warmed their almost-touching heads.

'He's in Jealousy,' Giselher said softly. 'In *The Chimera's Head*. Only a day's ride from here. What do you think of that?'

46

'The same as you,' Kayleigh snarled. 'Let's ride over and kill the whoreson.'

'Let's avenge Valdez,' Reef said. 'And Muchomorek.'

'Then various Hotspurns,' Iskra hissed, 'won't shove other people's fame and daring down our throats. We'll kill Bonhart, that scavenger, that werewolf. We'll nail his head above the inn door, to match the name! So everyone will see he wasn't a hard man, but a mere mortal like everyone else, one who finally took on someone better than himself. That'll show folk which gang is number one, from Korath to Pereplut!'

'They'll be singing songs about us at markets!' Kayleigh said heatedly. 'Why, and in castles!'

'Let's ride!' Asse slammed his hand down hard on the table, 'Let's ride and destroy the bastard.'

'And afterwards,' Giselher pondered, 'we'll think about that amnesty . . . that guild . . . Why are you twisting up your face, Kayleigh, as though you've bitten a louse? They're on our heels and winter's coming. Here's what I think, little Rats: let's winter, warming our arses by the fireplace, blanketed from the cold by the amnesty, swigging mulled amnesty beer. We'll see out this amnesty nice and politely . . . more or less . . . till the spring. And in the spring . . . when the grass peeps out from under the snow . . .'

The Rats laughed in unison, softly, ominously. Their eyes flared like those of real rats when they approach a wounded man incapable of defending himself at night in a dark alley.

'Let's drink,' Giselher said, 'to Bonhart's confusion! Let's eat that soup, and then go to bed. Rest, for we set off before sunrise.'

'That's right,' Iskra snorted. 'Let's follow Mistle and Falka's example. They've been in bed for an hour.'

The postal station keeper's wife trembled by the cauldron, hearing once again their soft, evil, hideous giggling.

*

Ciri raised her head. For a long time she said nothing, eyes fixed on the barely flickering flame of the lamp, where the last fish oil was burning down.

'I slipped out of the station like a thief,' she continued the story.

'Before dawn, in total darkness . . . But I didn't manage to flee unseen. Mistle must have woken when I was getting out of bed. She caught me in the stable, when I was saddling the horse. But she didn't show any surprise. And she didn't try to stop me. The sun was starting to rise . . .'

'Now it's not too far till *our* dawn,' yawned Vysogota. 'Time to sleep, Ciri. You can take up the story tomorrow.'

'Perhaps you're right.' She also yawned, stood and stretched vigorously. 'Because my eyelids are getting heavy. But at this pace, hermit, I'll never finish. How many evenings have we had together? At least ten. I'm afraid that the whole story might take a thousand and one nights.'

'We have time, Ciri. We have time.'

*

'Who do you want to run from, Little Falcon? From me? Or from yourself?'

'I've finished running. Now I want to catch up with something. Which is why I must return . . . to where everything began. I must. Please understand, Mistle.'

'So that was why . . . why you were so nice to me today. For the first time in so many days . . . The last time? To bid farewell? And then forget me?'

'I'll never forget you, Mistle.'

'You will.'

'Never. I swear. And it wasn't the last time. I'll find you. I'll come to you . . . I'll come in a golden carriage and six. With a retinue of courtiers. You'll see. I'll soon have . . . possibilities. Great possibilities. I'll change your fortunes . . . You'll see. You'll find out what I'll be capable of doing. Of changing.'

'You need great power to do that,' Mistle sighed. 'And tremendous magic . . . '

'And that's also possible.' Ciri licked her lips. 'Magic too . . . I can recover . . . everything I once lost can be restored. And be mine once more. I promise you, you'll be astonished when we meet again.'

Mistle turned her closely-cropped head away, eyes fixed on the pink and blue streaks the dawn had painted above the eastern edge of the world.

'Indeed,' she said quietly. 'I shall be astonished if we ever meet again. If I ever see you again, little one. Go. Let's not drag this out.'

'Wait for me,' Ciri sniffed. 'And don't get yourself killed. Think about the amnesty Hotspurn was talking about. Even if Giselher and the others don't want to . . . You think about it, Mistle. It may be a way to survive . . . Because I will come back for you. I swear.'

'Kiss me.'

The dawn broke. The light grew and it became colder and colder.

'I love you, Waxwing.'

'I love you, Little Falcon. Now go.'

*

'Of course, she didn't believe me. She was convinced I'd got cold feet, that I'd rush after Hotspurn to look for help, to beg for that tempting amnesty. How could she know what feelings had overcome me, as I listened to what Hotspurn had said about Cintra and my grandmamma Calanthe? And about how some "Cirilla" would become the wife of the Emperor of Nilfgaard? That same emperor who had murdered my grandmamma. And who had sent that black knight with feathers on his helmet after me. I told you, remember? On the Isle of Thanedd, when he held out his hand to me, I made him bleed! I ought to have killed him . . . But somehow I couldn't . . . I was a fool! Oh, never mind. Perhaps he bled to death on Thanedd . . . Why are you looking at me like that?'

'Go on. Tell me how you rode after Hotspurn, to recover your inheritance. To recover what belonged to you.'

'There's no need to sneer, no need to mock. Yes, I know it was stupid, I see it now, I saw it then too . . . I was cleverer in Kaer Morhen and in the temple of Melitele, there I knew that what had passed could not return, that I wasn't the Princess of Cintra but someone completely different, that I had no inheritance. All of that was lost and I had to reconcile myself to it. It was explained to me wisely and solemnly, and I accepted it. Calmly, too. And then it suddenly began to come back. First, when they tried to impress me with the Baron of Casadei's daughter's title . . . I'd never been bothered about such things, but suddenly I fell into a fury, put on airs and yelled that I was more titled and of better birth than she. And from then on I began to think about it. I felt the fury growing in me. Do you understand that, Vysogota?'

'I do.'

'And Hotspurn's story was the last straw. I was almost boiling with rage . . . I had been told so much about destiny in the past . . . But here was someone else about to benefit from my destiny, thanks to simple fraud. Someone had passed themselves off as me, as Ciri of Cintra, and would have everything, would live in the lap of luxury . . . I couldn't think of anything else . . . I suddenly realised I was hungry, cold, sleeping outdoors, that I had to wash in freezing streams . . . Me! When I ought to have a gold-plated bathtub! Water perfumed with spikenard and roses! Warmed towels! Clean bed linen! Do you understand, Vysogota?'

'I do.'

'I was suddenly ready to ride to the nearest prefecture, to the nearest fort, to those black-cloaked Nilfgaardians whom I so feared and whom I hated so much . . . I was ready to say, "*I* am Ciri, you Nilfgaardian morons. Your stupid emperor ought to take *me* as his wife. Some impudent fraud has been shoved into your emperor's arms, and that idiot hasn't realised he's being swindled". I was so determined I would have done it, given the opportunity. Without a thought. Do you understand, Vysogota?'

'I do.'

'Fortunately, I calmed down.'

'To your great fortune.' He nodded gravely. 'The matter of the imperial marriage bears all the hallmarks of a political scandal, a battle of factions or fractions. Had you revealed yourself, thwarting other influential forces, you wouldn't have escaped the dagger or poison.'

'I understood that too. And remembered it. I remembered it well. To reveal who I was would mean death. I had the chance to convince myself of it. But let us not get ahead of the story.'

They were silent for some time, working with the skins. A few days before, the catch had been unexpectedly good. Many muskrats and coypus, two otters and a beaver had been caught in the traps and snares. So they had a great deal of work.

'Did you catch up with Hotspurn?' Vysogota finally asked.

'I did.' Ciri wiped her forehead with her sleeve. 'Quite quickly, actually, because he was in no hurry. And he wasn't at all surprised when he saw me!'

*

'Miss Falka!' Hotspurn tugged at the reins, gracefully spinning the black mare around. 'What a pleasant surprise! Although I confess it's not such a great one. I expected it, I can't conceal that I expected it. I knew you would make the right choice, miss. A wise choice. I noticed a flash of intelligence in your lovely and charming eyes.'

Ciri rode closer, so that their stirrups almost touched. Then she hawked at length, leaned over and spat on the sand of the highway. She had learned to spit in that hideous but effective way when it was necessary to dampen somebody's enthusiasm.

'I understand,' Hotspurn smiled slightly, 'you wish to take advantage of the amnesty?'

'No.'

'To what, then, should I ascribe the joy which the sight of your comely face evokes in me, miss?'

'Must there be a reason?' she snapped. 'You said you'd be pleased to have company on the road.'

'Nothing has changed.' He grinned more broadly. 'But if I'm wrong about the issue of the amnesty, I'm not certain we should keep company. We find ourselves, as you see, at a crossroads. A junction, the four points of the compass, the need for a choice . . . Symbolism, as in that well-known legend. If you ride east you will not return . . . If you ride west you will not return . . . If you ride north . . . Hmm . . . Amnesty lies north of this post—'

'You can shove your amnesty.'

'Whatever you say, miss. So where, if I may ask, does your road lead? Which path from this symbolic crossroads will you choose? Master Almavera, artist of the needle, drove his mules westwards, towards the small town of Fano. The eastern highway leads to

51

the settlement of Jealousy, but I would very much advise against that.'

'The River Yarra,' Ciri said slowly, 'is the Nilfgaardian name for the River Yaruga, right?'

'Such a learned maiden–' he leaned over and looked her in the eye '–and she doesn't know that?'

'Can't you answer in a civilised fashion, when you're asked in a civilised fashion?

'I was only joking! Why bristle so? Yes, it's the same river. In elven and Nilfgaardian it's the Yarra, in the North it's the Yaruga.'

'And at the mouth of that river,' continued Ciri, 'lies Cintra?'

'That's right. Cintra.'

'From where we are now, how far is it to Cintra? How many miles?'

'Plenty. And it depends what kind of miles you count it in. Almost every nation has its own, so it's easy to make a mistake. It's more convenient, using the method of all wandering merchants, to calculate such distances in days. Reaching Cintra would take twenty-five to thirty days.'

'Which way? Due north?'

'Miss Falka seems very curious about Cintra. Why?'

'I want to ascend to the throne there.'

'Very well, very well.' Hotspurn raised his hand in a defensive gesture. 'I understood the gentle deflection, I won't ask any more questions. The most direct road to Cintra, paradoxically, doesn't lead due north, for wildernesses and boggy lakes would hinder your progress. First, you should head towards the town of Forgeham, and then north-west to Metinna, the capital of a country with exactly the same name. Afterwards you ought to ride across the plain of Mag Deira, on the merchant's road to the town of Neunreuth. Only from there should you head for the north road, which runs along the valley of the River Yelena. From there it's easy – military units and transports ply the road without let-up via Nazair and the Marnadal Stairs, which is a pass leading north to the Marnadal Valley. And the Marnadal Valley is Cintra.'

'Hmm . . . ' Ciri's eyes were fixed on the misty horizon, at the blurred line of black hills. 'To Forgeham and then north-west . . . You mean . . . Which way?'

'You know what, miss?' Hotspurn smiled slightly. 'I'm heading towards Forgeham, and then to Metinna. See, down that track, that line of yellow sand between those young pines? Ride that way with me, and you won't lose your way. Amnesty or no amnesty, but it will be pleasant to travel with such a charming maiden.'

Ciri measured him up with the coldest glance she could manage. Hotspurn bit his lip with a puckish smile.

'So?'

'Let's ride.'

'Bravo, Miss Falka. Wise decision. I said that you were as wise as you were beautiful. I was right.'

'Stop calling me "miss", Hotspurn. In your mouth it sounds insulting, and I won't let myself be insulted with impunity.'

'As you wish, miss.'

*

The day did not fulfil the beautiful dawn's promise. It was grey and wet. The damp fog dimmed the intensity of the autumnal leaves of the trees leaning over the road, displaying a thousand shades of ochre, red and yellow.

The damp air smelled of bark and mushrooms.

They rode at a walk over a carpet of fallen leaves, but Hotspurn often spurred his black mare to a gentle trot or canter. During those moments Ciri looked on in delight.

'Does she have a name?'

'No.' Hotspurn flashed his teeth. 'I treat my mounts functionally. I change them regularly and don't became attached to them. I think giving horses names is pretentious, if one doesn't run a stable. Do you agree with me? Blacky the horse, Fido the dog and Felix the cat. Pretentious!'

*

Ciri didn't like his gaze or ambiguous smiles, and especially disliked the slightly mocking tone he used when talking and answering questions. So she adopted a simple tactic – she remained silent, spoke in monosyllables and did not provoke him. When possible.

53

It was not always possible. Particularly when he talked about that amnesty of his. Thus when once again – and quite sternly – she expressed her reluctance, Hotspurn surprisingly changed his approach; he abruptly began trying to prove that in her case an amnesty was not necessary, it simply did not apply to her. The amnesty concerned criminals, he said, not victims of crimes. Ciri roared with laughter.

'You're a victim yourself, Hotspurn!'

'I was speaking seriously,' he assured her. 'Not in order to arouse your girlish glee, but to suggest a way of saving your skin in the event of being captured. Something like that won't work on the Baron of Casadei, nor can you expect clemency from the Varnhagens. The most favourable outcome is that they would hang you on the spot, quickly and, all being well, quite painlessly. Were you, however, to fall into the hands of the prefect and stood before the austere, but just, imperial law . . . Ha, then I would suggest the following line of defence: break down in tears and declare that you were the innocent victim of a coincidence.'

'And who would believe that?'

'Everybody would.' Hotspurn leaned over in the saddle and looked her in the eye. 'Because that's the truth. You *are* an innocent victim, Falka. You aren't even sixteen, so according to the empire's law you're a minor. You ended up in the Rats' gang by accident. It's not your fault that one of the bandits, Mistle, whose unnatural tastes are no secret, took a fancy to you. You were dominated by Mistle, sexually abused and forced to—'

'Now it's all clear,' Ciri interrupted, amazed by her own calm. 'It's finally clear what this is all about, Hotspurn. I've seen men like you before.'

'Indeed?'

'Just like every cockerel,' she said, still composed, 'your comb bristles at the thought of me and Mistle. Like every stupid tomcat it dawns in your stupid noggin to try to cure me of this sickness which is contrary to nature, to turn the deviant back onto the road of truth. But do you know what is truly disgusting and contrary to nature in all that? Your thoughts!'

Hotspurn observed her in silence, with a somewhat mysterious smirk on his thin lips.

54

'My thoughts, dear Falka,' he said a moment later, 'may not be decent, may not be nice, and they are obviously not innocent ... But, by the Gods, they are in keeping with nature. With my nature. You do me a disservice, thinking that my attraction to you has its basis in some ... perverted curiosity. Ha, you also do yourself a disservice, by not being aware – or not wanting to realise – that your captivating appeal and uncommon beauty are capable of bringing any man to his knees. That the charm of your glance—'

'Listen, Hotspurn,' she interrupted. 'Do you want to bed me?'

'What intelligence,' he said, spreading his hands. 'I'm simply lost for words.'

'Then I'll help you.' She spurred her horse a little, in order to look at him over her shoulder. 'Because I have plenty of words. I feel honoured. In other circumstances, who knows ... If you were someone else, ha! But you, Hotspurn, do not attract me at all. Nothing, simply nothing, about you attracts me. And actually, I'd say, it's the reverse: everything about you puts me off. You can see for yourself that in such circumstances the sexual act would be contrary to nature.'

Hotspurn laughed, also spurring on his horse. The black mare danced on the track, gracefully lifting her shapely head. Ciri fidgeted in the saddle, fighting with a strange feeling which had suddenly woken in her, somewhere deep in the pit of her stomach, but which quickly and doggedly struggled outside, onto her skin, quivering from the touch of her clothing. *I've told him the truth,* she thought. *I don't like him, by the devil, it's his horse I like, that black mare. Not him, but his horse ... What damned foolishness! No, no, no! Even if I wasn't thinking of Mistle, it would be ridiculous and stupid to yield to him just because the sight of that black mare dancing on the track excites me.*

Hotspurn let her ride closer and looked her in the eyes with a strange smirk. Then he jerked the reins again, making the mare take short steps, circle and walk gracefully sideways. *He knows,* thought Ciri, *the old rascal knows what I'm feeling.*

Damn it. I'm simply curious!

'Some pine needles,' Hotspurn said gently, riding up very close and extending a hand, 'have got caught in your hair. I'll remove them if you allow. And I'll add that the gesture springs from my gallantry, not from perverted lust.'

The touch – which came as no surprise to her at all – caused her pleasure. She was still very far from a decision, but just to be sure she reckoned the days from her last bleeding. Yennefer had taught her that; to count in advance and with a cool head, because afterwards, when things got hot, a strange aversion to counting developed, linked to a tendency to ignore the potential result.

Hotspurn looked her in the eye and smiled, just as though he knew that the reckoning had come out in his favour. *If only he weren't so old!* Ciri sighed. *He's got to be at least thirty . . .*

'Tourmalines,' said Hotspurn, his fingers gently touching her ear and earring. 'Pretty, but only tourmalines. I would gladly give you emeralds. They are precious and have a more intense green, which would suit your looks and the colour of your eyes much better.'

'Know,' she drawled, looking at him insolently. 'If it came to it, I'd demand emeralds in advance. Because no doubt it's not just horses you treat functionally, Hotspurn. No doubt after a heady night you'd think recalling my first name was pretentious. Fido the dog, Felix the cat and the maiden: Mary-Jane!'

''Pon my honour,' he laughed artificially, 'you can chill the most feverish desire, O Snow Queen.'

'I've been well schooled.'

*

The fog had lifted a little, but it was still gloomy. And soporific. Until the languorous mood was brutally interrupted by yelling and the thudding of hooves. Some horsemen rushed out from behind a clump of oaks they had just passed.

The two of them reacted as quickly and as smoothly as if they had been practicing it for weeks. They spurred and reined their horses around, breaking into a gallop, a furious dash, pressed to their horses' manes, urging their mounts on with shouts and kicks of their heels. Above their heads crossbow bolts whirred, and up came a shouting, a clanging and a thudding of hoofbeat.

'Into the trees!' Hotspurn yelled. 'Turn into the forest! Into the undergrowth.'

They turned without slowing. Ciri pressed herself harder and lower to her horse's neck, for the branches lashing her as she sped past threatened to knock her from the saddle. She saw a crossbow bolt flake a splinter from the trunk of an alder they were passing. She shouted at her horse to go faster, expecting the thud of a bolt in her back at any moment. Hotspurn, riding just in front of her, suddenly groaned strangely. They cleared a deep hollow and rode recklessly down a precipice into a thorny thicket. Just then Hotspurn slid from his saddle and tumbled into a cranberry bush. The black mare neighed, kicked, thrashed her tail and rushed on. Ciri did not think twice. She dismounted and slapped her horse on the rump. As it ran after the black mare she helped Hotspurn up. The two of them dived into the bushes, into an alder copse, fell over, tumbled down the slope and into some tall ferns at the bottom of the ravine. Moss cushioned their fall.

The thudding of their pursuers' hooves resounded from the precipice above them. Fortunately they were riding higher up through the forest, after the fleeing horses. It seemed that their disappearance among the ferns had gone undetected.

'Who are they?' Ciri hissed, pulling crushed russula mushrooms from under Hotspurn and shaking them from her hair. 'The prefect's men? The Varnhagens?'

'Common bandits . . .' Hotspurn spat out leaves. 'Thugs . . .'

'Offer them an amnesty,' she said, spitting sand. 'Promise them—'

'Be quiet. They'll hear.'

'Heeeyy! Heeeyyy! Over heeere!' they heard from above. 'Over on the leeeft! On the leeeft!'

'Hotspurn?'

'What?'

'You have blood on your back.'

'I know,' he answered coldly, pulling a wad of linen from his jacket and turning over on his side. 'Shove this under my shirt. By my left shoulder blade . . .'

'Where were you hit? I can't see the bolt . . .'

'It was an arbalest . . . Iron shot. The head of a horseshoe nail,

57

most probably. Leave it there, don't touch it. It's right by the backbone.'

'Dammit. What can I do?'

'Keep quiet. They're returning.'

Hooves pounded, someone whistled piercingly. Somebody yelled, called, and ordered somebody else to go back. Ciri listened intently.

'They're riding off,' she murmured. 'They've given up the chase. They didn't even catch the horses.'

'Good.'

'We won't catch them either. Will you be able to walk?'

'I won't have to.' He smiled, showing her a cheap-looking bracelet fastened to his wrist. 'I bought this trinket with the horse. It's magical. The mare has carried it since she was a foal. When I rub it, like this, it's as though I were calling her. As though she were hearing my voice. She'll run here. It'll take some time, but she'll come for certain. With a bit of fortune your roan will follow her.'

'And with a bit of bad luck you'll ride off by yourself?'

'Falka,' he said, becoming grave. 'I won't. I'm counting on your help. I'll have to be held up in the saddle. My toes are already going numb. I may lose consciousness. Listen: this ravine will lead you to a narrow river valley. You'll ride uphill, against the current, northwards. You'll carry me to a place called Tegamo. You'll find somebody there who'll know how to get this iron out of my back without me ending up dead or paralysed.'

'Is that the nearest village?'

'No. Jealousy is nearer, it's in a valley about twenty miles in the opposite direction, downstream. But don't go there under any circumstances.'

'Why?'

'Under no circumstances,' he repeated, frowning. 'It's not about me, it's about you. Jealousy means death for you.'

'I don't understand.'

'You don't have to. Simply trust me.'

'You told Giselher—'

'Forget Giselher. If you want to live, forget about all of them.'

'Why?'

'Stay with me. I'll keep my word, Snow Queen. I'll cover you with emeralds . . . I'll shower you in them. . .'

'Indeed, this is a wonderful time for making jokes.'

'It's always a good time for jokes.'

Hotspurn suddenly seized her, pulled her close and began to undo her blouse. Unceremoniously, but unhurriedly. Ciri pushed him away.

'Indeed!' she snapped. 'A wonderful time for that too!'

'It's always a good time for that. Especially for me, right now. I told you, it's my spine. There may be complications tomorrow . . .'

'What are you doing? Oh, damn it . . .'

This time she pushed him away harder. Too powerfully. Hotspurn blanched, bit his lip and groaned in pain.

'I'm sorry. But if somebody is wounded they ought to lie still.'

'Being close to you makes me forget the pain.'

'Stop that!'

'Falka . . . Be nice to a suffering man.'

'You'll really suffer if you don't take your hand away. This second!'

'Quiet . . . The thugs are liable to hear us . . . Your skin is like silk . . . Don't wriggle.'

Oh, dammit, thought Ciri, *let it be. In any case, what difference does it make? I'm curious. I can be curious. There's no real feeling in it. I'll treat him functionally and that's that. And forget him unpretentiously.*

She yielded to his touch and the pleasure it brought. She turned her head away, but decided that was exaggeratedly modest and fraudulently prudish; she didn't want to be a goody-goody being seduced. She looked him straight in the eyes, but that seemed too bold and provocative; she didn't want to be like that either. So she simply closed her eyes, hugged him around the neck and helped him with the buttons, because he was having difficulty with them and wasting time. The touch of fingers was joined by the touch of lips. She was close to forgetting about the entire world when Hotspurn suddenly froze stiff. For a while she lay patiently, remembering that he was wounded and the wound must be bothering him. But it went on a little too long. His saliva was cooling on her nipples.

'Hey, Hotspurn? Are you asleep?'

Something oozed onto her chest and side. She touched it with her fingers. Blood.

'Hotspurn!' she shoved him off her. 'Hotspurn, have you died?'

Foolish question, she thought. *I mean, I can see.*

I can see he's died.

*

'He died with his head on my breast.' Ciri turned her head away. The glow from the fireplace played red on her disfigured cheek. Perhaps there was a blush there too. Vysogota could not be certain.

'The only thing I felt then,' she added, still turned away, 'was disappointment. Does that shock you?'

'No. Actually not.'

'I understand. I'm trying not to embellish the story, not correct anything. Not keep anything back. Although occasionally I feel like it, especially that last part.' She sniffed, rubbing a knuckle into the corner of her eye.

'I covered him with branches and stones. Any old thing I could find, I confess. It grew dark, I had to sleep there. The bandits were still hanging around, I could hear their shouts and I was certain they weren't ordinary bandits. I just didn't know who they were hunting: me or him. But I had to stay quiet. The whole night. Until dawn. Next to a corpse. Brrr.'

'At dawn,' she began again a moment later, 'the sound of our pursuers had long since faded away and I could set off. I had a mount. The magical bracelet I took from Hotspurn's arm really worked. The black mare returned. Now she belonged to me. That was my present. That's the custom on the Isles of Skellige, did you know? A girl has the right to a costly gift from her first lover. So what if mine died before he managed to actually become my lover?'

*

The mare banged her front hooves on the ground, neighed and turned in profile as though ordering Ciri to admire her. Ciri could not suppress a sigh of admiration at the sight of the dolphin-like neck; straight and slender, but powerfully muscled, the small shapely head with its concave forehead, the high withers and her build of delightful proportions.

She approached cautiously, showing the mare the bracelet on her wrist. The mare gave a long drawn-out snort, flattened her twitching ears, but allowed herself to be caught by the bridle and stroked on her velvety nose.

'Kelpie,' Ciri said. 'You're as black and agile as a sea-kelpie. You're as magical as a kelpie. So you'll be "Kelpie". And I don't care if that's pretentious or not.'

The mare snorted, stuck her ears up, and shook her silky tail, which reached her hocks. Ciri – favouring a high saddle position – shortened the stirrup leathers and felt the unusual, flat saddle. It had no saddle tree or pommel. She fitted her boot to the stirrup and seized the horse by the mane.

'Nice and easy, Kelpie.'

The saddle, in spite of appearances, was quite comfortable. And for obvious reasons much lighter than standard cavalry saddles.

'Now,' Ciri said, patting the mare on her hot neck, 'let's see if you're as fleet as you are beautiful. If you're a real racer or just a hack. What do you say to a twenty-mile gallop, Kelpie?'

*

Had someone quietly crept up deep in the night to the remote cottage in the midst of the swamp with its sunken, moss-grown thatched roof, had they peered through the slits in the shutters, they would have seen a grey-bearded old man listening to the story told by a teenage girl with green eyes and ashen hair.

They would have seen the dying glow in the fireplace come alive and grow bright, as though sensing what would be told.

But that was not possible. No one could have seen it. The cottage of old Vysogota was well hidden among the reeds in the swamp. In a wilderness permanently covered in mist, where no one dared to venture.

*

'The stream's valley was level, and good for riding, so Kelpie ran like the wind. Of course, I wasn't riding uphill but downstream. I remembered that curious name: Jealousy. I recalled what Hotspurn had said to Giselher at the station. I understood why he had warned me about that village. There must have been an ambush in Jealousy. When Giselher made light of the offer of the amnesty and working for the guild, Hotspurn deliberately mentioned the bounty hunter quartered in the village. He knew the Rats would swallow the bait, ride there and fall into the trap. I had to get to Jealousy before them, cut off their route and warn them. Turn them back. All of them. Or at least just Mistle.'

'I conclude,' Vysogota mumbled, 'that you didn't manage to.'

'At that time,' she said softly, 'I thought that a large force, armed to the teeth, was waiting in Jealousy. In my wildest dreams it never occurred to me that the trap was a single man . . .'

She was silent, staring into the gloom.

'Nor did I have any idea what kind of man he was.'

*

Birka had once been a wealthy village, charming and picturesquely situated – its yellow thatch and red tiles crowded into a valley with steep, forested sides, which changed colour with the seasons. In autumn, especially, Birka delighted the artistic eye and sensitive heart.

It was like that until the settlement changed its name. Here is what happened:

A young farmer from a nearby elven colony was madly in love with the miller's daughter from Birka. The miller's prankish daughter ridiculed the elf's wooing and continued to sleep around with neighbours, friends and even relatives. They began to mock the elf and his blind love. The elf – somewhat untypically for his race – exploded with anger and vengeance, exploded horribly. One night, with a strong wind blowing the right way, he started a fire and burned Birka down.

The victims of the fire, now ruined, lost heart. Some roamed the world and others fell into idleness and drunkenness. The money gathered for the rebuilding of the village was regularly defrauded and squandered on drink, and the settlement became a vision of misery and despair: it was a jumble of ghastly, carelessly thrown together shacks beneath the bare and black-charred slope of the valley. Before the fire Birka had been oval-shaped, with a central square; now the few solidly built houses, granaries and a distillery formed something like a long main street, which was topped by the façade of *The Chimera's Head*, built by the efforts of the community and kept by the widow Goulue.

And for seven years no one had used the name 'Birka'. People said 'Flaming Jealousy', or for short; simply 'Jealousy'.

The Rats rode down the main street. It was a chill, overcast, gloomy morning.

People fled into their homes, hid in their sheds or their wattle-and-daub shacks. Those who had shutters slammed them closed, those who had doors bolted them. Whoever still had vodka drank it to give them courage. The Rats rode at a walk, ostentatiously slowly, stirrup against stirrup. An indifferent contempt was painted on their faces, but their narrowed eyes closely observed the windows, porches and alleyways.

'One bolt from a crossbow!' Giselher warned, loudly. 'One clang of a bowstring, and there'll be a bloodbath here!'

'And the red flame will be let slip!' Iskra added in her high, melodious soprano. 'Only earth and water will remain!'

Some of the villagers certainly had crossbows, but no one wanted to find out if the Rats' words were empty.

The Rats dismounted. They covered the final furlong separating them from *The Chimera's Head* on foot, side by side, their spurs, adornments and jewellery rhythmically jangling and clinking.

At the sight of them, three Jealousy residents, soothing the previous day's hangover with beer, bolted from the steps of the inn.

'Hope he's still here,' Kayleigh muttered. 'We've taken our time. There was no need for that rest, we should have come right away, even travelled at night . . .'

'Fool.' Iskra bared her little teeth. 'If we want bards to sing songs about this, it can't be done at night, in the darkness. People must see it! Morning is best, when everybody's still sober, right, Giselher?'

Giselher did not reply. He picked up a stone, swung and hurled it against the door of the inn.

'Come out, Bonhart!'

'Come out, Bonhart!' the Rats called in unison. 'Come out, Bonhart!'

Footsteps could be heard inside. Slow and heavy ones. Mistle felt a shiver crawling over the nape of her neck and her shoulders. Bonhart stood in the doorway.

The Rats involuntarily took a step back. The heels of their high boots dug into the ground and their hands shot to their sword hilts. The bounty hunter held his sword under one arm. That way he had his hands free; in one he held a peeled boiled egg and in the other a hunk of bread.

He slowly walked to the balustrade and looked down on them, from high up. He stood in the porch, and was huge. Immense, though he was as gaunt as a ghoul.

He looked at them, sweeping his watery eyes over each in turn. Then he bit off a morsel of egg and after it a piece of bread.

'Where's Falka?' he asked indistinctly. Bits of yolk fell from his moustache and lips.

*

'Run, Kelpie! Run, my beauty! Fast as you can!'

The black mare neighed loudly, extending her neck in a headlong gallop. A hail of gravel shot out from under her hooves, though it seemed as if they were barely touching the ground.

*

Bonhart stretched lazily, his leather jerkin creaking. He slowly pulled down and adjusted his elk-hide gloves.

'What could this be?' he grimaced. 'You want to kill me? And why?'

'For Muchomorek, for starters,' Kayleigh answered.

'And for our amusement,' said Iskra.

'And to get you off our backs,' Reef threw in.

64

'Aaaah,' Bonhart said slowly. 'So that's what it's about! And if I swear to leave you alone, will you leave me alone?'

'No, you grey cur, we will not.' Mistle smiled charmingly. 'We know you. We know you won't drop it, that you'll trudge along our trail and wait for a chance to stab one of us in the back. Come down!'

'Easy does it.' Bonhart smiled too, malevolently stretching his mouth wide beneath his grey whiskers. 'We can always find time to cavort around, there's no need to be hasty. First I'll make you an offer, Rats. I'll permit you to choose.'

'What are you mumbling about, you old fool?' Kayleigh shouted, crouching. 'Speak clearly!'

Bonhart nodded and scratched a thigh.

'There's a bounty on you, Rats. A goodly one. And life must go on.'

Iskra snorted and opened her eyes wide like a wildcat. Bonhart crossed his arms on his chest, holding his sword in the crook of his arm.

'That goodly reward,' he repeated, 'is for you dead, and it's a little larger for taking you alive. But, to tell the truth, it's all the same to me. I have nothing against you personally. I was thinking yesterday that I'd dispatch you all, for a bit of amusement and diversion, but you've come yourselves, saving me the bother. You've won my heart by so doing. Thus I shall let you choose. How do you prefer me to take you: the playful way or the painful way?'

The muscles on Kayleigh's jaw twitched. Mistle leaned over, ready to leap. Giselher caught her arm.

'He means to enrage us,' he hissed. 'Let the bastard talk.'

Bonhart snorted.

'Well?' he repeated. 'The easy way or the hard way? I advise the first. For you see, the easy way hurts much, much less.'

The Rats drew their weapons at the same instant. Giselher made a few crosscuts and struck a swordfighter's pose. Mistle spat copiously on the ground.

'Come down here, skinny old man,' she said, apparently calmly. 'Come here, you blackguard. We'll kill you like a grizzled old dog.'

'So you wish it the hard way,' Bonhart said, looking somewhere above the rooftops. He slowly drew his sword, throwing down his scabbard, and unhurriedly descended from the porch, his spurs clanking.

The Rats swiftly spread out across the street. Kayleigh went furthest to the left, almost to the wall of the distillery. Beside him stood Iskra, twisting her thin lips in her usual, dreadful smile. Mistle, Asse and Reef went off to the right. Giselher remained in the centre, staring at the bounty hunter from under narrowed eyelids.

'Very well, Rats.' Bonhart looked from side to side, looked up at the sky, and then raised his sword and spat on the blade. 'If we're to cavort, let us cavort. Let the music play!'

They leaped at each other like wolves, like lightning, silently, with no warning. Blades wailed in the air, filling the narrow street with the plaintive clang of steel. At first all that could be heard was the clang of sword hilts, gasps, groans and quickened breathing.

And then, suddenly and unexpectedly, the Rats began to scream. And die.

Reef lurched out of the melee first, his back smacking against a wall, splashing blood on the dirty whitewash. Asse reeled out after him, staggering, curled over and fell on his side, by turns bending and straightening his knees.

Bonhart whirled around and leapt like a mad thing, surrounded by the glint and whistle of his blade. The Rats backed away from him, lunging forward, slashing and jumping aside, furiously, fiercely, pitilessly. And ineffectively. Bonhart parried, struck, parried, struck, and attacked, attacked relentlessly, without respite, dictating the tempo of the bout. And the Rats backed away. And died.

Iskra, slashed in the neck, fell over in the mud, cowering like a kitten, blood gushing from an artery onto Bonhart's calves and knees as he walked past her. The bounty hunter parried the attacks of Mistle and Giselher with a broad swing, then whirled and carved Kayleigh open with a lightning-fast blow, striking him with the very tip of his sword; from collar bone to hip. Kayleigh released his sword, but did not fall, just curled up and seized his chest and belly in both hands, as blood trickled through his fingers. Bonhart once more whirled away from Giselher's thrust, parried Mistle's attack and smote Kayleigh again, this time turning the side of his head into scarlet pulp. The fair-haired Rat fell, splashing into a puddle of blood mixed with mud.

Mistle and Giselher hesitated for a moment. And instead of fleeing, yelled with a single voice, savagely and furiously. And leaped at Bonhart.

And found death.

*

Ciri burst into the settlement and galloped down the main street. Splashes of mud spurted from beneath the mare's hooves.

*

Bonhart shoved Giselher, who was lying by the wall, with his heel. The Rats' leader gave no sign of life. Blood had stopped gushing from his shattered skull.

Mistle, on her knees, searched for her sword, groping in the mud and dung with both hands, not seeing that she was kneeling in a quickly spreading puddle of red. Bonhart walked slowly over towards her.

'Noooooo!'

The hunter raised his head.

Ciri leaped from her speeding horse, staggered and dropped onto one knee.

Bonhart smiled.

'A she-rat,' he said. 'The seventh Rat. I'm glad you are here. I needed you to complete the set.'

Mistle had found her sword, but was unable to lift it. She wheezed and threw herself at Bonhart's feet. Her trembling fingers dug into the legs of his boots. She opened her mouth to scream, but instead of a cry, a shining crimson stream burst forth. Bonhart kicked her hard, knocking her over in the muck. Mistle, both hands now holding her mutilated belly, managed to raise herself again.

'Noooo!' Ciri screamed. 'Miiiistle!'

The bounty hunter paid no attention to her yell. He did not even turn his head. He swung his sword and struck vigorously, as though with a scythe. A powerful blow that jerked Mistle up from the ground and flung her over to the wall, as limp as a cloth doll, like a rag smeared with red.

A scream died in Ciri's throat. Her hands trembled as she reached for her sword.

'Murderer,' she said, astonished at the strangeness of her voice, at the strangeness of her lips, which had suddenly become horrendously dry.

'Murderer! Bastard!'

Bonhart observed her curiously, tilting his head slightly.

'Are you going to die too?' he asked.

Ciri walked towards him, skirting around him in a semi-circle. The sword in his raised and extended hands moved around, deceiving, beguiling.

The bounty hunter laughed loudly.

'Die!' he repeated. 'The she-rat wants to die!'

He moved around slowly, standing on the spot, not allowing himself to be lured into the trap of the semi-circle. But it was all the same to Ciri. She was boiling over with ferocity and hatred, trembling with the lust for murder. She wanted to strike that ghastly old man, feel her blade cut into his body. She wanted to see his blood gushing from severed arteries in the final beats of his heart.

'Well, little Rat.' Bonhart raised his bloody sword and spat on the blade. 'Before you die, show me what there is in you! Let the music play!'

*

'Truly, no one knows how that they did not slaughter each other during the first clash,' Nycklar, the son of the coffin maker said, six days later. 'They wanted to slaughter each other, that was clear to see. She to murder him and he her. They flew at each other, came together for a split second and there was a mighty clash of swords. They exchanged mebbes two, mebbes three blows each. There ain't a man what could of counted it, by sight or by hearing. So swiftly did they strike, m'lord, that not a man's eye nor ear could have grasped it. And how they danced and leaped around each other, like two weasels!'

68

Stefan Skellen, called Tawny Owl, listened attentively, playing with a knout.

'They leaped apart,' the boy went on, 'but neither of them was even grazed. The she-rat was as wrathful as the very Devil, and was hissing like a tomcat when someone wants to take his mouse away. But Mr Bonhart was wholly serene.'

*

'Falka,' Bonhart said, smiling and grinning like a veritable ghoul. 'Truly can you dance and whirl a blade! You have aroused my curiosity, wench. Who are you? Tell me, before you perish.'

Ciri panted. She felt terror beginning to seize her. She understood what she was up against.

'Tell me who you are, and I'll spare your life.'

She gripped her hilt more tightly. She had to, had to, get through his parries, slash him, before he closed up. She could not let him deflect her blows, she could not withstand his blows with her sword, she could not risk – even once more – the pain and paralysis which pierced and spread through her elbow and forearm when she parried. She could not waste energy dodging his blows, which were missing her by barely a hair's breadth. *Get through his defence*, she thought. *Right now. In this clash. Or die.*

'You will die, she-rat,' he said, moving towards her with his sword extended far out in front of him. 'Do you not fear? That is only because you know not what death looks like.'

Kaer Morhen, she thought, as she sprang. *Lambert. The comb. The somersault.*

She took three steps and performed a half-pirouette, and when he attacked she ignored his feint, threw a backward somersault, dropped into a nimble crouch and lunged at him, ducking under his blade and twisting her wrist for the cut, for a fearful blow, aided by a powerful twist of her hip. Suddenly she was seized by euphoria; she would feel the blade cutting into his body.

Instead, there was the hard, moaning impact of metal on metal. And a sudden flash in her eyes, a shock and pain in her head. She felt herself falling, felt herself hitting the ground. *He parried and twisted*, she thought. *I'm dying*, she thought. Bonhart kicked her in the belly. A second kick, accurately and painfully aimed at her elbow, knocked the sword from her hand. Ciri grabbed her head and felt a dull pain, but there was neither a wound nor blood beneath her fingers. *He hit me with his fist*, she thought to her horror. *I was just punched. Or struck with the pommel of his sword. He didn't kill me. He thrashed me like an unruly brat.*

She opened her eyes.

The hunter stood over her, terrible and gaunt as a skeleton, towering over her like a diseased, leafless tree, stinking of sweat and blood.

He seized her by the hair, lifted her violently, forced her to stand, but at once jerked her, knocking the ground from under her feet, and dragged her, wailing like the damned, towards Mistle, who was lying at the foot of the wall.

'So you don't fear death, do you?' he snarled, bending her head downwards. 'Then have a look, she-rat. That is death. That is how you die. Look, those are guts. That is blood. And that is shit. That's what's inside us all.'

Ciri tensed up, bent over, still gripped by his hand, and dry-retched hoarsely. Mistle was still alive, but her eyes were already misty, glazed, fishlike. Her hand, like a hawk's talons, clenched and unclenched, clawing the mud and dung. Ciri smelled the acrid, penetrating odour of urine. Bonhart cackled.

'That is how you'll die, little Rat. In your own piss!'

He released her hair. Ciri collapsed onto all fours, racked by dry, choking sobs. Mistle was right beside her. Mistle's hand, slender, delicate, soft; Mistle's hand . . .

It was no longer moving.

*

'He didn't kill me. He tied my hands to the hitching post.'

Vysogota sat motionless. He had been sitting like that for a long time. He was even holding his breath. Ciri continued her tale, but her voice was becoming more and more hushed, more and more unnatural, more and more unpleasant.

'He ordered the people who had gathered to bring him a sack of salt and a keg of vinegar. And a saw. I didn't know . . . I couldn't

understand what he meant to do . . . I still didn't know what he
was capable of. I was tied . . . to the hitching post . . . He called
some servants, ordered them to hold me by the hair . . . and by the
eyelids. He showed them how; so I couldn't turn my head away or
close my eyes . . . So I had to watch what he was doing. "You have
to take pains so the goods won't go off," he said. "So they won't
decay . . ."'

Ciri's voice cracked, stuck dryly in her throat. Vysogota, suddenly realising what he was hearing, felt the saliva well up in his
mouth like a flood wave.

'He cut off their heads,' Ciri said dully. 'With a saw. Giselher,
Kayleigh, Asse, Reef, Iskra . . . And Mistle. He sawed off their
heads . . . One after the other. In front of my eyes.'

*

If someone were to have quietly crept up that night to the remote
cottage in the midst of the swamp with its sunken, moss-grown
thatched roof, were they to have peered through the slits in the
shutters, in the dimly-lit interior they would have seen a grey-
bearded old man in a sheepskin coat and an ashen-haired girl with
her face disfigured by a scar on her cheek. They would have seen
the girl racked with sobs, choking on tears in the arms of the old
man, while he tried to calm her, awkwardly and mechanically
stroking and patting her trembling shoulders.

But it was not possible. No one could have seen it. The cottage
was well concealed amidst the marshes. In a wilderness ever covered in mist, where no one dared to venture.

71

I have often been asked what made me decide to write my memoirs. Many people seemed interested in the moment my memoirs began, namely what fact, event or incident gave rise to the writing. Formerly, I gave various explanations and often lied, but now, howbeit, I pay homage to the truth. For today, now that my hair has thinned and is going white, I know the truth is a precious seed, while a lie is but contemptible chaff.

And the truth is thus: the event which gave rise to everything, to which I owe the first notes, from which my subsequent life's work was formed, was the accidental discovery of paper and pencil among the things that my company and I stole from the Lyrian military convoys. It happened . . .

Dandelion, *Half a Century of Poetry*

CHAPTER THREE

. . . it happened on the fifth day after the September new moon, on the thirtieth day of our expedition, to be precise, reckoning from when we set out from Brokilon, and six days after the Battle on the Bridge.

Now, my dear future reader, I shall go back in time somewhat and describe the events which took place directly following the glorious Battle on the Bridge, which was so fraught with consequences. First though, I shall enlighten the considerable number of readers who know nothing about the Battle on the Bridge, either owing to their having other interests or as a result of their general ignorance. Let me clarify: that battle was waged on the last day of the month of August in the Year of the Great War in Angren, on the bridge connecting the two banks of the River Yaruga in the vicinity of a border post called the Red Timber Port. The sides of this armed conflict were: the Nilfgaardian Army; a corps from Lyria commanded by Queen Meve; and our glorious company. Which consisted of myself, i.e. the undersigned; and also the Witcher, Geralt; the vampire, Emiel Regis Rohellec Terzieff-Godefroy; the archer, Maria Barring, known as Milva; and Cahir Mawr Dyffryn aep Ceallach, a Nilfgaardian, who liked stubbornly to maintain that he was not such.

It may also be unclear to you, dear reader, why Queen Meve was in Angren, when it was believed she had perished during the Nilfgaardian incursion into Lyria, Rivia and Aedirn in July, which ended in the total conquest of those lands and their occupation by the imperial army. However, Meve had not perished in battle, as was thought, nor was she captured by Nilfgaard. Banding together a loyal mobile force from the surviving Lyrian Army under her colours and enlisting anyone she could, including mercenaries and common felons, the valiant Meve took up a partisan war against Nilfgaard. And the wildness of Angren suited guerrilla warfare perfectly; now striking from an ambuscade, now lurking in some undergrowth – for there was undergrowth in abundance in Angren. If truth be told, there is nothing worth mentioning in that land aside from undergrowth.

The regiment of Meve – now called the White Queen by her army – swiftly grew in might and acquired such daring that it was able to cross to the Yaruga's left bank, in order, to prowl freely and foment unrest far in the enemy's rear.

Now let us return to our sheep; that is, the Battle on the Bridge. The tactical situation was as follows. Queen Meve's partisans, having rampaged on the Yaruga's left bank, wanted to flee to the Yaruga's right bank, but happened upon the Nilfgaardians, who were rampaging along the Yaruga's right bank and wanted to flee to the Yaruga's left bank. We, from a central position, i.e. the very middle of the River Yaruga, happened upon the above and were surrounded on both sides, from the left and right, by armed men. Having nowhere to flee, we became heroes and covered ourselves in undying glory. The battle, incidentally, was won by the Lyrians, since they achieved what they had intended: i.e. a flight to the right bank. The Nilfgaardians bolted in an unknown direction and in so doing lost the battle. I realise that this all sounds passing confusing and I shall not omit to consult with some military theoretician on the text before publication. For the moment, I am relying on the authority of Cahir aep Ceallach, the only soldier in our company – and Cahir confirmed that winning battles by means of a rapid escape from the battlefield is permissible from the point of view of most military doctrines.

The contribution of our company to the battle was indisputably meritorious, but also had negative consequences. Milva, who was with child, met with a tragic misadventure. The rest of us were fortunate enough not to suffer any serious injuries. But neither did anyone profit, nor even receive any thanks. The exception being Geralt the Witcher. For Geralt the Witcher, in spite of his repeated, but clearly duplicitously professed, indifference and his frequently declared neutrality, displayed in the battle a fervour as great as it was exaggeratedly spectacular. In other words, he fought in a truly effective way, if not to say: for effect. He was noticed, and Meve, the Queen of Lyria, knighted him with her own hand. It quickly turned out that there was more unpleasantness than benefit from that accolade.

For I must tell you, gentle reader, that Geralt the Witcher was always a modest, prudent and composed man, with a soul as simple and uncomplicated as the shaft of a halberd. The unexpected promotion and apparent generosity of Queen Meve changed him, however, and had I not known him better, I would have said that it made him conceited. Instead of vanishing from the scene as quickly and anonymously as possible, Geralt became mixed up in the royal retinue, enjoyed his honour, took delight in the grace and favour, and relished his fame.

But fame and renown were the last things we needed. I shall remind those that do not remember that the very same Geralt the Witcher – now dubbed a knight – was being sought by the intelligence services of all the Four Kingdoms in connection with the matter of the sorcerers' rebellion on the Isle of Thanedd. Attempts were made to charge me – an innocent person, as honest as the day is long – with the crime of espionage. To that one ought to add Milva, who had collaborated with dryads and Scoia'tael, and who was embroiled – as it transpired – in the infamous massacre on the borders of Brokilon Forest. To that one ought to add Cahir aep Ceallach, a Nilfgaardian, a citizen of an enemy nation, whose presence on the wrong side of the battle would have been arduous to explain or justify. It so happened that the only member of our company whose curriculum vitae was not besmirched by political or criminal issues was the vampire. The exposure or identification of any one of us threatened us all with impalement on sharpened aspen stakes. Each day spent – initially, indeed, pleasantly, safely and with full bellies – in the shade of the Lyrian standards aggrandised that risk.

Geralt, when I emphatically reminded him of that, became somewhat dispirited, but put forward his arguments, of which he had two. Firstly, following her disagreeable accident, Milva still required care and attention, and there were barber-surgeons in the army. Secondly, Queen Meve's army was marching east, towards Caed Dhu. And our company, before it changed direction and became embroiled in the battle described above, had also been heading to Caed Dhu, for we hoped to obtain some information from the druids dwelling there to aid our search for Ciri. Patrols and lawless gangs prowling in Angren had driven us from our straight road to the aforementioned druids. Now, under the protection of the friendly Lyrian Army, in the grace and favour of Queen Meve, the way to Caed Dhu was wide open; why, it seemed straightforward and safe. I warned the Witcher that it only appeared so, that it was but a semblance and that royal favours are *deceptive and inconstant. The Witcher did not want to listen. But it was soon proved who was right. When news got out that a Nilfgaardian punitive expedition was marching towards Angren in great force from the Klamat Pass in the East, the Lyrian Army wasted no time in turning back towards the Mahakam Mountains in the North. As may easily be imagined, that change of direction did not suit Geralt in the slightest; he was hurrying to the druids, not to Mahakam! As naïve as a child, he ran to Queen Meve to obtain an exemption from the army and a royal blessing for his private business. And in that moment queenly love and favour ended, and admiration for the hero of the Battle for the Bridge vanished like so much smoke. The knight, Sir Geralt of Rivia, was reminded in a cool, though resolute, tone of his knightly duties towards the crown. The still ailing Milva, the vampire Regis and the undersigned were instructed to join the column of fugitives and civilians moving behind the convoy. Cahir aep Ceallach, a sturdy youth who in no way resembled a civilian, was given a white and blue sash and conscripted into a so-called free company, which meant a cavalry unit drawn from various bits of rabble picked up by the Lyrian corps on the road. In this way our company was sundered and everything suggested that our expedition was definitively and resoundingly over.*

As you might imagine, dear reader, it was not the end at all, nay, 'twas not even the beginning! Milva, once she had learned of this development, immediately declared herself fit and well. She was first to give the order to withdraw. Cahir flung his royal livery into the bushes and bolted from the free company, and Geralt fled the opulent tents of the select knighthood.

I shall not go on at length about the details, and modesty does not permit me the excessive display of my own − not insignificant − contribution to the undertaking. I merely state the fact: on the night of the fifth of September our entire company clandestinely took leave of Queen Meve's corps. Before parting from the Lyrian Army we stocked up liberally, without asking the quartermaster's permission for so doing. I consider the word 'theft' − as used by Milva − to be too blunt. For we deserved some sort of payment for our involvement in the memorable Battle of the Bridge. And if not a payment, then at least compensation and reparations for the losses we incurred! Passing over Milva's tragic accident, not counting Geralt and Cahir's cuts and

bruises, all our horses were killed or crippled, apart from my faithful
Pegasus and the skittish Roach, the Witcher's mare. Thus, in lieu of
compensation, we took three full-blooded cavalry steeds and one colt.
We also took various bits of tackle, whatever fell into our hands; for
the sake of fairness I shall add that we subsequently had to throw half
of it away. As Milva said, that can happen when you steal in the dark.
The most useful things were taken from the army stores by the vampire
Regis, who can see better in the dark than by day. Regis additionally
diminished the defensive capabilities of the Lyrian Army by one fat,
mousy-grey mule, which he led from the pen so expertly that not a
single beast snorted or stamped a hoof. Stories about animals smelling
vampires and reacting to their smell in panicked fear cannot thus be
believed; unless it refers to certain animals and certain vampires. I
shall add that we kept said mousy-grey mule for some time. Follow-
ing the loss of the colt, which later bolted in the forests of Riverdell,
alarmed by wolves, the mule carried what was left of our belongings.
The mule was called Draakul. It was so named by Regis immediately
after being stolen and so it remained. Regis was clearly entertained by
the name, which no doubt had some amusing significance in the culture
and speech of vampires, but which he did not wish to explain to us,
claiming it was an untranslatable pun.

In this way our company found itself on the road again, and the
previously lengthy list of folk who did not like us grew even longer.
Geralt of Rivia, an unblemished knight, had quit the ranks of the
knighthood before his promotion had been confirmed by a single deed,
and before the court heraldist had created a coat of arms for him.
Cahir aep Ceallach had already managed to fight in and desert from
both armies in the great conflict between Nilfgaard and the Nordlings,
earning a sentence of death in absentia in both. The rest of us were in
no better a situation. After all, a noose is a noose and the importance of
why one is to hang is extremely slight; whether for discrediting knightly
honour, desertion or christening an army mule 'Draakul'.

Let it not then astonish you, reader, that we made truly titanic
efforts to considerably increase the distance between us and Queen
Meve's corps. We rode south with all possible speed towards the
Yaruga, intending to cross to the left bank. Not only in order to put
the river between us and the queen and her partisans, but because the
wildernesses of Riverdell were less dangerous than war-torn Angren;

it would have been far more judicious to travel to the druids in Caed Dhu along the left and not the right bank. Paradoxically so – since the left bank of the Yaruga belonged to the hostile Nilfgaardian Empire. The father of the left-bank conception was Geralt the Witcher, who, after leaving the fraternity of swaggering knighthood, had regained the greater part of his reason, ability to think logically, and customary caution. The future was to show that the Witcher's plan was fraught with consequences and determined the fate of the entire expedition. But more about that later.

When we reached the Yaruga there were already plenty of Nilf-gaardians there who had crossed the reconstructed bridge at the Red Timber Port and were continuing the offensive against Angren; and probably further, against Temeria, Mahakam and the Devil only knows where else the Nilfgaardian general staff was planning to attack. Crossing the river right away was out of the question; we had to hide and wait for the army to move on. So for two whole days we hunkered in the riverside osiers, cultivating rheumatism and feeding the mosquitoes. To make matters worse, the weather soon declined: it drizzled, was windy as hell, and our teeth were chattering from the cold. I do not recall such a cold September among the many Sep-tembers engraved in my memory. It was then, my dear reader, having found paper and pencil among the supplies borrowed from the Lyrian convoys, to kill time and forget about our discomforts, that I began to record and immortalise some of our adventures.

The foul rainy weather and enforced inactivity spoiled our mood and prompted various dark thoughts. Particularly in the Witcher. Geralt had long since begun counting the days separating him from Ciri; and each day we were not on the road pushed him – in his opinion – further and further away from the girl. Now, in the wet osiers, in the cold and rain, the Witcher became gloomier and more evil with each passing hour. I also noticed he was limping heavily, and when he thought no one could see or hear he swore and hissed from the pain. For you ought to know, dear reader, that Geralt had suffered broken bones during the sorcerers' rebellion on the Isle of Thanedd. The frac-tures had knitted and been healed thanks to the magical efforts of the dryads of Brokilon Forest, but apparently had not stopped troubling him. Thus the Witcher was suffering, so to say, from both bodily and spiritual pain. It made him absolutely livid, so we steered clear of him.

And once again he was persecuted by dreams. On the morning of the ninth of September, while he was sleeping off his guard duty, he terrified us all by springing up with a cry and drawing his sword. It looked as though he were in a frenzy, but fortunately it subsided at once.

He went away, but was soon to return with a gloomy demeanour. He announced, in so many words, that he was breaking up the company with immediate effect and continuing on his way alone, since awful things were occurring somewhere, time was running out, it was becoming dangerous, and he didn't want to put anyone at risk or take responsibility for anyone. He talked and argued so tediously and unconvincingly that no one wanted to discuss it with him. Even the usually eloquent vampire dismissed him with a shrug, Milva by spitting, and Cahir with the terse reminder that he was responsible for himself, and that as far as risks went he did not carry a sword to give his belt ballast. Afterwards, however, everybody fell silent and stared knowingly at the undersigned, no doubt expecting me to avail myself of the opportunity and go back home. I probably do not have to say that they were most disappointed.

The incident persuaded us, nonetheless, to discard our lethargy and drove us to a bold deed; that of crossing the Yaruga. I confess that the undertaking aroused my anxiety, for the plan was to swim across at night; to quote Milva and Cahir, 'hanging on to the horses' tails'. Even if it had been a metaphor – and I suspect it was not – I somehow could not imagine it for myself or my steed, Pegasus, upon whose tail I would have to depend during the crossing. Swimming, to put it mildly, was – and is – not one of my strong points. Had Mother Nature wanted me to swim, in the act of creation and the process of evolution she would have equipped me with webbed fingers. And the same applied to Pegasus.

My fears turned out to be in vain, at least with regard to swimming behind a horse's tail. For we crossed using a different method. Who knows if it was not even more insane? We crossed in a truly impudent manner; beneath the reconstructed bridge at the Red Timber Port, under the very noses of the Nilfgaardian guard and patrols. The undertaking, it turned out, only appeared to be a demented effrontery and mortal gamble, and in reality passed off without a hitch. After the frontline units had crossed the bridge, transport after transport, vehicle after vehicle, flock after flock wandered this way and that.

81

There were also crowds of various kinds, including civilian flotsam and jetsam, among which our company did not stand out at all, nor were we conspicuous. Thus on the tenth day of September we all crossed to the left bank of the Yaruga, only once being hailed by the guard, at whom Cahir, wrinkling his brow imperiously, shouted back something menacing about imperial service, backing up his words with the classically military and ever effective 'for fuck's sake'. Before anyone had time to grow curious about us, we were already on the left bank of the Yaruga and deep in the Riverdell forest; for there was only a single highway there, heading south, and neither the direction nor the profusion of Nilfgaardians hanging around it suited us.

At our first camp in the forests of Riverdell I was also visited at night by a strange dream. Unlike Geralt's it was not about Ciri, but the sorceress Yennefer. The dream was curious, unsettling; Yennefer, in black and white as usual, was hovering in the air above a huge, grim mountain castle, and from below other sorceresses were shaking their fists and hurling abuse at her. Yennefer swirled the long sleeves of her dress and flew away, like a black albatross, over the boundless sea, straight into the rising sun. From that moment the dream transformed into a nightmare. On awaking the details vanished from my memory, and there remained only vague, not very sensible, images, but they were ghastly: of torture, screaming, pain, fear and death . . . In a word: horror.

I did not share that dream with Geralt. Not a word did I breathe of it. And rightly so, as it later turned out.

*

'She was called Yennefer! Yennefer of Vengerberg. And she was a most famous sorceress! May I not live to see the dawn if I lie!'

Triss Merigold shuddered and turned, trying to see through the crowd and blue smoke densely filling the tavern's main chamber. She finally rose from the table, somewhat regretfully abandoning a fillet of sole in anchovy butter, a local speciality and a genuine delicacy. She was not roaming the taverns and inns of Bremervoord to eat delicacies, however, but to obtain information. Apart from that, she had to watch her figure.

The crowd of people she had to squeeze among was already

dense and tight; in Bremervoord people loved stories and passed up no opportunity to listen to new ones. And the sailors who visited there in great numbers never disappointed; they always had a fresh new repertoire of sea tales. Naturally, the vast majority were invented, but that didn't make the slightest difference. A tale is a tale. And has its own rules.

The woman who was telling the story – and who had mentioned Yennefer – was a fisherwoman from the Isles of Skellige; stout, broad-shouldered, with close-cropped hair, and – like her four companions – dressed in a waistcoat of narwhal skin, worn to a sheen.

'It were the nineteenth day of the month of August, in the morning after the second night of the full moon,' the islander began, raising a mug of ale to her lips. Her hand, Triss noticed, was the colour of old brick, and her exposed, knotty arm must easily have measured twenty inches in girth. Triss's waist measured twenty-two.

'At the crack of dawn,' the fisherwoman continued, her eyes sweeping over her audience's faces, 'our smack put to sea, into the sound 'twixt An Skellig and Spikeroog, to the oyster grounds, where we usually set our salmon gillnets. We made great haste, for a storm were nigh, the heavens darkening cruelly from the West. We 'ad to pluck the salmon from the nets quick, for otherwise, as you knows yoursel', when at last, after a storm, you can venture forth to sea, only rotten, chewed heads remain in the nets, and all the catch is for naught.'

Her audience, residents of Bremervoord and Cidaris in the main, mostly living from the sea and dependent on it for their existence, nodded and murmured their understanding. Triss usually saw salmon in the form of pink slices, but also nodded and murmured, because she didn't want to stand out. She was there incognito, on a secret mission.

'We sail into port . . .' the fisherwoman went on, draining her mug and indicating that one of the listeners could buy her another. 'We sail in and are a-emptyin' the nets and blow me if Gudrun, Sturla's daughter, doesn't start yelling at the top of her voice! And pointing to starboard! We look, and summat's flying through the air, and it ain't a bird! My heart stopped for a tick, for at once I'm thinking it's a wyvern or young gryphon, they sometimes fly over

83

Spikeroog, true enough, but generally in the winter, usually with a west wind a-blowing. But meanwhile that black thing, if it don't splash into the water! And a wave shoves it! Direckly into our nets. It gets tangled up in the net and splashes around in the water like a seal, then all of us – we were eight fishwives in all – catch the net and heave it on board! And do our gobs fall open! Blow me if it ain't a woman! In a black gown, as black as any crow. She's all caught up in the net, 'twixt two salmon, of which one – as I live and breathe – must of weighed almost three stone!'

The fisherwoman from Skellige blew the froth from her refilled mug and took a deep draught. None of the listeners commented or expressed any disbelief, although not even the oldest among them could remember a salmon of such impressive weight being landed.

'The black-haired woman in the net,' the islander continued, 'is coughing, spitting seawater and thrashing about, and Gudrun, who's expecting, is frantically yelling "It's a kelpie! A kelpie! A havfrue!" But any fool could see it weren't no kelpie, for a kelpie would of ripped up the net long since; and besides, what monster would let itself be a-lugged onto a fishing smack? And it ain't no havfrue neither, for it don't 'ave a fishy tail, and a mermaid always 'as one! And it fell into the sea from the sky, didn't it, and who's seen a kelpie or havfrue flying in the sky? But Skadi, Una's daughter, she's always hasty, so she starts yelling "Kelpie!" too and ups and grabs the gaff! And aims at the net with it! And there's a blue flash from the net and Skadi squeals! The gaff goes left, she goes right, strike me down if I'm lying, she throws three somersets and bangs arse-down on the deck! Ha, turns out a sorceress in a net's worse than a jellyfish, a scorpena or a numbing eel! And on top o' that the witch starts cursing something 'orrible! And the net starts a-hissing, a-stinking and a-steaming, as she works 'er magic inside! We sees it won't be no picnic . . .'

The islander drained her mug and wasted no time in reaching for the next one.

'Ain't no picnic–' she belched loudly, and wiped her nose and mouth '–to catch a witch in a net! We can feel – as I live and breathe – that the magic's making the smack roll harder. No time to 'ang around! Britta, Karen's daughter, presses the net with 'er foot, and I grabs an oar and whack! Whack!! Whack!!!'

The ale splashed high and spilled over the table, and several mugs fell on the floor. The listeners wiped their cheeks and brows, but none of them uttered a word of complaint or admonishment. A tale is a tale. And has its own rules.

'The witch understood who she were up agin'.' The fisherwoman stuck out her ample bosom and gazed around defiantly. 'And that you can't fool around with the fishwives of Skellige! She said she were surrenderin' to us willin' like, and vowed not to cast any charms or incantations. And gave 'er name as Yennefer of Vengerberg.'

Her listeners murmured. Barely two months had passed since the events on the Isle of Thanedd, and the names of the traitors bribed by Nilfgaard were remembered. The name of the celebrated Yennefer too.

'We takes 'er,' the fisherwoman continued, 'to jarl Crach an Craite in Kaer Trolde on Ard Skellig. Never seen her after that. The jarl was away on an expedition, but they said when he returned he first received the witch harshly, but later treated her polite and courteous. Hmm . . . And I was just waiting to see what kind of surprise the sorceress would conjure up for me for whacking her with an oar. I thought she'd badmouth me before the jarl. But no. Never said a word, never complained, I know that. Honrable witch. Afterwards, when she killed herself I even felt sorry for 'er . . .'

'Yennefer's dead?' Triss screamed, so overwhelmed she forgot about the importance of remaining incognito and the secrecy of her mission. 'Yennefer of Vengerberg's dead?'

'Aye, she's dead,' the fisherwoman said, finishing her beer. 'Dead as a doornail. Killed 'erself with her own charms, making magic spells. Didn't 'appen long since, last day of August, just 'fore the new moon. But that's quite another story . . .'

*

'Dandelion! You're asleep in the saddle!'
'I'm not asleep. I'm thinking creatively!'

*

So we rode, dear reader, through the forests of Riverdell, heading East, towards Caed Dhu, searching for the druids who were meant to help us to find Ciri. I shall tell you how it went. Before that, though, for the sake of historical truth, I shall write a little about our company and each of its members.

The vampire Regis was more than four hundred years old. If he was not lying, it meant he was the oldest of us all. Of course, it might have been poppycock, but who could check? I preferred to suppose that our vampire was being truthful, for he had also declared that he had given up drinking people's blood irrevocably and for good. Owing to that declaration we fell asleep more calmly in our camps. I noticed that in the beginning, Milva and Cahir would fearfully and anxiously feel their necks after awaking, but they quickly stopped doing that. The vampire Regis was – or seemed to be – an utterly honourable vampire. If he said he would not drink their blood, then he would not.

He did possess flaws, however, which did not result at all from his vampiric nature. Regis was an intellectual, and liked to demonstrate it. He had the annoying habit of giving statements and truths with the tone and expression of a prophet, to which we swiftly stopped reacting, since the statements he gave were either genuine truths, or sounded like the truth, or could not be proved, which, in essence, amounted to the same thing. But what was truly unbearable was Regis's habit of answering a question before the person asking had finished formulating it – why, occasionally even before the questioner had begun formulating it. I always took that seeming expression of supposed high intelligence more as an expression of boorishness and arrogance; and those qualities, which suit university or courtly circles, are hard to bear in a companion with whom one travels stirrup by stirrup, day in day out, and who sleeps under the same blanket at night. Serious squabbles did not, however, occur, owing to Milva. Unlike Geralt and Cahir, whose inborn opportunism evidently allowed them to adapt to the vampire's mannerism, and even led them to compete with him in that regard, the archer Milva preferred simple and unpretentious solutions. When Regis, for the third time, gave her an answer to a question as she was halfway through asking, she cursed him roundly, using words and expressions capable of making even a hoary mercenary blush in embarrassment. Surprisingly enough it worked; the vampire lost his annoying mannerism in the blink of an eye. The conclusion thus *being that the most effective defence against intellectual domination is roundly to affront the domineering intellectual.*

Milva, it seems to me, had been greatly affected by her tragic accident – and loss. I write 'it seems to me' for I am aware that being a man I cannot imagine what such a loss means for a woman. Though I am a poet and a man of the quill, even my educated and trained imagination betrays me here and I can do nothing.

The archer swiftly regained her physical fitness, which could not be said for her mental state. It often happened that she would not utter a word throughout the whole day, from dawn to dusk. She would disappear and remain isolated, which worried everyone somewhat. Until finally a crisis occurred. Milva released the tension like a dryad or a she-elf; violently, impulsively and not very comprehensibly. One morning, in front of our eyes, she drew a knife and without a word cut off her plait just above her shoulders. 'It doesn't befit me, for I'm not a maiden,' she said, seeing our jaws hanging open. 'But nor am I a widow,' she added, 'so that's the end of my mourning.' From that moment on she was her old self; brusque, biting, mouthy and inclined to use unparliamentary language. From which we happily concluded that she had come through the crisis.

The third – and no less curious – member of the company was the Nilfgaardian, who kept trying to prove he was not one. He was called, so he claimed, Cahir Mawr Dyffryn aep Ceallach . . .

*

'Cahir Mawr Dyffryn, son of Ceallach,' Dandelion declared, pointing his pencil at the Nilfgaardian, 'I have reconciled myself with many things which I don't like, and actually can't stand, in this honourable company. But not with everything! I can't bear it when people look over my shoulder when I'm writing! And I don't intend to put up with it!'

The Nilfgaardian moved away from the poet, and after a moment's thought seized his saddle, sheepskin and blanket and dragged them over to Milva, who was dozing.

'I apologise,' he said. 'Forgive my obtrusiveness, Dandelion. I glanced involuntarily, out of pure curiosity. I thought you were creating a map or drawing up some tallies—'

'I'm not a bookkeeper!' the poet said, losing his temper and standing up. 'Nor am I a cartographer! But even if I were, it doesn't justify taking a sly look at my notes!'

'I have apologised,' Cahir repeated dryly, making his bed in the new place. 'I have reconciled myself with and become accustomed to many things in this honourable company. But I'm still accustomed to apologising only once.'

'Indeed,' the Witcher joined in, totally unexpectedly – for everyone, himself included – taking the side of the young Nilfgaardian. 'You've become devilishly touchy, Dandelion. One cannot fail to notice that it is somehow connected to the paper, which you have recently begun to deface with a bit of lead while we camp.'

'It's true,' Regis agreed, putting more birch branches on the campfire. 'Our minstrel has become touchy, not to say secretive, discreet and loving of solitude recently. Oh, no, having witnesses when performing his natural needs doesn't bother him at all which, in our situation, one cannot indeed be astonished by. His shameful secrecy and oversensitivity to being watched extends solely to his scribbled notes. Is, perhaps, a poem being written in our presence? A rhapsody? An epic? A romance? A canzone?'

'No,' Geralt retorted, shifting towards the fire and muffling his back with a blanket. 'I know him. It can't be verse, because he's not cursing, mumbling or counting the syllables on his fingers. He's writing in silence, so it must be prose.'

'Prose!' The vampire flashed his pointed fangs – which he usually tried not to do. 'A novel, perhaps? Or an essay? A morality play? Dammit, Dandelion! Don't torture us so! Reveal what you are writing.'

'My memoirs.'

'Your what?'

'From these notes,' Dandelion displayed a tube stuffed with paper, 'will arise the work of my life. My memoirs, bearing the title *Fifty Years of Poetry*.'

'Nonsensical title,' Cahir declared dryly. 'Poetry has no age.'

'And if one concedes that it does,' added the vampire, 'it is decidedly older than that.'

'You don't understand. The title means that the author of the

88

work has spent fifty years, no more and no less, in the service of Lady Poetry.'

'In that case, it's even more nonsensical,' said the Witcher. 'You aren't even forty yet. Your writing ability was thrashed into you in the temple elementary school, at the age of eight. Even if we allow that you were writing rhymes in school, you've not been serving Lady Poetry for longer than thirty years. But as I well know, for you've often told me about it, you only began seriously rhyming and composing melodies when you were nineteen, inspired by your love for Countess de Stael. That makes it the nineteenth year of your service, Dandelion. So how did you come up with this titular fifty years? Is it meant to be some kind of metaphor?'

'I,' the bard said, puffing up, 'trace broad horizons with my thought. I describe the present, but I pass into the future. I intend to publish this mighty work in some twenty or thirty years, and then no one will be able to cast doubt on the titular reckoning.'

'Ha. Now I get it. If anything astonishes me, it's the foresight. You aren't usually bothered about tomorrow.'

'Tomorrow still doesn't bother me much,' the poet declared with superiority. 'I'm thinking about posterity. About eternity!'

'From the point of view of posterity,' Regis observed, 'it isn't too ethical a beginning to write now, in advance. On the basis of the title, posterity has the right to expect a work written from a genuine fifty-year perspective, by a person with a genuine fifty-year store of knowledge and experience—'

'A person whose experience amounts to half a century,' Dandelion interrupted unceremoniously, 'must be – from the very nature of the case – a seventy-year-old, decayed old gimmer with his brain eroded by the hag of sclerosis. Someone like that should be sitting on the veranda breaking wind, not dictating their memoirs, for people would only laugh. I won't make that error. I'll write my biography at the height of my creative powers. Later, just before publication, I shall merely make cosmetic corrections.'

'It does have its merits,' Geralt said as he massaged and cautiously flexed his painful knee. 'Particularly for us. For though without doubt we appear in his work, though without doubt he has mauled us, in half a century we won't be especially concerned about it.'

'What's half a century?' the vampire smiled. 'A moment, a fleeting instant . . . Aha, Dandelion, a minor observation. In my opinion, *Half a Century of Poetry* sounds better than *Fifty Years*.'

'I don't deny it,' said the troubadour, crouching over a page and scribbling on it with a pencil. 'Thanks, Regis. Something constructive at last. Does anyone else have any comments?'

'I do,' Milva began unexpectedly, poking her head out from her blanket. 'Why are you goggling at me? Because I'm unlettered? But I'm not stupid! We're on an expedition, we're going to rescue Ciri, we're travelling through enemy lands with sword in hand. This rubbish of Dandelion's might fall into enemy mitts. And we know the poetaster, it's no secret he's a gasbag, a sensation-seeker as well as a gossip. So let him have a care with what he's scrawling. So we don't accidentally get hung because of his scribblings.'

'You're exaggerating, Milva,' the vampire said gently.

'Greatly, I'd say,' Dandelion continued.

'I'd say the same,' Cahir added carelessly. 'I don't know what it's like with the Nordlings, but in the Empire, possession of a manuscript isn't considered a *crimen*, nor is literary activity punishable.'

Geralt swept his eyes over him and snapped the stick he was playing with.

'But libraries are torched in cities captured by that cultured nation,' he said in an unaggressive tone, but with a distinct sneer. 'Never mind, though. Maria, I agree that you're exaggerating. Dandelion's scribblings, as usual, don't have any importance. Not regarding our safety.'

'Oh, sure!' said the archer, getting hot under the collar and sitting up. 'I know what I know! When the royal bailiff were taking a census round our way, my stepfather took to his heels, bolted into the forest and stayed there for a fortnight without poking his nose out. Wherever there's parchment there's a judgement, he used to say, and whoever's name is captured in ink today is broke on the wheel tomorrow. And he was right, the rotten bastard! I hope that whoreson's sizzling in hell!'

Milva threw off her blanket and – now quite wide awake – moved closer to the fire. It looked, Geralt observed, like another long fireside conversation was in the offing.

'You weren't fond of your stepfather, I deduce,' Dandelion observed after a moment's silence.

'I weren't,' Milva said, audibly grinding her teeth. 'For he were a rotten bastard. He made advances when mother wasn't looking, interfered with me. He wouldn't listen, so finally I couldn't stand it no more and took a rake to him, and when he fell over I gave him a kick or two, in the ribs and the privates. Two days later he were lying and spitting blood . . . So I decided to flee into the world, without waiting to see if he got better. Later I heard rumours he'd died, and mother soon after him . . . Oi, Dandelion! Are you writing that down? Don't you dare! Don't you dare, hear me?'

*

It was strange that Milva was trekking with us, and the fact that a vampire was accompanying us was astonishing. Nonetheless, strangest – if not simply incomprehensible – were the motives of Cahir, who had suddenly changed from an enemy into – if not a friend – then certainly an ally. The youngster had proved that at the Battle on the Bridge, unhesitatingly standing with sword in hand beside the Witcher against his countrymen. By this deed he gained our appreciation and conclusively dispelled our suspicions. In writing 'our', I have in mind myself, the vampire and the archer. For Geralt, though he had fought shoulder to shoulder with Cahir, though they had looked death in the eye side by side, was still mistrustful of the Nilfgaardian and did not like him. He did, admittedly, try to hide his resentment, but he was – as I believe I have already mentioned – as simple as a spear shaft, incapable of pretending, and his aversion crept out at every turn, like an eel from a rotten trap. The reason was clear: it was Ciri.

It had been my lot to be on the Isle of Thanedd that July new moon when the bloody battle took place between sorcerers loyal to the kings and traitors incited by Nilfgaard. The traitors were helped by the Squirrels – rebellious elves – and Cahir, son of Ceallach. Cahir had been on Thanedd, he had been sent there on a special mission; he was to have seized and abducted Ciri. Ciri wounded him defending herself; Cahir had a scar on his left hand, at the sight of which my mouth always went dry. It must have been hellishly painful and he still could not bend two of his fingers.

And after all that, we rescued him on the Ribbon, when his own countrymen were carrying him away to cruel torture in fetters. Why, I ask? For what misdeeds did they want to execute him? Or was it only for the defeat on Thanedd? Cahir is not garrulous, but I have a sensitive ear even for monosyllables. The lad is not yet thirty, but looks as though he were a high-ranking officer in the Nilfgaardian Army. Since he speaks the Common Speech impeccably, which is seldom found among Nilfgaardians, I think I know what kind of army Cahir served in and why he was promoted so quickly. And why he was sent on such strange missions. Including foreign ones.

For Cahir was the man who had tried once before to abduct Ciri. Almost four years before, during the massacre of Cintra. The destiny guiding the girl's fate had made itself felt for the first time. By coincidence I talked about this with Geralt on the third day after crossing the Yaruga, ten days before the Equinox, as we were negotiating the forests of Riverdell. That conversation, although very short, was fraught with unpleasant and worrying overtones. And at that moment there was writ on the face and in the eyes of the Witcher a harbinger of the horror which was to explode during the Equinox, after we were joined by the fair-haired Angoulême.

*

The Witcher wasn't looking at Dandelion. He wasn't looking ahead. He was looking at Roach's mane.

'Just before her death,' he began, 'Calanthe forced an oath on several of her knights. They were not to let Ciri fall into Nilfgaardian hands. During the flight, those knights were killed, and Ciri was left alone amidst corpses and conflagration, in the web of streets of the burning city. She would not have got out alive, that is beyond doubt. But he found her. Cahir. He carried her out of the pit of fire and death. He rescued her. Heroically! Nobly!'

Dandelion reined Pegasus back somewhat. They were riding at the rear, and Regis, Milva and Cahir were about a quarter of a furlong ahead, but the poet didn't want a single word of their conversation to reach the ears of their companions.

'The problem was,' the Witcher continued, 'that our Cahir was only acting nobly by order. He was noble as a cormorant is: he did not swallow the fish because he had a ring on his throat. He was meant to take the fish to his master. He failed, so the master was angry at the cormorant! The cormorant is now out of favour! Is that why he's searching for friendship in the company of fish? What do you think, Dandelion?'

The troubadour ducked in the saddle to avoid an overhanging linden branch. The branch already bore completely yellow leaves. 'But he saved her life, you said so yourself. Thanks to him Ciri left Cintra in one piece.'

'And she cried out in the night, seeing him in her dreams.'

'But he *did* save her. Stop dwelling on it, Geralt. Too much has changed, why, it changes every day. Brooding achieves nothing, save distress, which clearly does you no good. He rescued Ciri. That fact was, is, and will remain a fact.'

Geralt finally tore his gaze away from the horse's mane and raised his head. Dandelion glanced at his face and swiftly looked away.

'The fact remains a fact,' the Witcher repeated in an angry, metallic voice. 'Oh, yes! He yelled that fact in my face on Thanedd, and his voice stuck in his throat from terror, for he was staring at my sword edge. That fact and that cry were supposed to be the arguments which would stop me murdering him. Well, it did and I don't think it can now be undone. Which is a pity. For a chain ought to have been begun then, on Thanedd. A long chain of death, a chain of revenge, about which tales would still be told after a hundred years have passed. Tales which people will be afraid to listen to after dark. Do you understand that, Dandelion?'

'Not really.'

'Then to hell with you.'

*

That conversation was hideous and the Witcher's expression had been hideous too. Oh, I did not like it when he was in a mood such as that and went off on such a tack.

I must, though, confess that the vivid comparison with the cormorant had played its role. I began to worry. The fish in its beak, taken to be clubbed, gutted and fried! A truly nice analogy, joyful prospects . . .

However, good sense belied such fears. After all, if we were to con-tinue with the fishy metaphors, then who were we? Small fry. Small, bony fry. In exchange for such a meagre haul the cormorant Cahir could not count on imperial grace. In any case, he was far from the pike he wanted to be thought of as. He was small fry, just like us. When the war was raking both the earth and people's fates like an iron harrow, who was paying the slightest attention to small fry?

I am certain that no one in Nilfgaard remembers Cahir now.

*

Vattier de Rideaux, chief of the Nilfgaardian military intelligence, listened to the imperial reprimand.

'So,' Emhyr var Emreis continued scathingly, 'an institution which devours three times as much of the state budget as edu-cation, culture and the arts taken together is incapable of finding one man. This man simply disappears, goes into hiding, although I spend astronomical sums on an institution from which nothing has any right to remain concealed! One man, guilty of treason, blatantly mocks an institution to which I have given so many priv-ileges and funds as would give even innocent men sleepless nights. Oh, trust me, Vattier, when the council next speaks of trimming the funds for clandestine services, I shall prick up my ears. You may trust that!'

'Your Imperial Majesty,' Vattier de Rideaux croaked, 'will make, I have no doubt, the right decision, after weighing up all the pros and cons. Both the failures and the successes of the intelligence service. Your Majesty may also be certain that the traitor, Cahir aep Ceallach, will not escape punishment. I have taken steps—'

'I do not pay you for undertakings, but for results. And those are miserable, Vattier, miserable! What about Vilgefortz? Where the hell is Cirilla? What are you mumbling now? Louder!'

'I think Your Highness ought to wed the girl we are holding in Darn Rowan. We need that marriage, we need the legality of Cintra's sovereign fiefdom to subdue the Isles of Skellige and the rebels in Attre, Strept, Mag Turga and the Slopes. We need a gen-eral amnesty, peace at the rear and along supply lines . . . We need the neutrality of Esterad Thyssen of Kovir.'

94

'I know. But the girl from Darn Rowan is not Ciri. I cannot wed her.'

'May Your Imperial Majesty forgive me, but does it matter if she is not authentic? The political situation requires your nuptials. Urgently. The bride will be in a veil. And when we finally find the genuine Cirilla, the girls will simply be . . . exchanged.'

'Have you taken leave of your senses, Vattier?'

'The fake one was only shown briefly at court. No one has seen the real girl in Cintra for four years, and rumour has it she spent more time in Skellige than in Cintra. I guarantee that no one will see through the deceit.'

'No!'

'Your Imperial—'

'No, Vattier! Find the real Ciri! Pull your finger out. Find Ciri. Find Cahir. And Vilgefortz. Vilgefortz in particular. For he has Ciri, I'm certain of it'

'Your Imperial Highness . . .'

'Go on, Vattier! Speak!'

'At one time I suspected the so-called Vilgefortz case was nothing but a provocation. That the sorcerer had been murdered or is being imprisoned, and the spectacular and clamorous hunt allows Dijkstra to slander us and to justify his brutal repression.'

'I've had similar suspicions.'

'Ah, you have? This was not made public in Redania, but my agents inform me that Dijkstra found one of Vilgefortz's hideouts, and within in it evidence of the sorcerer's bestial experiments on people. To be precise, on human foetuses . . . and women with child. If Vilgefortz had Cirilla, I fear that continued searches for her—'

'Silence, dammit!'

'On the other hand,' Vattier de Rideaux quickly added, looking at the emperor's furious face, 'all of that may be disinformation. Intended to denigrate the sorcerer. That would be Dijkstra's style.'

'You're paid to find Vilgefortz and take Ciri from him, for God's sake! Not to digress and make conjectures! Where is Tawny Owl? Still in Geso? Why? He allegedly "left no stone unturned and looked into every hole in the ground". Allegedly the girl "is not there and never was". Apparently "the astrologer was either mistaken or is lying". Those are all quotations from his reports. What is he still doing there?'

'Coroner Skellen, I dare observe, undertakes none too transparent measures ... He is recruiting for his unit, the one Your Highness ordered him to set up, in Fort Rocayne, Maecht, where he has established his base. That unit, I take the liberty to add, is an extremely doubtful bunch. But it is odd that towards the end of August, Lord Skellen hired a notorious assassin—'

'What?'

'He engaged a hired thug, with instructions to eliminate a criminal gang marauding around Geso. A commendable act, but is it a task for the imperial coroner?'

'Is *invidia* speaking through you, Vattier, by any chance? And does it not give your reports colour and fervour?'

'I merely state the facts, Your Highness.'

'I want–' the emperor stood up abruptly '–to *see* the facts. I'm tired of *hearing* about them.'

*

It was an extremely hard day. Vattier de Rideaux was weary. In his schedule for that day he had planned an hour or two of paperwork, intended to protect him from drowning in pending documents, but the thought of it made him shudder. *No*, he thought, *easy does it. It can wait. I'm going home . . . No, not yet. My wife can wait. I'll go to Cantarella. To my gorgeous Cantarella, with whom I can relax so pleasantly.*

He quickly made up his mind. He simply rose, took his cloak and left, a gesture full of disgust holding off his secretary, who was trying to force a leather portfolio of urgent documents onto him. Tomorrow! Tomorrow is another day!

He left the palace by the rear exit, which opened onto the gardens, and walked along a path lined with cypresses. He passed an ornamental pond, where a carp introduced by Emperor Torres was approaching the venerable age of a hundred and thirty-two years, as testified by a golden commemorative medal attached to the gills of the immense fish.

'Good evening, viscount.'

Vattier released the dagger concealed in his sleeve with a short movement of his forearm. The hilt slid into his hand by itself.

'Very risky, Rience,' he said coldly. 'Very risky, showing your burned countenance in Nilfgaard. Even as a magical teleprojection.'

'You noticed? And Vilgefortz assured me that if you didn't touch me you wouldn't guess it was an illusion.'

Vattier put the dagger away. He had not guessed it was an illusion at all, but now he knew.

'You are too great a coward, Rience,' he said, 'to show yourself here in person. You know what would befall you if you did.'

'Is the emperor still so determined to seize me? And my master Vilgefortz?'

'Your insolence is disarming.'

'Go to hell, Vattier. We're still on your side, Vilgefortz and I. Well, I admit we tricked you with the counterfeit Cirilla, but it was done in good faith, in good faith, may I be drowned if I lie. Vilgefortz believed that since the real one had vanished, a fake one was better than none at all. We reckoned it was all the same to you—'

'Your insolence has stopped being disarming and has begun to be insulting. I have no intention of wasting time talking to an insulting mirage. When I finally get my hands on you we shall have a conversation, a long conversation. So until that time . . . *apage*, Rience.'

'What's come over you, Vattier? In the past, if even the Devil himself appeared to you, you wouldn't forget to investigate – before the exorcism – if you couldn't, by any chance, profit in some way.'

Vattier did not grace the illusion with a glance. Instead he watched the algae-covered carp idly churning up the sludge in the pond.

'Profit in some way?' he repeated slowly, pouting his lips contemptuously. 'From you? And what could you give me? The real Cirilla, perhaps? Perhaps your patron, Vilgefortz? Perhaps Cahir aep Ceallach?'

'Hold hard!' Rience raised an illusory hand. 'You mentioned him.'

'Who?'

'Cahir. We shall bring you Cahir's head. I, and my master, Vilgefortz . . .'

'Have mercy, Rience,' Vattier snorted. 'Reverse the order.'

'As you wish. Vilgefortz, with my humble help, will give you the head of Cahir, son of Ceallach. We know where he is and can pluck him out like a lobster from a pot, if you wish.'

'So you have such capabilities, well, well. Such good stool-pigeons in Queen Meve's army?'

'Are you testing me?' Rience grimaced. 'You really don't know? Must be the latter. Cahir, my dear viscount, is . . . We know where he is. We know where he's headed and in what company. You want his head? You shall have it.'

'A head,' Vattier smiled, 'which won't be able to tell anyone what really happened on Thanedd.'

'That's probably for the best,' said Rience cynically. 'Why give Cahir the chance to talk? Our task is to ease – not exacerbate – the animosity between Vilgefortz and the emperor. I shall bring you the mute head of Cahir aep Ceallach. We'll do it in such a way that it looks like your, and only your, achievement. Delivery in the next three weeks.'

The ancient carp in the fishpond fanned the water with its pectoral fins. That beast, thought Vattier, must be very wise. But why does it need that wisdom? It's still the same sludge and the same water lilies.

'Your price, Rience?

'A trifle. Where is Stefan Skellen and what is he plotting?'

*

'I told him what he wanted to know.' Vattier de Rideaux stretched out on the pillows, playing with a ringlet of Carthia van Canten's golden hair. 'You see, my sweet, one has to approach some matters wisely. And to approach them wisely means to conform. If one behaves differently, one won't get anything. Just the putrid water and foul-smelling sludge in a fishpond. And so what if the pond *is* made of marble and is three paces from the palace? Aren't I right, my sweet?'

Carthia van Canten, known by the pet-name of Cantarella, did not answer. Vattier in no way expected an answer. The girl was eighteen and – to put it mildly – no genius. Her interests, at least for the moment, were limited to making love with – at least for the moment – Vattier. Cantarella was a natural talent in sexual matters, combining enthusiasm and wholeheartedness with technique and artistry. That was not the most important thing about her, though.

Cantarella spoke little and seldom, while listening willingly and splendidly. With Cantarella one could unload oneself, relax, spiritually unwind and psychologically regenerate oneself.

'A man in this service can expect nothing but reprimands,' Vattier said bitterly. 'Just because he hasn't found some Cirilla or other! And is the fact that, thanks to the work of my men, the army is achieving successes unimportant? Does the fact that the general staff knows the enemy's every move mean nothing? And how many strongholds have my agents opened for the imperial forces, which would have taken weeks to storm? But no, there is no praise for that. Only some Cirilla or other is important!'

Puffing up angrily, Vattier de Rideaux took a glass of excellent Est Est of Toussaint from Cantarella's hands, a wine with a vintage that remembered the days when Emperor Emhyr var Emreis was a cruelly damaged little boy, devoid of any rights to the throne and Vattier de Rideaux was a young officer of the intelligence service, insignificant in the hierarchy.

It had been a good year. For wine.

Vattier sipped it, played with Cantarella's shapely breasts and went on. Cantarella listened splendidly.

'Stefan Skellen, my sweet,' muttered the chief of the imperial intelligence service, 'is a wheeler-dealer and a conspirator. But I shall know what he's up to before Rience gets there . . . I already have an agent there . . . Very close to Skellen . . . Very close . . .'

Cantarella untied the sash fastening Vattier's dressing gown, and leaned forward. Vattier felt her breath and moaned in anticipation of the pleasure. That's talent, he thought. And then the soft, hot touch of velvety lips drove all thoughts from his head.

Carthia van Canten slowly, deftly and skilfully supplied Vattier de Rideaux, the chief of the imperial intelligence service, with sexual bliss. That wasn't Carthia's only talent. But Vattier de Rideaux had no idea about her others.

He didn't know that despite appearances Carthia van Canten possessed a splendid memory and intelligence as lively as quicksilver.

Everything Vattier told her, every piece of information, every word he uttered, Carthia passed on to the sorceress Assire var Anahid the next day.

*

Yes, I would stake my head that everyone in Nilfgaard forgot about Cahir long ago, including his betrothed, if he had one.

But more about that later, for now we return to the day and place the Yaruga was crossed. We rode quite briskly eastwards, meaning to reach the region of the Black Forest known in the Elder Speech as Caed Dhu. For there dwelt the druids, who were capable of divining where Ciri was residing, or foretelling her location from the weird dreams that were vexing Geralt. We rode through Upper Riverdell, also known as Left Bank, a wild and deserted land situated between the Yaruga and the Slopes, set at the foot of the Amell Mountains, delineated to the east by the Dol Angra valley, and to the west by a boggy lakeland whose name has slipped my mind.

No one laid any specific claim to that land, and so it was never rightly known to whom it actually belonged or who governed it. In that respect, it seems, the successive monarchs of Temeria, Sodden, Cintra and Rivia – who, with varying results, treated Left Bank as a fiefdom of their kingdoms and occasionally tried to drive home their arguments using fire and sword – had some say. And subsequently the Nilfgaardian Army arrived from beyond the Amell Mountains and no one had anything more to say. Or any doubts about issues of fiefdom or territorial rights. Everything south of the Yaruga belonged to the Empire. As I write these words, plenty of lands to the north also belong to the Empire. Owing to a lack of precise information, I do not know how many or how far to the north.

Going back to Riverdell, permit me, dear reader, a digression concerning historical processes. The history of a given territory is often created and formed by accident, as a side effect of the conflicts between external forces. A given land's history is very often created by foreigners. Foreigners are the cause – but the effects are always invariably borne by the local people.

That rule fully applied to Riverdell.

Riverdell had its own folk, indigenous Riverdellers. The unceasing years of scrambles and struggles had transformed them into beggars and forced them to migrate. Their villages and settlements had gone up in smoke, and the ruins of homesteads and fields were transformed into fallow land and swallowed up by the wilderness. Trade fell into decline and caravans avoided the neglected roads and tracks. The few Riverdellers who remained turned into coarse boors. They mainly differed from wolverines and bears by the fact that they wore britches. At least some of them did. I mean some of them wore britches and some of them differed from the beasts. They were – generally speaking – an unobliging, crude and boorish nation.

And utterly devoid of a sense of humour.

*

The dark-haired daughter of the forest beekeeper tossed her plait over her shoulder, and resumed turning the quern with furious vigour. Dandelion's efforts were in vain; the poet's words seemed not to register with their audience. Dandelion winked at the rest of the company, pretending to sigh and raise his eyes to the ceiling. But he did not quit.

'Let me,' he repeated, grinning. 'Let me grind, while you fetch some ale from the cellar. There must be a hidden cellar somewhere around here and a keg in the vault. Am I right, fair one?'

'You might leave the wench alone, m'lord,' the forest bee-keeper's wife – a tall, willowy woman of astonishing beauty – said crossly as she busied herself around the kitchen. 'I already told 'ee there ain't no ale 'ere.'

'You bin told near a dozen times, m'lord,' the forest beekeeper said, backing up his wife, breaking off from his conversation with the Witcher and the vampire. 'I shall make you pancakes with honey, and then you'll eat. But leave the wench in peace to grind the corn for meal, for without meal even a sorcerer cannot make a pancake! Let 'er be, let 'er grind in peace.'

'Did you hear that, Dandelion?' called the Witcher. 'Leave the girl alone and go and do something useful. Or write your memoirs!'

'I fancy a drink. I fancy a drink before eating. I have some herbs, I'll brew myself an infusion. Granny, would there be any hot water in this cottage? Hot water, I'm asking. Would there be any?'

An old woman, the forest beekeeper's mother, sitting on the stove bench, raised her head from the sock she was darning.

'There would, petal, there would,' she muttered. 'Only it be cold b' now.'

Dandelion groaned and sat down, resigned, at the table, where the company was chatting with the beekeeper, whom they had happened upon in the forest early that morning. The beekeeper was short, thickset, swarthy and terribly hairy. No wonder, then, that he had given the company a scare when he loomed out of the undergrowth unexpectedly; they had taken him for a lycanthrope. To make it funnier still, the first to yell 'Werewolf! Werewolf!' had been the vampire, Regis. There was something of a commotion, but the matter was quickly cleared up, and the beekeeper, though at first sight surly, turned out to be hospitable and courteous. The company accepted the invitation to his homestead. His homestead – called, in forest-beekeeping jargon, a 'shanty' – stood in a cleared glade, where the beekeeper, his mother, his wife and their daughter lived. The latter two were women of exceptional, though somewhat curious, looks, clearly indicating that there was a dryad or hamadryad among their forebears.

During the conversations that ensued, the forest beekeeper at first gave the impression one could talk to him solely about bees, beehives carved into trees, hollows, rope harnesses, bear fences, beeswax, honey and honey-gathering, but that was just a semblance.

'With politics? And what should be happening with it? The same as usual. We 'ave to pay more and more duty. Three urns of honey, and an entire length of wax. I can barely supply it. I sit on my ropes from dawn to dusk, gouging out hollows . . . Who do I pay the duty to? To whoever calls, how am I to know who's in power now? Some time since, you know, they bin speakin' Nilfgaardian. I 'ear we're now an imporial provenance, or summat like 'at. They pay for the honey – if I sell any – in imporial coin, with the emprer's head struck on it. 'Is mush is more comely, though cruel, you'll know 'im right away. If you get my drift . . .'

Two dogs – one black and the other ruddy – sat facing the vampire, raised their heads and started to howl. The beekeeper's hamadryad wife turned back from the hearth and hit them with her broom.

'It be an evil sign,' the beekeeper said, 'when hounds howl in broad daylight. Kind of thing . . . What was I sposed to be talkin' 'bout?'

'About the druids of Caed Dhu.'

'Eh! So you wasn't jestin', m'lord? You rightly mean to go to the druids? Sick of life, are you? That way is death! He who dares to venture into the Mistletoers' clearings is seized, shoved into a wicker doll and roasted over a slow flame.'

Geralt looked at Regis and Regis winked at him. They both knew the popular rumours about the druids, and every last one was fabricated. Milva and Dandelion, though, began listening with greater curiosity than before. And evident alarm.

'There's some as say,' the forest beekeeper continued, 'that the Mistletoers are getting their own back, for the Nilfgaardians vexed 'em first, by entering their holy oak groves down in Dol Angra and by walloping the druids for no reason. Others say the druids started it, capturing and tormenting a couple of imporial men to death, and now Nilfgaard are getting their revenge. 'Ow it rightly is, no one knows. But one thing brooks no doubt; the druids catch people, puts 'em in the Wicker Woman and burns 'em. To venture among 'em is certain death.'

'We are not afraid,' Geralt said calmly.

'Certainly,' the forest beekeeper eyed the Witcher, Milva and Cahir up and down. Cahir was just entering the cottage, having groomed the horses. 'It is evident you are fearless folk, valorous and armed. Eh, wouldn't be no fear journeying with the likes of you . . . you know . . . But the Mistletoers ain't in the Black Grove presently, your toils and travels would be in vain. Nilfgaard pressed 'em, drove 'em from Caed Dhu. They ain't there presently.'

'How so?'

'Thus it is. The Mistletoers 'ave fled.'

'Fled where?

The forest beekeeper glanced at his hamadryad wife and said nothing for a moment.

'Fled where?' the Witcher repeated.

The beekeeper's tabby cat sat down before the vampire and miaowed frightfully. The hamadryad hit it with her broom.

'It be an evil sign when a tomcat mews in broad daylight,' the beekeeper mumbled, strangely embarrassed. 'But the druids . . . you know . . . They fled for the Slopes. Right enough. I speak the truth. To the Slopes.'

'A good sixty miles south,' Dandelion estimated in quite a casual – even cheerful – voice. But he fell silent when he saw the Witcher's expression.

Only the ominous miaowing of the cat, promptly driven outside, could be heard in the silence that fell.

'Well,' the vampire began, 'what difference does it make to us?'

*

The next morning brought more surprises. And riddles, which were quickly solved. 'A pox on it,' said Milva, who was the first to scramble out of the hay barrack, awoken by the commotion. 'Well, I'll be blowed. Look at that, Geralt.'

The clearing was full of people. At first glance it could be seen that five or six forest beekeeping families were gathered there. The Witcher's trained eye also picked out several fur trappers and at least one tar maker. Taken together, there were twelve men, ten women, ten adolescents of both sexes and the same number of little children. The gathering was equipped with six wagons, twelve oxen, ten cows and four goats, a fair number of sheep, and also plenty of dogs and cats, whose barking and miaowing could definitely be considered a bad omen in such circumstances.

'I wonder,' Cahir said, rubbing his eyes, 'what this means?'

'Trouble,' Dandelion replied, shaking the hay from his hair. Regis said nothing, but wore a curious expression.

'Please break your fast, noble lords,' said their friend the forest beekeeper, approaching the rick accompanied by a broad-shouldered man. 'Breakfast is ready. Milky porridge. And honey

'. . . And if I may introduce Jan Cronin, headman of us forest bee-keepers . . .'

'Pleased to meet you,' the Witcher lied, without returning the bow, partly because his knee was paining him intensely. 'And this crowd, how did they get here?'

'Type of thing . . .' the beekeeper scratched the back of his head. 'As you see, winter's coming . . . The trees have bear fences, the hollows have been gouged out . . . Time we returned to the Slopes and Riedbrune . . . Store away the honey, for winter, you know . . . But it is perilous to be in the forests . . . alone . . .'

The headman cleared his throat. The beekeeper glanced at Geralt's face and seemed to shrink a little.

'You are mounted and armed,' he grunted. 'Valorous and bold, anyone can see it. Wouldn't be no fear travelling with the likes of you . . . And it'd be commodious for you . . . We know every path, every track, every copse and holt . . . And we can feed you . . .'

'And the druids,' Cahir said coldly, 'have left Caed Dhu. And headed for the Slopes. Where you want to go. What a remarkable coincidence.'

Geralt walked slowly over to the forest beekeeper and grabbed him by the front of his coat. But a moment later thought better of it, released him and smoothed down his garments. He said nothing. And asked nothing. But in any case the beekeeper hurried to explain.

'I spoke the truth! I swear! May the earth swallow me up if I lie! The Mistletoers have gone from Caed Dhu! They ain't there!'

'And they're in the Slopes, are they?' Geralt growled. 'Where you are headed, you and this rabble of yours? And you want to travel with an armed escort? Speak, fellow. But take heed, the earth is indeed liable to cleave open!'

The beekeeper lowered his eyes and looked down apprehensively at the ground beneath his feet. Geralt kept meaningfully silent. Milva, finally understanding what it was all about, cursed foully. Cahir snorted contemptuously.

'Well?' the Witcher urged. 'Where were the druids making for?'

'Who knows, m'lord?' the beekeeper finally mumbled. 'But they may be in the Slopes . . . Just as well as they might be anywhere

105

else. There's a plenitude of mighty oak groves in the Slopes, and druids are fond of oaks . . .'

Aside from headman Cronin, both hamadryads – mother and daughter – were now standing behind the beekeeper. It's fortunate the daughter takes after her mother and not her father, the Witcher thought, for the beekeeper suits his wife as well as a wild boar suits a mare. He noticed that several more women were standing behind the hamadryads. They were much less comely, but were looking at him just as pleadingly.

He glanced at Regis, not knowing whether to laugh or curse. The vampire shrugged.

'Let me start by saying,' he said, 'that the forest beekeeper is right, Geralt. It is quite probable that the druids have gone to the Slopes. It is perfectly fitting terrain for them.'

'Is that probability–' the Witcher's gaze was very, very cold, '–sufficiently great, in your view, to prompt us to abruptly change our course and head off blindly with these folk here?'

Regis shrugged again.

'What difference does it make? Think it over. The druids are not in Caed Dhu, so we ought to eliminate that direction of travel. Neither can a return to the Yaruga, I venture, be an option. And so all remaining directions are equally good.'

'Really?' The temperature of the Witcher's voice now equalled his gaze. 'And which of those that remain, in your view, would be most advisable? The one with the forest beekeepers? Or a quite different one? Will you – in your infinite wisdom – undertake to stipulate that?'

The vampire turned slowly towards the forest beekeeper, the forest beekeeper headman, the hamadryads and the other women.

'What is it,' he asked gravely, 'you fear so much, good folk, that you seek an escort? What arouses this fear in you? Speak plainly.'

'Oh, m'lord,' Jan Cronin whined, and the most genuine horror appeared in his eyes. 'I'm glad you asked . . . Our way goes through the Dank Wilderness! And it's ghastly there, m'lord! There are, m'lord, brukolaks, vampyrodes, endryags, gryphoons and all kind of monstrosities! Why, barely two Sundays since, a leshy snatched my son-in-law, he only managed a rasp and that was him, dead.

Do you not wonder that we're afeared to go that way with our women and bairns? Eh?'

The vampire glanced at the Witcher and his face was very grave.

'My boundless wisdom,' he said, 'suggests I stipulate that the most advisable direction is whichever is most advisable for the Witcher.'

*

We set off northwards, towards the Slopes, a land lying at the foot of the Amell Mountains. We set off in a great procession which contained everything: young women, forest beekeepers, fur trappers, women, children, young women, domestic livestock, household paraphernalia, and young women. And a hell of a lot of honey. Everything was sticky from the honey, even the girls.

The train moved at walking and wagon speed, but the pace of the march did not falter, for we did not stray, but marched with ease – the beekeepers knew the tracks, paths and causeways between the lakes. But that knowledge came in useful, oh, how it did, for it began to drizzle and suddenly the whole of bloody Riverdell was plunged into a fog as thick as cream. Without the beekeepers we would surely have lost our way or sunk somewhere in the mire. Neither did we have to waste time or energy organising and preparing vittles – we were fed thrice a day, amply, if simply. And were permitted to laze around for some time after each repast.

In short, it was wonderful. Even the Witcher, that old sourpuss and bore, began to smile and enjoy life more, for he reckoned we were covering fifteen miles a day, which we had never once managed since leaving Brokilon. The Witcher had no work, for though the Dank Wilderness was so dank it would have been difficult to imagine anything danker, we did not encounter any monsters. Sure, at night spectres howled a little, forest weepers moaned and will o' the wisps capered on the bogs. But nothing remarkable.

It was a tiny bit worrying, in truth, that once again we were travelling in quite an accidentally chosen direction and once again without a precisely defined destination. But, as the vampire Regis articulated, it is better to go forward without an aim than loiter without an aim, and with surety much better than to retreat without an aim.

*

'Dandelion! Strap that tube of yours on securely! It would be a shame for half a century of poetry to break free and get lost in the ferns.'

'No fear! I shan't lose it, be certain of it. Nor let anyone take it from me! Anyone wanting this tube will have to wrest it from my cooling corpse. Might one know, Geralt, what provokes your peals of laughter? Let me hazard a guess . . . Congenital imbecility?'

*

It so happened that a team of archaeologists from the University of Castell Graupian, conducting excavations in Beauclair, dug through a layer of charcoal – indicating a great fire – to an even older layer, estimated to date from the 13th century. In that layer, a cavern formed by the remains of walls and sealed by clay and lime was excavated, and in it – to the great excitement of the scholars – were two perfectly preserved human skeletons: those of a woman and a man. Beside the skeletons – apart from weapons and countless small artefacts – was a tube made of hardened leather and measuring two and a half feet long. A coat of arms with faded colours depicting lions and lozenges was embossed on the leather. Professor Schliemann, a distinguished specialist in the sigillography of the Dark Ages, who was leading the team, identified the coat of arms as the emblem of Rivia, an ancient kingdom of unconfirmed location. The archaeologists' excitement reached its peak, since manuscripts were kept in similar tubes in the Dark Ages, when the container's weight permitted the supposition that there was plenty of paper or parchment preserved inside. The tube's excellent condition offered hope that the documents would be legible and throw light on the shadowy past. The centuries were about to speak! It was an exceptional surprise, a victory of science which could not be squandered. Linguists and scholars of extinct languages were prudently summoned from Castell Graupian, along with specialists capable of opening the tube without the risk of even the slightest damage to the valuable contents.

Meanwhile, rumours of 'treasure' had spread through Professor

Schliemann's team. It so happens that those words reached the ears of three characters, known as Zdyb, Billy Goat and Kamil Ronstetter, who'd been hired to dig out the clay. Convinced that the tube was literally stuffed full of gold and valuables, the three aforementioned diggers, under cover of darkness, swiped the priceless artefact and fled with it to the forest. Once there, they lit a small fire and sat down around it.

'What you waitin' for?' Billy Goat said to Zdyb. 'Open up that pipe!'

'Won't give,' Zdyb complained to Billy Goat. 'It's tight as a whoreson!'

'Stamp on the sodding bitch!' Kamil Ronstetter advised.

The hasp of the priceless find gave way under Zdyb's heel and the contents fell out onto the ground.

'Bugger the sodding bitch!' Billy Goat yelled in astonishment. 'What is it?'

The question was foolish, for at first sight it could be seen they were sheets of paper. For which reason Zdyb, rather than answer, took one of the sheets and brought it up to his nose. He examined the curious-looking signs for a long while.

'It's writing,' he finally stated authoritatively. 'They're letters!'

'Letters?' Kamil Ronstetter roared, paling in horror. 'Written letters? What a bitch!'

'Writing, meaning spells!' Billy Goat jabbered, his teeth chattering in terror. 'Letters, meaning witchery! Don't touch it, son-of-a-sodding-bitch! You might catch something from it!'

Zdyb didn't need telling twice, throwing the page onto the fire and nervously wiping his trembling hands on his britches. Kamil Ronstetter kicked the rest of the papers into the campfire – after all, children might chance upon that foul stuff. Then the three hurried away from that dangerous place. The priceless writing from the Dark Ages burned with a tall, bright flame. For a few short moments the centuries spoke with the soft whisper of paper blackening in the fire. And then the flame went out and darkness covered the earth.

Houvenaghel, Dominik Bombastus, b. 1239, became rich in Ebbing conducting trade on a great scale and settled in Nilfgaard; respected by previous emperors, he was appointed burgrave and director of mines in Venendal by Emperor Jan Calveit, and as reward for services rendered was given the office of mayor of Neveugen. A faithful imperial advisor, H. had the emperor's favour and also participated in many public affairs. d. 1301. While still in Ebbing, H. was engaged in numerous charitable works, supported the needy and impoverished, and founded orphanages, hospitals and nurseries, putting up plentiful sums for them. A great enthusiast of the fine arts and sport, he founded a comedic theatre and stadium in the capital, both of which bore his name. He was regarded as a model of probity, honesty and mercantile decency.

Effenberg and Talbot,
Encyclopaedia Maxima Mundi, Volume VII

CHAPTER FOUR

'Witness's surname and given name?'

'Selborne, Kenna. Beg pardon, I meant Joanna.'

'Profession?'

'Provider of diverse services.'

'Is the witness jesting? May the witness be reminded that she stands before the imperial tribunal in a trial of high treason! The lives of many people depend on the witness's testimony, since the penalty for treason is death! May the witness be reminded that she stands before the tribunal by no means as a free agent, but having been brought from a place of isolation in the citadel, and whether the witness returns there or is discharged depends inter alia on her testimony. The tribunal has taken the liberty of this lengthy lecture in order to show the witness how highly improper buffoonery and facetiae are in this chamber! They are not merely unpalatable, but also threaten very grave consequences. The witness has a half-minute to ponder this matter after which the tribunal shall pose the question once again.'

'Very well, Illustrious Judge.'

'Address us as "Your Honour". Witness's profession?'

'I'm a psionic, Your Honour. But mainly in the service of the imperial intelligence, I mean . . .'

'Please keep your answers brief and to the point. Should the court be desirous of further explanations we shall ask for them. The court is aware of the collaboration between the witness and the empire's secret service. For the record, what is the meaning of the term "psionic", which the witness used when giving her profession?'

'I've got pure aitch-es-pee, which means first category psi, without the gift of pee-kay. To be precise: I can hear other people's thoughts and speak remotely with a sorcerer, elf or other psionic. And I can give orders using thought. I mean: make someone do

113

what I want them to. I can also do pre-cog, but only when I'm under.'

'Please enter in the proceedings that the witness, Joanna Selborne, is a psionic, with the gift of hypersensory perception. She is a telepath and tele-empath, able to carry out precognition under hypnosis, but without the ability of psychokinesis. The witness is admonished that the use of magic and extrasensory powers in this chamber is strictly prohibited. We shall continue the hearing. When, where and in what circumstances did the witness encounter the matter of the person passing herself off as Cirilla, Princess of Cintra?'

'I only found out about some Cirilla or other when I was in the clink . . . I mean in a place of isolation, Illustrious Tribunal. While being investigated. I was made aware it was the same person as had been called Falka or the Cintran in my hearing. And the circumstances were such that I must state the order of events. For clarity, I mean. It was like this: I was accosted in a tavern in Etolia by Dacre Silifant, him, who's sitting over there . . . '

'Make note that the witness, Joanna Selborne, has indicated the accused Silifant without being prompted. Please continue.'

'Dacre, Illustrious Tribunal, recruited a hanza . . . I mean, an armed troop. Valiant to a man, and woman . . . Dufficey Kriel, Neratin Ceka, Chloe Stitz, Andres Vierny, Til Echrade . . . They're all dead, Your Honour . . . And of the ones what survived, most of them are sitting here, under guard . . . '

'Please state precisely when the meeting of the witness and the accused, Silifant, took place.'

'It was last year, in the month of August, somewhere near the end, I don't recall exactly. Well not in September, in any case, for that September, ha, is well embedded in my memory! Dacre, who'd learned about me from somewhere, said the hanza needed a psionic, one that wasn't afraid of magic, because we'd be dealing with sorcerers. The work, he said, was for the emperor and the empire, well-paid, furthermore, and the hanza would be commanded by none other than Tawny Owl himself.'

'When they say Tawny Owl, does the witness have in mind Stefan Skellen, the imperial coroner?'

'Yes, I do, indeed I do.'

114

'Please enter that in the proceedings. When and where did the witness encounter Coroner Skellen?'

'It was in September, on the fourteenth, in Fort Rocayne. Rocayne, Illustrious Tribunal, is a border watchtower, which guards the trade route from Maecht to Ebbing, Geso and Metinna. Our hanza – numbering some fifteen horse – was brought there by Dacre Silifant. So, taken together, there were twenty-two of us, as the others were already standing by in Rocayne, under the command of Ola Harsheim and Bert Brigden.'

*

The wooden floor boomed beneath heavy boots, spurs jingled and metal buckles clinked.

'Greetings, Sir Stefan!'

Tawny Owl not only did not stand up, he didn't even take his feet from the table. He just waved a hand in a very lordly gesture.

'At last,' he said curtly. 'You've kept me waiting a long time, Silifant.'

'A long time?' Dacre Silifant laughed. 'That's rich, Sir Stefan! You gave me, four Sundays to gather and bring here a good dozen of the best blades the empire and its dominions have produced. A year would be too little for the assembling of such a hanza! But I tossed it off in twenty-two days. That deserves praise, eh?'

'Let's refrain from praise,' Skellen said coolly, 'until I've seen this hanza of yours.'

'Why not now? Here are my – and now your, Sir Stefan – lieutenants: Neratin Ceka and Dufficey Kriel.'

'Hail, hail.' Tawny Owl finally decided to stand up, and his adjutants also rose. 'Let me introduce you, gentlemen . . . Bert Brigden, Ola Harsheim . . .'

'We know each other well.' Dacre Silifant grasped Ola Harsheim's right hand firmly. 'We put down the rebellion in Nazair under old Braibant. That was comical, eh, Ola? Eh, comical! The horses were hock-deep in blood! And Mr Brigden, if I'm not mistaken, from Gemmera? From the Pacifiers? Ah, there'll be comrades in the squad! I've got a few Pacifiers there.'

'I'm getting impatient to see them,' Tawny Owl interjected. 'May we go?'

'A moment,' Dacre said. 'Neratin, go and array the company, so they'll look their best before the honourable coroner.'

'Is it a he or she, that Neratin Ceka?' Tawny Owl squinted, watching the officer leave. 'A woman or a man?'

'Mr Skellen.' Dacre Silifant cleared his throat, but when he spoke his voice was steady and his eyes cold. 'I do not know exactly. He would appear to be a man, but I'm not certain. As to what kind of officer Neratin Ceka is, I'm certain. What you have deigned to ask me about would be significant were I to ask him – or her – for his – or her – hand. But that I do not intend. Neither do you, I expect.'

'You're right,' Skellen conceded after a moment's thought. 'So there's nothing to say. Let's go and scrutinise your gang, Silifant.'

Neratin Ceka, the individual of uncertain gender, had not wasted time. When Skellen and the officers went out into the fort's courtyard, the squad was standing in tidy array, aligned so that not a horse's muzzle extended further than a span. Tawny Owl gave a slight cough, content. A decent band, he thought. Ah well, were it not for official policy . . . Oh, to assemble a hanza like that and head for the marches, to plunder, rape, murder and burn . . . A man would feel young again . . . Pshaw, if it weren't for politics!

'Well, Sir Stefan?' Dacre Silifant asked, flushing with barely concealed excitement. 'How do you find them, these splendid sparrowhawks of mine?'

Tawny Owl's eyes travelled from face to face, from figure to figure. He knew some of them personally, for better or worse. Others, whose acquaintance he was now making, he had heard of. By reputation.

Til Echrade, a fair-haired elf, a scout of the Gemmerian Pacifiers. Rispat La Pointe, a sergeant from the same unit. Next, a Gemmerian: Cyprian Fripp the younger. Skellen had been present at the execution of Fripp the older. Both brothers had been famous for their sadistic proclivities.

Further away, leaning back easily in the saddle of a piebald mare, was Chloe Stitz, thief; occasionally hired and utilised by the secret service. Tawny Owl's eyes swiftly darted away from her insolent gaze and nasty smile.

116

Andres Vierny, a Nordling from Redania, a vicious killer. Stigward, a pirate, a renegade from Skellige. Dede Vargas an assassin by profession, the Devil only knew where he was from, Kabernik Turent, a murderer by vocation.

And others. Much the same. They're all akin, Skellen thought. A guild, a fraternity, where after killing the first five people they all become the same. The same movements, the same gestures, the same manner of speech, of movement and dress.

The same eyes. Impassive and cool, flat and immobile like the eyes of a snake, whose expression nothing – not even the most monstrous atrocity – was capable of changing.

'Well? Sir Stefan?'

'Not bad. A decent hanza, Silifant.'

Dacre blushed even more and saluted in the Gemmerian fashion, fist pressed against his calpac.

'I especially requested,' Skellen reminded him, 'several people who were no strangers to magic. Who fear neither spells nor sorcerers.'

'I remembered. Why, there's Til Echrade! And apart from him, see that tall maiden on that splendid chestnut, the one beside Chloe Stitz?'

'Bring her to me later.'

Tawny Owl leaned on the balustrade and rapped on it with the metal-tipped handle of his knout.

'Hail, company!'

'Hail, lord coroner!'

'Many of you,' Skellen began, when the echo of the gang's combined roar had died away, 'have worked with me before, know me and my requirements. Let them explain to those who don't know me what I expect from my subordinates, and what I do not tolerate from them. Then I shan't waste my breath needlessly.

'This very day some of you will receive your assignments and will ride out at dawn to execute them. In Ebbing. I remind you that Ebbing is an autonomous kingdom and we have no formal jurisdiction there, so I order you to act prudently and discreetly. You remain in the imperial service, but I forbid you from flaunting it, boasting about it or treating the local rulers arrogantly. You shall behave so as not to attract attention. Is that clear?'

'Yes sir, lord coroner!'

'Here, in Rocayne, you are guests and are to behave like guests. I forbid you from leaving your assigned quarters without an essential need. I forbid you from making contact with the fort's garrison. The officers will think up something so that boredom doesn't drive you to fury. Mr Harsheim, Mr Brigden, please show the troop their quarters!'

*

'I'd barely managed to get off me mare, Your Honour, than Dacre grabs me by the sleeve. Lord Skellen, he says, wants a word with you, Kenna. What to do? Off I go. Tawny Owl's sitting behind a table, feet up, whacking his knout against his bootleg. And without beating about the bush asks me if I'm the Joanna Selborne who was mixed up in the disappearance of the ship *The Southern Star*. I tells him nothing was ever proved. He bursts out laughing. "I like people, you can't pin anything on," he says. Then he asks if my aitch-es-pee, hypersensory perception, I mean, is innate. When I says aye, his mood darkened and he says: "I thought that talent of yours would come in useful with sorcerers, but first you'll have to deal with another mysterious personage".'

'Is the witness certain Coroner Skellen used those exact words?'

'I am. I'm a psionic, ain't I?'

'Please continue.'

'Our conversation was interrupted by a messenger, dusty from the road. He clearly hadn't spared his horse. He had urgent tidings for Tawny Owl, and Dacre Silifant says, as we was heading to our quarters, that he felt in his water that the messenger's tidings would shove us in the saddle before evening came. And 'e was right, Your Honour. Even before anyone had thought of dinner, half the hanza were saddled up. I got off that time; they took Til Echrade, the elf. I was content, for after those few days on the road my arse ached like buggery ... And to make matters worse my monthly had just started—'

'Will the witness please refrain from picturesque descriptions of her intimate complaints and keep to the subject. When did the witness learn the identity of the "mysterious personage" Coroner Skellen mentioned?'

'I'll tell you dreckly, but there has to be some order, don't there, for everything's getting so mixed up we won't ever untangle it! The ones who'd saddled their mounts in such haste before dinner raced from Rocayne to Malhoun. And brought back some teenage lad . . .'

*

Nycklar was angry with himself. So angry he felt like weeping.

If only he'd heeded the warnings given him by prudent folk! If only he'd remembered his proverbs, or at least the fable about the rook that couldn't keep its trap shut! If only he'd done what was to be done and returned home to Jealousy! But, oh no! Excited by the adventure, proud to be in possession of a fine steed, feeling the pleasant weight of coins in his purse, Nycklar couldn't resist showing off. Rather than going straight home to Jealousy, he rode to Malhoun, where he had loads of pals, including several maids, to whom he made advances. In Malhoun he strutted around like a gander in spring, kicked up a rumpus, cavorted, showed his horse off around the courtyard, and stood rounds in the inn, tossing money on the counter with the look and bearing of, if not a prince by blood, then at least a count.

And talked.

Talked about what had happened four days ago in Jealousy. He talked, constantly offering new versions, adding new information, confabulating, and ultimately lying through his teeth, which didn't bother his audience in the least. The inn's regulars – both locals and travellers – listened eagerly. And Nycklar went on, pretending to be well-informed. And placing himself ever oftener at the centre of the confabulated events.

On the third evening his own tongue landed him in trouble.

A deathly hush fell at the sight of the people entering the inn. And in that hush, the clank of spurs, the rattle of metal buckles and the scraping of scabbards sounded like a foreboding bell tolling misfortune from the top of a belfry.

Nycklar was not even given the chance to try playing the hero.

119

He was seized and escorted from the inn so fast he only managed to touch the floor with his heels about three times. His pals, who only the previous day – when he was paying for their drinks – had declared their undying friendship, were now practically sticking their heads under the tables, as though incredible marvels were occurring or naked women were dancing there. Even the deputy shire-reave – who was present in the inn – turned to face the wall and didn't breathe a word.

Nycklar didn't breathe a word either, not asking who, what or why. Terror turned his tongue into a stiff, dry board.

They put him on his horse and ordered him to ride. For several hours. Then there was a fort with a palisade and a tower. The courtyard was full of noisy, swaggering, well-armed mercenaries. And a chamber. And in the chamber were three men. A commander and two subordinates, it was immediately obvious. The commander, short, with blackish hair, and richly attired, was sober in his speech and admirably courteous. Nycklar listened with mouth agape as the commander apologised to him for the trouble and inconvenience and assured him he would suffer no harm. But he was not to be deceived. The men reminded him too much of Bonhart.

That observation turned out to be astonishingly accurate. For they were interested in Bonhart. Nycklar should have expected that. For, after all, it was his wagging tongue that had landed him in this quandary.

When prompted he began to talk. He was warned to speak the truth and not embellish it. He was warned courteously, but sternly and emphatically, and the one doing the warning, the richly attired one, played all the while with a metal-tipped knout, and his eyes were dark and evil.

Nycklar, the son of the coffin-maker from Jealousy, told the truth. The whole truth and nothing but the truth. About how, on the morning of the ninth day of September in the village of Jealousy, Bonhart, a bounty hunter, had wiped out the gang of Rats, sparing the life of only one bandit, the youngest, the one they called Falka. He told them how the whole of Jealousy had gathered to watch Bonhart torment and thrash his captive, but the folk were sorely disappointed, for Bonhart, astonishingly, did not kill or even torture Falka! He did no more than what a normal fellow does to his wife on returning home from the tavern on Saturday evening – just gave her a kicking, slapped her a few times, and nothing more.

The richly attired gentleman with the knout said nothing, and Nycklar told them how Bonhart had sawn the heads off the slaughtered Rats before Falka's eyes, and plucked the golden earrings set with gemstones from those heads like raisins from a bun. How Falka, tied to the hitching post, screamed and puked on seeing it. He told how afterwards Bonhart had buckled a collar around Falka's neck, like you would a bitch dog, and dragged her by it to *The Chimera's Head* inn. And then . . .

*

'And then,' said the lad, constantly licking his lips, 'the gentleman Bonhart called for ale, for he was sweating something awful and his throat was dry. And after that he cried that he had a fancy to give someone a good horse and a whole five florins. That's what he said, those were his very words. So I came forward at once, not waiting for anyone else to be quicker, for I wanted awful to have a horse and a little coin of my own. The old man gives me nothing, for he drinks whatever he makes on the coffins. So I comes forward and asks which horse – no doubt one of the Rats' – can I take? And his lordship Bonhart looks at me, till shivers ran through me and says, don't he, that the only thing I can take is a kick up the backside, for other things have to be earned. What to do? Don't look a gift horse in the mouth, says the proverb; well, the Rats' horses were standing at the hitching post, in particular that black mare of Falka's, a horse of rare beauty. So I bows and asks what must I do to earn the gift? And Mr Bonhart says that I must ride to Claremont, stopping off in Fano on the way. On the horse of my choosing. He must have known I had me eye on the black mare, for he forbad me from taking her. So I takes a chestnut with a white patch . . . '

'Less about horses' coats,' Stefan Skellen reprimanded dryly. 'And more hard facts. Tell us what Bonhart charged you to do.'

'His lordship Bonhart wrote some missives, and ordered me to hide them secure. He charged me to ride to Fano and Claremont, and there to hand over the letters to the indicated persons.'

'Letters? What was in them?'

'How should I know, gentle lord? Reading don't come easy to me, and the letters were sealed with Mr Bonhart's signet.'

'But for whom were the letters, do you recall?'

'Oh, indeed I do. Mr Bonhart ordered me to repeat it ten times, so I wouldn't forget. I got where I was to go without erring, and handed over the missives as instructed. They praised me for an able lad, and that honourable merchant even gave me a denar—'

'To whom did you deliver the letters? Speak plainly!'

'The first missive was for Master Esterhazy, a swordsmith and armourer from Fano. And the second was for the honourable Houvenaghel, a merchant from Claremont.'

'Did they open the letters in your presence? Perhaps one of them said something as he read? Rack your brains, lad.'

'I cannot recall. I didn't mark it then, and now I can't seem to remember . . .'

'Mun, Ola,' Skellen nodded at the adjutants, without raising his voice at all. 'Take the lout into the courtyard, drop his britches, and give him thirty solid lashes with a knout.'

'I remember!' the boy yelled. 'It's come back to me!'

'Nothing works on the memory,' Tawny Owl grinned, 'like nuts and honey, or a knout hovering over the arse. Talk.'

'When Houvenaghel read the missive in Claremont, there was another gentlemen there, a little chap, a veritable halfling. Mr Houvenaghel said to him . . . Erm . . . He said they'd written that soon there might be sport in the fleapit the like of which the world had never seen. That's what he said!'

'You aren't making this up?'

'I swear on my mother's grave! Don't have them flog me, gentle lord! Have mercy!'

'Well, well, get up, don't dribble on my boots! Here's a denar.'

'A thousand thanks . . . M'lord . . .'

'I said don't dribble on my boots. Ola, Mun, do you understand anything of this? What does a fleapit have in common with—'

'Bear pit,' Boreas Mun suddenly said. 'Not fleapit. Bear pit.'

'Aye!' the boy yelled. 'That's what 'e said! Just as though you'd been there, gentle lord!'

'A bear pit and sport!' Ola Harsheim hit one fist against the other. 'It's an agreed code, nothing too elaborate. It's easy. Sport – bear-baiting – is a warning about a pursuit or a manhunt. Bonhart was warning them to flee! But from whom? From us?'

'Who knows?' said Tawny Owl pensively. 'Who knows? We shall have to send men to Claremont . . . And to Fano also. You take care of that, Ola, give the squads their orders . . . Now listen, my lad . . .'

'Yes sir, gentle lord!'

'When you left Jealousy with Bonhart's letters, he was still there, I understand? And making ready to leave? Was he in haste? Did he say, perhaps, whither he was headed?'

'He did not. And neither could he make ready. He'd had his raiment – which was awful blood-spattered – cleaned and laundered, so he was only in a blouse and hose, but girt with a sword. Though I think he was hastening to leave. Why, he had thrashed the Rats and sawed them's heads off for the bounty, so he needs must ride and claim it. And, why, he'd captured that Falka too, to deliver her alive to someone. Why, that's his profession, ain't it?'

'This Falka . . . Did you have a good look at her? Why are you cackling, you ass?'

'Oh, gentle lord! Have a good look at her? I'll say I did! Every detail!'

*

'Disrobe,' Bonhart repeated, and there was something in his voice that made Ciri cringe involuntarily. But defiance immediately got the better of her.

'No!'

She didn't see the fist, she didn't even catch sight of its movement. She saw stars, the ground swayed, then shot from under her feet and suddenly thumped painfully against her hip. Her cheek and ear burned like fire; she realised she had not been punched, but struck with an open palm.

He stood over her and brought his clenched fist towards her face. She saw the heavy, skull-shaped signet, which a moment earlier had stung her face like a hornet.

123

'You owe me one front tooth,' he said icily. 'So the next time I hear the word "no" from you I'll knock two out right away. Get undressed.'

She stood up unsteadily and began to unfasten buckles and buttons with shaking hands. The villagers present in *The Chimera's Head* murmured, coughed and goggled. The widow Goulue, the alewife, bent down behind the counter, pretending to be looking for something.

'Strip off everything. To the last rag.'

They aren't here, she thought, undressing and staring blankly at the floor. *There's no one here. And I'm not here either.*

'Legs apart.'

I'm not here at all. What is about to happen won't touch me at all. Not at all. Not a bit.

Bonhart laughed.

'You flatter yourself, I think. I must dispel those illusions. I'm undressing you, little idiot, to check you haven't concealed any magical talismans, charms or amulets about your person. Not to enjoy your wretched nakedness. Don't start imagining the Devil knows what. You're a skinny kid, as flat as a pancake, and as ugly as the seven sins. Even if the urge was strong, I'd sooner tup a turkey.'

He walked over, spread her clothing around with the tip of his boot and sized it up.

'I said everything! Earrings, rings, necklace, bracelet!'

He gathered up her jewellery meticulously. He kicked her tunic with the blue fox-fur collar, gloves, coloured scarves and belt with silver chains into the corner.

'You won't parade around like a parrot or a half-elf from a whorehouse now! You can put on the rest of those rags. And what are you lot staring at? Goulue, bring some provender, I'm hungry! And you, fatso, see how my vestments are coming on!'

'I am the ealdorman here!'

'How convenient,' Bonhart drawled, and the ealdorman of Jealousy seemed to grow slimmer under his gaze. 'If anything has been damaged in the laundry I shall take measures against you, as a public servant. Off to the wash house! The rest of you, get out! And you, pipsqueak, why are you still standing here? You have the letters, the horse is saddled, so smartly to the highway and be gone! And remember: should you fail, lose the letters or mix up the addresses, I shall find you and cut you up so fine your own mother wouldn't recognise you!'

'I'm flying, m'lord! I'm flying!'

*

'That day,' Ciri pursed her lips, 'he beat me twice more. Once with his fist and once with a knout. Then he lost the urge. He just sat and stared at me without a word. His eyes were somehow . . . like those of a fish. Without eyebrows, without eyelashes . . . Somehow like watery orbs, with a black core sunk into each one. He stared hard at me and said nothing. That terrified me more than being beaten. I didn't know what he was plotting.'

Vysogota remained silent. Mice scampered around the chamber.

'He kept asking me who I was, but I said nothing. Just like when the Trappers caught me in Korath desert, this time too I fled deep into myself, inside, if you know what I mean. The Trappers said I was a doll then, and I was: a wooden doll, insensitive and lifeless. I was somehow looking down from above at everything that was being done to that doll. So what if they were hitting me, so what if they were kicking me, putting a collar on me like a dog? For it wasn't me, it wasn't me at all . . . Do you understand?'

'I do,' Vysogota nodded. 'I do understand, Ciri.'

*

'Then, Your Honour, it was our turn. The turn of our group. Neratin Ceka took command over us, and they also assigned Boreas Mun, a tracker, to us. Boreas Mun, Illustrious Tribunal, could track a fish in water, they say. That's how good he was! One time, they say, Boreas Mun—'

'The witness will refrain from digressions.'

'Beg pardon? Oh, yes . . . I get it. I mean they ordered us to ride to Fano at all speed. It was the morning of the sixteenth of September . . .'

*

Neratin Ceka and Boreas Mun rode at the head, and behind them, side by side, Kabernik Turent and Cyprian Fripp the younger, then Kenna Selborne and Chloe Stitz, and finally Andres Vierny and Dede Vargas. The latter two were singing a new and popular soldier's song, sponsored and endorsed by the Ministry of War. Even among soldier's songs it stood out by the horrifying paucity of its rhymes and alarming lack of respect for grammatical rules. It was entitled *At War*, since all the verses – and there were over forty of them – began with those words.

At war things can get quite rough,
Someone gets their head chopped off,
You come back from a drinking bout,
To see a cove with his guts hanging out.

Kenna softly whistled along. She was pleased to be among companions she had come to know well on the long journey from Etolia to Rocayne. After her conversation with Tawny Owl she had expected a random assignment, to be tagged onto a squad made up of Brigden and Harsheim's men. Til Echrade had been assigned to a squad like that, but the elf knew most of his new comrades, and they knew him. They rode at a walk, though Dacre Silifant had ordered them to race at full speed. But they were professionals. They had galloped, kicking up dust, while they could still be seen from the fort, then they'd slowed down. Tiring horses out and reckless gallops were good for tyros and amateurs, and haste, of course, only comes in useful for catching fleas!

Chloe Stitz, the professional thief from Ymlac, told Kenna about her erstwhile work with Coroner Stefan Skellen. Kabernik Turent and Fripp the younger reined in their horses and listened, often looking back.

'I know him well. I've served under him several times . . .'

Chloe stammered a little, aware of the suggestive nature of her words, but immediately laughed freely and carelessly.

'I've also served under his command,' she snorted. 'No, Kenna, don't worry. None of those demands from Tawny Owl. He didn't force himself on me, I looked for the opportunity and found it. But to be clear I'll say this: you won't gain his protection by doing that.'

'I'm not planning anything of the kind.' Kenna pouted, looking provocatively at the lewd smiles of Turent and Fripp. 'I won't be looking for an opportunity, but I'm not worried either. I'm not alarmed by any old thing. And certainly not by a cock!'

'That's all you talk about,' Boreas Mun said, reining back his dun stallion and waiting for Kenna and Chloe to catch up with him.

'We aren't riding off to fight with our cocks, ladies!' he added, continuing to ride beside the young women. 'Bonhart, let me tell you, has few equals with the sword. I'll be glad if it turns out there's no squabble or vendetta between him and Mr Skellen. And that everything blows over.'

'But I don't get it,' Andres Vierny admitted from the rear. 'Apparently we were to track down some sorcerer. That's why they gave us a psionic, this here Kenna. Wasn't it? Now, though, there's talk about some Bonhart and a girl!'

'Bonhart, the bounty hunter,' Boreas Mun said, 'had a compact with Mr Skellen. And let him down. Though he promised Mr Skellen he'd kill that girl, he let her live.'

'No doubt someone's paying more for her alive than Tawny Owl would for her dead.' Chloe Stitz shrugged. 'That's what bounty hunters are like. Don't go looking for honour among them!'

'Bonhart is different,' Fripp the younger, looking back, retorted. 'Bonhart never breaks his word.'

'Making it all the stranger that he's suddenly started.'

'And why,' Kenna asked, 'is that lass so prized? The one who was to be killed, but wasn't?'

'What business is it of ours?' Boreas Mun grimaced. 'We have our orders! And Mr Skellen has the right to demand his due. Bonhart was meant to have stuck Falka, and didn't. Mr Skellen has the right to demand that he accounts for it . . .'

'This Bonhart,' Chloe Stitz repeated with conviction, 'means to get more money for her alive than dead. There's your whole mystery.'

'The lord coroner,' Boreas Mun said, 'thought the same at first, that Bonhart had promised to supply Falka alive – for the sake of amusement and slow torture – to a baron from Geso, who was determined to punish the Rats' gang. But it turned out not to be true. No one knows who Bonhart is keeping Falka alive for, but it certainly ain't that baron.'

*

'Mr Bonhart!' The fat ealdorman of Jealousy lumbered into the tavern, puffing and panting. 'Mr Bonhart, there are armed men in the village! Riding horses!'

'What a sensation.' Bonhart wiped his plate with some bread. 'Now if they were riding monkeys, *that* would be remarkable. How many?'

'Four!'

'And where are my vestments?'

'Barely laundered . . . They haven't dried . . .'

'A pox on you. I'll have to greet our guests in my hose. But in truth, the quality of such a greeting suits that of the guests.'

He adjusted the belt and sword fastened over his hose, tucked the straps of his hose into his boot tops, and tugged the chain attached to Ciri's collar.

'On your feet, little Rat.'

When he led her out onto the porch, the four horsemen were already nearing the tavern. It was clear that they had ridden long over trackless terrain and through bad weather; their clothing, harnesses and horses were flecked with crusted-on dust and mud.

There were four of them, but they were leading a riderless horse. At the sight of it Ciri felt herself suddenly growing hot, though the day was very cool. It was her roan, still bearing her trappings and saddle. And a brow band, a gift from Mistle. The horsemen were among those who had killed Hotspurn.

They stopped outside the tavern. One, probably the leader, rode up, and raised his marten-fur calpac to Bonhart. He was swarthy and had a thin, black moustache on his upper lip like a line drawn in charcoal. His upper lip, Ciri noticed, curled every now and then; the tic meant he looked enraged the whole time. Perhaps he really was furious?

'Greetings, Mr Bonhart!'

'Greetings, Mr Imbra. Greetings, gentlemen.' Bonhart unhurriedly fastened Ciri's chain onto a hook on a post. 'Excuse my unmentionables, but I wasn't expecting you. A long road behind you, my, my . . . You've come all the way to Ebbing from Geso? And how is the honourable baron? In good health?'

'Fit as a fiddle,' the swarthy man replied indifferently, wrinkling his upper lip again. 'But there's no time to spend on idle chatter. We're in a hurry.'

'I–' Bonhart hauled up his belt and hose '–am not holding you back.'

'News has reached us that you slaughtered the Rats.'

'That is true.'

'And in accordance with your promise to the baron,' the swarthy man continued to pretend he could not see Ciri on the porch, 'you took Falka alive.'

'I'd say that that is also true.'

'You were lucky, where we were not.' The swarthy man glanced at the roan. 'Very well. We'll take the wench and head homeward. Rupert, Stavro, take her.'

'Not so fast, Imbra,' Bonhart raised a hand. 'You aren't taking anyone. And for the simple reason that I won't give her to you. I've changed my mind. I'm keeping the girl.'

The swarthy man called Imbra leaned over in the saddle, hawked and spat, impressively far, almost to the steps of the porch.

'But you promised His Lordship the baron!'

'I did. But I've changed my mind.'

'What? Do my ears deceive me?'

'The state of your ears, Imbra, is not my concern.'

'You stayed three days at the castle. You guzzled and gorged for three days on the promises given to His Lordship. The best wine from his cellar, roast peacock, venison, forcemeat, carp in cream. You slept like a king in a feather bed for three nights. And now you've changed your mind?'

Bonhart said nothing, maintaining an expression of indifference and boredom. Imbra clenched his teeth in order to suppress the twitching of his lips.

'You know, Bonhart, that we can take her from you by force?'

Bonhart's face, until that moment bored and amused, hardened instantly.

'Just try. There are four of you and one of me. And me in my

129

hose at that. But I don't have to don britches to deal with scoundrels like you.'

Imbra spat again, jerked his reins, and turned his horse around.

'The Devil take it, Bonhart, what's happened to you? You've always been renowned as a reliable, honest professional. Once given, you keep your word unfailingly. And now it turns out your word isn't worth shit! And since a man is judged by his words, then it turns out that you're a—'

'If the talk is of words,' Bonhart interrupted coldly, resting his hands on his belt buckle, 'then take heed, Imbra, that you don't let too coarse a word slip out by accident. For it might hurt when I shove it back down your throat.'

'You are bold against four! But will your boldness suffice against fourteen? For the Baron of Casadei will not let this insult slide!'

'I'd tell you what I'll do with your baron, but a crowd forms, and in it are women and children. So I shall merely tell you that in some ten days I shall stop in Claremont. Whomsoever wishes to pursue a right, avenge an insult or take Falka from me, let them come to Claremont.'

'I shall be there!'

'I shall be waiting. Now be off with you.'

*

'They feared him. They feared him terribly. I could feel the fear seeping from them.'

Kelpie whinnied loudly, jerking her head.

'There were four of them, armed to the teeth. And one of him, in darned long johns and a ragged old blouse with too-short sleeves. He would have been ridiculous, were he . . . Were he not so terrible.'

Vysogota remained silent, narrowing his eyes, which were watering from the wind. They were standing on a knoll rising above the Pereplut Marshes, not far from the spot where, two weeks earlier, the old man had found Ciri. The wind flattened the reeds and ruffled the water on the marshes.

'One of the four,' Ciri continued, letting her mare enter the water and drink, 'had a small crossbow by his saddle and his hand stretched out towards that crossbow. I could almost hear his thoughts and feel his terror. "Will I manage to cock it? And loose it? And what will happen if I miss?" Bonhart also saw that crossbow and that hand, he heard the same thoughts, I'm sure. And I'm sure the horseman wouldn't have been quick enough.'

Kelpie raised her head, snorted and jingled the rings of her curb bit.

'I was understanding better and better into whose hands I'd fallen. But I still couldn't understand his motives. I'd heard their conversation and remembered what Hotspurn had said before. That the Baron of Casadei wanted me alive and Bonhart had promised him that. And then he changed his mind. Why? Did he want to hand me over to somebody else who would pay more? Had he worked out who I really was? And meant to turn me over to the Nilfgaardians?

'We set off from the village before nightfall. He let me ride Kelpie. But he tied my hands and held me by the chain fixed to the collar the whole time. The whole time! And we rode, almost without stopping, a whole night and day. I thought I'd die of exhaustion. But *he* showed no tiredness at all. He isn't a man. He's the Devil incarnate.'

'Where did he take you?'

'To a little town called Fano.'

*

'When we entered Fano, Illustrious Tribunal, it was already gloomy, murky as you please, only the sixteenth of September, in truth, but the day was overcast and cold as hell, you'd of said it was November. We didn't have to search long for the armourer's workshop, for it was the largest farmstead in the entire town, and what's more, the ringing of hammers forging iron relentlessly sounded from it. Neratin Ceka . . . Master scribe, you write his name in vain, for I don't recall if I said, but Neratin is dead now, killed in a village called Unicorn—'

'Please do not instruct the clerk. Continue with your testimony.'

'Neratin knocked at the gate. He politely said who we were and what was our business, and asked politely to be heard. We were admitted. The swordsmith's workshop was a fine building, virtually a stronghold, with a palisade of pine timbers, towers of oaken planks, and inside planed larch on the walls—'

'The court is not interested in architectural details. Let the witness get to the point. Prior to that, however, please repeat the swordsmith's name for the records.'

'Esterhazy, Illustrious Tribunal. Esterhazy of Fano.'

*

The swordsmith, Esterhazy, looked long at Boreas Mun, unhurriedly answering the question posed to him. 'P'rhaps Bonhart was here,' he finally said, fiddling with a bone whistle hanging around his neck. 'And p'rhaps he wasn't? Who knows? This, gentlefolk, is a workshop where we forge swords. We shall answer any questions concerning swords eagerly, swiftly, elegantly and at length. But I see no reason to answer questions concerning our guests or customers.'

Kenna pulled a kerchief from her sleeve and pretended to wipe her nose.

'A reason can be found,' said Neratin Ceka. 'You may find one, Mr Esterhazy. Or I may. Would you choose?'

In spite of the semblance of effeminacy, Neratin's face could become hard and his voice menacing. But the swordsmith only snorted, continuing to toy with the whistle.

'Choose between a bribe and a threat? I would not. I consider the former and the latter worth only of being spat on.'

'Just one tiny piece of information,' Boreas Mun said, clearing his throat. 'Is that so much? We've known each other long, Mr Esterhazy, and Coroner Skellen's name is known to you—'

'It is,' the swordsmith cut in, 'it is indeed. The misdemeanours and exploits with which that name is associated are also known to us. But we are in Ebbing, an autonomous and self-governing kingdom. Only seemingly, perhaps, but nonetheless. Thus we shall tell you nothing. Continue on your way. As a consolation, we'll pledge to you that if in a week or a month someone asks about you, they will hear just as little.'

'But, Mr Esterhazy—'

'Must I make it clearer? Prithee, get out of here!'

Chloe Stitz hissed furiously, Fripp and Vargas' hands crept towards their hilts, and Andres Vierny laid his fist on the war hammer hanging at his thigh. Neratin Ceka did not move and his face did not even quiver. Kenna saw that his eye never left the bone whistle. Before they entered, Boreas Mun had warned them that the sound of the whistle was the signal for bodyguards – consummate men-at-arms – called 'quality controllers', who were waiting, concealed, in the swordsmith's workshop.

But, having foreseen everything, Neratin and Boreas had planned their next move. They had a trump up their sleeves.

Kenna Selborne. Psionic.

Kenna had already probed the swordsmith's mind, had gently pricked him with impulses and cautiously pervaded the tangle of his thoughts. Now she was ready. Pressing a kerchief to her nose – there always existed the danger of a nosebleed – she forced her way into his brain with a throbbing and a command. Esterhazy began to choke, flushed, and grasped the table he was sitting behind with both hands, as though he feared it would float away to distant lands along with the sheaf of invoices, the inkwell and the paperweight depicting a nereid cavorting with two tritons at once.

Keep calm, Kenna commanded, *it's nothing, nothing's the matter. You would simply like to tell us what we wish to know. For you know what interests us, and the words are positively bursting forth from you. So go on. Begin. You will see that you only need speak and the humming in your head, the roaring in your temples and the stabbing in your ears will cease. And the spasm in your jaw will also subside.*

'Bonhart,' Esterhazy said hoarsely, opening his mouth more often than would be expected from the syllabic articulation, 'was here four days ago, on the twelfth of September. He had a wench with him he called Falka. I was expecting his visit, for two days earlier a letter from him had been delivered . . .'

A trickle of blood seeped from his left nostril.

Speak, Kenna ordered. *Speak. Tell us everything. You can see what a relief it will be.*

*

133

The swordsmith Esterhazy scrutinised Ciri with curiosity, without getting up from the oaken table.

'It's for her,' he guessed, tapping a pen holder against the paper-weight depicting the weird group. 'The sword you requested in the letter. Right, Bonhart? Well, let's examine it then . . . Let's see if it agrees with what you wrote. Five feet, nine inches in height . . . And such she is. One hundred and twelve pounds in weight . . . Well, we'd have given her less than a hundred and twelve, but that's a minor detail. A hand, you wrote, which a number five glove would fit . . . Show me your hand, honourable maiden. Well, and that agrees, too.'

'With me everything always agrees,' Bonhart said dryly. 'Do you have any decent iron for her?'

'In my firm,' Esterhazy answered proudly, 'no other iron than decent is manufactured or offered. I understood it was to be a sword for combat, not for gala decoration. Ah, yes, you wrote that. Naturally, a weapon will be found for this maid without any diffi-culty. Swords of thirty-eight inches suit such a height and weight, standard manufacture. With that light build and small hand, she needs a mini-bastard with a hilt lengthened to nine inches, and a pommel. We could also suggest an elven taldaga or Zerrikanian sabre, or alternatively a light Viroledanian—'

'Show me the wares, Esterhazy.'

'Hot-tempered, are we, eh? Well, come this way. Come this way . . . Hey, Bonhart? What the Devil is this? Why are you pulling her on a leash?'

'Keep your snotty nose out of this, Esterhazy. Don't stick it where it doesn't belong, for you're liable to get it caught somewhere!'

Esterhazy, toying with the whistle hanging around his neck, looked at the hunter without fear or respect, though he had to crane his neck a good deal. Bonhart twisted his moustache and cleared his throat.

'I,' he said, a little more quietly, though still malevolently, 'don't meddle in your business or affairs. Does it surprise you that I demand reciprocity?'

'Bonhart.' The swordsmith did not even flicker an eyelid. 'When you leave my home and courtyard, when you close my gate behind you, then shall I respect your privacy, the secrecy of your affairs, the specifics of your profession. And I shall not meddle in them, be certain. But in my home I shall not allow you to abuse human dignity. Do you understand me? Outside my gate you may drag the wench behind a horse, if you wish. In my home you will remove that collar. Forthwith.'

Bonhart reached for the collar and unfastened it, unable to resist a tug which almost brought Ciri to her knees. Esterhazy, pretending he hadn't seen it, let the whistle slip from his fingers.

'That's better,' he said dryly. 'Let's go.'

They crossed a small passage into another, slightly smaller, courtyard adjoining the rear of the smithy, with one side opening out onto an orchard. There was a long table there, beneath a canopy resting on carved posts, where servants were just finishing laying out some swords. Esterhazy gestured for Bonhart and Ciri to walk up to the array.

'This is what I offer.'

They approached.

'Here,' Esterhazy pointed to a long row of swords on the table, 'we have my wares. All the blades were forged here. You can see the horseshoe, my punch-mark. Prices fall in the range of five to nine florins, since they're standard. These, though, lying here, are only assembled and finished by us. The blades are generally imported. Their origin can be told from the punches. The ones from Mahakam have crossed hammers stamped on them, those from Poviss a crown or a horse's head, and those from Viroleda a sun and the famous workshop's inscription. Prices start at ten florins.'

'And where do they end?'

'That varies. Oh, this one, for example, is an exquisite Viroledanian.' Esterhazy took up a sword from the table, gave a salute with it, and then moved to a fencing position, dextrously twisting his hand and forearm in a complicated sequence called an 'Angelica'. 'This one is fifteen. Antique workmanship, a collector's blade. Clearly made to order. The motif chiselled on the ricasso shows the weapon was intended for a woman.'

He turned the sword over, hand held in tierce, pointing the blade flat at them.

'As on all Viroleda blades, the traditional inscription: "Draw me not without reason; sheath me not without honour". Ha! They still

135

chisel such inscriptions in Viroleda. Throughout the wide world, these blades have been drawn by blackguards and oafs. Throughout the wide world, honour has gone way down in price, for it's an unprofitable commodity—'

'Don't talk so much, Esterhazy. Give her that sword, let her try it for size. Take the blade, girl.'

Ciri grasped the sword lightly, feeling the lizard-skin hilt cling firmly to her palm, and the weight of the blade urging her arm to wield and thrust.

'It's a mini-bastard,' Esterhazy reminded her. Needlessly. She knew how to use the long hilt, with three fingers on the pommel.

Bonhart took two steps backward, into the courtyard. He drew his sword from the scabbard and whirled it around until it hissed.

'Have at me!' he said to Ciri. 'Kill me. You have a sword and you have the opportunity. You have the chance. Make use of it. For I shan't soon give you a second.'

'Have you lost your mind?'

'Quiet, Esterhazy.'

She beguiled him with a glance to one side and a deceptive twitch of her shoulder, and struck like lightning, with a flat sinistre. The blade clanged so powerfully against the parry that Ciri staggered and had to leap to one side, banging her hip against the table with the swords. She involuntarily loosened her grip on the weapon, trying to regain her balance – knowing that at that moment he could have killed her without the slightest difficulty, had he so wished.

'You have lost your minds!' Esterhazy said, his voice raised. The whistle was in his hand again. The servants and craftsmen looked on in stupefaction.

'Put the iron aside.' Bonhart did not take his eyes off Ciri, utterly ignoring the swordsmith. 'Aside, I said. Or I'll hack off your hand!'

She obeyed after a moment's hesitation. Bonhart smiled ghoulishly.

'I know who you are, you viper. But I'll make you reveal it yourself. By word or deed! I'll make you reveal who you are. And then I'll kill you.'

Esterhazy hissed as though wounded.

'That sword—' Bonhart didn't even glance at him '—was too hefty for you. And because of it you were too slow. You were as slow as a pregnant snail. Esterhazy! What you gave her was too heavy by at least four ounces.'

The swordsmith was pale. His eyes ran from her to him, from him to her, and his face was strangely altered. At last he beckoned a servant and issued an order in hushed tones.

'I've something,' he said slowly, 'which ought to satisfy you, Bonhart.'

'Why, then, didn't you show it to me at once?' snarled the hunter. 'I wrote that I wanted something extraordinary. Perhaps you thought I can't afford a better sword?'

'I know what you can afford,' Esterhazy said with emphasis. 'I've known that for no little time. But why didn't I show you this one right away? I had no way of knowing who you would bring here . . . on a leash, with a collar around her neck. I couldn't guess who the sword was meant for and what it was to serve. Now I do.'

The servant had returned, bearing an oblong box.

'Come closer, girl,' Esterhazy said softly. 'Look.'

Ciri approached. And looked. And sighed audibly.

*

She unsheathed the sword with a deft movement. The fire from the hearth flared blindingly on the blade's wavily outlined edge, glowed red in the openwork of the ricasso.

'This is it,' said Ciri. 'As you've probably guessed. Hold it, if you wish. But beware, it's sharper than a razor. You feel how the hilt sticks to your hand? It's made from the skin of a flatfish which has a venomous spine on its tail.'

'A ray.'

'I guess. That fish has tiny teeth in its skin, so the hilt doesn't slide in the hand, even when it sweats. Look what's etched on the blade.'

Vysogota leaned over and examined it, squinting.

'An elven mandala,' he said soon after, raising his head. 'The so-called blathan caerme, or garland of destiny: stylised oak blossom, bridewort and broom flowers. A tower being struck by lightning – a symbol of chaos and destruction, for the Old Races ... And above the tower–'

'A swallow,' Ciri completed. 'Zireael. My name.'

*

'Indeed, a fine thing,' said Bonhart finally. 'Gnomish handiwork, that's clear at once. Only the gnomes forged such dark iron. Only the gnomes used undulating blades and only they open-worked their blades to reduce the weight ... Come clean, Esterhazy. Is it a replica?'

'No,' the swordsmith snapped. 'It's original. A genuine gnomish gwyhyr. The blade is more than two hundred years old. The finishing, naturally, is much more recent, but I wouldn't call it a replica. The gnomes of Tir Tochair made it to my order. Following ancient techniques, methods and patterns.'

'Dammit. It may be too dear for me after all. How much do you wish for this blade?'

Esterhazy was silent for some time. His face was inscrutable.

'I shall give it to her for nothing, Bonhart,' he finally said in hushed voice. 'As a gift. So that what is to come about, will come about.'

'Thank you,' said Bonhart, visibly astonished. 'Thank you, Esterhazy. A kingly gift, kingly indeed ... I accept, I accept. I am indebted to you ...'

'You are not. The sword is for her, not for you. Come here, girl with a collar on her neck. Examine the marks etched into the blade. You don't understand them, naturally. But I shall explain them to you. Look. The line delineated by destiny is winding, but leads to this tower. Towards annihilation, towards the destruction of established values, of the established order. But there, above the tower, do you see? A swallow. The symbol of hope. Take this sword. And may what is to come about, come about.'

Ciri cautiously extended a hand, and gently stroked the dark blade, its edge gleaming like a mirror.

'Take it,' Esterhazy said slowly, looking at Ciri with eyes wide open. 'Take it. Hold it, girl. Take it ...'

'No!' Bonhart suddenly barked, leaping up, seizing Ciri by the arm and shoving her suddenly and forcefully. 'Away!'

Ciri fell onto her knees, the gravel of the courtyard painfully pricking her hands, which she had to spread to keep her balance.

Bonhart slammed the box shut.

'Not yet!' he snarled. 'Not today! The time is not yet come!'

'Most evidently,' Esterhazy nodded calmly, looking him in the eyes. 'Aye, it most evidently hasn't come yet. Pity.'

*

'It was of little avail, Illustrious Tribunal, reading that sword-smith's thoughts. We were there on the sixteenth of September, three days before the full moon. And while we were returning from Fano to Rocayne, a patrol caught us up. Ola Harsheim and seven horse. Mr Harsheim ordered us to race as fast as we could to reach the rest of the unit. For the day before – the fifteenth of September – there had been a massacre in Claremont . . . I suppose I don't need to tell you; the illustrious tribunal doubtlessly knows about the massacre in Claremont . . .'

'Please testify, without worrying what the tribunal knows.'

'Bonhart was a day ahead of us. He brought Falka to Claremont on the fifteenth of September . . .'

*

'Claremont,' Vysogota nodded. 'I know that town. Where did he take you?'

'To a large house in the town square. With arcades and columns at the entrance. It was obvious at once that a wealthy man lived there . . .'

*

The chambers' walls were draped with sumptuous tapestries and splendid wall hangings depicting religious and hunting scenes, and idylls featuring disrobed women. The furniture gleamed with inlays and brass fittings, and one sunk ankle-deep into the carpets.

139

Ciri had no time to note the details, though, for Bonhart walked swiftly, dragging her by the chain.

'Greetings, Houvenaghel!'

Lit by the spectrum of colours cast by a stained-glass window, his back to a hunting tapestry, stood a man of impressive corpulence, attired in a kaftan dripping with gold and a fur-lined coat trimmed with karakul pelts. Although in the prime of his manhood, he had a bald pate and pendulous jowls like those of a great bulldog.

'Greetings, Leo,' he said. 'And you, lady—'

'That's no lady.' Bonhart showed him the chain and collar. 'No need to welcome her.'

'Politeness costs nothing.'

'Nothing but time.' Bonhart tugged the chain, walked up and unceremoniously patted the fat man's belly.

'You've put on a good deal,' he remarked. 'By my troth, Houvenaghel, were you to stand in the way it would be easier to jump over you than walk around.'

'Prosperity,' Houvenaghel explained jovially, shaking his cheeks. 'Greetings to you, greetings, Leo. 'Tis wonderful to host you, for I am most inordinate joyful today. My business affairs are going so admirably well that I feel like touching wood. The till's a-ringing! Only today, may this serve as an example, a captain in the Nilfgaardian reserve horse, the quartermaster responsible for supplying gear to the front, flogged me six thousand military bows, which I shall retail with a ten-fold profit to hunters, poachers, brigands, elves and diverse other freedom fighters. I also bought a castle from a local marquess . . .'

'Why the hell do you need a castle?'

'I must live regally. Getting back to my business affairs: one deal is quite simply thanks to you, Leo. A seemingly hopeless debtor paid me back. Quite literally a moment ago. His hands were shaking as he paid me. The fellow saw you and thought—'

'I know what he thought. Did you receive my letter?'

'I did.' Houvenaghel flopped down heavily, knocking the table with his belly and making the carafes and goblets on it ring. 'And I've prepared everything. Haven't you seen the handbills? The rabble must have torn them down . . . Folk are already heading for the theatre. The till's a-ringing . . . Sit you down, Leo. There's time. Let's talk, enjoy some wine . . .'

'I don't want your wine. It's army issue, no doubt, stolen from Nilfgaardian transports.'

'You must be jesting. It's Est Est from Toussaint, the grapes picked when our gracious emperor, Emhyr, was a mere nipper, shitting in his cradle. It was a good year. For wine. Cheers, Leo.'

Bonhart silently raised a toasting goblet. Houvenaghel smacked his lips, examining Ciri extremely critically.

'So this is the doe-eyed nymph,' he said at last, 'who is to guarantee the sport promised in your epistle? I know that Windsor Imbra is already nearing the town. And has with him several decent cut-throats. And a few local swordsmen have seen the bills . . .'

'Have you ever been disappointed by my wares, Houvenaghel?'

'Never, 'tis true. But neither have I had anything from you for a good while.'

'I work more seldom than in the past. I'm thinking about retiring entirely.'

'Capital is needed for that, from which to support oneself. I might have a way . . . Will you listen?'

'Only for want of other amusement.' Bonhart pulled a chair closer with his foot and made Ciri sit down.

'Have you ever thought of heading north? To Cintra, to the Slopes or across the Yaruga? Do you know that anyone who moves there and chooses to settle on captured territory is guaranteed a plot of eight oxgangs by the empire? And freedom from tax for a decade?'

'I,' replied the hunter calmly, 'am not cut out to be a farmer. I couldn't till the soil or breed cattle. I'm too sensitive. The sight of dung or worms makes me want to puke.'

'Me too.' Houvenaghel shook his jowls. 'The only thing I can tolerate in the whole of agriculture is distilling spirits. The rest is repugnant. They say agriculture is the basis of economics and guarantees prosperity. I consider it, however, contemptible and humiliating that something stinking of manure should determine my prosperity. I've taken some steps in that regard. One need not till the soil, Bonhart, one need not raise cattle on it. It's sufficient to own it. If one has enough of it one can extract decent profits from it. One can, believe me, live a life of ease. Yes, I've taken certain steps in that regard, hence, indeed, my question about a trip northwards. For you see, Bonhart, I would have work for you there. Permanent, well-paid, undemanding. And just right for a sensitive fellow like you: no dung, no worms.'

'I'm prepared to listen. Without committing to anything, naturally.'

'From the plots which the emperor guarantees the settlers, one can, with a bit of enterprise and a little seed capital, put together quite a decent latifundium.'

'I understand.' The hunter chewed his moustache. 'I understand what you're getting at. I already see what steps you're taking regarding your own prosperity. Do you see no difficulties?'

'Oh, I do. Of two kinds. Firstly, one has to find hired hands, who, pretending to be settlers, will travel north to receive the land from the distributing officers and take over the plots. Formally for themselves, but in practice for me. But I shall set about finding them. The second of the difficulties concerns you.'

'I'm all ears.'

'Some of the hired hands will take over the land and then be disinclined to give it up. They will forget about the agreement and the money they have taken. You wouldn't believe, Bonhart, how deeply fraud, wickedness and low motives are ingrained in human nature.'

'I would.'

'I will need someone to convince the dishonest that dishonesty doesn't pay. That it's punishable. And you could take care of that.'

'It sounds excellent.'

'It is. I have experience, I've already conducted rackets of this kind. Following the formal inclusion of Ebbing into the empire, when plots were distributed. And later, when the Enclosure Act came into force. Owing to that, Claremont – this charming little town – is on my land and thus belongs to me. The entire area belongs to me. Far, far away, to the mist-shrouded horizon. It's all mine. Three hundred oxgangs all told. That's over six thousand acres. Imperial acres, not peasant ones. Twenty-four thousand roods.'

"'O lawless empire, close to downfall",' Bonhart recited scorn-fully. 'An empire where everybody who steals has to fall. Its weakness lies in self-interest and self-seeking.'

'Its power and strength lie in it.' Houvenaghel shook his cheeks. 'You, Bonhart, confuse thievery with private enterprise.'

'Only too often,' admitted the bounty hunter detachedly. 'What do you say to this partnership, then?'

'Isn't it too early to be dividing up that land in the North? Per-haps, to be certain, we should wait until Nilfgaard wins the war?'

'To be certain? Don't jest. The result of the war is a foregone conclusion. Wars are won with money. The empire has it and the Nordlings don't.'

Bonhart cleared his throat meaningfully.

'While we're on the subject of money . . .'

'Ah yes.' Houvenaghel rummaged in the documents lying on the table. 'Here's a bank cheque for a hundred florins. Here is the deed of contract for the transfer of obligations, on the strength of which I shall receive the reward for the bandits' heads from the Varnhagens of Geso. Sign here. Thank you. You are also owed a percentage of the takings from the extravaganza, but the accounts have not yet been closed, the till's still a-ringing. There is great in-terest, Leo. Great, indeed. People in my town are awfully troubled by boredom and despondency.'

He broke off and looked at Ciri.

'I sincerely hope you aren't mistaken with regard to this person. That she will furnish us with wholesome amusement . . . And be willing to cooperate for the sake of our joint profit.'

'There won't be any profit for her–' Bonhart eyed up Ciri indif-ferently, '–she knows that.'

Houvenaghel grimaced and snorted.

'It's no good, no bloody good that she knows! She ought not to know! What's the matter with you, Leo? And if she's not willing to be sporting, if she turns out to be spitefully uncompliant? What then?'

The expression on Bonhart's face didn't change.

'Then,' he said, 'we'll unleash your mastiffs into the arena. They've always been compliant where sport's concerned, as I recall.'

*

Ciri was silent for a long time, rubbing her disfigured cheek.

'I was beginning to understand,' she finally said. 'I was beginning to realise what they wanted to do with me. I gathered myself, I was determined to escape at the first opportunity . . . I was prepared for any risk. But they didn't give me the chance. They were guarding me too well.'

Vysogota said nothing.

'They dragged me downstairs. The guests of that fat Houvenaghel were waiting there. More eccentrics! Where do all these grotesque odd fish come from, Vysogota?'

'They breed. Natural selection.'

*

The first of the men was short and chubby, more resembling a halfling than a human, and was even dressed like a halfling – modestly, pleasantly, neatly and in pastel colours. The second man – though no longer young – had the outfit and bearing of a soldier and a sword at his side. Silver embroidery depicting a dragon with batlike wings sparkled on the shoulder of his black jerkin. The woman was fair-haired and skinny, with a slightly hooked nose and thin lips. Her pistachio-coloured gown had a plunging neckline. Which wasn't very well advised. There wasn't much cleavage to show, apart from wrinkled and parchment-dry skin covered in a thick layer of rouge and white lead powder.

'Her Noble Ladyship the Marchioness de Nementh-Uyvar,' Houvenaghel said. 'Lord Declan Ros aep Maelchlad, captain in the Nilfgaardian reserve horse of His Mighty Emperorship of Nilfgaard. Lord Pennycuick, Mayor of Claremont. And this is Mr Leo Bonhart, my relative and former comrade.'

Bonhart bowed stiffly.

'So this is the little brigand who is to amuse us today,' said the skinny marchioness, staring intently at Ciri with her pale blue eyes. Years of drinking could be heard in her husky, seductive voice.

'Not too bad, I'd say. But nicely built . . . Quite a pleasant little bodikin.'

144

Ciri jerked, pushing off an obtrusive hand, paled with fury and hissed like a serpent.

'Please don't touch,' Bonhart said coldly. 'Don't feed it. Don't tease it. I take no responsibility.'

'A little bodikin–' the marchioness licked her lips, paying no attention to him '–can always be tied to a bed, to make it more amenable. Perhaps you'd sell her to me, Mr Bonhart, sir? My marquess and I like little bodikins like that, and Mr Houvenaghel is so reproachful when we seize local goose girls and peasant children. In any case, the marquess can't hunt children any longer. He can't run, because of those chancres and warts which have opened up in his crotch—'

'Enough, enough, Matilda,' Houvenaghel said softly but quickly, seeing the expression of growing disgust on Bonhart's face. 'We must leave for the theatre. Mr Mayor has just been informed that Windsor Imbra has reached the town with a squad of the Baron of Casadei's infantry. Which means it's time.'

Bonhart removed a flacon from a belt pouch, wiped the onyx table top with his sleeve and tipped out a small mound of white powder. He pulled on the chain, drawing Ciri closer.

'Do you know how to use it?'

Ciri clenched her teeth.

'Sniff it up. Or lick a finger and rub it into your gums.'

'No!'

Bonhart didn't even turn his head.

'You'll do it yourself,' he said softly, 'or I'll do it, only in a way that will supply everybody here with a bit of entertainment. You don't just have mucous membranes in your mouth and nose, little Rat, but in a few other amusing places. I'll call for servants, have you stripped naked and restrained, and I'll take advantage of those amusing places.'

The Marchioness de Nementh-Uyvar laughed gutturally, watching Ciri reaching for the narcotic with a trembling hand.

'Amusing places,' she repeated and licked her lips. 'What a fascinating idea. Worth trying one day! Hey, hey, girl, have a care, don't waste good fisstech! Leave some for me!'

*

The narcotic was much more powerful than the one she'd tried with the Rats. A little while after taking it, Ciri was overcome by a dazzling euphoria; contours were sharpened, light and colours pricked her eyes, smells irritated her nose, sounds became unbearably loud, and everything around her became unreal, as ephemeral as a dream. There were the steps, there were the tapestries stinking of thick dust, there was the husky laughter of the Marchioness de Nementh-Uyvar. There was the courtyard, rain drops falling quickly on her face, and the jerking of the collar she still had around her neck. There was an immense building with a wooden tower and a large, repulsively tawdry painting on the frontage. The painting depicted dogs baiting a monster – neither a dragon, a gryphon, nor a wyvern. There were people outside the entrance to the building. One was shouting and gesticulating.

'It's revolting! Revolting and sinful, Mr Houvenaghel, to be utilising a building which was once a place of worship for such an immoral, inhuman and disgusting practice! Animals also feel, Mr Houvenaghel! They also have their dignity! It's a crime to set animal against animal for the amusement of the common folk in the name of profit!'

'Calm yourself, you pious fellow! And don't meddle in my private enterprise! In any case, no animal shall be baited today. Not a single one! Exclusively people!'

'Oh. Then I do beg your pardon.'

Inside, the building was full of people sitting on rows of benches forming an amphitheatre. A pit had been dug in the centre, a circular depression measuring about ten yards across, shored up by hefty posts and topped with a balustrade. The stench and uproar were overwhelming. Again, Ciri felt a tug on the collar, somebody seized her under the arms, somebody shoved her. She suddenly found herself at the bottom of the pit, on firmly packed down sand.

In the arena.

The first rush had subsided, and now the narcotic was just stimulating her, sharpening her senses. Ciri pressed her hands over her ears – the crowd occupying the amphitheatre's benches roared, booed and whistled; the noise was unbearable. She noticed that her right wrist and forearm were tightly bound by a leather bracer. She couldn't recall it being fastened to her.

146

She heard the familiar hoarse voice, saw the skinny, pistachio-coloured marchioness, the Nilfgaardian cavalry captain, the pastel-toned mayor, Houvenaghel and Bonhart occupying a box perched above the arena. Her hands went to her ears again, as someone suddenly struck a copper gong.

'Look, good people! In the pit today there's no wolf, no goblin, no endrega! In the arena today is the murderous Falka from the Rats' gang! The ticket desk by the entrance is taking bets! Don't stint a penny, good people! You can't eat this amusement, you can't drink it, but if you skimp on it you'll not profit, you'll lose out!'

The crowd roared and applauded. The narcotic was working. Ciri trembled with euphoria. Her vision and hearing were registering everything, every detail. She could hear Houvenaghel's cackle, the marchioness' husky laugh, the mayor's grave voice, Bonhart's cold bass, the yelling of the animal-loving priest, the squealing of women and the crying of a child. She could see dark patches of blood on the posts encircling the arena and a stinking grill-covered hole gaping in it. And brutishly contorted faces, glistening with sweat, above the balustrade.

A sudden commotion, raised voices, curses. Armed men jostled the crowd, but ground to a halt, stopped by a wall of guards clutching partisans. She'd seen one of the men before – she remembered the swarthy face and the black moustache like a line drawn in charcoal on his upper lip, which quivered in a tic.

'Mr Windsor Imbra?' It was Houvenaghel's voice. 'Of Geso? Seneschal of His Noble Lordship, the Baron of Casadei? Greetings, greetings to our foreign guests. Take your places, the spectacle is about to begin. But don't forget, please, to pay at the entrance!'

'I'm not here for the sport, Mr Houvenaghel! I'm here on matters of service! Bonhart knows of what I speak!'

'Indeed? Leo? Do you know of what the seneschal speaks?'

'Do not jest! There are fifteen of us here! We've come for Falka! Hand her over, or things will turn ill!'

'I don't understand your excitation, Imbra.' Houvenaghel frowned. 'But I observe that this is not Geso, nor is it within the lands of that mandarin, your baron. Should you make a fuss and incommode us I shall have you driven away with knouts!'

'I wish to cause no offence, Mr Houvenaghel,' Windsor Imbra appealed. 'But the law is on our side! Bonhart, here present, promised Falka to His Grace, Baron of Casadei. He gave his bond. And now he must keep it!'

'Leo?' Houvenaghel said, jowls shaking. 'Do you know what he's talking about?'

'I do and I admit he's right.' Bonhart stood up, carelessly waving a hand. 'I shan't protest or cause any difficulties. The girl is here, as everybody sees. Whoever wishes to may take her.'

Windsor Imbra was dumbfounded. His lip trembled intensely. 'How is that?'

'The girl,' Bonhart repeated, winking at Houvenaghel, 'belongs to the man who wishes to take her from the arena. Alive or dead, as your taste dictates.'

'How is that?'

'Dammit, I'm gradually losing my patience!' Bonhart skilfully feigned anger. 'Nothing but "how is that"! Bloody parrot! How? However you wish! It's up to you; poison some meat and throw it to her as you would a she-wolf. But I can't guarantee she will devour it. She doesn't look stupid, does she? No, Imbra. Whoever wants her must take the trouble of going down to her. Down there, into the pit. You want Falka? Then claim her!'

'You wave Falka under my nose like a frog on a rod before a catfish,' Windsor Imbra growled. 'I don't trust you, Bonhart. I can smell the iron hook hidden in that bait!'

'I congratulate you on your sensitive nose.' Bonhart stood up, took the sword acquired in Fano from under the bench, drew it from the scabbard and threw it into the arena, so dexterously that the blade stuck vertically in the sand, two paces in front of Ciri. 'There's your iron. Out in the open, not concealed at all. I don't care for the wench, and whomsoever wants to may take her. If they're able.'

The Marchioness de Nementh-Uyvar laughed nervously.

'If they're able!' she repeated in her husky contralto. 'For now the bodikin has a sword. Bravo, Mr Bonhart. It seemed despicable to leave the bodikin defenceless and at the mercy of these good-for-nothings.'

'Mr Houvenaghel,' Windsor Imbra said with arms akimbo, not

148

gracing the skinny aristocrat with even a glance. 'This spectacle is being held under your patronage, for it's your theatre, after all. Just tell me one thing. By whose rules and principles are we to play – yours or Bonhart's?'

'By theatrical ones,' Houvenaghel cackled, shaking his belly and bulldog-like jowls. 'For though it's true that it's my theatre, the customer is always right, as he who pays the piper calls the tune! The customer sets the rules. While we merchants must act according to those rules: whatever the customer demands, we must give him.'

'Customer? You mean these folk?' Windsor Imbra gestured sweepingly across the packed auditorium. 'All these folk who have paid to marvel at these marvels?'

'Business is business,' Houvenaghel replied. 'If there a demand for something, why not sell it? Do folk pay for a wolf fight? For endrega and aardvark fights? For baiting a badger in a barrel, or a wyvern? Why are you so astonished, Imbra? Folk need circuses and spectacles as they do bread, why, more than bread. Many of those here had it taken from their mouths. Now look at them, how their eyes shine. They can't wait for the games to begin.'

'But at games,' Bonhart added, smiling spitefully, 'the appearances of sport must at least be observed. The brock, before the curs drag him from the barrel, may nip with its teeth; that's only sporting. And the girl has a blade. Let it also be sporting here. Well, good people? Am I right?'

The good people confirmed in an incoherent – though thunderous and joyful – chorus that Bonhart was absolutely right.

'The Baron of Casadei,' Windsor Imbra said slowly, 'will not be pleased, Mr Houvenaghel. I tell you he'll not be pleased. I don't know if it's worth your while picking a fight with him.'

'Business is business,' Houvenaghel repeated and jiggled his cheeks. 'The Baron of Casadei knows that very well. He has borrowed a deal of money from me at low interest, and when the time comes to borrow more, then we shall somehow smooth over our squabbles. But some foreign lord isn't going to interfere in my private enterprise. Wagers have been laid, people have paid to enter. Blood must soak into that sand, in that arena.'

'Must?' Windsor Imbra yelled. 'Bollocks! I'm itching to show

149

you that it doesn't need to at all! For I shall leave here and ride away, without looking back. Then you can spill your own blood! The very thought of supplying this rabble with amusement sickens me!'

'Let him go.' A character with a very low hairline in a horsehide jerkin emerged from the crowd. 'If it sickens him, let him go. It doesn't sicken me. They said whoever does for the she-rat takes the reward. I volunteer to enter the arena.'

'Not likely!' one of Imbra's soldiers, a short but wiry and well-built man, suddenly yelled. He had thick, unkempt and matted hair. 'We was first! Wasn't we, boys?'

'Yeah!' chimed in a second, a scrawny one with a pointed beard. 'We have priority! And don't let your sense of honour get the better of you, Windsor! What of it if the rabble is watching? Falka's in the pit, suffice to hold out a hand and take her. And let the peasantry goggle, we don't give a damn!'

'And we're ready to get something out of it too!' snickered a third, dressed in a doublet of vivid amaranth. 'Let's make sport of it, am I right, Mr Houvenaghel? Let's make a contest of it! As long as a reward's on offer!'

Houvenaghel grinned and nodded, proudly and majestically jiggling his pendulous cheeks.

'Well then,' asked the one with the goatee curiously, 'are there any wagers?'

'As of now,' the merchant laughed, 'no one has wagered on the result! As of now it's three to one, since none of you dares enter the enclosure.'

'Huuuh!' Horsehide yelled. 'I dare! I'm minded!'

'Out of the way, I said!' Matted Hair roared back. 'We was first and we have first crack. Come on, what are we waiting for?'

'How many can go in at one time?' Amaranth tightened his belt. 'Or is only one at a time allowed?'

'You whoresons!' Quite unexpectedly, the pastel mayor suddenly roared in a powerful voice utterly incongruent with his build. 'Perhaps ten of you want to take on the one of her? On horseback, perhaps? Riding chariots, perhaps? Perhaps you want to borrow a catapult from the armoury in order to hurl boulders at the wench from afar? Eh?'

'Very well, very well,' Bonhart interrupted, after swiftly consulting with Houvenaghel. 'Let it be sport, but let there be entertainment too. We'll say two at a time. You may enter in pairs.'

'But the reward,' Houvenaghel warned, 'will not be doubled! If it's two, you'll have to share.'

'In pairs? Two at a time?' Matted Hair flung his cape from his shoulders. 'Are you ashamed, boys? She's just a wench!' He spat on the ground. 'Stand back. I'll go myself and take her down. Big deal!'

'I want Falka alive!' protested Windsor Imbra. 'A pox on your fights and duels! I won't go along with Bonhart's circus, I want the wench! Alive! You two go in, you and Stavro. And haul her out of there.'

'As for me,' Stavro, the one with the goatee, said, 'it's an insult for two of us to take on that scrawny thing.'

'The baron's florins will make that insult more palatable. But only if she's alive!'

'The baron's a miser,' Houvenaghel cackled, wobbling his belly and bulldog's jowls. 'He doesn't have an ounce of sporting spirit in him. Nor the desire to reward that spirit in others! I, though, champion sport. And hereby increase the reward. Whomsoever enters the arena alone and leaves it on his own two feet, will be paid, by this very hand, from this very coffer, not twenty but thirty florins!'

'So what are we waiting for?' yelled Stavro. 'I'm going first!'

'Not so fast!' the short mayor roared once again. 'The wench has but thin linen on her back! So cast off that brigandine, soldier. This is sport!'

'A pox on you!' Stavro stripped off the studded kaftan, then pulled his shirt off over his head, revealing a scrawny chest and arms as hairy as a baboon. 'A pox on you, m'lords, and your sodding sport! I'll go in the buff! Shall I take off me britches too?'

'And your braies!' the Marchioness de Nemeth-Uyvar croaked seductively. 'Then we'll see if you're only manly in word!'

Rewarded by thunderous applause and naked to the waist, Stavro drew his weapon and threw one leg over the barrier, watching Ciri intently. Ciri folded her arms over her chest. She didn't even take a step towards the sword plunged into the sand. Stavro hesitated.

'Don't do it,' said Ciri, very softly. 'Don't make me . . . I won't let you touch me.'

'Don't begrudge me, wench.' Stavro clambered over the barrier. 'I've nothing against you. But business is—'

He didn't complete the sentence, for Ciri was already on him, was already holding Swallow, as she had named the gnomish gwyhyr. She used a very simple, downright childish attack and feint called 'three little steps' – but Stavro was taken in by it. He took a step backwards and raised his sword involuntarily, and was then at her mercy – after stepping back he was leaning against a post and Swallow's blade was an inch from the tip of his nose.

'That move,' Bonhart explained to the marchioness, shouting over the roaring and applause, is called "three little steps, a feint and a lunge in tierce". A cheap trick, I'd expected something more refined from the wench. Though one must admit, if she'd wanted it, the fellow would already be dead.'

'Kill 'im! Kill 'im!' the spectators bellowed, and Houvenaghel and Mayor Pennycuick pointed their thumbs downwards. The blood had drained from Stavro's face, and the pimples and pock-marks on his cheeks were repugnantly visible.

'I told you not to make me,' Ciri hissed. 'I don't want to kill you! But I won't let anyone touch me. Go back where you came from.'

She moved back, turned around, put down her sword and looked up towards the box.

'Are you toying with me?' she cried, voice breaking. 'Do you mean to force me to fight? To kill? You can't do it! I won't fight!'

'Hear that, Imbra?' Bonhart's sneering voice resounded in the silence. 'Clear profit! And no risk! She won't fight. Thus you can take her from the arena and deliver her alive to the Baron of Casadei, so he can freely amuse himself with her. You can take her without any danger! With your bare hands!'

Windsor Imbra spat. Stavro, still standing with his back pressed against the post, panted, gripping his sword. Bonhart laughed.

'But I, Imbra, bet a diamond to a walnut that you can't.'

Stavro took a deep breath. The girl standing with her back to him appeared distracted, preoccupied. He was seething with rage, shame and hatred. He couldn't control himself. He attacked. Swiftly and treacherously.

152

The audience didn't notice the swerve or reverse thrust. All they saw was the rushing Stavro making a truly balletic leap, after which – less balletically – he fell belly and face down in the sand; sand which was immediately stained red with blood.

'Instinct takes the upper hand!' Bonhart shouted over the crowd. 'Reflexes come into play! Eh, Houvenaghel? What did I say? You'll see, the mastiffs won't be needed!'

'What a splendid and profitable spectacle,' Houvenaghel said, closing his eyes in bliss.

Stavro raised himself on trembling arms, jerked his head, cried out, croaked, puked blood and slumped down on the sand.

'What's that blow called, Mr Bonhart, sir?' the Marchioness de Nementh-Uyvar asked huskily and sensuously, rubbing her knees together.

'That was improvised.' The teeth of the bounty hunter – who didn't even look at the marchioness – flashed from beneath his lips. 'An exquisite, inspired and, I'd say, visceral improvisation. I've heard of a place where they teach that kind of improvised butchery. I'll wager our maiden knows it well. Now I know who she is.'

'Don't make me!' Ciri screamed, a truly ghastly note trembling in her voice. 'I don't want to! Understand? I don't want to!'

'You hellish slut!' Amaranth nimbly vaulted the barrier, circling the arena to distract Ciri from Matted Hair, who was entering from the opposite side. Horsehide cleared the barrier behind Matted Hair.

'That's fighting dirty!' roared the halfling-sized Mayor Penny-cuick, who was sensitive to fair play, and the crowd yelled with him.

'Three against one! That's unfair!'

Bonhart laughed. The marchioness licked her lips and began to wriggle her legs more urgently.

The threesome's plan was simple – pin the retreating girl against the posts. Then two would block and the third one kill. Nothing came of it, for a simple reason. The girl didn't retreat but attacked.

She slipped between them with a balletic pirouette, so lightly she almost didn't touch the sand. She struck Matted Hair in passing,

153

precisely where he ought to be struck: in the carotid artery. The blow was so subtle it didn't jar her rhythm. She ducked away in a reverse feint, so swiftly that not a single drop of the blood gushing from Matted Hair's neck in a two-yard stream fell on her. Amaranth, behind her, aimed to slash across the back of her neck, but his treacherous blow clanged against a lightning-fast parry of her blade, held up behind her. Ciri unwound like a spring, slashing with both hands, amplifying the blow's power with a jerk of her hips. The dark gnomish blade was like a razor, and cut his abdomen open with a hiss and a squelch. Amaranth howled and flopped forward onto the sand, curling up in a ball. Horsehide leaped at Ciri and thrust towards her throat, but she dodged, spun fluidly and struck from close quarters with the middle of the blade, mutilating his eye, nose, mouth and chin.

The spectators yelled, whistled, stamped their feet and bayed for more. The Marchioness de Nementh-Uyvar thrust both hands between her clenched thighs, licked her shining lips and laughed in her nervous drinker's contralto. The captain of the Nilfgaardian reserve horse was as wan as vellum. A woman tried to cover the eyes of her child as he wriggled free. A grizzled old man in the front row vomited loudly and spasmodically, and hung his head between his knees.

Horsehide sobbed, holding his face, as blood mixed with snot and spit poured through his fingers. Amaranth rolled around, squealing like a stuck hog. Matted Hair stopped scrabbling against a post slippery with blood, spurting from him in the rhythm of his heartbeat.

'Heeelp meeee,' Amaranth howled, tightly clutching his innards spilling out of his belly. 'Comraaaades! Heeeelp meeee!'

'Bheeeh . . . bhooo . . . bheeeeh . . .' Horsehide spat and snorted blood.

'Fin-ish-'im-off! Fin-ish-'im-off!' chanted the audience, stamping their feet to the rhythm. The puking old man was shoved from the bench and kicked towards the gallery.

'A diamond to a walnut,' Bonhart's sneering bass resounded amongst the racket, 'that none will now dare enter the arena. A diamond to a walnut, Imbra! What am I saying – even to an empty walnut shell!'

'Kill 'em!' A roaring, thumping of feet and clapping. 'Kill 'em!'

'Noble maiden!' Windsor Imbra shouted, gesturing his subordinates to go forward. 'Let them remove the wounded! Let them enter the arena and take them, before they bleed to death! Have a heart, noble maiden!'

'A heart,' Ciri repeated with effort, only then feeling the adrenaline strike her. She got herself quickly under control, with a series of well-drilled breaths.

'Come in and take them,' she said. 'But come in unarmed. Have a heart as well. Just this once.'

'Noooo!' the crowd roared and chanted. 'We-want-blood! We-want-blood!'

'You rotten bastards!' Ciri turned around gracefully, sweeping her gaze over the stands and benches. 'You despicable swine! You scoundrels! You lousy whoresons! You want blood? Come here, come down, taste it and smell it! Lick it up before it clots! Bastards! Vampires!'

The marchioness groaned, trembled, fluttered her eyelashes and softly nestled up to Bonhart, without taking her hands from between her thighs. Bonhart grimaced and shoved her away from him, not bothering to be gentle. The crowd howled. Someone threw a half-chewed sausage into the arena, someone else a boot, and yet another chucked a gherkin, aimed at Ciri. She sliced the gherkin in two with a flourish of her sword, provoking an even louder roar.

Windsor Imbra and his men picked up Amaranth and Horsehide. When Amaranth was touched, he howled, while Horsehide fainted. Matted Hair and Stavro no longer showed any signs of life. Ciri moved back, to stand as far away as the arena permitted. Imbra's men also did their best to stay away from her.

Windsor Imbra stood motionless. He waited until they had heaved out the dead and wounded. He looked at Ciri through narrowed eyes, his hand on the hilt of his sword, which – despite his promise – he had not removed on entering the arena.

'No,' she warned, barely moving her lips. 'Don't make me. Please.'

Imbra was pale. The crowd stamped their feet, roared and howled.

'Don't listen to her!' Bonhart shouted over the racket again. 'Draw your sword! Otherwise it'll get out that you're a coward and a turd! From the Alba to the Yaruga everyone will be talking about how Windsor Imbra ran from a slip of a girl with his tail between his legs!'

Imbra's blade slid an inch from the scabbard.

'Don't,' said Ciri.

The blade went back in.

'Coward!' roared someone from the crowd. 'Shithead! Chicken heart!'

His face impassive, Imbra walked to the edge of the arena. Before seizing the hands of his comrades reaching down from above, he turned back one last time.

'You probably know what you're in for, wench,' he said softly. 'You probably already know what Leo Bonhart is. You probably already know what Leo Bonhart's capable of. What excites him. You'll be shoved out into the arena to kill for the amusement of the swine and scum in here. And even worse than them. And when the fact that you can kill stops amusing them, when Bonhart tires of doing violence to you, then they'll kill you too. They'll send so many to face you, you won't be able to watch your back. Or they'll set dogs on you. And the dogs will tear you apart, and the rabble in the stands will sniff blood and applaud. You'll expire on this blood-stained sand. Like the men you slaughtered today. You'll remember my words.'

Oddly, it was only then that she noticed the small escutcheon on his enamel gorget.

A silver unicorn rampant on a black field.

A unicorn.

Ciri lowered her head. She looked at her sword's openwork recasso.

Everything suddenly went quiet.

'By the Great Sun,' Declan Ros aep Maelchlad, the captain of the Nilfgaardian reserve horse, abruptly began. 'No. Don't do that, girl. *Ne tuv'en que'ss, luned!*'

Ciri slowly turned Swallow around in her hand and rested the pommel on the sand. She went down on one knee. Holding the blade with her right hand, she aimed the point with her left

156

towards her breastbone. The blade cut through her clothing and pricked her at once.

Just don't cry, thought Ciri, pushing harder and harder down on the sword. Just don't cry, there's nothing to cry over. One quick thrust and it will all be over . . . It will all be over . . .

'You won't do it.' Bonhart's voice resounded in the complete silence. 'You won't do it, witcher girl. In Kaer Morhen you were taught how to kill, so you kill like a machine. Instinctively. To kill yourself you need character, strength, determination and courage. And they couldn't teach you that.'

*

'He was right,' Ciri said with effort. 'I couldn't.'

Vysogota remained silent. He was holding a coypu pelt. Motionless. Had been for a long time. He had almost forgotten about the pelt as he listened.

'I chickened out. I was a coward. And I paid for it. As every coward pays for it. In pain, dishonour and hideous humiliation. And an absolute revulsion towards myself.'

Vysogota said nothing.

*

Had someone crept up to the cottage with the sunken thatched roof that night, had they peered through the slits in the shutters, they would have seen in the dimly lit interior a grey-bearded old man and an ashen-haired girl sitting by the fireplace. They would have noticed that the two of them were staring silently into the glowing, ruby coals.

But no one could have seen it. For the cottage with the sunken, moss-grown thatched roof was well hidden among the fog and the mist, in a boundless swamp in the Pereplut Marshes where no one dared to venture.

Whosoever sheds man's blood, by man shall his blood be shed.

Genesis, 9:6

Verily, great self-righteousness and great blindness are needed to call the gore pouring from the scaffold justice.

Vysogota of Corvo

CHAPTER FIVE

'What seeks the Witcher on my territory?' Fulko Artevelde, the Prefect of Riedbrune, repeated the question, now clearly impatient with the lengthening silence. 'Whence is the Witcher coming? And whither is he headed? With what purpose?'

That's what comes of playing at good deeds, thought Geralt, looking at the prefect's face, which was marked with thickened scars. That's what comes of playing the noble witcher out of compassion for a bunch of shabby forest folk. That's what comes of the desire for luxury and sleeping in taverns, where there's always a nark. That's what comes of travelling with a loudmouthed poetaster. Here I sit, in a room like a windowless cell, on a hard interrogation chair bolted to the floor, and on the chair's back – it's impossible not to notice – are cuffs and leather straps. For binding the arms and restraining the neck. They haven't been used yet, but they're there.

How the bloody hell do I get myself out of this pickle now?

*

After five days of trekking with the Riverdellian forest beekeepers they finally emerged from the wilderness onto a boggy reed bed. It stopped raining, the wind dispersed the mists and clammy fog, the sun broke through the clouds. And mountain peaks sparkled snow-white in the glare.

If a short while ago the River Yaruga had signified to them a clear dividing line, a border, the crossing of which represented an evident passage to the next, more serious, stage of the expedition, it was even more so now; the sense that they were approaching a limit, a barrier, a place which could only be turned back from. They all felt it, Geralt above all – it could only be thus, since from dawn to dusk they had been faced with a mighty, jagged

161

range of mountains barring their way, rising up in front of them to the south, and gleaming with snow and glaciers. The Amell Mountains. And rising even above the saw-toothed Amell was the forbiddingly majestic obelisk of Mount Gorgon, Devil Mountain, as angular as the blade of a misericorde. They did not talk about it, didn't discuss it, but Geralt felt what everybody was thinking. For when he looked at the Amell range and Gorgon, the thought of continuing the journey southwards seemed sheer insanity.

Fortunately, it suddenly turned out there would be no need to head south.

This news was brought to them by the shaggy forest beekeeper, owing to whom they had acted as the train's armed escort for the previous five days. The husband and father of the comely hama-dryads, next to whom he looked like a wild boar beside two mares. He who had tried to deceive them by saying the druids of Caed Dhu had gone to the Slopes.

It was the day after their arrival in Riedbrune, a town teeming like an anthill and the destination of the forest beekeepers and trappers from Riverdell. It was the day after parting with the forest beekeepers, for whom the Witcher was no longer needed. He hadn't expected to see any of them again. His astonishment was thus all the greater.

For the forest beekeeper began with effusive expressions of gratitude and the handing to Geralt of a full pouch of mainly small change; his witcher's fee. He accepted it, feeling on him the somewhat mocking gaze of Regis and Cahir, to whom he had occasionally moaned during the trek about human ingratitude and stressed the pointlessness and stupidity of selfless altruism.

And then the excited beekeeper literally shouted out the news. 'The, you know, Mistletoers, I mean the druids, are camped, dear Master Witcher, in the oak groves by Loch Monduirn, a lake, get my drift, thirty-five miles from here in a westerly direction.'

The beekeeper had heard these tidings at a honey and bees-wax trade market from a relative living in Riedbrune, while the relative had been given the information from a diamond prospec-tor acquaintance of his. When the beekeeper learned about the druids he ran as quickly as he could to tell the Witcher. And now he was glowing with happiness, pride and a sense of importance, like every liar when his lies accidentally turn out to be true.

At first, Geralt had intended to make for Loch Monduirn without a moment's delay, but the company protested vehemently. Being in possession of the money from the beekeepers – declared Regis and Cahir – and being in a town where anything could be bought, they ought to stock up on vittles and supplies. And buy extra arrows, added Milva, because they was always demanding game from her and she weren't going to shoot whittled sticks. And spend at least one night in a bed in an inn, added Dandelion, and retired to that bed bathed and pleasantly tipsy on ale.

The druids, they chorused, won't run away.

'Utter coincidence though it may be,' added the vampire Regis with a curious smile, 'our company is on exactly the right road, and heading in exactly the right direction. For since we are clearly and absolutely destined to encounter the druids, a day or two's delay makes no difference.'

'And as regards haste,' he added philosophically, 'the impression that time is quickly running out is customarily a warning signal enjoining one to reduce the pace, and proceed slowly and with due prudence.'

Geralt didn't protest or argue with the vampire's philosophy, although the weird nightmares he was being haunted by still inclined him towards haste. Despite his being unable to recollect them after waking.

It was the seventeenth of September and a full moon. Six days remained until the autumn Equinox.

*

Milva, Regis and Cahir took upon themselves the task of making purchases and acquiring the necessary equipment. Geralt and Dandelion, however, were to reconnoitre and gather information in the town of Riedbrune.

Situated in a bend in the River Nevi, Riedbrune was a small town, if one only took into consideration the densely-grouped brick and wooden buildings inside the ring of earthen embankments bristling with a palisade. But the serried buildings inside the embankments were currently merely the centre of the town, and no more than a tenth of the population could live there. Nine tenths resided in the noisy ocean of ramshackle huts, shacks, cabins, sheds, tents and wagons serving as dwellings which surrounded the embankments.

The Witcher and the poet were served by a cicerone in the form of the beekeeper's relative; young, artful and arrogant, a typical specimen of an urban layabout, who'd been born in the gutter and was no stranger to bathing nor slaking his thirst there. This stripling was like a trout in a crystal-clear mountain stream in the urban hubbub, throng, grime and stench, and the chance to show someone around his repugnant town clearly delighted him. Unconcerned that nobody was asking him any questions, the guttersnipe gave enthusiastic explanations. He explained that Riedbrune was an important stage for Nilfgaardian settlers travelling northwards after the endowment pledged by the emperor: six oxgangs or roughly one hundred and twenty acres. And on top of that a ten-year tax moratorium. For Riedbrune lay at the mouth of the Dol Nevi valley which cuts through the Amell Mountains, via the Theodula pass linking the Slopes and Riverdell with Mag Turga, Geso, Metinna and Maecht; all countries for many years subordinate to the Nilfgaardian Empire. The town of Riedbrune, explained the guttersnipe, was the last place where the settlers could depend on something else and not just themselves, their womenfolk and what they had on their wagons. Which was why most of the settlers remained camped outside the town for quite some time, gathering their strength before the last push to the banks of the Yaruga and beyond. And many of them, he added, with the pride of a slum patriot, settled in the town permanently, because the town was, why, culture, not some yokelish dump stinking of dung.

In truth, the town of Riedbrune's stench drew on many smells; dung included.

Geralt had been there, years before, but couldn't recognise it. Too much had changed. Previously, there hadn't been so many cavalrymen in black armour and cloaks with silver emblems on their spaulders. Previously, the Nilfgaardian tongue had not been heard on all sides. Previously, there hadn't been a quarry outside the town, where now ragged, dirty, haggard and bloodied

164

people split boulders into ashlars and rubble, whipped by black-uniformed overseers.

A large force of Nilfgaardian soldiers are stationed here, explained the guttersnipe, but not permanently, only during breaks in marches and searches for partisans of the Free Slopes organisation. They'll be setting up a powerful Nilfgaardian garrison here when a great, stone stronghold is constructed on the site of the old castle. A stronghold built of stone hard-won from the quarry. The people splitting the stone are prisoners of war. From Lyria, from Aedirn, and lately from Sodden, Brugge and Angren. And Temeria. Four hundred prisoners are employed here in Riedbrune. A good five hundred work in the ore quarries, underground and open-cast mines in the vicinity of Belhaven and over a thousand are building bridges and levelling roads in the Theodula pass.

There had also been a scaffold in the town square when Geralt had visited, but a much more modest one. There hadn't been so many devices arousing hideous associations on it, and there hadn't been so many revolting and putrid decorations hanging from the gallows, stakes, forks and poles.

That's thanks to Mr Fulko Artevelde, the prefect recently installed by the military authorities, explained the guttersnipe, looking at the scaffold and the fragments of human anatomy gracing it. Mr Fulko has given the hangman business again. There's no fooling around with Mr Fulko, he added. He's a stern master.

The diamond prospector – the guttersnipe's mate, who they found in the tavern – didn't make a good impression on Geralt. For he happened to be in that tremblingly pale, half-sober, half-drunk, half-real, almost nightmarish state which drinking for several nights and days without stopping puts a fellow into. The Witcher's heart sank. It looked as though the sensational news about the druids might have originated in simple delirium tremens.

The drink-sodden prospector answered their questions astutely, however, and with good sense. He wittily retorted to Dandelion's accusation that he didn't look like a diamond prospector by saying that he would if he ever found a diamond. He described the dwelling place of the druids by Loch Monduirn explicitly and precisely, without exaggerated embellishment or an overinflated fantasising manner. He took the liberty of asking what his interlocutors wanted from the druids and, when treated to a contemptuous silence, warned them that entering the druidic oak groves meant certain death, since the druids were wont to grab intruders, shove them in a basket called the Wicker Woman and burn them alive to the accompaniment of prayers, chants and incantations. The groundless rumour and foolish superstition, it turned out, had dogged the druids, resolutely keeping up, never lagging more than two furlongs behind.

Further conversation was interrupted by nine soldiers in black uniforms with the sign of the sun on their spaulders, armed with guisarmes.

'Would you be,' asked the sergeant commanding the soldiers, tapping his calf with an oaken truncheon, 'the witcher Geralt?'

'Yes,' Geralt answered after a moment's reflection. 'I would.'

'You'll be coming along with me, then.'

'How can you be sure I will? Am I under arrest?'

The soldier looked at him in a seemingly endless silence, but somehow strangely without respect. No doubt his eight-man escort gave him the nerve to look in that manner.

'No,' he said at last. 'You aren't under arrest. I received no order to arrest you. If I'd received an order my question would have been different, sir. Very different.'

Geralt adjusted his sword belt rather ostentatiously.

'And my answer,' he said icily, 'would have been different, too.'

'Now, now, gentlemen,' Dandelion decided to step in, putting on an expression, which, in his opinion, was the smile of a seasoned diplomat. 'Why that tone? We're honest men, we needn't fear the powers that be, why, we're willing to help them. Whenever the opportunity arises. But by virtue of that we deserve something from authority, don't we, officer? If only something as tiny as an explanation of why our civic freedoms are being curtailed.'

'There's a war on, sir,' the soldier replied, not in the least bit disconcerted by the torrent of words. 'Freedom, as the name suggests, is a matter for peacetime. Any reasons will be elucidated by His Lordship the Prefect. I carry out orders, so don't get into discussions with me.'

'Fair enough,' the Witcher conceded and gave the troubadour a slight wink. 'Then lead us to the prefecture, good soldier.

166

Dandelion, go back to the others and tell them what's happened. Do the necessary. Regis will know what to do.'

*

'What's a witcher doing in the Slopes? What do you seek?'

The person asking the questions was a broad-shouldered, dark-haired man with a face rutted with scars and a leather patch over his left eye. In a dark alleyway, the sight of that cyclopean face was capable of wresting a moan of terror from many a breast. But how unjust, when it was the face of Mr Fulko Artevelde, Prefect of Riedbrune, the highest ranking custodian of law and order in the entire region.

'What does a witcher seek in the Slopes?' repeated the highest ranking custodian of law and order in the entire region.

Geralt sighed and shrugged, feigning indifference.

'You know, of course, the answer to your question, prefect. You could only have gleaned the fact that I'm a witcher from the Riverdell forest beekeepers who hired me to protect them on their march. And being a witcher, in the Slopes, or anywhere else, I'm generally in search of the chance to work. So I'm journeying in the direction suggested by the patrons who hired me.'

'Logical,' Fulko Artevelde nodded. 'On the face of it at least. You parted company with the beekeepers two days ago. But you intend to continue your travels southwards, in somewhat peculiar company. With what aim?'

Geralt didn't lower his eyes, but steadily returned the burning gaze of the prefect's only eye.

'Am I under arrest?'

'No. Not for the time being.'

'Then the purpose and direction of my travel is my private business.'

'I suggest frankness and openness, nonetheless. If only in order to prove you don't feel in any way guilty and don't fear either the law, or any authority guarding it. I'll repeat the question: what is behind your expedition, witcher?'

Geralt pondered this briefly.

'I'm trying to reach the druids who were abiding in Angren, but

167

have probably moved into these parts. It would have been easy to learn that from the beekeepers I was escorting.'

'Who hired you to deal with the druids? The guardians of nature haven't burned one too many people in the Wicker Woman, have they?'

'Fairy tales, rumours, superstitions. Strange for an enlightened person like yourself. I want information from the druids, not their blood. But really, prefect, it seems to me I've been too frank, in order to prove I don't feel guilty.'

'It's not about your guilt. At least not just about it. I'd like, nevertheless, a tone of mutual congeniality to prevail in our talk. For in spite of appearances, the aim of this talk is, among others, to save you and your companions' lives.'

'You have provoked my sincere curiosity, m'lord prefect,' answered Geralt after some time, 'Among other things. I shall hear out your explanations with truly rapt attention.'

'I don't doubt it. We'll get to those explanations, but gradually. In stages. Have you ever heard, master witcher, of the tradition of turning imperial evidence? Do you know what that is?'

'I do. Weaselling out of one's responsibilities by fingering one's comrades.'

'A gross simplification,' Fulko Artevelde said without smiling, 'typical, actually, for a Nordling. You often disguise gaps in your education with sarcastic or exaggerated simplifications which you consider witty. Imperial law operates here in the Slopes, master witcher. More precisely, imperial law is going to operate here when rank lawlessness has been utterly extirpated. The best way to fight lawlessness and criminality is the scaffold, which you surely saw in the town square. But occasionally the offer to turn imperial evidence also works.'

He made a dramatic pause. Geralt didn't interrupt.

'Quite recently,' the prefect continued, 'we managed to lure a gang of juvenile criminals into an ambush. The brigands offered resistance and were killed . . . '

'But not all of them, right?' Geralt conjectured, bluntly, becoming a little bored by all this oratory. 'One was taken alive. They were promised a reprieve if they turned imperial evidence. I mean if they started grassing. And they grassed me up.'

'Why such a deduction? Have you had any contact with the local criminal underworld? Now or in the past?'

'No. I haven't. Not now, or in the past. So forgive me, lord prefect, but the whole matter is either a complete misunderstanding or humbug. Or a trap directed against me. In the latter case I would suggest we don't waste any more time and proceed to the nub of the matter.'

'It appears that the thought of a trap troubles you,' the prefect observed, furrowing his scarred brow. 'Could you, perhaps, in spite of your assurances, have some reason to fear the law?'

'No. I'm beginning, though, to fear that the fight against crime is being conducted hurriedly, wholesale and not meticulously enough, without painstaking inquiries to determine guilt or innocence. But well, perhaps that's just an exaggerated simplification, typical of a dull Nordling. And this Nordling continues not to understand in what way the Prefect of Riedbrune is saving his life.'

Fulko Artevelde observed him in silence for a moment, then clapped his hands.

'Bring her in,' he ordered the soldiers who'd appeared at his signal.

Geralt calmed himself with several breaths, for suddenly a certain thought made his heart race and his adrenaline flow. A moment later he had to take several more breaths, and even – astonishingly – had to make a Sign with his hand out of sight beneath the table. And the effect – astonishingly – was none. He felt hot. And cold.

For the guards had shoved Ciri into the room.

'Well I never,' said Ciri, right after she'd been sat down in a chair and had her hands handcuffed behind the backrest. 'Look what the cat's dragged in!'

Artevelde made a brief gesture. One of the guards, a huge fellow with the face of a slow-witted child, drew his arm back in an unhurried swing and struck Ciri in the face so hard it made the chair rock.

'Forgive her, Your Lordship,' said the guard apologetically and astonishingly mildly. 'She's young and foolish. Skittish.'

'Angoulême,' Artevelde said slowly and emphatically. 'I promised you I'd hear you out. But I meant I'd listen to your answers to my questions. Not to your badinage. You will be rebuked for your lack of respect. Understand?'

'Sure, nuncle.'

The gesture. The slap. The chair rocked.

'Young,' mumbled the guard, rubbing his hand on his hip. 'Skittish . . .'

From the young woman's snub nose – Geralt could see now that it wasn't Ciri and was astonished at his mistake – trickled a thin stream of blood. The young woman sniffed hard and smiled predatorily.

'Angoulême,' the prefect repeated. 'Do you understand me?'

'Yes sir, Mr Fulko.'

'Who's this, Angoulême?'

The girl sniffed again, inclined her head and fixed Geralt with her huge eyes. Hazel, not green. Then she shook her untidy mane of flaxen hair, causing it to fall onto her forehead in unruly locks.

'Never seen him before.' She licked the blood which dripped onto her lip. 'But I know who he is. Anyway, I already told you that, Mr Fulko; now you know I wasn't lying. His name's Geralt. He's a witcher. He crossed the Yaruga about ten days ago and he's heading for Toussaint. Right, my white-haired nuncle?'

'She's young . . . Skittish . . .' said the guard quickly, looking somewhat anxiously at the prefect. But Fulko Artevelde just grimaced and shook his head.

'You'll still be fooling about on the scaffold, Angoulême. Very well, let's go on. With whom, according to you, was Geralt the Witcher travelling?'

'I've already told you that too! With a comely fellow called Dandelion, who's a troubadour and carries a lute. And a young woman, who has dark blonde, chin-length hair. I don't know her name. And another man, without a description, his name wasn't mentioned either. Four of them in all.'

Geralt rested his chin on his knuckles, observing the girl with interest. Angoulême didn't lower her gaze.

'What eyes you have,' she said. 'Creepy peepers!'

'Continue, Angoulême, continue,' Mr Fulko urged, scowling. 'Who else belonged to this witcher's cohort?'

'No one. I said there were four of them. Not been listening, nuncle?'

The gesture, the slap, the trickle. The guard kneaded his hip, but refrained from any more comments about the skittishness of youth.

'You lie, Angoulême,' said the prefect. 'How many of them are there, I ask for the second time?'

'Whatever you say, Mr Fulko. Whatever you say. As you wish. There's two hundred of 'em. Three hundred! Six hundred!'

'Lord prefect.' Geralt forestalled the order to strike. 'Let's leave it, if we may. What she said is precise enough to show she's not lying; at most lacking in information. But where did she get her facts? She declared she's never seen me before. It's the first time I've seen her too. I give my word.'

'Thank you,' Artevelde frowned at him, 'for your help with the investigation. How valuable. When I start interrogating you I count on your being equally eloquent. Angoulême, did you hear what the gentleman said? Speak. And don't make me encourage you.'

'It was said,' replied the girl as she licked the blood dripping from her nose, 'that if the authorities were informed about a planned crime, if it was revealed who was planning villainy, there'd be clemency. So I'm telling you, ain't I? I know about a crime being prepared and I want to forestall the evil deed. Listen to what I say: Nightingale and his hanza are waiting in Belhaven for this here witcher and are planning to club him to death there. A half-elf gave them the contract. A stranger, no one knows where the hell he's from, no one knows him. The half-elf said it all: who he is, what he looks like, where he's from, when he'll arrive, in what company. He warned that the Witcher's no mug but an old hand, so not to play the hero, but stab him in the back, down him with a crossbow or better yet poison him, if he eats or drinks somewhere in Belhaven. The half-elf gave Nightingale some money. A lot of money. And promised there'd be more after the job's done.'

'After it's done,' Fulko Artevelde remarked. 'So the half-elf is still in Belhaven? With Nightingale's gang?'

'Perhaps. I don't know. It's over a fortnight since I escaped from Nightingale's hanza.'

'So would that be the reason you're grassing them up?' the Witcher smiled. 'Settling scores?'

The young woman's eyes narrowed and her swollen mouth twisted. 'Leave my sodding scores out of this, nuncle! And me grassing is saving your life, right? Some thanks would be in order!'

'Thank you.' Geralt again prevented the beating. 'I only meant to remark that if you're settling scores, it diminishes your credibility to turn imperial evidence. People grass to save their skin and their life, but they lie when they want revenge.'

'Our Angoulême has no chance of saving her life,' Fulko Artevelde interjected. 'But she wants, naturally, to save her skin. To me that's an absolutely credible motive. Well, Angoulême? You do want to save your skin, don't you?'

The girl pursed her lips and visibly blanched.

'The boldness of a criminal,' said the prefect contemptuously, 'and of a snot-nosed kid at the same time. Swoop down in numbers, rob the weak, kill the defenceless, oh, yes. Look death in the eye, not so easy. That's beyond you.'

'We shall see,' she snarled.

'We shall,' nodded Fulko gravely. 'And we shall hear. You'll bellow your lungs out on the scaffold, Angoulême.'

'You promised me clemency.'

'And I shall keep my promise. If what you have testified proves to be the truth.'

Angoulême jerked on the chair, pointing at Geralt with a movement seemingly of her whole, slim body.

'And that?' she yelled. 'What's that? Isn't that the truth? Let him deny he's a witcher and he's Geralt! Let him say I'm not credible! Let him ride to Belhaven, and you'll have better proof that I'm not lying! You'll find his corpse in some gutter in the morning. But then you'll say I didn't prevent a crime, so the clemency'll still come to nothing! That right? You're fucking swindlers! Nothing but swindlers!'

'Don't hit her,' said Geralt. 'Please.'

There was something in his voice that checked the raised hands of the prefect and the guard. Angoulême sniffed, looking at him piercingly.

'Thanks, nuncle,' she said. 'But beating's nothing much. If they

172

want, let 'em carry on. I've been beaten since a child, I'm used to it. If you want to be kind, confirm I'm telling the truth. Let them keep their word. Let them sodding hang me.'

'Take her away,' Fulko ordered, quietening Geralt, who was about to protest, with a gesture.

'She is of no use to us,' he explained, once they were alone. 'I know everything and you shall have your explanations. And then I shall ask for reciprocity.'

'First of all,' the Witcher's voice was cold, 'explain what that noisy exit was all about. Ending with that curious request to be hanged. If she's turned imperial evidence the girl's done her work, hasn't she?'

'Not yet.'

'How is that?'

'Homer Straggen, nicknamed Nightingale, is an exceptionally dangerous scoundrel. Cruel and brazen, cunning and clever, and a lucky rogue. His impunity emboldens others. I must put an end to it. Which is why I made a deal with Angoulême. I promised her that if, as a result of her testimony, Nightingale is captured and his gang broken up, she will hang.'

'I beg your pardon?' The Witcher's astonishment was genuine. 'Is that what you call turning imperial evidence here? The noose in exchange for collaboration with the authorities? And what for refusing to collaborate?'

'Impalement. Preceded by gouging out the eyes and tearing the bosom with red-hot pincers.'

The Witcher didn't say a word.

'It is called exemplary terror,' Fulko Artevelde continued. 'Absolutely imperative in the fight against crime. Why do you clench your fists, so hard I can almost hear your knuckles grinding? Perhaps you favour humane killing? You can afford that luxury. You mainly fight creatures, which, however ridiculous it sounds, also kill humanely. I cannot afford it. I've seen merchants' convoys and homes pillaged by Nightingale and his like. I've seen what's done to people to make them reveal hiding places or magical passwords to jewel cases and strong boxes. I've seen the women Nightingale has taken a knife to just to check they weren't concealing valuables. I've seen worse things done to people simply for the sake of

173

wanton amusement. Angoulême, whose fate moves you so, took part in such merriment – that is certain. She was in the gang long enough. And were it not for sheer accident and the fact she fled the gang no one would have found out about the ambush in Belhaven, and you would have learned of it some other way. Perhaps she'd have shot you in the back with a crossbow.'

'I don't like speculation. Do you know why she fled the gang?'

'Her evidence in that regard was vague, and she didn't want to divulge it to my men. But it's no secret that Nightingale is one of those men who restrict women to a, let us say, primitively natural role. If he can't do it any other way, he forces that role on women. Certainly generational conflicts contributed to it. Nightingale is a mature man, while Angoulême's last gang were urchins like her. But those are speculations; in actual fact, it interests me not. And why, may I ask, do you care? Why has Angoulême evoked such interest from the moment you saw her?'

'Strange question. The girl informs me about an attempt on my life being planned by her former comrades on the orders of some half-elf. A sensational matter in itself, since I have no long-standing feuds with any half-elves. The girl knows only too well what company I ride with. Including such details as the trouba-dour being called Dandelion, and that the woman has cut off her plait. That plait, particularly, makes me suspect lies or a trap in this. It wouldn't have been hard to seize and question one of the forest beekeepers I've been journeying with for the last week. And swiftly stage a—'

'That will do!' Artevelde slammed his fist on the table. 'You race too far ahead, sir. You're accusing me of engineering some-thing here? To what end? To deceive or ensnare you? And who are you that you so fear provocation and ensnarement? Only the thief fears the truth, m'lord witcher. Only the thief!'

'Give me another explanation.'

'No, you give me one, sir!'

'Regrettably, I have none.'

'I might say something,' the prefect smiled maliciously. 'But for what? Let's be clear. I'm not interested in who wants to see you dead or why. I don't care where that person came by such interest-ing information about you, including your comrade's hair colour and length. I shall go further: I might have not informed you at all about the plot on your life, witcher. I could simply have treated your company as utterly ignorant bait for Nightingale. Lurked, waited until the Nightingale swallowed the hook, line and sinker. And then seized him as my own. For it's him I'm interested in, him I want. And if you met your maker? Ha, a necessary evil, incidental!'

He fell silent. Geralt made no comment.

'Know you, master witcher,' the prefect continued after a pause, 'that I swore to myself that the law would rule on my turf. At any cost, and using any methods, *per fas et nefas*. For the law is not jurisprudence, not a weighty tome full of articles, not philosophical treatises, not peevish nonsense about justice, not hackneyed platitudes about morality and ethics. The law means safe paths and highways. It means backstreets one can walk along even after sundown. It means inns and taverns one can leave to visit the privy, leaving one's purse on the table and one's wife beside it. The law is the sleep of people certain they'll be woken by the crowing of the rooster and not the crashing of burning roof timbers! And for those who break the law; the noose, the axe, the stake and the red-hot iron! Punishments which deter others. Those that break the law should be caught and punished. Using all available means and methods . . . Eh, witcher? Is the disapproval written on your countenance a reaction to the intention or the methods? The methods, I think! For it's easy to criticise methods, but we would all prefer to live in a safe world, wouldn't we? Go on, answer!'

'There's nothing to say.'

'Oh, I believe there is.'

'Mr Fulko,' Geralt said calmly, 'the world you envision quite pleases me.'

'Indeed? Your expression suggests otherwise.'

'The world you envision is made for a witcher. A witcher would never be short of work in it. Instead of codes, articles and peevish platitudes about justice, your idea creates lawlessness, anarchy, the licence and self-serving of princelings and mandarins, the officiousness of careerists wanting to endear themselves to their superiors, the blind vindictiveness of fanatics, the cruelty of assassins, retribution and sadistic vengeance. Your vision is a world where people are afraid to venture out after dark; not for fear of cut-throats, but of the guardians of public order. For, after all, the result of all great crackdowns on miscreants is always that the miscreants enter the ranks of the guardians of public order en masse. Your vision is a world of bribery, blackmail and entrapment, a world of turning imperial evidence and false witnesses. A world of snoopers and coerced confessions. Informing and the fear of being informed upon. And inevitably the day will come in your world when the flesh of the wrong person will be torn with pincers, when an innocent person is hanged or impaled. And then it will be a world of crime.

'In short,' he finished, 'a world where a witcher would be in his element.'

'Well, well,' Fulko Artevelde said after moment's silence, rubbing his eye socket through the leather patch. 'An idealist! A witcher. A professional. A hired killer. But an idealist, nonetheless. And a moralist. That's dangerous in your profession, witcher. A sign you begin to outgrow your profession. One day you'll hesitate to despatch a striga. For what if it's innocent? What if it's blind vengeance and blind fanaticism? I don't wish it on you. But what if, one day . . . I don't wish this on you either, though it is possible . . . what if someone close to you is harmed in a cruel and sadistic way? Then I'd willingly return to this conversation, to the issue of the punishment fitting the crime. Who knows if we would then differ so greatly in our views? But today – here, now – that is not the subject of our consideration or discussion. Today we shall talk about hard facts. And you're a hard fact.'

Geralt raised an eyebrow slightly.

'Though you were scornful about my methods and my vision of a world of law, you shall aid me, my dear witcher, in the fulfilling of that vision. I repeat: I swore to myself that those who break the law will get their just desserts. All of them. From the minor felon who cheats with dishonest scales at the market, to he who swipes a cargo of bows and arrows meant for the army on the highway. Highwaymen, cutpurses, thieves, robbers. Terrorists from the Free Slopes organisation, who grandly call themselves "freedom fighters". And Nightingale. Above all Nightingale. A fitting punishment must befall Nightingale; the method is inconsequential.

176

As long as it's quick. Before an amnesty is declared and he weasels out . . . Witcher, I've been waiting months for something that'll let me get one step ahead of him. That'll let me nudge him, make him trip up and make the decisive error which will be his undoing. Shall I continue, or do you follow?'

'I do, but go on.'

'The mysterious half-elf, seemingly the initiator and instigator of the attempt, warned Nightingale about a witcher, advocated caution, advised against a cavalier attitude or swaggering arrogance and bravado. I know he had his reasons. The warning will come to nothing, though. Nightingale will make a mistake. He will attack a witcher who's been forewarned and is prepared to defend himself. A witcher who's waiting to be attacked. And it'll be the end of the robber Nightingale. I wish to strike a bargain with you, Geralt. You shall be my informer. Don't interrupt; it's a simple agreement. Each side will meet their obligations. You put paid to Nightingale. While in exchange, I . . .'

He was silent for a while, smiling slyly.

'I shan't ask you who you are, where you're from, or where and why you journey. I shan't ask why one of you speaks with a barely detectable Nilfgaardian accent, and why sometimes dogs and horses bristle at your party's approach. I shan't order the roll of papers to be taken from the troubadour Dandelion, nor shall I check what they say. And I shall only inform imperial counter-intelligence about you when Nightingale is dead or in my dungeon. Or even later. Why hurry? I'll give you time. And a chance.'

'A chance to do what?'

'To reach Toussaint. That ridiculous fairy-tale duchy, whose borders even the Nilfgaardian counter-intelligence don't dare violate. And then much may change. There'll be an amnesty. There may be a truce on the far side of the Yaruga. Maybe even lasting peace.'

The Witcher was silent for a long time. The prefect's disfigured face was unmoving. His eye shone.

'Agreed,' Geralt finally said.

'Without haggling? Without conditions?'

'I have two.'

'How could it be otherwise? Go on.'

'I must first ride west for a few days. To Loch Monduirn. To the druids, since—'

'Are you making an ass of me?' Fulko Artevelde interrupted abruptly. 'Do you mean to gull me? West? Everyone knows where your route takes you! Including Nightingale, who is right now laying an ambush on your road. To the south, in Belhaven, at a spot where the Nevi valley cuts the Sansretour valley leading to Toussaint.'

'Does that mean . . . '

'. . . that the druids aren't by Loch Monduirn? No, nor have they been for almost a month. They headed down the Sansretour valley to Toussaint, under the protective wings of Duchess Anarietta of Beauclair, who has a weakness for freaks, loonies and oddballs. Who gladly gives asylum to such in her little fairy-tale land. You know that as well as I do, witcher. Don't try to dupe me!'

'I won't try,' Geralt said slowly. 'I give you my word that I won't. I set out for Belhaven tomorrow.'

'Haven't you forgotten something?'

'No, I haven't forgotten. My second condition: I want Angoulême. You'll rush through her amnesty and release her from the dungeon. This witcher informer needs your informer. Quickly. Do you agree or not?'

'I do,' Fulko Artevelde replied almost at once. 'I have no choice. Angoulême is yours. For I know you're only cooperating for her sake.'

*

The vampire, riding at Geralt's side, listened attentively and didn't interrupt. The Witcher wasn't disappointed by his perspicacity.

'There are five or us, not four,' he concluded as soon as Geralt had finished his account. 'We've been travelling in a group of five since the end of August; the five of us crossed the Yaruga. And Milva only cut off her plait in Riverdell, about a week ago. Your fair-haired protégée knows about Milva's plait. But said four not five. Bizarre.'

'Is that the strangest part of this bizarre story?'

'Far from it. The strangest thing is Belhaven. The town where the ambush has reputedly been laid for us. A town set deep in the mountains, on the path through the Nevi valley and the Theodula pass—'

'—and we never planned to go there,' the Witcher finished, spurring on Roach, who was beginning to fall behind. 'Three weeks ago, when that highwayman Nightingale took the job to kill me from some half-elf, we were in Angren, heading to Caed Dhu, fearful of the Ysgith bogs. We didn't even know we'd have to cross the Yaruga. Dammit, we didn't know that this morning—'

'We did,' the vampire interrupted. 'We knew we were looking for the druids. We knew that just as clearly this morning as three weeks ago. That mysterious half-elf is preparing an ambush on the road leading to the druids, certain we'll take that road. He simply—'

'Has a better idea than us which way that road leads,' it was the Witcher's turn to interrupt. 'How does he?'

'We shall have to ask. Which is precisely why you took the prefect's offer, isn't it?'

'Naturally. I'm counting on being able to have a chat with Mr Half-Elf.' Geralt smiled hideously. 'Before that happens, doesn't any explanation suggest itself to you? Or simply come to mind?'

The vampire observed him in silence for some time.

'I don't like what you're saying, Geralt,' he said at last. 'I don't like what you're thinking. I consider it an inopportune thought. Taken hurriedly, without reflection. Resulting from prejudice and resentment.'

'How else can one explain—'

'Any way,' Regis interrupted him with a tone Geralt had never heard from him. 'Any way but like that. Don't you think, for example, there's a possibility your fair-haired protégée is lying?'

'Hey, there, nuncle!' called Angoulême, riding behind them on the mule called Draakul. 'Don't accuse me of lying if you can't prove it!'

'I'm not your uncle, dear child.'

'And I'm not your dear child, nuncle!'

'Angoulême,' Witcher turned around in the saddle. 'Be quiet.'

'If you say so.' Angoulême calmed down immediately. 'You're allowed to give me orders. You got me out of that hole, wrested

179

me from Mr Fulko's talons. I obey you, you're now the leader, the head of the hanza . . . '

'Be quiet please.'

Angoulême muttered under her breath, stopped urging Draakul on and remained at the rear, particularly since Regis and Geralt had put on speed to catch up with Dandelion, Cahir and Milva, who were riding in the vanguard. They were heading towards the mountains, along the bank of the River Nevi, whose waters, turbid and yellowish-brown following the last rains, rolled swiftly over rocks and shelves. They weren't alone. They frequently passed or overtook troops of Nilfgaardian cavalry, lone horsemen, settlers' wagons or merchants' caravans.

The Amell Mountains rose up to the south, closer and closer and more and more menacing. And the pointed needle of Gorgon, Devil Mountain, was enveloped in the clouds which quickly covered the whole sky.

'When are you going to tell them?' the vampire asked, indicating with a glance the threesome riding ahead of them.

'When we make camp.'

*

Dandelion was the first to speak when Geralt had finished his account.

'Correct me if I'm wrong,' he said. 'But that girl, Angoulême, whom you have so cheerfully and carelessly added to our company, is a criminal. To save her from her well-deserved penalty you've agreed to collaborate with the Nilfgaardians. You've hired yourself out. Why, not just yourself – you've hired us all out. We are all to assist the Nilfgaardians capture or kill somebody. Some local brigand. In short: you, Geralt, have become a Nilfgaardian mercenary, a bounty hunter, a hired assassin. And we've been promoted to the rank of your acolytes . . . Or perhaps your fam—'

'You have an incredible talent for over simplification, Dandelion,' Cahir muttered. 'Have you really not understood what this is about? Or are you just talking for talking's sake?'

'Silence, Nilfgaardian. Geralt?'

'Let me begin by saying,' the Witcher threw a stick he'd been

180

playing with for some time onto the fire, 'that no one's forced to help me with my plans. I can handle it by myself. Without acolytes or famuli.'

'You're audacious, nuncle,' Angoulême began. 'But Nightingale's hanza numbers twenty-four stout blades. They won't take fright at a witcher, and where it concerns swordsmanship, even if it were true what they say about witchers, no witcher could deal with two dozen by himself. You saved my life, so I'll repay you likewise. With a warning. And with help.'

'What the bloody hell is a hanza?'

'*Aen hanse,*' Cahir explained. 'In our tongue it's an armed gang, but one linked by bonds of friendship—'

'A company?'

'Precisely. I see the word has entered the local slang here—'

'A hanza's a hanza,' Angoulême interrupted. 'In our lingo: a gang or hassa. What are we on about here? That was a serious warning. One man has no chance against the entire hanza. To make matters worse, one who knows neither Nightingale, nor anyone in Belhaven or the surroundings, neither foes, friends, nor allies. Who knows not the roads leading to the town – and there are various. I say: the Witcher won't cope. I don't know what customs prevail among you, but I won't leave the Witcher alone. As Nuncle Dandelion said, he cheerfully and carelessly took me into your company, even though I'm a criminal. My hair still stinks of the cell; there was no way of washing it. The Witcher, and no other, got me out of that cell and into the daylight. I'm grateful to him for that. Which is why I won't leave him alone. I'll lead him to Belhaven, to Nightingale and that half-elf. I'm going with him.'

'Me too,' Cahir said at once.

'And me and all!' Milva barked.

Dandelion pressed to his chest the tube with the manuscripts which, lately, he wouldn't be parted from for a single moment. He lowered his head. He was evidently struggling with his thoughts. And the thoughts were winning.

'Stop meditating, poet,' Regis said kindly. 'For there's nothing to be ashamed of. You're even less cut out to participate in a bloody swordfight than I am. We weren't taught to carve up our neighbours with a blade. Furthermore . . . Furthermore, I'm . . . '

He raised shining eyes towards the Witcher and Milva.

'I'm a coward,' he confessed curtly. 'If it's not necessary, I don't want to go through what we had on the ferry and the bridge again. Never. For which reason I request to be left out of the fighting team heading to Belhaven.'

'You lugged me from that ferry and that bridge on your back,' Milva began softly, 'when infirmity robbed me of my legs. If there'd been a coward there, instead of you, he'd have left me and fled. There was no coward, though. Only you, Regis.'

'Well said, aunty,' said Angoulême with conviction. 'I have no clue what you're on about, but well said.'

'I'm no aunt of yours!' Milva's eyes flashed ominously. 'Have a care, miss! If you call me that again, you'll see!'

'What will I see?'

'Quiet!' the Witcher barked harshly. 'That's enough, Angoulême! I need to take all of you to task, I see. The time of lurching blindly towards the horizon is over, for now there might be something just over the horizon. The time for decisive action has arrived. Time for throats to be cut. For at last there's someone to attack. Those who haven't understood till now, let them understand – we finally have a clear-cut enemy within reach. The half-elf who wants us dead is an agent of forces hostile to us. Thanks to Angoulême we've been forewarned, and forewarned is forearmed, as the proverb has it. I have to get my hands on that half-elf and wring from him whose orders he's acting on. Do you finally understand, Dandelion?'

'I'd say,' the poet began calmly, 'that I understand more and better than you. Without any attacking or wringing needed, I surmise that the mysterious half-elf is acting on Dijkstra's orders. The same Dijkstra you lamed on Thanedd by smashing his ankle. Following Marshal Vissegerd's report, Dijkstra doubtless considers us Nilfgaardian spies. And following our flight from the corps of Lyrian partisans, Queen Meve has assuredly added a few points to the list of our crimes . . .'

'You're mistaken, Dandelion,' Regis softly interjected. 'It's not Dijkstra. Or Vissegerd. Or Meve.'

'Then who?'

'Any judgement or conclusion now would be premature.'

182

'Agreed,' the Witcher drawled icily. 'Which is why the matter needs to be examined in situ. And conclusions drawn first-hand.'

'And I,' Dandelion said, not giving up, 'still judge it a stupid and risky idea. It's good we've been warned about the ambush, that we know about it. Now that we know, let's give it a wide berth. Let that elf or half-elf wait for us as long as he wishes, and we'll hurry along our own road—'

'No,' the Witcher interrupted. 'That's the end of the discussion, my little chicks. The end of anarchy. The time has come for our . . . hanza . . . to have a ringleader.'

Everyone, not excluding Angoulême, looked at him in expect-ant silence.

'Angoulême, Milva and I,' he said, 'will make for Belhaven. Cahir, Regis and Dandelion will ride into the Sansretour valley and go to Toussaint.'

'No,' Dandelion said quickly, gripping his tube more tightly. 'Not a chance. I can't—'

'Shut up. This isn't a debate. It was an order from the hanza's leader! You're going to Toussaint with Regis and Cahir. You'll wait for us there.'

'Toussaint means death for me,' the troubadour declared em-phatically. 'If I'm recognised in Beauclair, at the castle, I'm dead. I have to tell you—'

'No you don't,' the Witcher interrupted bluntly. 'It's too late. You could have turned back, but you didn't want to. You remained in the company. In order to rescue Ciri. Am I right?'

'You are.'

'So you'll ride with Regis and Cahir down the Sansretour valley. You'll wait for us in the mountains, without crossing the Toussaint border for now. But if . . . if the necessity arises, you'll have to cross it. For the druids, the ones from Caed Dhu, Regis's acquaintances, are allegedly in Toussaint. So if the necessity arises, you'll get information about Ciri from the druids and set off to get her . . . alone.'

'What do you mean alone? Do you anticipate—'

'I'm not anticipating, I'm bearing in mind the possibility. Just in case, so to speak. As a last resort, if you prefer. Perhaps it'll all go well and we won't have to show up in Toussaint. But in the event . . . well, then it's important that a Nilfgaardian force doesn't follow you to Toussaint.'

'Well, it won't,' Angoulême cut in. 'It's strange, but Nilfgaard respects Toussaint's marches. I've hidden from pursuers there before. But the knights there are no better than the Black Cloaks! Refined and courteous in their speech, but quick to seize the sword or lance. And they patrol the marches ceaselessly. They're called knights errant. They ride alone, or in twos or threes. And they persecute the rabble. Which means us. Witcher, one detail needs changing in your plans.'

'What?'

'If we are to make for Belhaven and cross swords with Nightingale, you and Sir Cahir should go with me. And let aunty go with them.'

'Why so?' Geralt calmed Milva with a gesture.

'You need men for that job. Why are you raging, aunty? I know what I'm talking about! When the time comes, it may be necessary to act with menace, rather than force itself. And none of Nightingale's hanza will be scared of a band of three, where there are two women to one man.'

'Milva rides with us.' Geralt clenched his fingers around the archer's forearm, who was genuinely infuriated. 'Milva, not Cahir. I don't want to ride with Cahir.'

'Why's that?' Angoulême and Cahir asked almost at the same time.

'Precisely,' Regis said slowly. 'Why?'

'Because I don't trust him,' the Witcher said bluntly.

The silence which fell was unpleasant, weighty; almost tangible. From the forest, near which a merchants' caravan and a group of other travellers had made camp, came raised voices, shouts and singing.

'Explain,' Cahir said at last.

'Somebody has betrayed us,' Witcher said dryly. 'After our conversation with the prefect and Angoulême's revelations, there's no doubt about it. And if one thinks it over carefully, one comes to the conclusion that there's a traitor among us. And it takes little pondering to guess who.'

'It seems to me,' Cahir frowned, 'that you have taken the liberty to suggest that the traitor is me?'

'I don't deny that such a thought has occurred to me,' the Witcher's voice was cold. 'There's much to suggest it. It would explain much. Very much.'

'Geralt,' said Dandelion. 'Aren't you going a mite too far?'

'Let him speak.' Cahir curled his lip. 'Let him speak. Let him feel free.'

'It puzzled us,' Geralt swept his gaze over his companions' faces, 'how there could have been an error in the reckoning. You know what I'm talking about. That there are five of us and not four. We thought someone had simply made a mistake: the mysterious half-elf, the brigand Nightingale or Angoulême. But if we reject that then the following possibility suggests itself: the company numbers five, but Nightingale is only meant to kill four. Because the fifth is the assassins' accomplice. Someone who keeps them constantly informed about the company's movements. From the start, from the moment the celebrated fish soup was eaten and the company was formed. And we invited a Nilfgaardian to join us. A Nilfgaardian who must catch Ciri, must hand her over to Emperor Emhyr, for his life and further career depends on it . . . '

'So I wasn't wrong, then,' Cahir said slowly. 'I'm a traitor after all. A lousy, two-faced turncoat?'

'Geralt,' Regis began again. 'Excuse my frankness, but your theory is riddled with holes. And your thought, as I've already told you, is inopportune.'

'I'm a traitor,' Cahir repeated, as though he hadn't heard the vampire's words. 'As I understand it, however, there is no proof of it, only vague circumstantial evidence and the Witcher's speculations. As I understand it, the burden of proving my own innocence falls on me. So I'll have to prove I'm not what I appear to be. Is that right?'

'Don't be pompous, Nilfgaardian,' snapped Geralt, standing before Cahir and glaring at him. 'If I had proof of your guilt, I wouldn't be wasting time talking. I'd have filleted you like a herring already! Do you know the principle of *cui bono*? So answer me: who, aside from you, had even the slightest reason to betray me? Who, aside from you, would have gained anything from it?'

185

A loud and long-drawn-out crack resounded from the merchants' camp. A firework exploded in a burst of red and gold, rockets shot out a swarm of golden bees and coloured rain fell against the black sky.

'I'm not what I appear,' said the young Nilfgaardian in a powerful, resonant voice. 'Unfortunately, I can't prove it. But I can do something else. Do what befits me, what I have to do, when I'm being slandered and insulted, when my honour is besmirched and my dignity sullied.'

His attack was as swift as lightning, but it still wouldn't have surprised the Witcher had it not been for Geralt's aching knee, which hampered his movements. Geralt was unable to dodge, and the gloved fist smashed him in the jaw with such force he fell backwards and tumbled straight into the campfire, throwing up clouds of sparks. He leaped up, too slow again owing to the pain in his knee. Cahir was already upon him. Again the Witcher didn't even manage to duck; the fist rammed into the side of his head, and colourful fireworks flared up in his eyes, even more glorious than the ones the merchants had set off. Geralt swore and pounced on Cahir, wrapped his arms around him and knocked him to the ground. They rolled around in the gravel, thumping and pummelling each other.

And all in the eerie and unnatural light of the fireworks bursting in the sky.

'Stop it!' Dandelion yelled. 'Stop it, you bloody fools!'

Cahir artfully knocked the ground out from under Geralt, and smote him in the teeth as he was trying to get up. And punched him again. Geralt crouched, tensed and kicked him, not in his crotch where he had aimed, but in the thigh. They grappled again, fell and rolled over, thumping one another wherever they could, blinded by the punches and the dust and sand getting into their eyes.

Then suddenly they came apart, rolling in opposite directions, cowering and shielding their heads from the blows raining down on them.

Having unfastened her sturdy, leather belt, Milva had seized it by the buckle, wound it around her fist, fallen on the fighters and begun to flog them with lusty blows, with all her might,

186

sparing neither the strap nor her arm. The belt whistled and fell with a dry crack first on Cahir's then on Geralt's arms, back and shoulders. When they parted, Milva hopped from one to the other like a grasshopper, thrashing them evenly, so that neither of them received any less or any more than the other.

'You thick thickheads!' she yelled, cracking Geralt across the back. 'You doltish dolts! I'll teach you both a lesson!'

'Enough?' she yelled even louder, lashing Cahir's arms, with which he was shielding his head. 'Had enough? Calmed down now?'

'Stop!' the Witcher howled. 'Enough!'

'Enough!' echoed Cahir, who was huddled up in a ball. 'That'll do!'

'That will suffice,' said the vampire. 'That really will suffice, Milva.'

The archer was panting heavily, wiping her forehead with her fist, belt still wound around it.

'Bravo,' said Angoulême. 'Bravo, aunty.'

Milva turned on her heel and thrashed her across the shoulders with all her might. Angoulême screamed, sat down and burst into tears.

'I told you,' Milva puffed, 'not to call me that. I told you!'

'It's all right!' In a somewhat shaking voice Dandelion reassured the merchants and travellers, who had run over from the neighbouring campfires. 'Just a misunderstanding between friends. A lovers' tiff. It's already been patched up!'

The Witcher probed a wobbly tooth with his tongue and spat out the blood dripping from his cut lip. He felt the welts beginning to rise on his back and shoulders, and his ear – which had been lashed by the strap – seeming to swell to the dimensions of a cauliflower. Beside him, Cahir clumsily hauled himself up from the ground, holding his cheek. Broad, red marks quickly spread over his exposed forearm.

Rain smelling of sulphur – ash from the last firework – was falling on the ground.

Angoulême sobbed woefully, holding her shoulders. Milva threw aside her belt, then after a moment's hesitation knelt, embraced and hugged her without a word.

187

'I suggest,' said the vampire frigidly, 'that you shake hands. I suggest never, ever, revisiting this matter.'

Unexpectedly, a gale came down from the mountains in whispered gusts in which it seemed some kind of ghastly howling, crying and wailing could be heard. The clouds being blown across the sky took on fantastic shapes as the crescent moon turned as red as blood.

*

They were woken before dawn by a furious chorus of goatsucker nightjars and the whirring of their wings.

They set off just after the rising of the sun, which later lit up the snows on the mountain peaks with blinding flame. They had left much earlier than that, before the sun had appeared from behind the peaks. Actually, before it appeared, the sky had become overcast.

They rode amongst forests, and the road led higher and higher, which was discernible in the tree species. The oak and hornbeam finished abruptly, and they rode into a gloom of beech lined with fallen leaves, smelling of mould, cobwebs and mushrooms. The mushrooms were in abundance. The damp year end had yielded a plentiful harvest. In places, the forest floor literally vanished beneath the caps of ceps, morels and agarics.

The beechwood was quiet and looked as though most of the songbirds had flown away to their mysterious winter haven. Only crows at the edge of the undergrowth cawed, feathers dripping.

Then the beech ended and spruce replaced it. The scent of resin filled the air.

More and more often they encountered bald hillocks and stone runs, where they were caught by strong winds. The River Nevi foamed over steps and cascades. Its water – in spite of the rain – had turned crystal clear.

Gorgon loomed up on the horizon. Ever closer.

All year long, glaciers and snows flowed from the angular sides of the huge mountain, which meant Gorgon always looked as though it were clad in white sashes. The peak of Devil Mountain was constantly swathed in veils of clouds, like the head and neck of an enigmatic bride. Sometimes, though, Gorgon shook her white raiment like a dancer. The sight was breathtaking, but brought death – avalanches ran from the peak's sheer walls, wiping out everything in their path, down to the scree at the foot and further down the hillside, to the highest spruce stands above the Theodula pass, above the Nevi and Sansretour valleys, above the black circles of mountain tarns. The sun, which in spite of everything had managed to penetrate the clouds, set much too quickly – it simply hid behind the mountains to the west, setting light to them with a purple and golden glow.

They stopped for the night.

The sun rose.

And the time came for them to part.

*

Milva carefully wrapped a silk scarf around her head. Regis put on his hat. Yet again he checked the position of the sihill on his back and the daggers in his boots.

Beside them, Cahir was whetting his long Nilfgaardian sword. Angoulême tied a woollen band around her forehead and slipped a hunting knife – a present from Milva – into her boot. The archer and Regis saddled up their horses. The vampire handed Angoulême the reins to his black, while he mounted the mule Draakul.

They were ready. Only one thing remained to be taken care of.

'Come here, everybody.'

They approached.

'Cahir, son of Ceallach,' Geralt began, trying not to sound pompous. 'I wronged you with unfounded suspicion and behaved shabbily towards you. I hereby apologise, before everyone, with bowed head. I apologise and ask you to forgive me. I also ask you all for forgiveness, as I shouldn't have made you watch or listen to it.

'I vented my fury and resentment on Cahir and all of you. It was caused by knowing who betrayed us. I know who betrayed and abducted Ciri, whom we aim to rescue. I'm angry because I'm talking about a person who was once very close to me.

'Where we are, what we're planning, what route we're taking

189

and whither we're heading . . . all was uncovered with the help of scanning, detecting magic. It's none too difficult for a mistress of magic to remotely detect and observe a person who was once well-known and close, with whom they had a long-term psychic contact which permits the creation of a matrix. But the sorcerer and sorceress of whom I speak made a mistake. They've revealed themselves. They made an error when counting the members of the company, and that error betrayed them. Tell them, Regis.'

'Geralt may be right,' Regis said slowly. 'Like every vampire, I'm invisible to magical visual probing and scanning; that is, to a detecting spell. A vampire may be tracked using an analytical spell, from close up, but it is not possible to detect a vampire with a remote, scanning spell. The detection will report that there's no one there. Thus only a sorcerer could be mistaken regarding us: to register four people, where there were actually five; that is, four people and one vampire.'

'We shall exploit the sorcerers' error,' the Witcher continued. 'Cahir, Angoulême and I shall ride to Belhaven to talk to the half-elf who hired assassins to kill us. We won't ask the half-elf on whose orders he's acting, for we know that already. We'll ask him where the sorcerers on whose orders he is acting are. When we learn their location we'll go there. And exact our revenge.'

Everybody was silent.

'We stopped counting the date, so we haven't even noticed it's the twenty-fifth of September. Two days ago it was the night of the Equinox. The Equinox. Yes, that's exactly the night you're thinking about. I see your dejection, I see what your eyes are saying. We received a signal, that dreadful night, when the merchants camping beside us were keeping their courage up with aqua vitae, singing and fireworks. You probably had a less distinct sense of foreboding than Cahir and I, but you're speculating too. You suspect. And I'm afraid your suspicions are well founded.'

The crows flying over the moorland cawed.

'Everything indicates that Ciri is dead. She perished, two nights ago, at the Equinox. Somewhere far from here, alone amongst hostile people; strangers.

'And all that's left to us is vengeance. A cruel and bloody revenge, about which stories will still be told a hundred years hence.

Stories which folk will be afraid to listen to after nightfall. And the hand of any who would repeat such a crime will tremble at the thought of our vengeance. We shall give a horrible example of terror! Using the ways of Mr Fulko Artevelde, wise Mr Fulko, who knows how blackguards and scoundrels should be treated. The illustration of terror we shall give will astonish even him!

'So let us begin and may Hell assist us! Cahir, Angoulême, to horse. We ride up the Nevi, towards Belhaven. Dandelion, Milva, Regis, make for Sansretour, towards Toussaint's borders. You won't get lost, Gorgon will point the way. Goodbye.'

*

Ciri stroked the black cat, which had returned to the cottage in the swamp, as is customary with all cats in the world, when its love of freedom and dissolution had been undermined by cold, hunger and discomfort. Now it was lying in the girl's lap and arching its back against her hand with a purr signifying profound bliss. The cat couldn't have cared less about what the girl was saying.

'It was the only time I dreamed of Geralt,' Ciri began. 'From the time we parted on the Isle of Thanedd, from the Tower of the Seagull, I'd never seen him in a dream. So I thought he was dead. And then suddenly came that dream, like the ones I used to have, dreams which Yennefer said were prophetic, precognitive; that they either show the past or the future. That was the day before the Equinox. In a small town whose name I don't recall. In a cellar where Bonhart had locked me. After he'd flogged me and made me admit who I am.'

'Did you divulge to him who you are?' Vysogota raised his head. 'Did you tell him everything?'

'I paid for my cowardice,' she swallowed, 'with humiliation and self-contempt.'

'Tell me about your dream.'

'In it I saw a mountain; lofty, sheer, and sharp, like a stone knife. I saw Geralt. I heard what he was saying. Exactly. Every word, as though he were with me. I remember I wanted to call out and say it wasn't like that at all, that none of it was true, that he'd made an awful mistake . . . That he'd got everything wrong! That

191

it wasn't the Equinox yet, so even if I happened to have died on the Equinox, he shouldn't have declared me dead earlier, when I was still alive. And he shouldn't have accused Yennefer or said such things about her . . . '

She was silent for a time, stroking the cat and sniffing hard.

'But I couldn't say a word. I couldn't even breathe . . . As though I was drowning. And I awoke. The last thing I saw, that I recall from that dream, was three riders. Geralt and two others, galloping along a ravine, with water gushing from its walls . . .'

Vysogota said nothing.

*

Had someone crept up to the shack with the sunken, moss-grown thatched roof after nightfall, had they peered through the gaps in the shutters, they would have seen a grey-bearded old man listening raptly to a story told by an ashen-haired girl in the dimly lit interior, her cheek disfigured by a nasty scar.

They would have seen a black cat lying on the girl's lap, purring lazily, demanding to be stroked – to the delight of the mice scampering around the room.

But no one could have seen it. For the cottage with the sunken, moss-grown thatched roof was well hidden among the fog, in the boundless Pereplut Marshes, where no one dared to venture.

It is well known that when a witcher inflicts pain, suffering and death he experiences absolute ecstasy and bliss such as a devout and normal man only experiences during sexual congress with his wedded spouse, ibidem cum ejaculatio. This leads one to conclude that, also in this matter also, a witcher is a creature contrary to nature, an immoral and filthy degenerate, born of the blackest and most foul-smelling Hell, since surely only a devil could derive bliss from suffering and pain.

Anonymous, *Monstrum, or a description of a witcher*

CHAPTER SIX

They left the main track leading along the Nevi valley and took a short cut through the mountains. They rode as quickly as the track would allow. It was narrow and winding, hugging fantastically-shaped rocks covered in patches of colourful moss and lichen. They rode between vertical rocky cliffs, from which ragged ribbons of cascades and waterfalls tumbled. They rode through ravines and gorges, across small rickety bridges over precipices at the bottom of which streams seethed with white foam.

The angular blade of Gorgon seemed to rear up directly above their heads. The peak of Devil Mountain was not visible, but shrouded in the clouds and fog cloaking the sky. The weather – as happens in the mountains – worsened in the course of a few hours. It began to drizzle bitingly and disagreeably.

When dusk fell, the three of them nervously and impatiently looked around for a shepherd's bothy, a tumbledown barn or even a cave. Anything that would protect them from the weather during the night.

*

'I think it's stopped raining,' Angoulême said hopefully. 'It's only dripping from the holes in the roof now. Tomorrow, fortunately, we'll be near Belhaven, and we can always sleep in a shed or a barn on the outskirts.'

'Aren't we entering the town?'

'Out of the question. Mounted strangers on horses are conspicuous and Nightingale has plenty of informers in the town.'

'We were thinking about using ourselves as bait—'

'No,' she interrupted. 'That's a rotten plan. The fact that we're together will arouse suspicion. Nightingale's a cunning bastard and news of my capture has certainly spread. And if anything alarms him, it'll also reach the half-elf.'

'So what do you suggest?'

'We skirt around the town from the east, from the mouth of the Sansretour valley. There are ore mines there. I've a mate who works in one of them. We'll visit him. Who knows, with a bit of luck the visit might prove profitable.'

'Could you speak more plainly?'

'I'll tell you tomorrow. In the mine. So as not to jinx it.'

Cahir threw some birch branches on the fire. It had been raining all day and no other fuel would have burned. But the birch, though wet, crackled a little and then flared up in a tall, blue flame.

'Where are you from, Angoulême?'

'From Cintra, Witcher. It's a country by the sea, by the mouth of the Yaruga—'

'I know where Cintra is.'

'So why do you ask, if you know all that? Do I fascinate you so?'

'A little, let's say.'

They fell silent. The fire crackled on.

'My mother,' Angoulême finally said, staring into the flame, 'was a Cintran noblewoman, from a high-ranking family, I believe. The family had a sea-cat in its coat of arms. I'd show it to you, I used to have a little medallion with that bloody sea-cat on it, from my mother, but I lost it at dice . . . That family, though – sod them and their sea-cat – disowned me, because my mother was said to have slept with some churl, a stableman, I believe, and so I was a bastard, a disgrace, an ignominious stain on their honour. They gave me away to be raised by distant relatives. Admittedly they didn't have a cat, dog or any other fucker on their arms, but they weren't bad to me. They sent me to school and generally didn't beat me . . . Though they reminded me pretty often who I was. A bastard, conceived in the straw. My mother visited me maybe three or four times when I was small. Then she stopped. And to be honest, I didn't give a shit . . . '

'How did you fall among criminals?'

'You sound like an examining magistrate!' she snorted, contorting her face grotesquely. 'Among criminals, pshaw! Fallen from virtue, huh?'

She grunted, rummaged around in her bosom and took something out which the Witcher couldn't see clearly.

'One-eyed Fulko,' she said indistinctly, rubbing something vigorously into her gum and inhaling, 'isn't a bad old fellow. He took what he took, but left the powder. Want a pinch, Witcher?'

'No. I'd rather you didn't take it either.'

'Why?'

'I just would.'

'Cahir?'

'I don't use fisstech.'

'Well, it's clear I've landed up with a couple of goody-goodies.' She shook her head. 'You'll probably start preaching that I'll go blind, deaf and bald from this stuff, I suppose? And give birth to a crippled child?'

'Leave it, Angoulême. And finish the story.'

The young woman sneezed loudly.

'Very well, as you wish. Where was I . . . ? Aha. The war broke out, you know, with Nilfgaard. My relatives lost everything, had to abandon their house. They had three children of their own, and I'd become a burden to them, so they gave me away to an orphanage. It was run by the priests of some temple or other. It was a jolly place, as it happens. A bordello, a whorehouse, simple as that, for people who like their fruit tart and with white pips, get it? Young girls. And young boys too. So when I joined them I was too grown up, adult, there were no takers for me . . . '

Quite unexpectedly she blushed with shame, visible even in the firelight.

'Well, almost none,' she added through clenched teeth.

'How old were you then?'

'Fifteen. I met one girl and five boys there, my age and a bit older. And we teamed up in no time. We knew, didn't we, the legends and tales. About Mad Dea, about Blackbeard, about the Cassini brothers . . . We wanted to get out on the road, to taste freedom, to maraud! So what, we told ourselves, if they feed us twice a day? Does that give some lechers the right to screw us—'

'Language, Angoulême! Keep it in moderation.'

The girl hawked noisily and spat into the campfire.

'Prig! Very well, I'll get to the point, because I don't feel like talking. We found knives in the orphanage kitchen. We just had to whet them well on a stone and strop them on a belt. We made some excellent clubs from the turned legs of an oaken chair. All we needed was horses and coin, so we waited for two perverts, regular customers, old buggers of, ugh, at least forty. They came, sat down, sipped wine and waited for the priests to tie the chosen kid to a special contraption, as was customary . . . But they didn't get their oats that day!'

'Angoulême.'

'All right, all right. In short: we knifed and clubbed to death those two lecherous creeps, three priests and a page; the only one not to bolt, he was guarding the horses. We roasted the temple warden's soles until he changed his mind about giving us the key to the coffer, but we spared his life, because he was a nice old gaffer, always kind to us. And we took to the road to plunder. We had our ups and downs, won some, lost some, we gave and took some beatings. Full bellies, empty bellies. Ha, more often empty. I've eaten everything that crawls, anything you can fucking catch. And things that fly? I even ate a child's kite once, because it was made of flour and water paste.'

She fell silent, then distractedly messed up her flaxen hair.

'What's past is past. I'll just say this: no one who escaped with me from the orphanage is still alive. The last two, Owen and Abel, were dispatched a few days ago by Mr Fulko's pikemen. Abel surrendered, like me, but they stuck him anyway, even though he'd thrown down his sword. They spared me. Don't think it was out of the goodness of their hearts. They'd already spread-eagled me on a cloak, but an officer ran up and stopped their sport. And then you saved me from the scaffold . . . '

She was silent for a time.

'Witcher?'

'Yes.'

'I know how to express gratitude. So if you'd ever like to . . . '

'Excuse me?'

'I'll go and look over the horses,' Cahir said hurriedly and rose, wrapping himself in his cloak. 'I'll take a walk . . . around the place . . . '

The girl sneezed, sniffed, and cleared her throat.

198

'Not a word, Angoulême,' Geralt warned her, genuinely angry, genuinely confused, genuinely embarrassed. 'Not another word!'

She gave a slight cough again.

'Do you really not want me? Not even a bit?'

'You've already tasted Milva's strap, little punk. If you're not quiet this instant, you'll get a second helping.'

'I won't say another thing.'

'Good girl.'

*

Pits and holes – shored up and lined with planks, connected by footbridges, ladders and scaffolding – gaped in a hillside covered in misshapen and twisted pine trees. Catwalks supported by criss-crossed posts protruded from the holes. People were busily pushing carts and wheelbarrows along some of the catwalks. The contents of the carts and wheelbarrows – which at first sight seemed to be dirty, stony soil – were being tipped from the catwalks into a great quadrangular trough, or rather a complex of increasingly small troughs divided up by shutters. Water, supplied from a forested hillock along gutters supported on low trestles, gushed through them, and yet more channelled it away down towards a cliff.

Angoulême dismounted and indicated to Geralt and Cahir to do likewise. Leaving their mounts by a fence, they headed towards the buildings, wading through mud beside the leaking gutters and pipes.

'It's an iron ore washing plant,' Angoulême said, pointing at the equipment. 'The ore is carted out of those mineshafts, tipped into the troughs and rinsed with water from the stream. The ore settles on the sifter, and it's taken from there. There are tons of mines and washing plants around Belhaven. And the ore is carted down the valley to Mag Turga, where there are bloomeries and forges, because there are more forests there and you need wood for smelting—'

'Thanks for the lesson,' Geralt cut her off sourly. 'I've seen a few mines in my lifetime; I know what's needed for smelting. Why have we come here?'

'To have a chat with one of my mates. The foreman here. Follow

199

me. Ah, I can see him! Over there, outside the joiner's shop. Let's go.'

'You mean that dwarf?'

'Yeah. He's called Golan Drozdeck. As I said, he's—'

'The foreman here. You said. You didn't say, though, what you want to chat with him about.'

'Look at your boots.'

Geralt and Cahir obediently examined their footwear, which was covered in sludge of a strange, reddish hue.

'The half-elf we're seeking,' Angoulême anticipated the question, 'had the same crimson mud on his shoes when he was talking to Nightingale. Get it?'

'I do now. And the dwarf?'

'Don't say a word to him. I'll do the talking. He should take you for types that don't talk, just cleave. Look tough.'

They didn't have to make a special effort. Some of the miners who were watching quickly looked away, others froze with mouths open. The ones in their way hurriedly stood aside. Geralt guessed why. He and Cahir still had visible bruises, cuts and swellings – vivid tokens of their fight and the hiding Milva had given them. They looked like types who took pleasure from punching each other in the face, and wouldn't need much persuasion to punch someone else.

The dwarf, Angoulême's mate, was standing outside a building bearing the sign 'joinery shop' and painting something on a board made of two planed staves. He saw them coming, put down his brush and tin of paint and scowled. Then an expression of utter amazement suddenly appeared behind his paint-spattered beard.

'Angoulême?'

'What cheer, Drozdeck?'

'Is it you?' The dwarf's hairy jaw fell open. 'Is it really you?'

'No. It isn't. It's the freshly resurrected prophet Lebioda. Ask me another, Golan. A more intelligent one, perhaps.'

'Don't mock, Flaxenhair. I never expected to see you again. Mulica were 'ere five days since, he says they nabbed you and stuck you on a stake in Riedbrune. He vowed it were true!'

'Everything has its benefits,' the girl shrugged. 'Next time

200

Mulica borrows some money and vows he'll pay it back you'll know what his vow's worth.'

'I knew that before,' the dwarf replied, blinking quickly and twitching his nose like a rabbit. 'I wouldn't lend 'im a broken farthing, even if he bent down and licked my boots. But you're alive and kicking, I'm glad, I'm glad. Hey! Perhaps you'll pay back your debt too, eh?'

'P'raps. Who knows?'

'And who've you got with you? Eh, Flaxenhair?'

'Sound fellows.'

'Righto, mates . . . And where are the gods leading you?'

'Astray, as usual.' Angoulême, unconcerned by the Witcher looking daggers at her, sniffed up a pinch of fisstech, rubbing the rest into her gum. 'Fancy a snort, Golan?'

'I should say.' The dwarf took and inhaled a pinch of the narcotic.

'Truth be told,' the girl continued, 'I'm thinking about going to Belhaven. You don't know if Nightingale and his hanza are hanging around somewhere there?'

Golan Drozdeck cocked his head.

'You, Flaxenhair, should stay out of Nightingale's way. He's as pissed off with you, they say, as a wolverine roused from his winter sleep.'

'Blow that! And when the news reached him that I'd been spitted on a palisade by a two-horse team, didn't his heart change? Didn't he regret it? Didn't he shed a tear, foul his beard with snot?'

'Not at all. I heard he said: "Angoulême's finally got what she had coming to her: a stake up the arse".'

'Oh, the boor. Vulgar, loutish chump. Prefect Fulko would call him the arse end of society. To me he's what comes out of the arse!'

'You'd be better off, Flaxenhair, saying things like that out of his earshot. And not hanging around Belhaven, give it a wide birth. And if you have to enter the town, better go in disguise—'

'Hey, Golan, don't teach your grandmother to suck eggs.'

'Wouldn't dream of it.'

'Then listen, dwarf.' Angoulême rested a boot on a step leading to the joinery shop. 'I'll ask you a question. Don't hurry with the answer. Think it over well.'

'Ask away.'

'A half-elf hasn't caught your eye recently, by any chance? A stranger, not from round here?'

Golan Drozdeck breathed in, sneezed loudly and wiped his nose on his wrist.

'A half-elf you say? What half-elf?'

'Don't play the fool, Drozdeck. The one who hired Nightingale for a contract. A contract killing. Of a witcher . . . '

'A witcher?' Golan Drozdeck laughed, picking his board up from the ground. 'Well I never! Believe it or not, we're looking for a witcher. Look, we're painting signs and putting them up all around here. See: "Witcher wanted, decent pay, board and lodgings included. Particulars at the office of the Petite Babette ore mine". How's it spelt, anyway? "Particulars" or "putticulars"?'

'Just paint it out and write "details". What do you need a witcher at the mine for?'

'Now she's asking. Monsters, of course.'

'Like what?'

'Vespertyls and barbegazis. They're running rampant in the lower galleries.'

Angoulême glanced at Geralt, who nodded to confirm he knew what that was about. And coughed meaningfully to signal that she ought to get back to the subject.

'Getting back to the subject –' the girl understood at once '– what do you know about that half-elf?'

'I don't know nothing about no 'alf-elf.'

'I told you to think it over well.'

'So I did.' Golan Drozdeck suddenly assumed a sly expression. 'And I decided it doesn't pay to know anything about this case.'

'Meaning?'

'Meaning, it's shaky here. The ground's shaky and the times are shaky. Gangs, Nilfgaardians, partisans from the Free Slopes . . . And diverse foreign elements, half-elves. Each one raring to commit assault . . . '

'Meaning?' Angoulême wrinkled her nose.

'Meaning you owe me money, Flaxenhair. And rather than pay it back, you're getting deeper into debt. Serious debt, because you might get a whack on the head for what you're asking, and not with a bare hand, but an axe. What kind of business is that for me? Will it pay if I *do* know something about the half-elf, eh? Will I get anything out of it? For if it's only risk and no profit—'

Geralt had had enough. The conversation was boring him, the jargon and the dwarf's mannerisms annoying him. As quick as lightning he caught the dwarf by the beard, yanked down and pushed him over. Golan Drozdeck tripped over the can of paint and fell. The Witcher leaped on him, pressed his knee against his chest and flashed a knife in front of his eyes.

'You may profit,' he growled, 'by escaping with your life. Talk.'

Golan's eyes looked as though they would pop out of their sockets and go for a stroll.

'Talk,' Geralt repeated. 'Tell us what you know. Otherwise, when I slash your throat open you'll drown before you bleed to death.'

'The Rialto . . . ' the dwarf stammered. 'The Rialto pit . . . '

*

The Rialto mine didn't differ very much from the Petite Babette mine, or from the other mines and quarries that Angoulême, Geralt and Cahir had passed on the way, which were called Autumn Manifest, Old Mine, New Mine, Juliet Mine, Celestine, Common Cause and Lucky Pit. Work was in full swing in all of them, soil and ore being carted out of every shaft and pit to be tipped onto a sluice and washed in the sifters. There was an abundance of the characteristic red mud in all of them.

Rialto was a large mine, located near the top of the hill. The crown had been sliced away and formed a quarry. The actual washing station was located on a terrace carved out of the hillside. Here, at the foot of a vertical wall – in which shafts and drifts gaped – was a sluice, sifters, gutters and other mining paraphernalia. There was also a veritable village of wooden huts, sheds, shacks and hovels covered in bark.

'I don't know anyone here,' said the girl, tying her reins to the fence. 'But let's try and talk to the overseer. Geralt, if you could, maybe don't seize him by the throat immediately or threaten him with a shiv. First we'll talk—'

'Don't teach your grandmother to suck eggs, Angoulême.'

They didn't get as far as talking. They didn't even reach the building where they suspected the overseer had his office. They ran straight into five horsemen in the square where the ore was being loaded onto wagons.

'Oh, shit,' said Angoulême. 'Oh, shit. Look what the cat dragged in.'

'What's up?'

'They're Nightingale's men. Here to extort protection money ... and they've recognised me ... Dammit! Now we're in the shit . . . '

'Can't you lie our way out of it?' Cahir muttered.

'I wouldn't count on it.'

'Why?'

'I skinned Nightingale when I escaped from the hanza. They won't forgive me for that. But I'll try . . . Be quiet. Keep your eyes open and stay alert. For anything.'

The horsemen rode up, with two of them at the head; a fellow with long, grizzly hair, wearing a wolfskin, and a young beanpole with a beard, clearly grown to cover acne scars. They feigned indifference, but Geralt noticed veiled flashes of hatred in the glances they were casting at Angoulême.

'Flaxenhair.'

'Novosad. Yirrel. Greetings. Nice out today. Pity about the rain.'

The grizzly-haired man dismounted, or rather leaped down from the saddle, briskly swinging his right leg over his horse's head. The others also dismounted. Grizzled Hair handed his reins to Yirrel, the beanpole with the beard, and came closer.

'Well, well,' he said. 'Our big-mouthed little magpie. Looks like you're alive and well?'

'Alive and kicking.'

'You brazen little upstart! There was a rumour you were kicking, but on a stake. Rumour has it One-Eyed Fulko caught you. Rumour has it you sang like a bird when you were tortured, told them everything they asked!'

'Rumour has it,' Angoulême snapped, 'that your mother only charged her customers four shillings, but no one would give her more than two.'

The brigand spat at her feet contemptuously. Angoulême hissed again, just like a cat.

'Listen, Novosad,' she said insolently, arms akimbo. 'I need to talk something over with Nightingale.'

'Interesting. Likewise he with you.'

'Shut your trap and listen, while I still feel like talking. Two days ago, a mile outside Riedbrune, me and these companions of mine slaughtered that witcher the contract's out for. Get it?'

Novosad glanced knowingly at his comrades and then pulled up his sleeves, scrutinising Geralt and Cahir.

'Your new companions,' he drawled. 'Ha, I see from their faces they're no choirboys. They killed the witcher, you say? How? A stab in the back? Or in their dreams?'

'That's a minor putticular.' Angoulême grimaced like a little monkey. 'The major putticular is that the witcher is six feet under. Listen, Novosad. I don't want to quarrel with Nightingale or get in his way. But a deal's a deal. The half-elf gave you an advance on the contract, so I shan't demand it, that's your money, for costs and for your trouble. But the second instalment – which the half-elf promised after the job was done – that's mine by right.'

'By right?'

'Yes!' Angoulême ignored his sarcastic tone. 'We carried out the contract and killed the witcher, proof of which we can show the half-elf. Then I'll take what's mine and head off into the sunset. I don't mean to compete with Nightingale, because the Slopes aren't big enough for the both of us. Tell him that, Novosad.'

'Is that all?' Stinging sarcasm again.

'And a kiss,' Angoulême snorted. 'You can hold your arse out on my behalf, *per procura*.'

'I've a better idea,' Novosad declared, glancing at his companions. 'I'll drag your arse to him, Angoulême. I'll deliver you to him in fetters, and then he'll discuss and straighten everything out with you. And settle up. Everything. The question is who owns the money from the half-elf Schirrú's contract. And your repayment for what you stole. And that the Slopes aren't big enough for all of us. Everything will be sorted out the same way. In fine detail.'

'There's one snag.' Angoulême lowered her hands. 'How do you plan to take me to Nightingale, Novosad?'

'Like this!' The brigand held out a hand. 'By the neck!'

Geralt's sihill was out in a flash and under Novosad's nose.

'I advise against it,' he snarled.

Novosad sprang back, drawing his sword. Yirrel drew a curved sabre with a hiss from the scabbard on his back. The others followed their example.

'I still advise against it,' the Witcher said.

Novosad swore. His eyes swept over his comrades. Arithmetic wasn't his strong point, but he calculated that five was considerably more than three.

'Get 'em!' he yelled, lunging at Geralt. 'Kill 'em!'

The Witcher evaded the blow with a half-turn and slashed him viciously across the temple. Even before Novosad had fallen, Angoulême ducked forward with a short jab, her knife whistled in the air and Yirrel reeled away, the bone handle jutting from beneath his chin. The brigand dropped his sabre and jerked the knife from his throat with both hands, spurting blood, but Angoulême sprang up to kick him in the chest and knocked him to the ground. Meanwhile, Geralt had struck another bandit. Cahir hacked the next one to death; something shaped like a slice of watermelon dropped from the robber's skull after a powerful blow of his Nilfgaardian blade. The last thug fled and jumped onto his horse. Cahir tossed up his sword, seized it by the blade and hurled it like a javelin, striking the brigand right between the shoulder blades. The horse neighed and jerked its head, sat hard on its haunches and stamped its hooves, dragging the corpse over the red mud, its hand tangled up in the reins.

The whole thing took less than five heartbeats.

'Heeey!' yelled somebody from among the buildings. 'Heeeelp! Heeeelp! Murder, vicious killers!'

'Troops! Call out the troops!' shouted another miner, shooing away children who – as is the immemorial custom of all the world's children – had appeared from nowhere to watch and get in the way.

'Someone run and call the army!'

Angoulême picked up her knife, wiped and sheathed it.

'Let them run, by all means!' she shouted back, looking around.

'What is it, quarrymen, are you blind or what? That was self-defence! They fell on us, the bloody thugs! Don't you know them? Haven't they done you enough harm? Haven't they extorted enough from you?'

She sneezed loudly. Then she tore the purse from the belt of the still twitching Novosad and leaned over Yirrel.

'Angoulême.'

'What?'

'Leave it.'

'Why should I? It's spoils! Short of money?'

'Angoulême . . . '

'You,' a voice suddenly shouted. 'This way, please.'

Three men stood in the open doorway to a barrack serving as the tool store. Two of them were heavies with low foreheads and closely-cropped hair, of undoubtedly limited intelligence. The third – the one who'd shouted to them – was a very tall, dark-haired, handsome man.

'I couldn't help overhearing the conversation preceding the incident,' the man said. 'I found it hard to believe you'd killed a witcher, thinking it empty bragging. I don't think that now. Step inside.'

Angoulême drew an audible intake of breath. She glanced at the Witcher and nodded barely perceptibly.

The man was a half-elf.

*

The half-elf Schirrú was tall – well over six feet. He wore his dark hair tied on his neck in a ponytail falling down his back. His mixed blood was betrayed by his eyes, which were large, almond-shaped and yellowish-green, like a cat's.

'So you killed the Witcher,' he said again, smiling repulsively. 'Forestalling Homer Straggen, also called Nightingale? Fascinating, fascinating. Put simply, I ought to pay you fifty florins. The second instalment. Which means Straggen received his two score and ten florins for nothing. For you surely can't suppose he'll give it up.'

'How I settle accounts with Nightingale is my business,' said

207

Angoulême, sitting on a crate and swinging her legs. 'The contract on the Witcher was a one-off commission. And we carried out that commission. We did, not Nightingale. The Witcher's in the ground. His company, all three of them, are in the ground. In other words: job done.'

'At least that's what you claim. How did it happen?'

Angoulême kept swinging her legs.

'I'll write my life story when I'm old,' she declared in her usual impudent tone. 'I'll describe how this, that and the other took place. You'll have to hold on until then, Mr Schirrú.'

'It shames you that much, then,' the half-breed remarked coldly. 'So, you did the deed foully and treacherously.'

'Does that bother you?' Geralt asked.

Schirrú looked at him intently.

'No,' he answered after a moment. 'Geralt the Witcher of Rivia didn't deserve a better fate. He was a simpleton and a fool. If he'd had a finer, more honest and honourable death, legends would have sprung up around him. But he didn't merit a legend.'

'Death is always the same.'

'Not always.' The half-elf turned his head, trying to catch a glimpse of Geralt's eyes, shaded by his hood. 'Not always, I assure you. I presume *you* dealt the mortal blow.'

Geralt didn't reply. He felt the overwhelming urge to grab the cross-breed by the ponytail, knock him to the floor and wring every detail out of him, knocking his teeth out one by one with his sword pommel. He held himself back. Good sense suggested Angoulême's hoax might bear better results.

'As you wish,' said Schirrú, not getting an answer. 'I won't insist on a report about the course of events. It's clearly difficult for you to talk about it, and there's clearly not very much to boast about. Supposing, of course, that your silence doesn't stem from something quite different . . . For example, that nothing at all occurred. Do you perhaps have any proof of the veracity of your words?'

'We cut off the Witcher's right hand,' Angoulême replied impassively. 'But later a raccoon took it and devoured it.'

'So we have only this.' Geralt slowly unbuttoned his shirt and drew out his medallion with the wolf's head. 'The Witcher wore it around his neck.'

'May I?'

Geralt didn't hesitate for long. The half-elf hefted the medallion in his palm.

'*Now* I believe,' he said slowly. 'The gewgaw emanates powerful magic. Only a witcher could have had something like this.'

'And a witcher,' Angoulême continued, 'wouldn't have let it be taken from him while he was still breathing. It's rock-solid evidence. So slap the cash on the table, mester.'

Schirrú carefully put the medallion away, took a wad of papers from his bosom, put them down on the table and spread them out with a hand.

'Over here, please.'

Angoulême hopped off the crate and walked over, mocking him and swinging her hips. She leaned over the table. As quick as a flash, Schirrú grabbed her hair, slammed her down on the table and shoved a knife to her throat. The girl didn't even have time to cry out.

Geralt and Cahir already had their swords in their hands. But it was too late.

The half-elf's assistants – the musclemen with low foreheads – were holding iron hooks. But they were in no hurry to come closer.

'Drop your swords,' Schirrú snarled. 'Both of you; swords on the floor. Or I'll widen the slut's smile.'

'Don't listen—' Angoulême began – and ended with a shriek as the half-elf ground his fist into her hair. And scored her skin with a dagger; a glistening red wavy line trickled down the girl's neck.

'Swords on the ground! I'm serious!'

'Perhaps we could talk this out?' Geralt, heedless of the rage seething inside him, decided to stall for time. 'Like civilised folk?'

The half-elf laughed venomously.

'Talk it out? With you, Witcher? I was sent here to finish you off, not talk. Yes, yes, freak. You were lying, putting on a song and dance, but I recognised you the moment I saw you. You'd been described precisely to me. Can you guess who described you so precisely? Who gave me precise instructions about where and in what company I'd find you? Oh, I'm certain you've guessed.'

'Release the girl.'

'But I don't just know you from the description,' Schirrú

continued, with no intention of releasing Angoulême. 'I've seen you before. I even tracked you once. In Temeria. In July. I followed you on horseback to the town of Dorian and to the chambers of the jurists Codringher and Fenn. Ring any bells?'

Geralt twisted his sword so that the blade flashed in the half-elf's eyes.

'I wonder,' he said icily, 'how you mean to get out of this stalemate, Schirrú? I see two solutions. The first: you let go of the girl right away. The second: you kill the girl . . . And a second later your blood paints the walls and ceiling a pretty red.'

'Your weapons,' Schirrú brutally yanked Angoulême's hair, 'will be lying on the ground before I count to three. Then I start butchering the slut.'

'We'll see how much you manage to cut off. Not much, I reckon.'

'One!'

'Two!' Geralt had begun his own reckoning, whirling the sihill in a hissing moulinet.

The thudding of hooves, the neighing and snorting of horses and yelling reached them from outside.

'And what now?' Schirrú laughed. 'That's what I was waiting for. It's not stalemate but checkmate! My friends have arrived.'

'Really?' said Cahir, looking through the window. 'I see the uniforms of the imperial light horse.'

'Checkmate indeed, but against you,' said Geralt. 'You lose, Schirrú. Release the girl.'

'Like hell.'

The barrack doors yielded to kicks and about a dozen men entered, most of them in identical black uniforms. They were led by a fair-haired, bearded man with a silver bear on his spaulder.

'Que aen suecc's?' he asked menacingly. 'What's going on here? Who answers for this brawl? For the bodies in the yard? Speak up this minute!'

'Commander—'

'Glaeddyvan vort! Drop your swords!'

They obeyed, for crossbows and arbalests were being aimed at them. Released by Schirrú, Angoulême meant to spring up from the table, but suddenly found herself in the grasp of a stocky, colourfully dressed bruiser with bulging frog eyes. She tried to cry out, but the bruiser clamped a gloved fist over her mouth.

'Let's abstain from violence,' Geralt suggested coolly to the commander with the bear. 'We aren't criminals.'

'Well I never.'

'We're acting with the knowledge and permission of Mr Fulko Artevelde, the Prefect of Riedbrune.'

'Well I never,' repeated the Bear, signalling for Geralt and Cahir's swords to be picked up and confiscated. 'With the knowledge and permission. Of Mr Fulko Artevelde. The esteemed Mr Artevelde. Hear that, lads?'

His men – those dressed in the black and colourful clothes – cackled in unison.

Angoulême struggled in the grip of Frog-Eyes, vainly trying to scream. Needlessly. Geralt already knew. Even before the smiling Schirrú began to shake the hand proffered to him. Even before the four black-uniformed Nilfgaardians seized Cahir and three others aimed their crossbows straight at his face.

Frog-Eyes pushed Angoulême into the arms of his comrades. The girl sagged in their grasp like a ragdoll. She didn't even try to offer any resistance.

The Bear walked slowly over to Geralt and suddenly slammed him in the crotch with his armoured-gloved fist. Geralt bent over but didn't fall. Cold fury kept him on his feet.

'Then the news that you aren't the first asses to be used by One-Eyed Fulko for his own purposes may console you.' said the Bear, 'Profitable business deals – like the one I'm carrying out here with Mr Homer Straggen, known by some as "Nightingale" – are a thorn in his side. It pisses Fulko off that I've recruited Homer Straggen into the imperial service and appointed him commander of the volunteer mines defence company to expedite those deals. Unable, thus, to avenge himself officially, he hires a variety of rogues.'

'And witchers,' a smiling Schirrú interjected scathingly.

'Outside,' said the Bear loudly, 'five bodies are getting soaked in the rain. You murdered men in the Imperial service! You disrupted the work of this mine! I have no doubt about it: you're spies, saboteurs and terrorists. Martial Law applies here. I hereby summarily sentence you to death.'

Frog-Eyes cackled. He walked over to Angoulême, who was being held up by the bandits, grasped one of her breasts, and squeezed it hard.

'Well then, Flaxenhair?' he croaked, and it transpired that his voice was more froglike than his eyes. His bandit soubriquet – assuming he'd christened himself with it – showed a sense of humour. But if it was an alias intended to disguise it was extremely effective.

'We meet again, then!' the froglike Nightingale croaked, pinching Angoulême in the breast. 'Happy?'

The girl groaned in pain.

'Where are the pearls and stones you stole from me, you whore?'

'One-Eyed Fulko took them for safe keeping!' Angoulême yelled, ineffectually pretending that she wasn't afraid. 'Go and claim them back!'

Nightingale croaked and goggled his eyes – now he looked like a genuine frog, which any moment would start catching flies with its tongue. He pinched Angoulême even harder. She struggled and groaned even more pathetically. Through the red fog of fury covering Geralt's eyes the girl had once again begun to resemble Ciri.

'Take them,' the Bear ordered impatiently. 'To the yard with them.'

'He's a witcher,' said one of the bandits from Nightingale's mines defence company, hesitantly. 'He's a hard case! How can we take him with our bare hands? He's liable to cast a charm on us, or summat else . . . '

'No fear.' A smiling Schirrú patted his pocket. 'Without his witcher's amulet he's unable to work magic, and I have it. Take him.'

*

There were more armed Nilfgaardians in black cloaks in the yard, and more of Nightingale's colourful hassa. A clutch of miners had also gathered. The ubiquitous children and dogs were also milling around.

Nightingale suddenly lost control of himself, quite as though a devil had possessed him. Croaking furiously, he punched

Angoulême, and when she fell, kicked her repeatedly. Geralt strained in the grip of the bandits and was hit on the back of the neck with something hard for his pains.

'They said,' croaked Nightingale, hopping over Angoulême like a frantic toad, 'that you'd had a stake shoved up your backside in Riedbrune, you little strumpet! You were destined for the stake then and you'll expire on the stake today! Boys, find a post and sharpen it to a spike. Look lively!'

'Mr Straggen.' The Bear grimaced. 'I see no reason to indulge in such a time-consuming and bestial execution. The prisoners ought simply to be hanged . . . '

He fell silent under the evil gaze of the froglike eyes.

'Be quiet, captain,' croaked the bandit. 'I pay you too much for you to make improper remarks. I promised Angoulême a foul death and now I'm going to deliver it. Hang those two if you must. I'm not bothered about them—'

'But I am,' Schirrú interrupted. 'I need them both. Especially the Witcher. Especially him. And since skewering the girl will take some time, I shall make use of it.'

He walked over and fixed his feline eyes on Geralt.

'You ought to know, freak,' he said, 'that it was *I* that dispatched your comrade, Codringher, in Dorian. I did it on the orders of my lord, Master Vilgefortz, whom I've served for many years. But I did it with immense pleasure.

'The old rogue Codringher,' the half-elf continued, without getting a reaction, 'had the audacity to stick his nose into Master Vilgefortz's affairs. I gutted him with a knife. And I torched that loathsome monstrosity Fenn among his papers and roasted him alive. I could have simply stabbed him, but I devoted a little time and effort to listen to his howling and squealing. And howl and squeal he did, I swear, like a stuck piglet. There was nothing, absolutely nothing, human in that howling.

'Do you know why I'm telling you all this? Because I could also simply knife you or order you stabbed to death. But I shall put in a little time and effort. And listen as you howl. You said death is always the same? You'll soon see it isn't. Hey boys, heat up some pitch in a tar kettle. And fetch a chain.'

Something smashed against the corner of the barracks and

213

exploded with a red flash and a frightful crash. A second vessel containing petroleum – Geralt recognised it by the smell – landed plumb in the tar kettle, and a third shattered just beside the men restraining the horses. It boomed and belched fire and the horses fell into a frenzy. There was a turmoil and from it rushed a howling dog in flames. One of Nightingale's bandits suddenly spread his arms and keeled over in the mud with an arrow in his back.

'Long live the Free Slopes!'

Figures in grey mantles and fur hats loomed at the top of the hill, on the scaffoldings and the catwalks. More missiles, trailing wakes of flames and smoke behind them like fireworks fell onto the people, horses and mine buildings. Two flew into the workshop; onto the floor strewn with shavings and sawdust.

'Long live the Free Slopes! Death to the Nilfgaardian invaders!'

Arrow fletchings and crossbow bolts sang.

One of the black-uniformed Nilfgaardians tumbled down under his horse, one of Nightingale's bandits fell with his throat pierced, and one of the close-cropped musclemen dropped with a bolt in his nape. The Bear sprawled with a ghastly groan. An arrow had hit him in the chest, under the sternum, beneath the gorget. The arrow had been stolen – though no one could have known that – from a military convoy and was standard issue of the imperial army, slightly adapted. The wide, two-bladed arrowhead had been filed in several places with the aim of fragmentation.

The arrowhead fragmented beautifully in the Bear's guts.

'Down with the tyrant Emhyr! The Free Slopes!'

Nightingale croaked, grabbing his arm, grazed by a bolt.

One of the children rolled over in the mud, pierced through by an arrow from one of the less accurate freedom fighters. One of the men holding Geralt dropped. One of the men holding Angoulême fell over. The girl wrested herself free of the second, drew a knife from her boot in an instant, swung hard and slashed. In her frenzy she missed Nightingale's throat, but mutilated his cheek splendidly, almost down to the teeth. Nightingale croaked more gratingly than usual, and his eyes bulged more bulgingly. He slumped to his knees, blood spurting between hands clutching his face. Angoulême gave an unearthly scream and leaped forward to finish the job, but couldn't, for another bomb exploded between her and Nightingale, belching fire and clouds of foul-smelling smoke.

Fire roared all around and a fiery pandemonium raged. Horses thrashed, whinnied and kicked. The bandits and Nilfgaardians yelled. The miners ran in a panic – some fled and others tried to put out the blazing buildings.

Geralt had managed to pick up his sihill, which the Bear had released. He jabbed it into the forehead of a tall woman in a chain mail vest, who was aiming a blow at Angoulême with a morning star as she rose to her feet. He sliced open the thigh of a black-uniformed Nilfgaardian running at him with a half-pike. He then slashed the throat of the next one who simply happened to be in the way.

Right alongside him, a frantic, scorched horse rushing blindly knocked over and trampled another child.

'Seize the horse! Seize the horse!' Cahir was now right beside him, and created room for them both with great swings of his sword. Geralt wasn't listening or looking. He slew another Nilfgaardian. He looked around for Schirrú. Angoulême, on bended knee, shot a crossbow she'd picked up, sending the bolt – at a distance of three paces – into the belly of a bandit from the mines defence company who was coming for her. Then she sprang to her feet and hung onto the bridle of a horse running by.

'Grab one of them, Geralt!' Cahir yelled. 'And ride!'

The Witcher slit open another Nilfgaardian from breastbone to hip with a downward stroke. He shook blood from his eyebrows and eyelashes with a sharp jerk of his head. 'Schirrú! Where are you, you bastard?'

A stroke. A cry. Warm drops on his face.

'Mercy!' howled a lad in a black uniform, kneeling in the mud. The Witcher hesitated.

'Wake up!' yelled Cahir, grabbing him by the shoulders and shaking him hard. 'Control yourself! Are you in a frenzy?'

Angoulême was returning at a gallop, dragging another horse by the reins. She was being followed by two riders. One of them fell – hit by the arrow of a fighter for the freedom of the Slopes. The other was hurled from the saddle by Cahir's sword.

Geralt leaped into the saddle. And then he saw Schirrú in the light of the blaze, summoning the panicked Nilfgaardians to him-self. Beside the half-elf, Nightingale, croaking and bawling out curses with his bloody maw, looked like a veritable cannibal troll.

Geralt roared furiously, reined his horse around and whirled his sword.

Beside him, Cahir shouted and swore, wobbling in the saddle, blood from his forehead pouring over his eyes and face.

'Geralt! Help me!'

Schirrú had gathered a group around him, and was yelling and ordering them to shoot their crossbows. Geralt slapped his horse on the rump with the flat of his sword, ready for a suicidal charge. Schirrú had to die. Nothing else meant anything. Or mattered. Cahir meant nothing. Angoulême meant nothing . . .

'Geralt!' Angoulême yelled. 'Help Cahir!'

He came to his senses. And was ashamed.

Geralt held Cahir up, supported him. Cahir wiped his eyes with a sleeve, and the blood instantly poured over them again.

'It's nothing – a scratch . . . ' His voice shook. 'Ride, Witcher . . . follow Angoulême . . . Ride!'

From the foot of the mountain came a great cry and a crowd armed with picks, crowbars and axes came rushing out. For miners from the neighbouring mines of Common Cause and Lucky Pit were hurrying to help their mates and comrades from the Rialto colliery. Or from some other. Who could possibly know?

Geralt kicked his horse with his heels. They rode at a gallop, recklessly, *ventre à terre*.

*

They pounded on, not looking back, hugging their horses' necks. Angoulême had landed the best horse, a small but fleet and sturdy bandit steed. Geralt's horse, a bay with Nilfgaardian trappings, was beginning to snort and wheeze and was having difficulty hold-ing its head up. Cahir's horse, also an army beast, was stronger and tougher, but what of that when its rider was causing problems, swaying in the saddle, mechanically clenching with his thighs and bleeding profusely onto his mount's mane and neck.

But they galloped on.

Angoulême, who had pulled ahead, was waiting for them on a bend, in a place where the road went downhill, winding amongst rocks.

'Our pursuers . . . ' she panted, smearing dirt on her face, 'will come after us, they won't give up . . . The miners saw which way we fled. We oughtn't to stay on the highway . . . We have to head into the forests, get off the road . . . Lose them . . .'

'No,' the Witcher protested, anxiously listening to the sounds coming from the horse's lungs. 'We must stay on the highway . . . Take the straightest and shortest route to Sansretour.'

'Why?'

'There's no time to talk. Let's ride! Squeeze what you can from the horses . . . '

They galloped on. The Witcher's bay wheezed.

*

The bay wasn't fit to ride any further. It was barely walking, legs as stiff as boards, panting hard, the air escaping from it in a hoarse wheezing. It finally fell over on its side, kicked stiffly, looked at its rider; and there was reproach in its cloudy eye.

Cahir's horse was in somewhat better shape, but Cahir's condition was worse. He simply fell from the saddle, raised himself, but only onto his hands and knees, and retched spasmodically, though his stomach was empty.

When Geralt and Angoulême tried to touch his bloodied head he screamed.

'Dammit,' said the girl. 'It's quite a haircut they've given him.'

The skin of the young Nilfgaardian's forehead and temple, along with the hair, was detached from the skull along a considerable length. Were it not for the fact that the blood had formed a sticky clot, the loose patch would probably have fallen off all the way to his ear. It was a gruesome sight.

'How did that happen?'

'They threw a hatchet right at him. To make it even funnier, it wasn't a Nilfgaardian, nor any of Nightingale's men, but one of the quarrymen.'

'Doesn't matter who threw it.' The Witcher bound Cahir's

head tightly with a torn-off shirtsleeve. 'It matters, luckily, that he was a poor shot, and he just scalped him, rather than smashing his skull in. But Cahir took a hefty whack in the pate. And the brain felt it too. He won't stay upright in the saddle, even if the horse could bear his weight.'

'What shall we do then? Your horse has died, his is almost dead, and the sweat's dropping off mine . . . And they're on our trail. We can't stay here . . .'

'We have to stay here. Me and Cahir. And Cahir's horse. You ride on. Hard. Your horse is strong, it can withstand a gallop. And even were you to exhaust it . . . Angoulême, somewhere in Sansretour valley Regis, Milva and Dandelion are waiting for us. They don't know anything of this and may fall into Schirrú's clutches. You have to find them and warn them, and then all four of you must ride as fast as you can to Toussaint. You won't be followed there. I hope.'

'What about you and Cahir?' Angoulême bit her lip. 'What will happen to you? Nightingale isn't stupid. When he sees a half-dead riderless horse he'll rake over every hollow in the region! And you won't get far with Cahir!'

'Schirrú – for he's the one pursuing us – will follow your trail.'

'Do you think so?'

'I'm certain. Go.'

'What will aunty say when I show up without you?'

'You'll explain. But not to Milva; to Regis. Regis will know what's to be done. And we . . . When Cahir's mop dries a bit harder onto his pate, we'll make for Toussaint. We'll meet up there somehow. Very well, don't dally. Get on your horse and ride. Don't let our pursuers get any closer. Don't let them hunt you by sight.'

'Don't teach your grandmother to suck eggs. Look after yourselves! Farewell!'

'Farewell, Angoulême.'

*

He didn't move too far from the road. He couldn't deny himself a glance at their pursuers. And in fact he didn't fear any trouble from them, knowing they wouldn't waste time and would pursue Angoulême.

He wasn't mistaken.

The riders who thundered into the pass less than a quarter of an hour later stopped, admittedly, at the sight of the dead horse, shouted, argued, trotted around the roadside bushes, but returned almost at once to the road to resume their pursuit. They clearly believed that two of the three fugitives were now riding one horse and it would be possible to catch them quickly if they didn't dawdle. Geralt saw that some of the pursuing horses weren't in the best of shape either.

There weren't too many black cloaks of the Nilfgaardian light horse among them. Nightingale's colourful brigands predominated. Geralt couldn't see if Nightingale himself was taking part in the hunt, or if he'd stayed behind to treat his mutilated face.

When the hoof beats of the vanishing pursuers had faded away, Geralt stood up from his hiding place in the bracken, lifted and held up the moaning and groaning Cahir.

'The horse is too feeble to bear you. Will you be able to walk?'

The Nilfgaardian made a noise which might as easily have been agreement or disagreement. Or something else. But he shuffled forward, and that was the main idea.

They went down to the stream bed in the ravine. Cahir negotiated the final few yards of the slippery slope in a rather chaotic descent. He crawled to the stream, drank, and poured the icy water copiously over the bandage on his head. The Witcher didn't hurry him. He was breathing heavily himself, gathering his strength.

He walked upstream, supporting Cahir and pulling the horse at the same time, wading in the water and stumbling on pebbles and fallen tree trunks. After some time Cahir stopped cooperating, stopped shuffling his legs obediently – in fact he stopped moving them at all, so the Witcher simply dragged him. It was impossible to continue like that, particularly since the stream bed was obstructed by rocks and waterfalls. Geralt grunted and lifted the wounded man onto his back. Neither did pulling the horse make life any easier. When they finally emerged from the ravine, the Witcher simply collapsed on the wet forest floor and lay, panting, completely drained, beside the groaning Cahir. He lay there for a long time. His knee had begun to throb again with intense pain.

Cahir finally started to show signs of life once more, and soon after – astonishingly – got up, swearing and holding his head. They set off. Cahir marched bravely at first. Then slowed. Then slumped down.

Geralt heaved him onto his back again and lugged him, grunting, slipping over the stones. Pain shot through his knee, and fiery, black bees seemed to flash in front of his eyes.

'Just a month ago . . .' Cahir moaned from his back. 'Who'd have thought you'd be lugging me like this . . .'

'Quiet, Nilfgaardian . . . You're heavier when you talk . . .'

When they finally made it to the rocks and the rock walls, it was almost dark. The Witcher didn't look for or find a cave – he fell exhausted by the first opening he came across.

*

Human skulls, ribs, pelvises and other bones were strewn around on the cave floor. But – more importantly – there were also dry branches there.

Cahir was feverish, trembling and shivering. He endured the sewing of the patch of skin to his skull using twine and a crooked needle manfully and fully conscious, with his faculties intact. The crisis came later, during the night. Geralt lit a fire in the cave, disregarding safety considerations. Actually, outside it was drizzling and a strong wind was blowing, so it was unlikely that anybody was wandering around watching out for the glare of a fire. And he had to keep Cahir warm.

The fever lasted the entire night. He trembled, moaned and raved. Geralt enjoyed no sleep – he kept the fire burning. And his knee hurt like hell.

*

A young and sturdy fellow, Cahir came around the following morning. He was pale and sweaty, and the heat of his fever could still be felt. His chattering teeth somewhat complicated articulation. But what he said was comprehensible. And he spoke lucidly.

He was complaining of a headache – a fairly normal symptom for someone whose scalp has been torn from their head by an axe.

Geralt divided his time between anxiously catnapping and catching rainwater dripping from the rocks in beakers he had fashioned from birch bark. Thirst was tormenting both him and Cahir.

*

'Geralt?

'Yes?'

Cahir tidied up the wood in the fire using a femur he'd found.

'When we were fighting in the mine . . . I was scared.'

'I know.'

'For a moment it looked as though you'd gone berserk. That nothing mattered to you any longer . . . Aside from killing . . .'

'I know.'

'I was afraid,' he calmly finished, 'that you'd butcher Schirrú to death in your frenzy. And we wouldn't get any information out of a dead man, would we?'

Geralt cleared his throat. He was growing to like the young Nilfgaardian more and more. He was not only brave, but smart too.

'You did right, sending Angoulême away,' Cahir continued, his teeth chattering only slightly. 'It isn't for girls . . . Not even for girls like her. We'll sort it out, the two of us. We'll ride down our pursuers. But not in order to slaughter them in a berserker frenzy. What you said about revenge that time . . . Geralt, even in vengeance there must be some method. We'll catch up with that half-elf . . . And force him to tell us where Ciri is . . .'

'Ciri's dead.'

'Not true. I don't believe she's dead . . . And you don't either. Admit it.'

'I don't want to believe it.'

A gale was whistling outside and the rain was whispering. It was cosy in the cave.

'Geralt?

'Yes.'

'Ciri's alive. I've had dreams again . . . Yes, something happened at the Equinox, something dreadful . . . Yes, without doubt, I felt and saw it . . . But she's alive . . . She's definitely alive. Let's hurry . . . But not to avenge and murder. To find her.'

'Yes. Yes, Cahir. You're right.'

'And you? Don't you have dreams now?'

'I do,' he said bitterly. 'But seldom since we crossed the Yaruga. And I remember nothing after waking. Something has ended in me, Cahir. Something has burned out. Something has ruptured in me . . .'

'Never mind, Geralt. I shall dream for both of us.'

*

They set off at dawn. It had stopped raining. It even seemed that the sun was trying to find a hole in the greyness enveloping the sky.

They rode slowly, on the single horse with the Nilfgaardian military trappings.

The horse trudged over the pebbles, moving at a walk along the bank of the Sansretour, the small river leading to Toussaint. Geralt knew the way. He had been there once. A long, long time ago; much had changed since then. But the valley had not changed, and neither had the Sansretour stream, which, the further they went, become more and more the River Sansretour. Neither the Amell Mountains, nor the obelisk of the Gorgon, Devil Mountain, had changed.

There were certain things that simply didn't change.

*

'A soldier doesn't question his orders,' said Cahir, feeling the dressing on his head. 'Doesn't analyse them, doesn't ponder over them, doesn't wait for them to be explained to him. That's the first thing they teach a soldier where I come from. So you can understand that not for a second did I ever question an order which was issued to me. The thought of *why* I had to capture a Cintran princess didn't even cross my mind. An order's an order. I was cross, naturally, because I wanted to taste fame, fighting against the knighthood, against the regular army . . . But working for the intelligence service is also treated as an honour where I come from.

222

If it had only concerned a more taxing task, a more important prisoner . . . But a girl?'

Geralt threw a trout's spine onto the fire. Before nightfall they had caught enough fish in a stream flowing into the Sansretour to eat their fill. The trout were spawning and easy to catch.

He listened to Cahir's account, and the curiosity in him struggled with a feeling of profound hurt.

'It was essentially chance,' Cahir went on, gazing into the flames. 'Pure chance. There was – as I found out later – a spy at the Cintran court, a valet. When we'd captured the city and were preparing to encircle the castle the spy stole out and gave a sign that he would try to get the princess out of the city. Several squads like mine were formed. By accident, it was my group the men spiriting Ciri away ran into.

'A chase through the streets began, in quarter that was already on fire. It was sheer hell. Nothing but the roar of flames, walls of fire. The horses didn't want to go there, and the men, what can I say, were in no hurry to urge them. My subordinates – there were four of them – began to claim I'd gone mad, that I was leading them to their doom . . . I barely managed to wrest back control . . .

'We pursued them through that fiery bedlam and caught up with them. We suddenly had them before us: five mounted Cintrans. And a bloody fight began, before I could tell them to watch out for the girl. Who ended up on the ground at once anyway, as the man who was carrying her perished first. One of my men lifted her up and onto his horse, but he didn't get far, for one of the Cintrans stabbed him through the back. I saw the blade pass an inch from Ciri's head and she fell in the mud again. She was dazed with fear; I saw her cuddling up to the dead man, saw her trying to crawl under him . . . Like a kitten by its dead mother . . .'

He fell silent and swallowed audibly.

'She didn't even know she was cuddling up to the enemy. To a hated Nilfgaardian.'

'We ended up alone, she and I,' he continued a moment later, 'and all around us corpses and fire. Ciri was grovelling in a puddle, and the water and blood were beginning to steam. A house collapsed, and I could see very little through the sparks and smoke. The horse wouldn't go any closer. I called to her, appealed to her to come to me. My voice had almost gone, trying to outshout the conflagration. She saw and heard me but didn't react. The horse wouldn't move, and I couldn't control it. I had to dismount. There was no way I could lift her with one arm, and I had to hold the reins with the other; the horse was struggling so much it almost threw me. When I lifted her she began to scream. Then she tensed up and fainted. I wrapped her in my cloak which I had wetted in a puddle; in mud, muck and blood. And we rode on. Straight through the fire.

'I don't know by what miracle we managed to get out of there. But a breach in the wall suddenly appeared and we were by the river. Unluckily, it turned out, for it was the spot the fleeing Nordlings had chosen. I discarded my officer's helmet, for they would have recognised me right away by it, even though the wings had burned off. The rest of my clothing was so blackened it couldn't have betrayed me. But had the girl been conscious, had she screamed, they would have put me to the sword. I was lucky.

'I rode a few furlongs with them, and then fell back and hid in the bushes by a river bearing dead bodies.'

He fell silent, coughed slightly, and felt his bandaged head with both hands. And blushed. Or was it merely the glare of the flames?

'Ciri was so dirty. I had to undress her . . . She didn't resist, didn't scream. She just trembled, eyes closed. Each time I touched her to clean her or dry her, she tensed and stiffened . . . I know, I ought to have spoken to her, calmed her . . . But suddenly I couldn't find the words in your language . . . In my mother's language, which I've known from a child. Unable to find the words, I tried to calm her by touch, by gentleness . . . But she stiffened and whimpered . . . Like a baby . . .'

'That haunted her in her nightmares,' Geralt whispered.

'I know. Mine too.'

'What then?'

'She fell asleep. So did I. From fatigue. When I woke she wasn't beside me. She was nowhere to be seen. I don't recall the rest. Those who found me claimed I was running around in circles howling like a wolf. They had to tie me up. When I'd calmed down, I was taken in hand by intelligence agents, Vattier de Rideaux's subordinates. They wanted to know about Cirilla. Where she was,

where she fled to, how she gave me the slip, why I let her escape.
And again, from the beginning: where was she, where had she fled
to . . . ? Infuriated, I yelled something about the emperor hunting
a little girl like a sparrowhawk. For that I spent a year locked up
in the citadel. But then I was back in grace, for I was needed. On
Thanedd, they needed someone who spoke the Common Speech
and knew what Ciri looked like. The emperor wanted me to go to
Thanedd . . . And not to fail this time. But bring him Ciri.'

He was silent for a time.

'Emhyr gave me a chance. I could have refused. It would have
meant absolute, total, perpetual disfavour and oblivion, but I
could have declined if I'd wanted. But I didn't decline. For you
see, Geralt . . . I couldn't forget her.

'I won't lie to you. I saw her constantly in my dreams. And
not as the skinny child she was by the river, when I undressed
and washed her. I saw her . . . and I still see her . . . as a woman;
comely, aware, provocative . . . With such details as a crimson rose
tattooed on her groin . . . '

'What are you talking about?'

'I don't know. I don't know myself . . . But that's how it has
been and is yet. I see her in my dreams, just as I saw her in my
dreams back then . . . That is why I volunteered for the mission to
Thanedd. That's why I wanted to join you afterwards. I . . . I want
to see her . . . again. I want to touch her hair again, look into her
eyes . . . I want to gaze on her. Kill me if you will. But I won't pretend any longer. I think . . . I think I love her. Please don't laugh.'

'I don't feel like laughing.'

'So that's why I'm riding with you. Do you understand?'

'Do you want her for yourself or for your emperor?'

'I'm a realist,' he whispered. 'I mean, she won't want me. But as
the emperor's spouse I could at least see her.'

'As a realist,' the Witcher snapped, 'you should remember we
have to find and rescue her first. Assuming your dreams aren't
lying and Ciri is really still alive.'

'I'm aware of that. And should we find her? What then?'

'We shall see. We shall see, Cahir.'

'Don't deceive me. Be frank. You won't let me take her, will
you?'

He didn't reply. Cahir didn't repeat the question.

'Until then,' he asked coolly, 'may we be comrades?'

'We may, Cahir. I apologise again for back there. I don't know what came over me. I've never seriously suspected you of treachery or duplicity.'

'I'm not a traitor. I'll never betray you, Witcher.'

*

They rode along a deep gorge, which the swift-flowing and wide Sansretour – now a river – had carved out of the hills. They rode east towards the border of the Duchy of Toussaint. Gorgon, Devil Mountain, rose above them. To look at the summit they would have had to crane their necks.

But they didn't.

*

First they smelled smoke, then a moment later beheld a campfire, with spits over it and filleted trout roasting on them. They then beheld a solitary individual sitting beside the fire.

Not long before, Geralt would have mocked, mercilessly ridiculed and thought a complete idiot anyone who would have dared claim that he – a witcher – would feel great joy at the sight of a vampire.

'Oho,' Emiel Regis Rohellec Terzieff-Godefroy said placidly, adjusting the spits. 'Look what the cat dragged in.'

*The **Knocker**, likewise called a knacker, coblynau, bucca, polterduk, karkorios, rübezahl, or pustecki, is a form of kobold, which, nonetheless, the **K.** considerably surpasses in magnitude and strength. The **K.** as a rule also wears a great beard, which kobolds habitually do not. The **K.** dwells in adits, vertical shafts, spoil heaps, precipices, tenebrous hollows, inside rocks, in diverse grottos, caves and stone wildernesses. Wherever it dwells, natural riches such as metal, ore, carbon, salt or petroleum are surely buried in the earth. Thus, one may often encounter a **K.** in mines, particularly abandoned ones, although it is also likely to appear in active ones. It is a vicious scourge and pest, a curse and veritable divine retribution for miners and quarrymen, whom the vexatious **K.** leads astray. By knocking on the rock it beguiles and frightens, obstructs galleries, steals and spoils mining equipment and all kinds of belongings, and is also inclined to strike one on the head a place of concealment. But it may be bribed, to curb its mischief-making, by placing in a dark gallery or shaft some bread and butter, a smoked cheese, or a flitch of smoked gammon; but best of all is a demijohn of alcohol, since the **K.** is extremely greedy for such.*

Physiologus

CHAPTER SEVEN

'They're safe,' assured the vampire, spurring on his mule, Draakul. 'All three of them. Milva, Dandelion and, of course, Angoulême, who drove us into the Sansretour valley just in time and told us everything, not stinting with her colourful expressions. I've never understood why the majority of human curses and insults refer to the erotic sphere. Sex is wonderful and associated with beauty, joy and pleasure. How can the names of the sexual organs be used as a vulgar synonym for—'

'Drop the subject, Regis,' Geralt interrupted.

'Of course, I apologise. Warned by Angoulême about the approaching brigands, we crossed the marches of Toussaint without delay. Milva, admittedly, wasn't overjoyed, and was spoiling to turn tail and bring you both aid. I managed to dissuade her. And Dandelion, astonishingly, rather than enjoy the asylum afforded by the borders of the duchy, clearly had his heart in his mouth . . . You don't by any chance know what he fears so in Toussaint?'

'I don't, but I can guess,' Geralt replied sourly. 'It wouldn't be the first place where our dear friend the bard has been up to no good. He has settled down now somewhat, for he moves in decent society, but nothing was sacred to him in his youth. Only urchins and women who had climbed to the tops of tall trees were safe from him. Husbands regularly held grudges against the troubadour for unknown reasons. There is doubtless a man in Toussaint for whom the sight of Dandelion will bring back memories . . . But these are essentially trifling matters. Let's return to the facts. What of our pursuers? I hope—'

'I don't think,' Regis smiled, 'that they followed us into Toussaint. The border is teeming with errant knights, who are extremely bored and hankering for a fight. Furthermore, we and a group of pilgrims we bumped into on the border ended up in the sacred grove of Myrkvid. And that place is fearsome. Even the pilgrims and infirm people who make for Myrkvid from the most distant corners to be healed stop in the settlement near the forest edge, not daring to go deeper. There are rumours that any who dare enter the sacred oak groves end up burned over a slow flame in the Wicker Hag.'

Geralt inhaled.

'You mean—'

'Of course,' the vampire interjected again. 'The druids are in the grove of Myrkvid. The ones who were previously in Caed Dhu, Angren, later journeyed to Loch Monduirn, and finally to Myrkvid in Toussaint. We were fated to find them. Did I say we were? I don't recall.'

Geralt sighed deeply. Cahir, riding at his back, also sighed.

'That friend of yours, is he among those druids?'

The vampire smiled once more.

'Not he, but she,' he explained. 'Indeed, she is. She has even been promoted. She leads the entire Circle.'

'Is she the hierophantess?'

'She is the flaminika. That's the highest druidic title when borne by a woman. Only men may be hierophants.'

'True, I'd forgotten. So am I to understand that Milva and the rest—'

'Are now in the care of the flaminika and her Circle.' The vampire – as was his custom – answered the question while it was being asked, after which he set about answering a question not yet asked.

'I, however, hurried to meet you. For a mysterious thing occurred. The flaminika – to whom I began to present our case – didn't let me complete it. She said she knew everything. That she had been anticipating our arrival for some time—'

'Really?'

'I couldn't hide my disbelief either.' The vampire reined in the mule, stood up in his stirrups and looked around.

'Are you seeking somebody or something?' asked Cahir.

'I'm no longer searching, I've found it. Let's sit down.'

'I'd prefer to—'

'Let's sit down. I'll explain everything.'

They had to raise their voices to be able to converse over the roar of a waterfall tumbling from a considerable height down the vertical wall of a rocky precipice. Down below, where the waterfall had hollowed out a largish lake, a black cave mouth gaped in the rock. The Witcher stared at it.

'Yes, right there,' Regis confirmed the Witcher's suspicion. 'I rode here to meet you, for I was instructed to direct you there. You will have to enter that cave. I told you, the druids knew about you, knew about Ciri, knew about our mission. And they learned about it from someone who lives down there. That person – if one is to believe the druidess – wishes to talk to you.'

'"If one is to believe the druidess",' Geralt repeated sneeringly. 'I've been in these parts before. I know what dwells in the deep caves beneath Devil Mountain. There are various denizens there. But it's impossible to talk to the vast majority of them, except with a sword. What else did your druidess say? What else am I to believe?'

'She gave me clearly to understand –' the vampire's black eyes bored into Geralt '– that she isn't generally fond of individuals who destroy and kill flora and fauna, and of witchers in particular. I explained that at the present moment you are a more of a titular witcher. That you absolutely don't pester flora or fauna, as long as the aforementioned doesn't pester you. The flaminika, you ought to know, is an extremely shrewd woman, and noted that you have abandoned witcherhood, not as a result of ideological changes, but because you were compelled to by circumstances. I know very well, she said, that misfortune has befallen a person close to the Witcher. The Witcher was thus forced to abandon witcherhood and go to her rescue . . . '

Geralt didn't comment, but his gaze was expressive enough to make the vampire hurry to explain.

'She declared, and I quote: "The Witcher-who-is-not-a-witcher will prove he is capable of humility and sacrifice. He will enter the sombre mouth of the earth. Unarmed. Having laid down all weapons, all sharp iron. All sharp thoughts. All aggression, fury, anger and arrogance. He will enter in humility. And then in the abyss, the humble not-witcher will find answers to the questions which torment him. He will find answers to many questions. But should the Witcher remain a witcher, he will find nothing".'

Geralt spat towards the waterfall and the cave.

'It's a game,' he declared. 'A jest! A prank! Soothsaying, sac-rifice, mysterious encounters in caverns, answers to questions . . . You can only encounter such hackneyed devices from ragged wandering storytellers. Somebody's mocking me. At best. And if it's not mockery—'

'I would not call it mockery under any circumstances,' Regis said firmly. 'None at all, Geralt of Rivia.'

'What, then, is it? One of those notorious druidic peculiarities?'

'We shan't know,' Cahir chipped in, 'until we find out. Come on, Geralt, we'll enter together—'

'No.' The vampire shook his head. 'The flaminika was cate-gorical in this respect. The Witcher must enter alone. Without a weapon. Give me your sword. I shall look after it during your absence.'

'To hell with that—' Geralt began, but Regis interrupted his flow of words with a rapid gesture.

'Give me your sword.' He held out a hand. 'And if you have any other weapons leave them with me too. Remember the flaminika's words. No aggression. Sacrifice. Humility.'

'Do you know who I will encounter down there? Who . . . or what . . . is waiting for me in that cave?'

'No, I don't. Various creatures inhabit the subterranean corri-dors beneath Gorgon.'

'I may be struck down!'

The vampire softly cleared his throat.

'That cannot be ruled out,' he said gravely. 'But you must take that risk. I know you will, of course.'

*

Geralt was not disappointed – as he had expected, the entrance to the cave was filled with an impressive heap of skulls, ribs, tibulas and other bones. There was no stench of putrefaction, however. The mortal remains were clearly ancient and functioned as decor-ations intended to scare away intruders.

At least so he thought.

He entered the darkness and the bones crunched and grated beneath his feet.

His vision quickly adjusted to the gloom.

He was in a gigantic cave, a rocky cavern whose dimensions the eye was unable to take in, for its proportions broke up and vanished in the forest of stalactites suspended from the ceiling in striking festoons. Stalagmites, stocky and squat at the base, becoming slender towards the top, rose white and pink from the colourful, shimmering gravel glistening with water on the cave floor. Some of their points reached well above the Witcher's head. Some of them were fused with stalactites, forming columns of stalagnates. No one called out. The only audible sounds were from the water, which echoed as it splashed and dripped.

He walked on, slowly, straight ahead, into the gloom, between the columns of stone. He knew he was being watched.

He felt the lack of the sword on his back intensely, importunately and distinctly – like the lack of his recently knocked-out tooth.

He slowed.

What a moment earlier he had taken as rounded boulders lying at the foot of some stalagmites now goggled great, glowing eyes at him. Great maws opened and conical fangs flashed in the matted mass of grey and brown shaggy, dust-covered hair.

Barbegazis.

He walked slowly, and stepped cautiously. Barbegazis of all sizes were everywhere. They lay in his way, with no intention of yielding. Though they had behaved extremely peacefully until that moment, he was nonetheless uncertain as to what would happen if he trod on one of them.

The stalagnates were like a forest, so there was no way of walking straight; he had to weave around them. Above, water dripped from the ceiling bristling with needles of stalactites.

The barbegazis – more and more of them were appearing – accompanied him as he walked, waddling and rolling over the cave floor. He could hear their monotonous babbling and puffing. He smelled their pungent, sour scent.

He had to stop. In his way, between two stalagmites, in a place he couldn't pass around, lay a large echinops, bristling with masses of long spines. Geralt swallowed. He knew only too well that the echinops was capable of shooting its spines a distance of ten feet. The spines had a peculiar property – once stuck into the body they

233

broke off and the sharp tips penetrated and worked they way in deeper and deeper until they finally reached a sensitive organ.

'Stupid witcher,' he heard in the gloom. 'Cowardly witcher! He's frit, ha, ha!'

The voice sounded odd and weird, but Geralt had heard similar voices many times. Creatures not accustomed to communicating using articulated speech spoke like that, they accented and intoned strangely, drawing out the syllables unnaturally.

'Stupid witcher! Stupid witcher!'

He refrained from comment. He bit his lip and carefully moved past the echinops. The monster's spines swayed like a sea anemone's tentacles. But only for a moment, then the echinops stopped moving and once again seemed nothing more than a clump of bog grass.

Two immense barbegazis waddled across his path, jabbering and growling. From the ceiling came the flapping of webbed wings and a hissing cackle, unerringly signalling the presence of vampyrodes and vespertyls.

'He's come here, a murderer, a killer! A witcher!' The same voice which had spoken previously reverberated in the gloom. 'He's come down here! He dared! But he has no sword, the killer. So how means he to kill? With his gaze? Ha, ha!'

'Or maybe,' came a second voice, with even more unnatural articulation, 'we kill him? Haaaa?' The barbegazis babbled in a noisy chorus. One of them, as large as a mature pumpkin, rolled closer and closer and snapped its teeth right by Geralt's heels. The Witcher stifled the curse pressing itself against his lips and walked on. Water dripped from the stalactites, jingling with a silvery echo.

Something seized his leg. He refrained from pushing it roughly away.

The strange creature was small, not much larger than a Pekinese dog. It resembled a Pekinese a little, too. At least, its face did. The rest of it was like a small monkey. Geralt had no idea what it was. He had never seen anything like it.

'Wi-tcha!' sang the almost-Pekinese, in a high-pitched voice, but quite distinctly, clutching Geralt's boot. 'Wi-tch-tcha. Ba-stard!'

'Get off,' he said through clenched teeth. 'Get off my boot or I'll kick your arse.'

The barbegazis babbled louder, more urgently and menacingly. Something lowed in the darkness. Geralt didn't know what it was. It sounded like a cow, but the Witcher bet it wasn't.

'Wi-tcha, the ba-stard.'

'Let go of my boot,' he repeated, fighting to control himself. 'I came here unarmed, in peace. You're bothering me—'

He broke off and choked on a wave of repellent fetor, making his eyes water and his hair curl. The strange Pekinese-like creature digging into his calf goggled and defecated right on his boot. The hideous stink was accompanied by even more hideous noises.

He swore appropriately to the situation and shoved the aggressive creature away with his foot. Much more gently than he should have. But what he was expecting happened anyway.

'He kicked the little one!' something roared in the darkness, above the literally thunderous jabbering and howling of the barbegazis. 'He kicked the little one! He harmed something smaller than himself!'

The nearest barbegazis rolled right over to his feet. He felt the gnarled and steely claws grabbing and immobilising him. He didn't fight back; he was resigned to his fate. He wiped his befouled boot on the fur of the largest and most aggressive one. He sat down, tugged by his clothes.

Something large descended a stalagnate, jumping down onto the cave floor. He knew at once what it was. A knocker. Stocky, pot-bellied, hairy, bow-legged, at least two yards across the shoulders, with an even broader ruddy beard. The knocker's approach was heralded by the ground shaking, as though not a knocker but a Shire horse was approaching. Each of the monster's callused and wide feet were – however ridiculous it sounds – a foot and a half long.

The knocker leaned over him and its breath smelled of vodka. The rascals distil hooch here, Geralt thought mechanically.

'You hit someone smaller than you, witcher,' the knocker said, breathing his foul breath into Geralt's face. 'You harmed a small, gentle, innocent creature without cause. We knew you couldn't be trusted. You're aggressive. You have the instincts of a murderer. How many of our kind have you killed, you scoundrel?'

He didn't deign to answer.

'Ooooh!' The knocker breathed alcohol fumes harder. 'I've dreamed of this since I was a child! Since I was a child! My dream has finally come true. Look to the left.'

Like an idiot he looked. And was punched in the teeth with a right hook so hard he saw an intense brightness.

'Oooooh!' The knocker bared huge crooked teeth from the mass of his reeking beard. 'I've dreamed of this since I was a child! Look to the right.'

'Enough.' A loud and sonorous order resounded from somewhere in the depths of the cave. 'Enough of this fun and games. Let him go, please.'

Geralt spat blood from his cut lip. He cleaned his boot in a small stream of water flowing down the rock. The almost-Pekinese grinned at him sneeringly, but from a safe distance. The knocker also grinned, massaging its fist.

'Go, witcher,' it growled. 'Go to him, since he summons you. I shall wait. For you will have to return this way, after all.'

*

The cave he entered was – astonishingly – full of light. Through openings in the ceiling, bristling with stalactites, shone crisscrossing columns of brightness, drawing from the rocks and dripstone formations a kaleidoscope of brilliance and colour. Furthermore, a magical ball blazing with light – amplified by reflections in the quartz on the walls – was suspended in the air. In spite of all this illumination the end of the cave faded into the gloom, and black darkness loomed in the vista of the colonnade of stalagnates.

An immense cave painting was in the process of being created on the wall, which nature had seemingly prepared for that purpose. The painter was a fair-haired elf dressed in a paint-smudged mantle. His head seemed to be ringed by a luminous halo in the magical-natural brilliance.

'Sit down,' said the elf, without wresting his gaze away from the painting. He gestured to a boulder with a wave of his brush. 'They didn't harm you, did they?'

'No. Not really.'

'You'll have to forgive them.'

'Indeed. I will.'

'They're a bit like children. They were awfully glad you were coming.'

'I noticed.'

Only then did the elf glance at him.

'Sit down,' he repeated. 'I shall be at your disposal shortly. I'm just finishing.'

What the elf was finishing was a stylised animal, probably a bison. For the moment only its outline was complete – from its splendid horns to its equally magnificent tail. Geralt sat down on the boulder indicated and swore to be patient and meek – to the bounds of his abilities.

The elf, softly whistling through clenched teeth, dipped his brush into a bowl of paint and coloured his bison purple with swift flourishes. After a moment's thought he painted tiger stripes on the animal's side.

Geralt watched in silence.

Finally the elf took a step back, admiring the fresco which now depicted an entire hunting scene. The striped purple bison was being pursued in wild leaps by skinny human figures with bows and spears, painted with careless brushstrokes.

'What's it meant to be?' asked Geralt, unable to contain himself.

The elf glanced at him in passing, sticking the clean end of the brush in his mouth.

'It is,' he declared, 'a prehistoric painting executed by the primitive people who lived in this cave thousands of years ago and who mainly lived by hunting the purple bison, which became extinct long ago. Some of the prehistoric hunters were artists and felt a profound artistic need to immortalise what was in their hearts.'

'Fascinating.'

'It most certainly is,' the elf agreed. 'Your scholars have roamed through caves like this for ages, searching for traces of primitive man. And whenever they find something like this they are inordinately fascinated. For it is proof that you aren't strangers in this land and in this world. Proof that your forebears have lived here for centuries; thus proof that this world belongs to their heirs. Why, every race has the right to some roots. Even your – human

– race, whose roots should be sought in the treetops, after all. Ha, an amusing quip, don't you think? Worthy of an epigram. Are you fond of light poetry? What do you think I ought to add to the painting?'

'Draw huge, erect phalluses on the primitive hunters.'

'That's a thought.' The elf dipped his brush in the paint. 'The phallic cult was typical for primitive civilisations. It could also serve as the birth of a theory that the human race is yielding to physical degeneration. Its forebears had phalluses like clubs, but their descendants were left with ridiculous, vestigial little pricks . . . Thank you, Witcher.'

'Don't mention it. It was somehow in my heart. The paint looks very fresh for something prehistoric.'

'In three or four days the colours will fade due to the salt exuded by the wall and the painting will look so prehistoric you won't believe it. Your scholars will wet themselves with joy when they see it. Not one of them, I swear, will see through my deceit.'

'They will.'

'How is that?'

'You won't be able to resist signing your masterpiece, will you?'

The elf laughed dryly.

'Quite right! You've seen through me. Oh, fire of vanity, how difficult it is for an artist to quell you. I've already signed the cave painting. Right here.'

'That isn't a dragonfly?'

'No. It's an ideogram denoting my name. I am Crevan Espane aep Caomhan Macha. For convenience I use the alias Avallac'h, and you may also address me as such.'

'I shall be sure to.'

'You, though, are called Geralt of Rivia. You're a witcher. Presently you are not, however, destroying monsters or beasts, but are busy hunting for missing girls.'

'News spreads astonishingly quickly. Astonishingly far. And astonishingly deep. You allegedly foresaw that I'd show up here. You can foretell the future, I gather?'

'Anyone,' Avallac'h wiped his hands on a rag, 'can foretell the future. And everyone does it, for it is simple. It is no great art to foretell it. The art is in foretelling it accurately.'

'An elegant deduction, worthy of an epigram. You, naturally, can prophecy accurately.'

'And often. I, my dear Geralt, know much and am capable of much. Actually, my academic title – as you, humans, would say – indicates that. It reads in full "Aen Saevherne".'

'A Sage – a Knowing One.'

'Precisely.'

'And willing, I hope, to share that knowledge?'

Avallac'h said nothing for a moment.

'Share?' he finally drawled. 'With you? Knowledge, my dear, is a privilege, and privileges are only shared with one's equals. And why would I, an elf, a Sage, a member of the elite, share anything with a descendant of a creature that appeared in the universe barely five million years ago, having evolved from an ape, a rat, a jackal or some other such mammal? A creature that took around a million years to discover that one can execute some sort of operation with a gnawed bone using its two hairy hands? After which it shoved the bone up its rectum and shrieked for joy?'

The elf fell silent, turning and fixing his gaze on his painting.

'Why indeed,' he repeated, 'do you dare to think I would share any knowledge at all with you, human? Tell me!'

Geralt wiped the rest of the shit from his boot.

'Because, perhaps,' he replied dryly, 'it is inevitable?'

The elf spun around.

'What,' he asked through clenched teeth, 'is inevitable?'

'Perhaps –' Geralt didn't feel like raising his voice '– for the reason that a few years will pass and people will simply take all knowledge for themselves, heedless of whether anyone wants to share it with them or not? Including knowledge which you, elf and Sage, cunningly conceal behind cave paintings? Counting on the fact that people will not want to take pickaxes to that wall, painted with the false evidence of primitive human existence? Eh? O, my fire of vanity?'

The elf snorted. Quite cheerfully.

'Oh, yes,' he said. 'It would be vanity truly carried to stupidity to believe you wouldn't smash something. You smash everything. But what of it? What of it, man?'

'I don't know. Tell me. And if you don't think it fit, I'll take myself off. Ideally through a different exit, since your mischievous chums are waiting for me by the other one, longing to crack my ribs.'

'By all means.' The elf spread his arms wide in a sudden movement, and the rock wall opened with a grinding and a cracking, brutally splitting the purple bison in two. 'Leave this way. Tread towards the light. Metaphorically or literally, that is usually the right way.'

'A bit of a shame,' Geralt muttered. 'I liked the frescoes.'

'You must be jesting,' the elf said after a brief silence, sounding quite astonishingly kindly and friendly. 'The fresco won't be harmed. I shall close the rock with an identical charm, and not even the trace of a crack will remain. Come. I'll go out with you, I shall escort you. I've reached the conclusion that I have something to tell you. And show you.'

It was dark inside, but the Witcher knew right away that the cave was immense – he could tell from the temperature and air currents. The gravel they walked over was wet.

Avallac'h conjured light in the elven fashion, simply using a gesture, without uttering a spell. A glowing ball rose towards the ceiling and the formations of rock crystal in the cave walls sparkled in a myriad of reflections and gleams. Shadows danced. The Witcher gasped involuntarily.

It wasn't the first time he'd seen elven sculptures and statues, but the impression was the same each time. That the figures of elves and she-elves frozen in mid-movement, in mid-flicker, weren't the work of a sculptor's chisel, but the result of a powerful spell, able to change living tissue into the white marble of Amell. The nearest statue depicted a she-elf sitting with her feet tucked beneath her on a basalt slab. The she-elf was turning her head away, as though alarmed by the patter of approaching steps. She was utterly naked. The white marble, polished to a milky brilliance, meant one virtually felt the warmth emanating from the statue.

Avallac'h stopped and leaned against one of the columns marking the way among an avenue of statues.

'You have seen through me for a second time, Geralt,' he said softly. 'Yes, you were right, the bison cave painting *was* camouflage. Intended to discourage hacking and drilling through the

240

wall. Intended to defend everything in here from plunder and devastation. Every race – the elven too – has a right to its roots. What you see here are our roots. Tread carefully, please. It is essentially a graveyard.'

The reflections of light dancing over the rock crystals drew further details from the gloom. Beyond the avenue of statues could be seen colonnades, stairways, amphitheatrical galleries, arcades and peristyles. Everything made of white marble.

'I want it,' Avallac'h continued, stopping and indicating with a hand, 'to survive. Even when we depart, when this whole continent and this whole world ends up under a mile-thick layer of ice and snow, Tir ná Béa Arainne will endure. We shall leave this place, but one day we shall return. We elves. We are promised this by Aen Ithlinnespeath, the Ithlinne Aegli aep Aevenien prophecy.'

'Do you really believe in it? In that prophecy? Does your fatalism really run so deep?'

'Everything –' the elf looked not at him, but at the marble columns covered with reliefs as delicate as cobwebs '– has been foreseen and prophesied. Your arrival on the continent, the war, the shedding of elven and human blood. The rise of your race, your decadence. The battle between the rulers of the North and the South. And the king of the South shall rise up against the kings of the North and overrun their lands like a flood, they will be crushed, and their nations devastated . . . And so shall begin the extinction of the world. Do your recall Ithlinne's text, Witcher? Who is far shall die at once; who is near shall fall from the sword; who hides shall die of hunger, who survives shall perish from the frost . . . For Tedd Deireadh, the Time of the End, the Time of the Sword and the Battle Axe, the Time of Contempt, the Time of the White Cold and the Wolfish Snowstorm shall come . . . '

'Poetry.'

'Do you prefer it less poetic? As a result of a change in the angle of the sun's rays, the margin of permafrost will shift – significantly. Then the mountains will be crushed and pushed back southwards by the ice sliding from the North. Everything will be buried under snow. Under a thick layer more than a mile deep. And it will become very – *very* – cold.'

'We'll wear warm britches,' Geralt said without emotion. 'Sheepskins. And fur hats.'

'You took the words right out of my mouth,' the elf agreed calmly. 'And you'll survive in those hats and britches, in order to return one day, dig holes and poke around in these caves, to wreck and plunder. Ithlinne's prophecy doesn't say so, but I know it. It's impossible to utterly destroy humans and cockroaches; at least one pair always remains. As far as we elves are concerned, Ithlinne is more explicit: only those who follow the Swallow will survive. The Swallow, the symbol of spring, is the saviour, the one who will open the Forbidden Door, signal the way of salvation. And make possible the world's rebirth. The Swallow, the Child of the Elder Blood.'

'You mean Ciri?' Geralt burst out. 'Or Ciri's child? How? And why?'

Avallac'h seemed not to hear.

'The Swallow of the Elder Blood,' he said again. 'From her blood. Come. And look.'

The statue Avallac'h pointed at stood out even among the other astoundingly realistic statues; most captured mid-movement or mid-gesture. The white marble she-elf reclining on the slab gave the impression that – having been awoken – she was about to sit up and get to her feet. Her face was turned towards the empty place by her side, and her raised hand seemed to be touching something invisible.

There was an expression of calm happiness on the she-elf's face.

It was a long time before Avallac'h broke the silence.

'That is Lara Dorren aep Shiadhal. It's not a grave, naturally, but a cenotaph. Does the statue's position surprise you? Support was not gained for the plan to carve both of the legendary lovers in marble. Lara and Cregennan of Lod. Cregennan was a man; it would be sacrilege to waste Amell marble on a statue of him. It would be blasphemy to erect a statue of a man here, in Tir ná Béa Arainne. On the other hand, it would be an even greater crime to deliberately destroy the memory of this emotion. So a happy medium was found. Formally . . . Cregennan is not here. And yet he is. In Lara's aspect and pose. The lovers are together. Nothing was able to separate them. Neither death, nor oblivion . . . Nor hatred.'

It seemed to the Witcher that the elf's indifferent voice had changed for a moment. But that would have been impossible. Avallac'h approached the statue and stroked the marble arm with a cautious, gentle movement. Then he turned around and the usual, slightly sneering smile reappeared on his angular face.

'Do you know, Witcher, what the greatest snag of longevity is?'

'No.'

'Sex.'

'What?'

'You heard right. Sex. After almost a hundred years it becomes boring. There's nothing in it to fascinate or excite any longer, nothing that has the exciting appeal of novelty. It has all been done already . . . In this or that way, but it has happened. And then suddenly comes the Conjunction of the Spheres and you, people, appear here. Human survivors, come from another world, from your former world, which you managed utterly to destroy with your still-hirsute hands, barely five million years after evolving as a species. There's only a handful of you, your life expectancy is ridiculously low, so your survival depends on the pace of reproduction. Thus unbridled lust never leaves you, sex totally governs you; it's a drive more powerful even than the survival instinct. To die? Why not, if one can fuck around beforehand. That is your entire philosophy.'

Geralt didn't interrupt or comment, although he felt a strong desire to.

'And what suddenly happens?' Avallac'h continued. 'Elves, bored by she-elves, court the always-willing human females. Bored she-elves give themselves, out of perverse curiosity, to human males, always full of vigour and verve. And something happens that no one can explain: she-elves, who normally ovulate once every ten or twenty years, when copulating with a man begin to ovulate with each powerful orgasm. Some hidden hormone, or combination of hormones, became active. She-elves suddenly understand they can, in practice, only have children with humans. So, owing to the she-elves, we didn't exterminate you when we were still the more powerful race. And later you were more powerful and began to exterminate us. But you still had allies in the she-elves. For they were the advocates of coexistence and cooperation . . . and they didn't want to admit that essentially it was about commingling.'

'What does that –' Geralt cleared his throat '– have to do with me?'

'With you? Absolutely nothing. But with Ciri, a great deal. For Ciri is a descendant of Lara Dorren aep Shiadhal, and Lara Dorren was an advocate of coexistence with humans. Chiefly with one human. Cregennan of Lod, a human sorcerer. Lara Dorren coexisted with Cregennan often and effectively. To put it more simply: she became pregnant.'

The Witcher kept silent this time too.

'The snag was that Lara Dorren wasn't an ordinary she-elf. She was genetic potential. Especially prepared. The result of many years' work. In combination with another charge – an elven one, naturally – she was meant to bear an even more special child. Engaging with the seed of a man, she ruined that chance, wasted hundreds of years' planning and preparation. At least so it was thought at the time. No one supposed that the cross-breed begat by Cregennan could inherit anything positive from its pure-blood mother. No, such a misalliance could not bring any good—'

'For which reason,' Geralt interjected, 'he was severely punished.'

'Not the way you think.' Avallac'h glanced at him. 'Although the relationship between Lara Dorren and Cregennan caused incalculable damage to the elves, and it could have turned out well for humans, it was, however, humans – and not elves – who murdered Cregennan. Humans – and not elves – brought Lara to ruin. Thus it was, despite the fact that many elves had reason to hate the lovers. Personally, too.'

For the second time, the slight change in the elf's voice puzzled Geralt.

'One way or another,' Avallac'h continued, 'the peaceful co-existence burst like a soap bubble, and the races went for each other's throats. A war began which endures until today. And meanwhile Lara's genetic material . . . exists, as you've probably guessed. And has even developed. Unfortunately, it mutated. Yes, yes. Your Ciri is a mutant.'

This time, again, the elf didn't wait for a comment.

'Of course, the sorcerers had a hand in this, cleverly combining

244

breeding individuals into pairs, but it got out of control. Few can guess how Lara Dorren's genetic material regenerated so powerfully in Ciri, what the trigger was. I think it is known by Vilgefortz, the one who gave you a hiding on Thanedd. The sorcerers who experimented with Lara and Riannon's progeny, running a veritable breeding farm, didn't get the expected results, so they became bored and abandoned the experiment. But the experiment continued; just spontaneously. Ciri, the daughter of Pavetta, the granddaughter of Calanthe, the great-great-granddaughter of Riannon, was Lara Dorren's true descendant. Vilgefortz learned about it, probably by accident. It is also known about by Emhyr var Emreis, the Emperor of Nilfgaard.'

'And you know about it.'

'I know more about it than the two of them. But that means nothing. The mill of destiny is turning, the querns of fate are grinding . . . Whatever is destined must occur.'

'So what must occur?'

'Whatever is destined to. That which was determined above, in the metaphorical sense, of course. Something that is determined by the action of an unerringly functioning mechanism, at the root of which lies the Purpose, the Plan and the Result.'

'That's either poetry or metaphysics. Or the one and the other, for they are occasionally difficult to distinguish. Are any hard facts possible? If only a very few? I'd love to discuss this and that with you, but it so happens I'm in a hurry.'

Avallac'h gave him a long look.

'And where are you hurrying to? Ah, forgive me . . . You, it seems to me, haven't understood anything I've said to you. So I'll tell you straight: your great rescue expedition is meaningless. It has lost all meaning.

'There are several reasons,' the elf continued, looking at the Witcher's granite-like face. 'Firstly, it's too late now, the serious evil has already occurred; you're no longer in a position to save the girl from it. Secondly, now that she has taken the right road, the Swallow will cope wonderfully by herself. She carries too mighty a force inside her to fear anything. She doesn't need your help. And thirdly . . . Hmmm . . . '

'I'm still all ears, Avallac'h. All ears!'

'Thirdly ... Thirdly, someone else will help her now. You can't be so arrogant as to think that the girl's destiny is exclusively bound to you.'

'Is that all?'

'Yes.'

'Then farewell.'

'Wait.'

'I said I'm in a hurry.'

'Let's suppose for a moment,' the elf said serenely, 'that I know what will happen, that I can see the future. What if I tell you what is to happen, what will happen anyway, irrespective of the efforts you make? Of the initiatives already undertaken? What if I told you that you could search for a peaceful place on earth and stay there, doing nothing, waiting for the inevitable consequences of the course of events. Would you choose to do something like that?'

'No.'

'What if I communicated to you that your activities – testifying to your lack of faith in the unwavering mechanisms of the Purpose, Plan and Result – may, though the likelihood is slight, indeed change something, but only for the worse? Would you reconsider? Oh, I see from your expression that you wouldn't. Then I'll simply ask you: why not?'

'Do you really want to know?'

'I do.'

'Because I don't believe in your metaphysical platitudes about goals, plans and preordained ideas of creators. Nor do I believe in the celebrated prophecy of Ithlinne or other prophecies. I consider them, if you can imagine it, the same bullshit and humbug as your cave painting. The purple bison, Avallac'h. Nothing more. I don't know if you can't – or won't – help me. Nonetheless, I don't feel resentment towards you . . . '

'You say I can't or don't want to help you. And how might I help?'

Geralt pondered for a moment, absolutely aware that much depended on how the question was put.

'Will I get Ciri back?'

The answer was immediate.

'You will. Only to lose her at once. And to be clear: forever;

irrevocably. Before it comes to that, you will lose everybody who accompanies you. You will lose one of your companions in the next few weeks, perhaps even days. Perhaps even hours.'

'Thank you.'

'I haven't finished yet. The direct effect of your interference in the grinding querns of the Purpose and the Plan will be the death of tens of thousands of people. Which, as a matter of fact, doesn't matter much, since soon after, tens of millions of people will lose their lives. The world as you know it will simply vanish, cease to exist, in order – after a suitable time has passed – to revive in a totally different form. But in fact no one has, nor will have, any influence on it, no one is capable of preventing it nor staving off the course of events. Not you, not I, not sorcerers nor Sages. Not even Ciri. What do you say to that?'

'Purple bison. All the same, I thank you, Avallac'h.'

'While we're about it,' the elf shrugged, 'I'm somewhat curious as to what a pebble falling in the gears of the querns might accomplish . . . May I do anything else for you?'

'Not really. Because you can't show me Ciri, I imagine?'

'Who said so?'

Geralt held his breath. Avallac'h headed towards the cave wall with rapid steps, indicating the Witcher to follow him.

'The walls of Tir ná Béa Arainne –' he pointed to the sparkling rock crystals '– have special qualities. And I, though I say it as shouldn't, have special abilities. Place your hands on this. Fix your gaze on it. Think intensively. About how much she needs you right now. And declare, so to speak, the mental willingness to help. Think about how you want to run and rescue her, be beside her; something like that. The image should appear by itself. And be distinct. Look, but refrain from impulsive reactions. Say nothing. It will be a vision, not communication.'

He obeyed.

The first images, in spite of the promise, weren't distinct. They were vague, but so brutal that he stepped back involuntarily. A severed hand on a table . . . Blood splashed on a glazed surface . . . Skeletons on skeleton horses . . . Yennefer, in manacles . . .

A tower? A black tower? And behind it, in the background . . . The northern lights?

And suddenly, without warning, the image became all too clear.

'Dandelion!' Geralt yelled. 'Milva! Angoulême!'

'Eh?' Avallac'h took an interest. 'Ah, yes. You seem to have spoiled everything.'

Geralt leaped back from the cave wall, almost falling over on a basalt plinth.

'It doesn't bloody matter!' he cried. 'Listen, Avallac'h, I must get to that druidic forest as quickly as possible . . .'

'Caed Myrkvid?'

'Very likely! My companions are in mortal danger there! They're fighting for their lives! Other people are also in danger . . . What's the quickest way . . . ? Oh, dammit! I'm going back for my sword and horse—'

'No horse,' the elf calmly interrupted, 'is capable of carrying you to the Myrkvid grove before nightfall—'

'But I—'

'I haven't finished yet. Go and get your legendary sword, and meanwhile I'll find you a mount. A perfect steed for mountain tracks. It's a somewhat unusual one, I'd say . . . But with its help you'll be in Caed Myrkvid in less than half an hour.'

*

The knocker reeked like a horse – but that was where the similarity ended. Geralt had once seen in Mahakam a mountain goat-riding contest organised by dwarves, which had seemed to be a totally reckless sport. But it was only now, as he sat on the back of the knocker as it hurtled insanely up the cliff, that he learned what true recklessness was.

In order not to fall off, he dug his fingers tightly into the rough shaggy coat and squeezed his thighs against the monster's fleecy sides. The knocker stank of sweat, urine and vodka. It flew as though possessed, the earth thudding under the impact of its gigantic feet, as though its soles were of bronze. Slowing slightly, it climbed up hillsides and pelted down them so fast the wind howled in Geralt's ears. It rushed across ridges, mountain paths and ledges so narrow Geralt kept his eyes tightly closed so as not to look down. It cleared waterfalls, cascades, chasms and clefts too extreme even for a mountain goat, and each successful leap was accompanied by a savage and deafening roar. That is, more savage and deafening than the knocker's usual roar – which was something it did almost constantly.

'Don't race like that!' The rush of air shoved the words back down his throat.

'Why not?'

'You've been drinking!'

'Uuuaaahaaaaaaaa!'

They raced on. The wind whistled in his ears.

The knocker reeked.

The clatter of immense feet on rock fell silent. Instead, rock fields and scree rattled. Then the ground became less rocky, and something that might have been a dwarf pine flashed by. Then a blur of green and brown, for the knocker was loping in insane bounds through a fir forest. The scent of resin mingled with the monster's stench.

'Uaaahaaaaaa!'

The firs ceased and fallen leaves whispered. Now red, now claret, ochre and golden.

'Slow down!'

'Uaaaahahhahaha!'

The knocker cleared a pile of fallen trees with a huge bound. Geralt almost bit his tongue off.

*

The breakneck ride ended as unceremoniously as it had begun. The knocker dug its heels into the ground, roared, and tossed the Witcher onto the leaf-strewn forest floor. Geralt lay still for a while and couldn't even curse, from lack of breath. Then he stood up, hissing and rubbing his knee, which had begun to throb again.

'You never fell off,' the knocker stated with surprise in its voice. 'Well, well.'

Geralt didn't comment.

'We've arrived.' The knocker pointed with one shaggy paw. 'That's Caed Myrkvid.'

Beneath them was a basin, densely filled with mist. The tops of great trees showed through the haze.

'That fog,' the knocker anticipated the question, sniffing, 'isn't natural. What's more I can smell smoke from over there. If I were you, I'd hurry. Eeeh, I'd go with you . . . I'm sick with the desire to fight! And I dreamed as a child of one day charging at people with a witcher on me back! But Avallac'h forbad me from showing myself. It's to do with the safety of our whole tribe. . . '

'I know.'

'Don't bear a grudge that I smacked you in the mouth.'

'I don't.'

'You're alright. For a human.'

'Thank you. For the lift too.'

The knocker bared his teeth among his red beard, and breathed vodka.

'The pleasure's all mine.'

*

The fog lying on Myrkvid Forest was dense and had an irregular shape, calling to mind a heap of whipped cream squeezed onto a cake by a lunatic cook. The fog reminded the Witcher of Brokilon – the Forest of the Dryads was often covered by a similarly dense, protective and camouflaging magical haze. Like Brokilon it had the dignified and menacing atmosphere of an ancient forest, here at the edge consisting predominantly of alder and beech.

And just like in Brokilon, right at the edge of the forest, on the leaf-strewn road, Geralt almost tripped over a corpse.

*

The cruelly massacred people weren't druids or Nilfgaardians, and they certainly didn't belong to Nightingale and Schirrú's hassa. Before Geralt had even spied the outlines of wagons in the fog, he recalled that Regis had spoken of pilgrims. It appeared that for some the pilgrimage had not ended happily.

The stench of smoke and burning, unpleasant in the damp air, became more and more distinct, and pointed the way. Soon after, the way was also indicated by voices. Cries. And the discordant music of fiddles. Geralt made haste.

A wagon stood on the rain-softened road. More bodies lay beside the wheels.

One of the bandits was rummaging around the wagon, chucking objects and tackle onto the road. Another was holding the unharnessed horses and a third was stripping a foxskin coat from a dead pilgrim. A fourth was sawing a fiddle with a bow – evidently found among the loot – and utterly failing to get even a single pure note from the instrument.

The cacophony came in useful. It muffled Geralt's steps.

The music broke off abruptly, the fiddle stings whined piercingly, the brigand slammed down onto the leaves and spattered them with blood. The one holding the horses didn't even manage to shout; the sihill severed his windpipe. The third brigand didn't manage to jump down from the wagon. He fell, yelling, with his femoral artery carved open. The last one even managed to draw his sword. But not to raise it.

Geralt shook blood from the fuller with his thumb.

'Yes, boys,' he said to the forest and the scent of smoke. 'This was a stupid idea. You oughtn't to have listened to Nightingale and Schirrú. You should have stayed at home.'

*

He soon came across further wagons and further victims. Druids in bloodstained white robes also lay among the numerous mutilated pilgrims. The smoke from the now close fire crawled low over the ground.

This time, the brigands were more vigilant. He only managed to stalk one of them, who was occupied pulling cheap rings and bracelets from the bloody hands of a murdered woman. Geralt, without hesitation, slashed the bandit, the bandit roared, and then the remaining men – brigands mixed up with Nilfgaardians – attacked him, yelling.

He dodged into the forest, to the foot of the nearest tree, so the trunk would protect his back. But before the brigands could run over, hooves thudded, and from the bushes and fog emerged a mighty horse draped in a caparison with a red and gold diagonal chequered pattern. The horse was carrying a rider clad in full armour, a snow-white cloak, and a helmet with a perforated pig-faced visor. Before the bandits could compose themselves, the knight was already breathing down their necks and carving every which way with his sword, and blood was gushing in fountains. It was a splendid sight.

Geralt didn't have time to watch, however, having two on his hands himself: a brigand in a cherry-red jerkin and a black-uniformed Nilfgaardian. The brigand exposed himself as he lunged, so Geralt slashed him across the face, and the Nilfgaardian – seeing teeth flying – took to his heels and vanished into the fog.

Geralt was almost trampled by the horse in the chequered caparison, now running and riderless.

Without delaying, he leaped through the undergrowth towards cries, curses and thudding.

Three bandits had dragged the knight in the white cloak from the saddle and were trying to kill him. One of them, standing with legs astride, was smiting with a poleaxe; the second was striking with a sword; and the third – small and red-haired – was hopping beside them like a hare, seeking a chance and an unprotected place where he could stab with his bear spear. The knight – lying on his back – was yelling incomprehensibly from inside his helmet and deflecting the blows with a shield held in both hands. The shield sank lower with each blow; it was almost resting on his breastplate. There was no doubt. One or two more blows and the knight's innards would burst through every slit in his armour.

Geralt was in the thick of it in three bounds, slashing the hopping red-head with the bear spear across the nape and carving open the belly of the one with the poleaxe. The knight, agile in spite of his armour, whacked the third brigand in the knee with the shield rim, and pummelled him thrice in the face as he lay on the ground until blood sprayed across his shield. He rose onto his knees, fumbled among ferns in search of his sword, buzzing like a great iron-plated drone. He suddenly saw Geralt and froze.

'In whose hands am I?' He trumpeted from deep within his helmet.

'In no one's. The men lying there are also my foes.'

'Aha . . .' The knight tried to raise his visor, but the metal plate was bent and the mechanism had blocked. ''Pon my word! Thank you a hundredfold for your succour.'

'I thank you. For it was you who came to my aid.'

'Indeed? When?'

He didn't see anything, thought Geralt. He hadn't even noticed me through the holes in that iron pot.

'What is your name?' the knight asked.

'Geralt. Of Rivia.'

'Coat of arms?'

'It is not the time, sir knight, for heraldry.'

''Pon my word, 'tis the truth, stout-hearted Sir Geralt.' Having found his sword the knight stood up. His chipped shield – like the horse's caparison – was decorated with a gold and red diagonal chequered pattern, the letters A and H alternating in the fields.

'They are not my ancestral arms,' he boomed in explanation. 'They are the initials of my suzerain lady, Duchess Anna Henarietta. I'm called the Chequered Knight. I'm a knight errant. And forbidden from revealing my name or arms. I have taken knightly vows. 'Pon my word, thanks again for the help, sir knight.'

'The pleasure's all mine.'

One of the defeated bandits groaned and rustled in the leaves. The Chequered Knight leaped and pinned him to the ground with a mighty thrust. The brigand's arms and legs waved like a spider impaled on a pin.

'Let us hurry,' the knight said. 'The rabble is still raging here. 'Pon my word, it's not time to repose yet!'

'True,' Geralt agreed. 'There's a gang marauding through the forest, killing pilgrims and druids. My friends are in a predicament . . .'

'Excuse me for a moment.'

A second brigand was showing signs of life. He was also vigorously pinned and his turned-up feet cut such a caper that his boots fell off.

''Pon my word!' The Chequered Knight wiped his sword on the moss. 'These good-for-nothings are loath to depart this life! Let it not astound you, sir knight, that I'm finishing off the wounded. 'Pon my word, I've not done it for many years. But these imps recover so swiftly an honest fellow may only envy them. Ever since I happened to cross swords with the same rascal thrice in a row, I began to finish them off more meticulously. Once and for all.'

'I understand.'

'I – you see – am errant. But not, 'pon my word, erratic! Oh, it's my horse. Come here, Bucephalus!'

*

The forest became more open and brighter; great oaks with spreading but thin crowns began to predominate. They could now smell the smoke and stench of the fire nearby. And a moment later they could see it.

Three cottages with thatched roofs – an entire small settlement – were on fire. The tarpaulins of the nearby wagons were also on fire. Corpses were lying between the wagons; from a distance it was evident that many were wearing white druidic gowns.

The bandits and Nilfgaardians, drumming up courage by yelling, and concealed behind wagons they were pushing in front of them, were attacking a large house on stilts leaning against the trunk of a gigantic oak. The house was built from robust beams with a shingle roof down which the torches thrown by the bandits were harmlessly rolling. The besieged house was defending itself and striking back effectively – before Geralt's eyes one of the brigands leaned imprudently out from behind a wagon and fell as though struck by lightning with an arrow in his skull.

'Your friends,' the Chequered Knight displayed his acuity, 'must be in that building! 'Pon my word, they're in desperate straits! Onward! Let us hasten to their aid!'

Geralt heard screeching yells and orders, and recognised the robber Nightingale with his bandaged cheek. He also glimpsed the half-elf Schirrú, hiding behind some Nilfgaardians in black cloaks. Suddenly horns roared, so loudly that leaves fell from the oak trees. The hooves of war horses rumbled and the swords and armour of charging knights flashed. The robbers fled, yelling, in all directions.

''Pon my word!' the Chequered Knight roared, spurring on his

254

horse. 'It's my comrades! They're ahead of us! Attack, so a little glory will be left for us! Smite, kill!'

Galloping ahead on Bucephalus the Chequered Knight fell on the fleeing robbers, hacked down two in a flash, and scattered the rest like a hawk among sparrows. Two of them turned towards Geralt, and the Witcher dealt with them in the blink of an eye.

A third shot at him with a Gabriel.

A certain Gabriel, a craftsman from Verden, had invented and patented a miniature crossbow. He advertised them with the slogan "Defend yourself". His handbill declared "Banditry and violence are rampant among us. The law is powerless and inept. Defend yourself! Don't leave home without a handy Gabriel crossbow. A Gabriel is your guardian, a Gabriel will protect you and your dear ones from bandits."

Sales were phenomenal. Soon every bandit packed a Gabriel during robberies.

Geralt was a witcher and could dodge a bolt. But he'd forgotten about his painful knee. His evasive manoeuvre was an inch late, and the leaf-shaped point gashed his ear. The pain blinded him, but just for a moment. The brigand was too slow to reload and defend himself. The furious Witcher slashed him across the hands, and then disembowelled him with a sweeping flourish of his sihill.

Geralt hadn't even managed to wipe the blood from his ear and neck when he was attacked by a small character as agile as a weasel, with unnaturally shining eyes, armed with a curved Zerrikanian sabre which he was twirling with admirable skill. He parried two of Geralt's blows, and the fine steel of the two blades rang and showered sparks. The weasel was alert and keen-eyed – he noticed at once that the Witcher was limping. He immediately began to circle and attack from a more favourable position. He was astonishingly quick. The sabre's blade seemed to wail as he made dangerous diagonal thrusts. Geralt was finding it more and more difficult to avoid the blows. He was limping worse and worse, forced to stand on his aching leg.

The weasel suddenly hunched forward, jumped, and made a dexterous feint and lunge, slashing diagonally downwards. Geralt parried obliquely and deflected. The bandit spun nimbly, moving from his stance to a nasty cut from below, when he suddenly goggled, sneezed loudly and covered himself in snot, dropping his guard for a moment. The Witcher jabbed him fast in the neck and the blade went in as far as the vertebrae.

'Well, who'll tell me now,' he panted, looking at the twitching corpse, 'that taking drugs isn't bad for your health?'

A bandit attacking him with a raised club tripped and fell face down in the mud, an arrow sticking out of the back of his head.

'I'm coming, Witcher!' Milva screamed. 'I'm coming! Hold on!'

Geralt turned, but there was no one left to hack. Milva had shot the only brigand remaining in the vicinity. The rest fled into the forest, pursued by the colourful knighthood. Several were being tormented by the Chequered Knight on Bucephalus. He caught them, and his terrible raging could be heard from the forest.

One of the black-uniformed Nilfgaardians, not finished off precisely, suddenly leaped to his feet and bolted. Milva raised and tautened her bow in a second. The fletchings howled and the Nilfgaardian fell on the leaves with a grey-feathered arrow between his shoulder blades. The archer sighed heavily.

'We'll hang for this,' she said.

'Why do you think so?'

'This is Nilfgaard, isn't it? And it's the second month I've been mainly shooting at Nilfgaardians.'

'This is Toussaint, not Nilfgaard.' Geralt felt the side of his head, and took away a bloody hand.

'Dammit. What is it? Have a look, Milva.'

The archer examined it carefully and critically.

'Your ear's been torn off,' she finally said. 'Nothing to worry about.'

'Easy for you to say. I was fond of that ear. Help me to bind it with something, it's dripping down my collar. Where are Dandelion and Angoulême?'

'In the cottage, with the pilgrims . . . Oh, a pox on it . . . '

Hooves pounded, and from the mist emerged three riders on warhorses, cloaks and pennants fluttering as they galloped. Before their war cries resounded, Geralt had grabbed Milva by the arm and pulled her under a wagon. There was no fooling around with someone charging with a lance, which gave the riders an effective range of ten feet in front of their horse's head.

'Get out!' The knights' mounts churned the earth around the wagon with their horseshoes. 'Drop your weapons and get out!'

'We're going to hang,' Milva murmured. She might have been right.

'Ha, thugs!' one of the knights, bearing a shield with a black bull's head on a silver field, roared . 'Ha, rogues! 'Pon my word, you shall hang!'

''Pon my word!' crowed the other, with a uniformly blue shield, in a youthful voice. 'We'll carve them up on the spot!'

'Hi, I say! Stop!'

The Chequered Knight emerged from the fog on Bucephalus. He had finally managed to lift his twisted visor, from beneath which luxuriant flaxen moustaches now peeped.

'Free them with all haste!' he called. 'They are not bandits, but upright and honest folk. The lady manfully acted in defence of the pilgrims. And that fellow is a goodly knight!'

'A goodly knight?' Bull's Head raised his visor and scrutinised Geralt extremely incredulously. ''Pon my word! It cannot be!'

''Pon my word!' The Chequered Knight thumped an armoured fist into his breastplate. 'It can, I give my word! This doughty fellow saved my life when I was in need, after I was flung to the ground by ne'er-do-wells. He is called Geralt of Rivia.'

'Arms?'

'I'm forbidden from revealing them,' the Witcher grunted. 'I can share neither my true name nor my arms. I have taken knightly vows. I am the errant Geralt.'

'Oooh!' a familiar insolent voice suddenly yelled. 'Look what the cat dragged in. Ha, I told you, aunty, that the Witcher would come and rescue us!'

'And just in time!' shouted Dandelion, approaching with Angoulême and a small group of terrified pilgrims. He was carrying his lute and the ever-present tube of scrolls. 'And not a second too soon. You have a fine sense of drama, Geralt. You ought to write plays for the stage!'

He suddenly fell silent. Bull's Head leaned over in his saddle and his eyes shone.

'Viscount Julian?'

'Baron de Peyrac-Peyran?'

257

Two more knights emerged from behind the oaks. One, in a great helm adorned with a very good likeness of a white swan with outstretched wings, was leading two prisoners in a lasso. The other knight, errant, but practical, was preparing a noose and looking for a suitable bough.

'Neither Nightingale,' Angoulême noticed the Witcher's expression, 'nor Schirrú. Pity.'

'Pity,' Geralt admitted. 'But we'll try to correct that. Sir knight . . .'

But Bull's Head – or rather Baron de Peyrac-Peyran – wasn't paying any attention to him. He only had eyes, it seemed, for Dandelion.

''Pon my word,' he drawled. 'My eyes do not deceive me! It's Viscount Julian in person. Ha! The Duchess *will* be pleased!'

'Who is Viscount Julian?' the Witcher asked curiously.

'That would be me,' Dandelion muttered. 'Don't interfere, Geralt.'

'Lady Henrietta *will* be pleased,' Baron de Peyrac-Peyran repeated. 'Ha, 'pon my word! We shall take you all to Beauclair Castle. But no excuses, viscount. I won't hear of any excuse!'

'Some of the brigands fled,' Geralt spoke in quite a cool tone. 'I suggest we catch them first. And then think about what to do with this day – so interestingly begun. What say you, baron?'

''Pon my word,' said Bull's Head, 'nothing will come of it. Pursuit is impossible. The criminals fled across the stream, and we mustn't put a foot over it, not even a scrap of hoof. That part of the Myrkvid Forest is an inviolable sanctuary, in accordance with the compacts entered into with the druids by Her Majesty Duchess Anna Henarietta, who benignly reigns over Toussaint—'

'The robbers bolted in there, dammit!' Geralt interrupted, growing furious. 'They're going into that inviolable sanctuary to kill! And you're telling me about some compacts—'

'We've given our knightly word!' It seemed a mutton head would have suited Baron de Peyrac-Peyran's shield better than a bull's head. 'We are forbad! Compacts! Not a single step onto druidic territory!'

'If they're forbidden, well that's too bad,' Angoulême snorted, pulling two bandit horses by their bridles. 'Drop that empty talk,

258

Witcher. Let's go. I still have unfinished business with Nightingale and you, I think, would like to talk some more with the half-elf.'

'I'm with you,' said Milva. 'I'll just find some mare or other.'

'Me too,' Dandelion muttered. 'I'm with you too . . . '

'Oh, no, no, no!' called the bull-headed baron. ''Pon my word, Viscount Julian will ride with us to Beauclair Castle. The duchess wouldn't forgive us if after meeting you we didn't bring you to her. I shan't stop the rest of you, you are free in your plans and ideas. As the companions of Viscount Julian, Her Grace, Lady Henarietta, would have gladly received you with all due respect and invited you to stay at the castle, but why, if you scorn her hospitality. . . '

'We scorn it not,' Geralt interrupted, with a menacing glance restraining Angoulême, who was making insulting gestures with her hand behind the baron's back. 'Far be it from us to scorn it. We shall not fail to pay our respects and due homage to the duchess. But first we will accomplish what we must accomplish. We also gave our word; one might say that we've also made compacts. Once we have carried them out we shall make for Beauclair Castle. We shall unfailingly go there.'

'If only,' he added knowingly and with emphasis, 'to ensure that no disgrace or dishonour befalls our comrade, Dandelion. I meant Julian, by thunder.'

''Pon my word!' the baron suddenly laughed. 'No disgrace nor dishonour will befall Viscount Julian, I'm prepared to give my word on it! For I omitted to tell you, viscount, that Duke Raymund died of apoplexy two years past.'

'Ha, ha!' Dandelion shouted, beaming all over. 'The duke kicked the bucket! These truly are marvellous and joyous tidings! I mean, I meant to say, sorrow and grief, a great loss . . . May the earth lie lightly on him . . . If that is the case, let's ride with all haste to Beauclair, noble knights! Geralt, Milva and Angoulême, I'll see you in the castle!'

*

They forded the stream and spurred the horses into the forest, among spreading oaks and stirrup-high ferns. Milva found the trail of the fleeing gang without difficulty. They rode as quickly as they could, for Geralt feared for the druids. He was afraid the survivors of the gang, feeling safe, would want to seek vengeance on the druids for the massacre sustained from the knights errant of Toussaint.

'Well, Dandelion's come up trumps,' Angoulême suddenly said. 'When Nightingale's men surrounded us in that cottage, he told me what he feared in Toussaint.'

'I'd guessed,' Witcher replied. 'I just didn't know he'd aimed so high. The duchess, ho!'

'It was a good few years ago. And Duke Raymund, the one who croaked, had apparently sworn he'd tear out the poet's heart, have it roasted and make his inconstant duchess eat it for supper. Dandelion's lucky he didn't fall into the duke's clutches while he was still alive. We're also lucky . . .'

'That remains to be seen.'

'Dandelion claims that Duchess Henarietta is madly in love with him.'

'Dandelion always claims that.'

'Shut your traps!' Milva snapped, reining in her horse and reaching for her bow.

A brigand rushed blindly towards them, without a hat, weaving from oak to oak. He was running, falling over, getting up and running again. And screaming. Shrilly, dreadfully, awfully.

'What the . . . ?' Angoulême asked in astonishment.

Milva tautened her bow in silence. She didn't shoot, but waited until the brigand approached and rushed straight for them, as though he couldn't see them. He ran between the horses of the Witcher and Angoulême. They saw his face, as white as a sheet and contorted in horror. They saw his bulging eyes.

'What the . . . ?' Angoulême repeated.

Milva recovered from her astonishment, turned in the saddle and sent an arrow into the fleeing man's back. The brigand roared and tumbled into the ferns.

The earth shook, making acorns fall from a nearby oak.

'I wonder,' said Angoulême, 'what he was fleeing from . . .'

The earth shook again. The bushes rustled and broken branches cracked.

'What is it?' Milva stammered, standing up in her stirrups. 'What is it, Witcher?'

Geralt looked, saw it and sighed loudly. Angoulême also saw it. And paled.

'Oh, fuck!'

Milva's horse also saw it. It neighed wildly, reared and then bucked. The archer flew from the saddle and sprawled heavily onto the ground. The horse raced into the forest. Without a second thought the Witcher's steed rushed after it, unfortunately choosing a path under an overhanging oak branch. The branch toppled the Witcher from the saddle. The impact and the pain in his knee almost made him lose consciousness.

Angoulême managed to stay in control of her frenzied horse the longest, but finally she too ended up on the ground and her horse fled, almost trampling Milva as she was getting up.

And they saw more clearly the thing that was coming for them. And absolutely, absolutely lost their astonishment at the animals' panic.

The creature resembled a gigantic tree, a branching, ancient oak; perhaps it *was* an oak. But if so it was a very unusual oak. Instead of standing somewhere in a clearing among fallen leaves and acorns, instead of letting squirrels scamper over it and linnets shit on it, this oak was marching briskly through the forest, stamping its sturdy roots steadily and waving its boughs. The stout trunk – or torso – of the monster had a diameter of more or less four yards, and the hollow gaping in it was probably not a hollow, but its maw, for it was snapping with a sound like the slamming of a heavy door.

Though the ground trembled beneath its terrible weight, making it difficult for them to keep their balance, the creature was loping through the ravines quite nimbly. And it wasn't doing it aimlessly.

In front of their eyes the monster swung its boughs, swished its branches and plucked from a pit a bandit who was cowering there, just as deftly as a stork plucks a frog hidden in the grass. Entwined in the branches, the thug hung among the boughs, howling pitifully. Geralt saw that the monster was carrying three brigands caught in the same way. And one Nilfgaardian.

261

'Run . . .' he moaned, vainly trying to stand. He felt as though someone was banging a white-hot nail into his knee with the rhythmic blows of a hammer. 'Milva . . . Angoulême . . . Run . . .'

'We won't leave you!'

The tree creature heard them, stamped its roots joyfully and rushed towards them. Angoulême, vainly trying to lift Geralt, swore hideously. With trembling hands, Milva tried to nock an arrow on the bowstring. Quite pointlessly.

'Run away!'

It was already too late. The tree creature was upon them. Paralysed by terror, they could now see its prey: four robbers, hanging in a tangle of branches. Two were still alive, for they were emitting hoarse croaks and kicking their legs. The third, probably unconscious, was hanging limply. The monster was clearly trying to catch its prey alive. But it had been unsuccessful with the fourth, and it had inadvertently squeezed too hard – which was obvious from its victim's bulging eyes and distended tongue, which was flopping down over a chin soiled with blood and vomit.

The next second they were hanging in the air, tangled in the branches, all three of them howling to high heaven.

'Graze, graze, graze,' they heard from below, near the roots. 'Graze, graze, Little Tree.'

A young druidess in a white robe with a flower wreath on her head strode behind the tree creature, driving it lightly with a leafy twig.

'Don't harm them, Little Tree, don't squeeze. Gently. Graze, graze, graze.'

'We aren't brigands . . .' Geralt grunted from above, barely able to produce a sound from his chest, which was being crushed by the bough. 'Order it to let us go . . . We're innocent . . .'

'They all say that.' The druidess shooed away a little butterfly fluttering around her brow. 'Graze, graze, graze.'

'I've pissed myself . . .' Angoulême whimpered. 'I've bloody pissed myself!'

Milva only wheezed. Her head was lolling on her chest. Geralt swore vilely. It was the only thing he could do.

Driven by the druidess, the tree creature ran jauntily through the forest. During the run, all of the prisoners – at least those that were conscious – teeth were chattering to the rhythm of the creature's leaps, so loudly it echoed.

After a short while they were in a large clearing. Geralt saw a group of white-robed druids, and besides them another tree creature. The other had a poorer collection – only three bandits hung from its boughs, and probably only one was still alive.

'Oh, criminals, malefactors, oh, contemptible ones!' declaimed one of the druids from below. He was an old man resting on a long crosier. 'Observe carefully. See what punishment befalls criminals and base individuals in Myrkvid Forest. Look on and remember. We shall release you, that you might tell others about what you will soon behold. As a warning!'

In the very centre of the clearing stood a cage woven from wicker, a great, human-shaped effigy upon a huge pile of logs and faggots. The cage was full of yelling and struggling people. The Witcher could clearly hear the frog-like croaking of the robber Nightingale, hoarse with terror. He saw the face of the half-elf Schirrú, as white as a sheet and contorted in panicked fear, pressed against the wicker lattice.

'Druids!' Geralt yelled, puting all his strength into the cry, in order to be heard despite the general clamour. 'Lady flaminika! I am the Witcher Geralt!'

'I beg your pardon?' responded a tall, thin woman with hair the colour of grey steel falling over her back, bound around her brow with a wreath of mistletoe.

'I am Geralt . . . The Witcher . . . A friend of Emiel Regis . . .'

'Again, please. I didn't catch that.'

'Geraaaaalt! A friend of the vampiiiire's!'

'Oh! You ought to have said so at once!'

At a sign from the druidess, the tree creature put them on the ground. Not very gently. Milva was unconscious, with blood dripping from her nose. Geralt stood up with difficulty and kneeled before her.

The steely-haired flaminika stood beside them and gave a slight cough. Her face was very lean, even haggard, evoking unpleasant associations of a skull covered in skin. Her cornflower-blue eyes were kind and gentle.

'I believe she has broken ribs,' she said, looking at Milva. 'But

263

we shall soon remedy that. Our healers will give her help immediately. I regret what has happened. But how was I to know who you were? I didn't invite you to Caed Myrkvid or give my permission for you to enter our sanctuary. Emiel Regis vouched for you, admittedly, but the presence of a witcher in our forest, a paid killer of living creatures . . .'

'I shall get out of here without a moment's delay, honourable flaminika,' Geralt assured her. 'As soon as I—'

He broke off, seeing druids with flaming torches walking up to the pyre and the effigy full of people.

'No!' he cried, clenching his fists. 'Stop!'

'That cage,' said the flaminika, seeming not to hear him, 'was originally meant to serve as a winter manger for starving animals, was meant to have stood in the forest, stuffed with hay. But when we seized those scoundrels, I recalled the nasty rumours and calumnies which people spread about us. Very well, I thought, you can have your Wicker Hag. You made it up as a horrific nightmare, so I shall treat you to that nightmare . . .'

'Order them to stop,' the Witcher gasped. 'Honourable flaminika . . . Don't set light to it . . . One of the bandits has important information for me . . .'

The flaminika folded her arms on her chest. Her cornflower-blue eyes were still soft and gentle.

'Oh, no,' she said dryly. 'No chance. I don't believe in the institution of turning imperial evidence. Wriggling out of a punishment is immoral.'

'Stop!' The Witcher yelled. 'Don't set fire to it! Stooo—'

The flaminika made a short gesture with her hand and Little Tree, still standing nearby, stamped down its roots and laid a bough on the Witcher's shoulder. Geralt sat down with a thump.

'Light it!' the flaminika ordered. 'I'm sorry, Witcher, but it must be thus. We druids cherish and venerate life in all its forms. But sparing the lives of criminals is sheer stupidity. Only terror deters criminals. So we shall give them an example of it. I pin great hopes on not having to repeat this example.'

The brushwood caught fire in an instant. The pyre belched smoke and flames leaped up. The yelling and screaming coming from the Wicker Hag made the Witcher's hair stand on end. Of

264

course, it was impossible among the cacophony – made louder by the crackle of the fire – but it seemed to Geralt that he could make out Nightingale's desperate croaking and the high-pitched, pain-filled shrieks of the half-elf Schirrú.

The half-elf had been right, he thought. Death isn't always the same.

And then – after a terribly long time – the pyre and the Wicker Hag mercifully exploded into an inferno of roaring fire, a fire in which nothing could survive.

'Your medallion, Geralt,' said Angoulême, standing beside him.

'Eh?' He cleared his throat, for his throat was tight. 'What did you say?'

'Your silver medallion with the wolf. Schirrú had it. Now you've lost it forever. It'll melt in that heat.'

'Too bad,' he said a moment later, looking into the flaminika's cornflower-blue eyes. 'I'm no longer a witcher. I've stopped being a witcher. I've learned that now. On Thanedd, in the Tower of the Seagull. In Brokilon. On the bridge on the Yaruga. In the cave beneath Gorgon. And here, in Myrkvid Forest. No, I'm not a witcher now. So I'll have to learn to manage without my medallion.'

The king loved the queen boundlessly, and she loved him with all her heart. Something so fair had to finish unhappily.

Flourens Delannoy, *Fairy Tales and Stories*

Delannoy, *Flourens, linguist and historian b. 1432 in Vicovaro, in the years 1460–1475 secretary and librarian to the imperial court. Indefatigable scholar of legends and folktales, he wrote many treatises considered classics of ancient language and literature of the Empire's northern regions. His most important works are:* Myths and Legends of the Peoples of the North; Fairy Tales and Stories; The Surprise, or the Myth of the Elder Blood; A Saga about a Witcher, *and* The Witcher and the Witcher Girl, or the Endless Search. *From 1476 professor at the academy in Castell Graupian, where d. 1510.*

Effenberg and Talbot,
Encyclopaedia Maxima Mundi, Volume IV

CHAPTER EIGHT

A strong wind blew in from the sea, ruffling the sails, and a drizzle like thin hail stung the voyagers' faces painfully. The water in the Great Canal was leaden, rippled by the wind and flecked by a rash of rain.

'Come this way, sire. The boat is waiting.'

Dijkstra sighed heavily. He was thoroughly sick of the sea voyage. He'd been delighted by those few moments on the hard and solid rock wharf, and he was pissed off at the thought of stepping onto a wobbly deck once again. But what else to do? Lan Exeter, Kovir's winter capital, differed fundamentally from the world's other capital cities. In the harbour of Lan Exeter, travellers arriving by sea disembarked onto the stone quay only to immediately embark onto another craft; a slender many-oared boat with a highly upturned prow and slightly lower stern. Lan Exeter was built on the water, in the wide estuary of the River Targo. The city had canals instead of streets – and all municipal transportation was by boat.

He got in, greeting the Redanian ambassador waiting for him by the gangway. The boat was pushed away from the quay, the oars struck the water evenly, the boat moved off and picked up speed. The Redanian ambassador said nothing. *Ambassador*, Dijkstra thought mechanically. For how many years had Redania been sending ambassadors to Kovir? A hundred and twenty, at most. For a hundred and twenty years Kovir and Poviss had been foreign to Redania. Though it hadn't always been that way.

From time immemorial Redania had treated the countries in the North, on the Gulf of Praxeda, as part of its fiefdom. Kovir and Poviss were – it was said at the Tretogorian court – the greatest protectorates in the "Crown dominions". Successive earls were called Troydenids, since they were descended – or so they claimed – from their common forebear, Troyden. Prince Troyden

269

had been the natural brother of Radovid I, King of Redania, later called the Great. Even in his youth Troyden was already a lewd and extremely beastly character. People were afraid when they realised he would develop with time. King Radovid – no exception in this regard – detested his brother like the plague. He thus appointed him Earl of Kovir in order to be rid of him, to move him as far away as possible. And nowhere was further away than Kovir.

Earl Troyden was formally a liegeman of Redania, but an atypical one – he didn't bear any feudal obligations or duties. Why, he didn't even have to take the ceremonial feudal oath! All that was demanded of him was a pledge of 'no interference'. Some said that Radovid simply pitied his brother, knowing that the Koviran "protectorate" couldn't afford to pay tax or raise armies. Others, though, claimed Radovid simply wanted the earl out of his sight – the thought that his younger brother might turn up in Tretogor in person with money or military aid made him sick. No one knew what was true, but so it was, and so it remained. Many years after the death of Radovid I, the law established by the great king was still binding in Redania. Firstly, the county of Kovir was a vassal, but did not have to pay or serve. Secondly, the Koviran inheritance was in the exclusive control of the House of Troyden. Thirdly, Tretogor did not interfere in the affairs of the House of Troyden. Fourthly, members of the House of Troyden were not invited to Tretogor for ceremonies celebrating state holidays. Fifthly, nor for any other occasion.

Essentially, few knew and few were interested in what went on in the North. News about conflicts between Kovir and smaller northern rulers reached Redania, mainly by a roundabout route through Kaedwen. About alliances and wars; with Hengfors, Malleore, Creyden, Talgar and other lands with difficult-to-remember names. Someone conquered someone else and swallowed them up, someone allied with someone else in a dynastic union, someone routed and subjugated someone else. Essentially: no one knew who, whom or why.

However, news about wars and battles lured to the North a whole myriad of brawlers, adventurers, thrill seekers and other restless spirits, looking for plunder and the chance to blow off steam. They were drawn there from all the corners of the world, even from countries as distant as Cintra and Rivia. But they were above all citizens of Redania and Kaedwen. Entire cavalry squadrons came to Kovir, in particular from Kaedwen; rumour even trumpeted that the notorious Aideen, the rebellious, illegitimate daughter of the Kaedwenian monarch, rode at the head of one of them. In Redania it was said that designs were forming at the court in Ard Carraigh for the annexation of the northern county and severing it from the Redanian crown. Some even began clamouring for armed intervention.

Tretogor, however, ostentatiously announced that the North didn't interest it. As the royal jurists deemed, the principle of mutuality applied – the Koviran state had no obligations to the crown, so the crown wouldn't come to Kovir's aid. All the more so since Kovir had never asked for any help.

Meanwhile, Kovir and Poviss had emerged stronger and more powerful from the wars waged in the North. Few knew about that back then. A clearer signal of the North's growing might was a more and more vigorous export market. For decades it had been said of Kovir that the land's only wealth was sand and sea water. That joke was recalled when production from the Koviran foundries and salt works virtually monopolised the world's glass and salt markets.

But although hundreds of people drank from glasses with the mark of the Koviran foundries and seasoned their soup with Poviss salt, in people's awareness it was still an extremely distant, inaccessible, harsh and hostile land. And, above all, foreign.

In Redania and Kaedwen, rather than 'go to Hell' people said 'get to Poviss'. If you don't like working for me, a master would say to his unruly journeymen, 'the path's clear to Kovir'. 'We won't have Koviran order here', shouted a schoolmaster at his disobedient and boisterous pupils. 'Go mouth off in Poviss', called a farmer to his son when he was critical of his forefathers' ard and swidden agriculture.

If anyone doesn't like the old order, 'the road's open to Kovir'!

The recipients of these statements slowly – very slowly – began to ponder them and soon noticed that indeed nothing, absolutely nothing, was barring their way to Kovir and Poviss. A second wave of emigration set off for the North. Just like the previous one, this one mainly consisted of discontented mavericks who were different and wanted things done differently. But this time they weren't troublemakers and misfits at odds with life. Well, at least not all of them.

Scholars who believed in their theories, although they had been shouted down and called demented, headed North. Technicians and constructors, convinced that contrary to popular opinion it was possible to build the machines and devices invented by the scholars. Sorcerers, for whom the use of magic to erect breakwaters wasn't a sacrilegious offence. Merchants for whom the prospect of a growth in turnover was capable of exploding the rigid, static and short-sighted limits of risk. Farmers and stock breeders, convinced that one could create fertile fields from even the worst soil, that it was always possible to breed varieties of animals in a given climate.

Miners and geologists, for whom the bleakness of Kovir's barren mountains and rocks was an infallible signal that if there was such paucity on the surface there must be wealth beneath, also headed North. For nature loves equilibrium.

There *was* wealth beneath those wastes.

A quarter of a century passed – and Kovir had extracted as many minerals as Redania, Aedirn and Kaedwen taken together. Only Mahakam surpassed Kovir in the extraction and processing of iron ore, but transports full of metal serving the production of alloys went from Kovir to Mahakam. Kovir and Poviss accounted for a quarter of the world's yield of silver, nickel, lead, tin and zinc, half of the extraction of copper ore and native copper, three quarters of the yield of manganese, chromium, titanium and tungsten ores, and the same amount of metals occurring only in their native form: platinum, ferroaurum, kryobelitium and dimeritium.

And more than eighty per cent of the world's gold production.

Gold, with which Kovir and Poviss bought what didn't grow or wasn't bred in the North. And what Kovir and Poviss didn't pro-duce. Not because they were unable to or didn't have the expertise, but because it didn't pay. A craftsman from Kovir or Poviss – the son or grandson of an immigrant who went there with a bindle on his back – now earned fourfold that of his counterpart in Redania or Temeria.

Kovir traded and wanted to trade with the whole world, on a greater and greater scale. But it couldn't.

Radovid III became king of Redania, and shared with Radovid the Great – his great-grandfather – the same name as well as the same cunning and miserliness. That king – called the Bold by fawners and hagiographers, and Rufus by everybody else – had observed what none before him had wanted to. Why didn't Redania have a single farthing of the gigantic trade engaged in by Kovir? Why, Kovir was just a meaningless county, a fiefdom, a tiny jewel in the Redanian crown. It was time the Koviran vassal began to serve its suzerain!

A wonderful opportunity occurred to do so; Redania had a border dispute with Aedirn, as usual concerning the Pontar valley. Radovid III was determined to take up arms and began to prepare for it. He promulgated a special tax for military purposes, called the 'Pontar tithe'. All of his subjects and vassals were to pay it. Without exception. Kovir included. Rufus rubbed his hands. Ten per cent of Kovir's income; that was something!

Redanian emissaries made for Pont Vanis, imagined as a small town with a wooden palisade. They communicated astonishing news to Rufus on their return.

Pont Vanis wasn't a small town. It was a great city, the summer capital of Kovir, whose ruler, King Gedovius, sent King Radovid the following answer:

The Kingdom of Kovir is no one's vassal. Redania's petitions and claims are groundless and based on the dead letter of a law which never had any force. The kings of Redania have never been the overlords of Kovir, for the rulers of Kovir – as can easily be checked in the annals – have never paid Redania tribute, have never carried out military servitude and, most importantly, have never been invited to celebrations of state holidays. Or any others.

Therefore, the King of Kovir informed the emissaries – with regret – that he could not recognise King Radovid as his seigneur or suzerain, much less pay him a tithe. Nor could any of the Koviran vassals or arriere vassals – which were subject exclusively to the Koviran suzerainty.

In short: let Redania mind its own business and not stick its nose into the affairs of Kovir, a sovereign kingdom.

273

Cold fury welled up in Rufus. A sovereign kingdom? A foreign land? Very well. We shall deal with Kovir as we would any foreign province.

Redania, along with Kaedwen and Temeria – incited by Rufus – applied against Kovir a retaliatory tax and ruthless right of storage. A merchant from Kovir, heading southward, had to, whether he liked it or not, put all his goods on sale in one of Redania's cities and sell it or return home. That same constraint faced a merchant from the distant South, when making for Kovir.

Redania demanded heavy duty on goods which Kovir shipped by sea, even if they were not calling at Redanian or Temerian ports. Koviran ships, naturally, didn't want to pay – and only those who didn't manage to escape paid. The game of cat and mouse begun on the sea quickly led to an incident. A Redanian patrol craft tried to arrest a Koviran merchant, two Koviran frigates appeared, the patrol craft went up in flames. There were casualties.

The line had been overstepped. Radovid decided to discipline his disobedient vassal. A four-thousand strong Redanian army crossed the River Braa, and an expeditionary force from Kaedwen invaded Caingorn.

After a week, the two thousand surviving Redanians crossed the Braa the other way, and the poorly-equipped survivors of the Kaedwenian corps trudged home across the passes of the Kestrel Mountains. This had revealed a further purpose which the northern gold served. Kovir's permanent army consisted of twenty-five thousand professionals seasoned by combat – and banditry – as well as mercenaries drafted from the far corners of the world, unreservedly loyal to the Koviran crown for their exceptionally generous pay and a pension guaranteed by contract. Prepared for any risk for the exceptionally generous bonuses paid out after every victorious battle. Further, these wealthy soldiers were led in battle by experienced, able – and now extremely wealthy – commanders whom Rufus and King Benda of Kaedwen knew very well; they were the same ones who not long before had served in their armies, but had unexpectedly retired and gone abroad.

Rufus was no fool and could learn from his mistakes. He quelled his swaggering remaining generals, who were demanding a crusade, ignored the merchants calling for a starvation blockade, and mollified Benda of Kaedwen, who was greedy for blood and revenge for the extermination of his elite unit. Rufus initiated negotiations unrestrained by the prospect of humiliation, by the bitter pill he had to swallow; Kovir agreed to talks, but on their territory, in Lan Exeter. He had to eat humble pie.

They sailed to Lan Exeter like petitioners, thought Dijkstra, wrapping himself in his cloak. *Like humble supplicants. Quite like me today.*

The Redanian squadron sailed into the Gulf of Praxeda and headed towards the Koviran coast. From the deck of the flagship *Alata*, Radovid, Benda of Kaedwen – and the hierarch of Novigrad accompanying them in the role of mediator – observed in astonishment the breakwaters extending into the sea, above which rose the walls and sturdy bastions of the fortress guarding access to the city of Pont Vanis. And sailing north from Pont Vanis, towards the mouth of the River Targo, the kings saw port alongside port, shipyard beside shipyard, harbour by harbour. They saw a forest of masts and the blinding white of sails. Kovir, it turned out, was prepared for blockades, embargos and duty wars. Kovir was clearly ready to dominate the seas.

Alata sailed into the broad mouth of the Targo and dropped anchor in the stony jaws of the outport. But – to the kings' astonishment – one more trip by water awaited them. The city of Lan Exeter didn't have streets, but canals. The Great Canal, leading from the harbour straight to the royal residence, was the main artery and axis of the metropolis. The kings transferred to galleys decorated in scarlet and gold garlands and a coat of arms on which Rufus and Benda recognised in amazement the Redanian eagle and the Kaedwenian unicorn.

As they travelled along the Great Canal, the kings and their retinues looked around and kept silent. Actually, it ought to be said they were rendered speechless. They'd been wrong to think they knew what wealth and splendour were, that they couldn't be astonished by manifestations of affluence or any display of luxury. They went down the Great Canal, passing the impressive Admiralty building and the Merchants' Guild. They floated alongside promenades packed with colourful and finely attired crowds. They

275

travelled between avenues of magnificent aristocratic residences and merchants' townhouses, reflecting in the canal's water a spectrum of splendidly embellished, but exceptionally narrow, façades. In Lan Exeter tax was paid on a house's frontage; the wider the frontage, the higher the tax.

On the steps leading down to the canal of Ensenada Palace, the royal winter residence, the only building with a wide frontage, was already waiting for them a welcoming committee and the royal couple: Gedovius, the king of Kovir, and his wife, Gemma. The couple welcomed the new arrivals courteously, politely . . . and uncharacteristically. Dear uncle, Gedovius greeted Radovid. Darling grandfather, Gemma smiled to Benda. Gedovius was a Troydenid, after all. Gemma, however, it turned out was descended from the rebellious Aideen, in whose veins flowed the blood of the kings of Ard Carraigh, who had fled from Kaedwen.

The proven consanguinity improved the mood and evoked affection, but didn't help in the negotiations. By and large what followed were not negotiations. The 'children' briefly stated their demands. Their 'grandfathers' heard them out. And then signed a document, which posterity called the First Exeter Treaty. To distinguish it from those entered into later. The First Treaty also bears a name in keeping with the first words of its preamble: *Mare Liberum Apertum.*

The sea is free and open. Trade is free. Profit is sacred. Love the trade and profit of your neighbour like your own. To hinder someone's trading and profiting is to break the laws of nature. And Kovir is no one's vassal. It's a sovereign, autonomous – and neutral – kingdom.

It didn't look as if Gedovius and Gemma wanted – even, say, in the name of politeness – to make a single concession, even the slightest, nothing that would have rescued Radovid and Benda's honour. Nonetheless, they did. They agreed for Radovid – during his lifetime – to use in official documents the title of King of Kovir and Poviss, and Benda – during his lifetime – the title of King of Caingorn and Malleore.

Of course, with the proviso *de non preiudicando.*

Gedovius and Gemma reigned for twenty-five years; the royal branch of the Troydenids ended with their son, Gerard. Esteril

Thyssen ascended to the Koviran throne. And founded the House of Thyssen.

The kings of Kovir were soon after bound by blood ties to all the other dynasties of the world, and they all steadfastly abided by the Exeter Treaties. They never interfered with their neighbours' affairs. They never raised the issue of foreign succession, though often historical turbulence meant that the king or prince of Kovir had all possible grounds to judge himself the rightful successor to the throne of Redania, Aedirn, Kaedwen, Cidaris or even Verden or Rivia. The mighty Kovir didn't attempt territorial annexations or conquests, nor did it send gunboats armed with catapults and ballistae into foreign waters. It never seized the privilege of ruling the waves. *Mare Liberum Apertum*; a sea free and open for trade was sufficient for Kovir. Kovir believed in the sanctity of trade and profit.

And in absolute, unswerving neutrality.

Dijkstra put up the beaver collar of his cloak, protecting his nape from the wind and the lashing rain. He looked around, shaken from his contemplations. The water in the Great Canal looked black. In the drizzle and fog, even the Admiralty building – the boast of Lan Exeter – looked like a barracks. Even the merchants' townhouses had lost their usual sumptuousness – and their narrow frontages seemed narrower than normal. *Perhaps they are sodding narrower*, thought Dijkstra. *If King Esterad has raised the tax, the sly householders may have narrowed their houses.*

'Has the weather been so plague-stricken for long, Your Excellency?' he asked, just to interrupt the annoying silence.

'Since the middle of September, Count,' answered the ambassador. 'Since the full moon. It looks as though winter will come early. It has already snowed in Talgar.'

'I thought,' said Dijkstra, 'the snow never melted in Talgar.'

The ambassador glanced at him, as if to make sure it was a joke and not ignorance.

'In Talgar –' now he showed off his wit '– the winter begins in September, and ends in May. The remaining seasons are spring and autumn. There's also the summer . . . it usually falls on the first Tuesday after the August new moon. And lasts until Wednesday morning.'

Dijkstra didn't laugh.

'But even there,' the ambassador turned gloomy, 'snow at the end of October is a sensation.'

The ambassador – like most of Redania's aristocracy – couldn't stand Dijkstra. He considered the need to receive and entertain the arch-spy as a personal affront, and the fact that the Regency Council had charged Dijkstra and not him with negotiations with Kovir as a mortal insult. It sickened him that he, de Ruyter of the most celebrated branch of the de Ruyter family, Grafs for nine generations, should have to address a churl and upstart as 'Count'. But as an experienced diplomat he concealed his resentment masterfully.

The oars rose and fell rhythmically, and the boat glided swiftly along the canal. They had just passed the bijou – but extremely tasteful – palace of Culture and Art.

'Do we sail to Ensenada?'

'Yes, Count,' confirmed the ambassador. 'The minister of foreign affairs stressed emphatically that he wished to see you immediately on arrival, which is why I'm taking you directly to Ensenada. In the evening I shall send a boat to the palace, for I would like to entertain you over supper—'

'Your Excellency will deign to forgive me,' Dijkstra interrupted, 'but my duties won't allow me to take you up on it. I have a prodigious amount of matters to deal with and little time, so I must manage them at the cost of pleasure. We shall sup another day. In happier, more peaceful times.'

The ambassador bowed and furtively sighed with relief.

*

He entered Ensenada, naturally, by a rear entrance. For which he was very glad. An impressive but damned long staircase of white marble led straight from the Great Canal to the main entrance of the royal winter residence, beneath a magnificent frontage supported on slender columns. The stairs leading to one of the numerous rear entrances were incomparably less spectacular, but far easier to negotiate. In spite of that, Dijkstra, as he walked, bit his lip and swore softly under his breath, so that the major-domo, lackeys and guardsmen escorting him wouldn't hear.

More stairs and more climbing awaited him inside the palace. Dijkstra cursed again *sotto voce*. Probably the damp, cold and uncomfortable position in the boat was why his leg, with its smashed and magically healed ankle, had begun to make itself known with a dull, nagging pain. And a nasty memory. Dijkstra ground his teeth. He knew that the Witcher – the man responsible for his suffering – had also had his bones broken. He had profound hopes that they also pained the Witcher and wished in his heart of hearts that it would pain him as long and as severely as possible.

Dusk had already fallen outside and Ensenada's corridors were dark. The route Dijkstra was taking behind a silent major-domo was, nonetheless, lit by a sparse row of lackeys with candlesticks. And outside the doors of the chamber to which the major-domo was leading him stood guardsmen with halberds, so erect it seemed spare halberds had been stuck up their backsides. The lackeys with candles stood more densely there, so the luminance was blinding. Dijkstra was somewhat astonished by the pomp with which he was being received.

He entered the chamber and immediately stopped being astonished. He bowed low.

'Greetings to you, Dijkstra,' said Esterad Thyssen, King of Kovir, Poviss, Narok, Velhad and Talgar. 'Don't stand by the door, come closer. Put etiquette aside, it's an unofficial audience.'

'Your Majesty.'

Esterad's wife, Queen Zuleyka, responded to Dijkstra's reverential bow with a slightly absent-minded nod, not interrupting her crocheting for a moment.

There wasn't a soul in the chamber apart from the royal couple.

'Precisely.' Esterad had noticed his glance. 'Just the two of us will chat. I beg your pardon, just the three of us. For something tells me it'll be better this way.'

Dijkstra sat down on the scissors chair indicated, opposite Esterad. The king was wearing a crimson ermine-trimmed cape and a matching velvet chapeau. Like all the men of the Thyssen clan he was tall, powerfully built and devilishly handsome. He always looked robust and healthy, like a sailor just returned from the sea; one could almost smell the seawater and cold, salt wind coming from him. As with all the Thyssens it was difficult to determine his exact age. Judging by his hair, skin and hands – the features which most clearly express one's age – Esterad might have passed for forty-five. Dijkstra knew the king was fifty-six.

'Zuleyka.' The king leaned over towards his wife. 'Look at him. If you didn't know he was a spy, would you give credence to it?'

Queen Zuleyka was short, quite stout and pleasantly plain. She dressed in quite a typical way for women of her looks, which was based on selecting elements of attire so that no one would guess she wasn't her own grandmother. Zuleyka achieved this effect by wearing loose-fitting gowns, dull of cut and grey-brown of tone. On her head she wore a bonnet inherited from her ancestors. She didn't use any makeup and didn't wear any jewellery.

'The Good Book,' she spoke in a quiet and sweet little voice, 'teaches us circumspection in judging our neighbours. For one day they will judge us, too. Let's hope not on the basis of appearance.'

Esterad Thyssen favoured his wife with a warm look. It was widely known that he loved her boundlessly, with a love which for twenty-nine years of marriage hadn't dimmed a jot. On the contrary, as the years passed it blazed brighter and hotter. Esterad, it was claimed, had never betrayed Zuleyka. Dijkstra couldn't really believe in anything so unlikely, but himself had tried three times to plant on – or virtually place under – the king stunning female agents, candidates for favourites, superb sources of information. Nothing had come of it.

'I like to speak bluntly,' said the king, 'therefore I shall reveal at once, Dijkstra, why I've decided to talk to you personally. There are several reasons. Firstly, I know you won't shrink from bribery. I'm certain, by and large, of my ministers, but why put them to the test, lead them into temptation? What kind of bribe did you intend to offer the minister of foreign affairs?'

'A thousand Novigradian crowns,' the spy responded without batting an eyelid. 'Were he to haggle, I'd have gone up to a thousand five hundred.'

'And that's why I like you,' Esterad Thyssen said after moment's silence. 'You're a dreadful whoreson. You remind me of my youth. I look at you and see myself at your age.'

Dijkstra thanked him with a bow. He was just eight years

younger than the king. He was convinced that Esterad was well aware of it.

'You're a dreadful whoreson,' the king repeated, growing serious. 'But a respectable and decent one. And that's a rarity in these rotten times.'

Dijkstra bowed once more.

'You see,' Esterad continued, 'in every country one may encounter people who are blind fanatics for the idea of social order. People committed to an idea, prepared to do anything for it. Including crime, for to them the aim justifies the means and changes the meaning of concepts. They don't murder, they rescue order. They don't torture, they don't blackmail: they safeguard the national interest and fight for order. For such people, the life of an individual – should that individual violate the dogma of the established order – is not worth a farthing or a shrug. People like that don't acknowledge the fact that the society they serve is made up of individuals. People like that are availed of the so-called "broad" view . . . and such a view is the most certain way of not noticing other people.'

'Nicodemus de Boot,' Dijkstra blurted out.

'Close, but wide of the mark.' The king of Kovir bared his alabaster-white teeth. 'It was Vysogota of Corvo. A lesser known, but also able, ethicist and philosopher. Read him. I recommend it. Perhaps one of his books has survived in Redania. Perhaps you didn't burn them all? Come, come, let's get to the point. You, Dijkstra, are also unscrupulous in your use of intrigue, bribery, blackmail and torture. You don't bat an eyelid when condemning someone to death or ordering an assassination. That fact you do it for the kingdom you faithfully serve does not excuse you or make you any more pleasant in my eyes. Not in the slightest. Be aware of that.'

The spy nodded as a sign that he was.

'You are, though,' Esterad continued, 'as it's been said before, a whoreson of upright character. And that's why I like and respect you, why I've granted you a private audience. For you, Dijkstra, having had a million opportunities, have never done anything for private gain or stolen so much as a ha'penny from the state coffers. Not even a farthing. Zuleyka, look! Is he blushing, or am I deceived?'

281

The queen raised her head from her crocheting.

'Their righteousness shall be known from their modesty.' She quoted a passage from the Good Book, although she must have seen that not even a trace of a blush had appeared on the spy's features.

'Very well,' Esterad said. 'To business. Time to move to state affairs. He, Zuleyka, crossed the sea motivated by his patriotic duty. Redania, his fatherland, is threatened. Chaos rages there, following the tragic death of King Vizimir. Redania is now governed by a band of aristocratic idiots, calling themselves the Regency Council. That band, my Zuleyka, will do nothing for Redania. In the face of danger it will either bolt or begin obsequiously to grovel before the pearl-trimmed slippers of the Nilfgaardian Emperor. That band despises Dijkstra, for he's a spy, a murderer, an upstart and a boor. But Dijkstra crossed the sea to save his country. Demonstrating who really cares about Redania.'

Esterad Thyssen fell silent, exhaled loudly, wearied by his speech, and adjusted his crimson chapeau, which had slipped down slightly over his nose.

'Well, Dijkstra,' he continued. 'What ails your kingdom? Aside from a shortage of money, naturally?'

'Aside from a shortage of money,' the spy's face was inscrutable, 'all are well, thank you.'

'Aha,' the king nodded. His chapeau once more slipped down over his nose and had to be adjusted again. 'Aha. I comprehend.'

'I comprehend,' he continued. 'And I applaud the idea. When one has money, one may purchase medicaments for every affliction. The crux is to have the money. Which you do not. If you did, you wouldn't be here. Do I understand correctly?'

'Impeccably.'

'And how much do you need, I wonder?'

'Not much. A million bizants.'

'Not much?' Esterad Thyssen grasped his chapeau in both hands in an exaggerated gesture. 'You call that not much? Oh, my!'

'But for Your Royal Highness,' the spy mumbled, 'such a sum is a trifle—'

'A trifle?' The king released his chapeau and raised his hands towards the ceiling. 'Oh, my! A million bizants is a trifle. Do you

282

hear, Zuleyka, what he's saying? And do you know, Dijkstra, that to have a million and not to have a million, is two million together? I understand, I comprehend, that you and Philippa Eilhart are looking desperately and feverishly for an idea to defend yourselves against Nilfgaard, but what do you want? Do you plan to buy the whole of Nilfgaard?'

Dijkstra did not reply. Zuleyka crocheted on. For a moment Esterad pretended to be admiring the nude nymphs on the ceiling.

'Come along.' He suddenly rose and nodded to the spy. They walked over to a huge painting portraying King Gedovius sitting astride a grey horse, pointing out something which wasn't included on the canvas to the army with his sceptre, probably indicating the right direction. Esterad fished a tiny, gilded wand from his pocket, tapped the frame of the picture with it, and murmured a spell in hushed tones. Gedovius and his grey horse vanished, and a relief map of the known world appeared. The king touched a silver button in the corner of the map with his wand and magically transformed the scale, narrowing the visible sweep of the world to the Yaruga Valley and the Four Kingdoms.

'The blue is Nilfgaard,' he explained. 'The red is you. What are you gawping at? Look here!'

Dijkstra tore his gaze away from the other paintings – chiefly nudes and seascapes. He wondered which was the magical camouflage for another notorious map of Esterad's: the one which depicted Kovir's military and trade intelligence service, an entire network of bribed informers and blackmailed individuals, agents, operational contacts, saboteurs, hired killers, moles and active resident spies. He knew such a map existed; he had been trying unsuccessfully for many years to gain access to it.

'The red is you,' Esterad Thyssen repeated. 'Looks pretty hopeless, doesn't it?'

Yup, pretty hopeless, Dijkstra admitted to himself. Lately he had been continuously looking at strategic maps, but now, on Esterad's relief map, the situation seemed even worse. The blue squares formed themselves into the shape of terrible dragon's jaws, liable at any moment to snatch and crush the small, miserable red squares in its great teeth.

Esterad Thyssen looked around for something that might serve as a pointer for the map, finally drawing a decorative rapier from the nearest panoply.

'Nilfgaard,' he began his lecture, pointing appropriately with the rapier, 'has attacked Lyria and Aedirn, declaring an assault on the border fort Glevitzingen as a *casus belli*. I'm not going to investigate who really attacked Glevitzingen wearing which disguise. It's also senseless to speculate how many days or hours Emhyr's armed operation occurred before the analogical undertakings by Aedirn and Temeria. I shall leave that to the historians. I'm more interested in the situation today and what it will be tomorrow. At this very moment Nilfgaard is in Dol Angra and Aedirn, shielded by a buffer in the shape of the elven dominium in Dol Blathanna, bordering with that part of Aedirn which King Henselt of Kaedwen, speaking vividly, tore from Emhyr's teeth and himself devoured.'

Dijkstra made no comment.

'I shall also leave a moral judgement of King Henselt's campaign to the historians,' Esterad continued. 'But a single glance at the map is sufficient to see that by annexing the Northern Marches Henselt barred Emhyr's way to the Pontar Valley. He secured Temeria's flank. And yours, the Redanians. You ought to thank him.'

'I did,' Dijkstra muttered. 'But quietly. King Demawend of Aedirn is our guest in Tretogor. And Demawend has quite a precise moral judgement of Henselt's deed. He customarily expresses it in blunt and ringing words.'

'I can imagine,' the King of Kovir nodded. 'Let's leave it for now, and glance at the South, at the River Yaruga. Attacking in Dol Angra, Emhyr simultaneously secured his flank by concluding a separatist treaty with Foltest of Temeria. But immediately after the end of the military operations in Aedirn the emperor broke the pact without further ado and struck Brugge and Sodden. Through his cowardly negotiations Foltest gained two weeks of peace. Sixteen days to be precise. And it's the twenty-sixth of October today.'

'It is.'

'Thus the situation on the twenty-sixth of October is as follows. Brugge and Sodden occupied. The strongholds of Razvan and Mayena fallen. Temeria's army defeated in the Battle of Maribor and repulsed northwards. Maribor besieged. This morning it was still holding out. But it's already late evening, Dijkstra.'

'Maribor will hold out. The Nilfgaardians didn't manage to seal it off.'

'True. They advanced too far, they overextended their supply lines, they're imprudently exposing their flanks. They will call off the siege before the winter, withdrawing towards the Yaruga, shortening the front. But what will happen in the spring, Dijkstra? What will happen when the grass peeps out from under the snow? Come closer. Look at the map.'

Dijkstra looked.

'Look at the map,' the king repeated. 'And I shall tell you what Emhyr var Emreis will do in the spring.'

*

'They will begin an offensive on an unparalleled scale,' announced Carthia van Canten, adjusting her golden curls in front of the looking glass. 'Oh, I know that information isn't sensational in itself. Old women enliven their laundry at every town well with stories about the spring offensive.'

Assire var Anahid was unusually tetchy and impatient today, but nonetheless managed not to ask why, in that case, she was bothering her with such unsensational information. But she knew Cantarella. And if Cantarella started talking about something she had her reasons. And she usually finished her statements with conclusions.

'I know a little more than the hoipolloi, however,' Cantarella continued. 'Vattier told me everything, about the entire council with the emperor. And in addition brought me a whole briefcase of maps. When he fell asleep I examined them . . . Shall I go on?'

'But of course, my dear.' Assire squinted.

'The thrust of the main strike is, of course, Temeria. The border of the River Pontar, along the line Novigrad-Vizima-Ellander. A force of the Central Army, under the command of Menno Coehoorn, will strike. A force of the Eastern Army will secure the flank, striking the Pontar Valley and Kaedwen from Aedirn . . .'

'Kaedwen?' Assire raised an eyebrow. 'Is that the end of the fragile friendship struck up during the sharing of spoils?'

'Kaedwen is threatening the right flank.' Carthia van Canten pouted slightly with her full lips. Her doll-like face was in striking contrast to the strategic grasp she was demonstrating. 'The strike is of a preventive character. Assigned units of a group from the Eastern Army are to bind King Henselt's army, to remove any thoughts of helping Temeria.

'The Verden special operations group will strike in the west,' the blonde woman continued, 'with the task of capturing Cidaris and tightly sealing off the blockade of Novigrad, Gors Velen and Vizima. For the General Staff is taking into account the necessity of besieging those three strongholds.'

'You didn't name the two armies' commanders.'

'The Eastern Group, Ardal aep Dahy.' Cantarella smiled slightly. 'The Verden Group, Joachim de Wett.'

Assire raised her eyebrows.

'How interesting,' she said. 'Two princes, offended by the removal of their daughters from Emhyr's matrimonial plans. Our emperor is either very naive, or very cunning.'

'If Emhyr knows anything about a plot by the princes,' said Cantarella, 'it's not from Vattier. Vattier told him nothing.'

'Go on.'

'The offensive will be on an unprecedented scale. Taken together, including front line units, reserves, auxiliary and rear services, over three hundred thousand men will be taking part in the operation. And elves, naturally.'

'Scheduled start date?'

'Not yet set. Supplies are a key issue. Supplies means clear roads, and no one can predict when the winter will finish.'

'What else did Vattier speak of?'

'He was complaining, poor thing.' Cantarella flashed her little teeth. 'Complaining that the emperor had abused and reprimanded him again. Publically. The reason again was the mysterious disappearance of Stefan Skellen and his entire unit. Emhyr publically called Vattier a clot, said he was a head of a department which, rather than making people disappear without trace, are surprised by such disappearances. He constructed on the subject a malicious

286

equivoque which Vattier, sadly, wasn't able to repeat exactly. Then the emperor asked Vattier in jest if his failure meant some other secret organisation had been set up, kept confidential even from him. Our imperator is sharp. He's close to the target.'

'He is,' Assire murmured. 'What else, Carthia?'

'The agent Vattier had in Skellen's unit – who also vanished – was called Neratin Ceka. Vattier must have thought very highly of him, because he's extremely dejected over his disappearance.'

I, thought Assire, *am also left dejected by the disappearance of Jediah Mekesser. But I, unlike Vattier de Rideaux, will find out what happened.*

'And Rience? Has Vattier met him again?'

'No. He didn't mention it.'

They were both briefly silent. The cat in Assire's lap purred loudly.

'Madam Assire.'

'Yes, Carthia?'

'Will I have to play the role of the foolish lover much longer? I'd like to return to my studies, devote myself to scholarly work—'

'Soon,' Assire interrupted. 'Just a little longer. Hold on, my child.'

Cantarella sighed.

They finished their conversation and bade each other farewell. Assire var Anahid shooed the cat from the armchair and reread the letter from Fringilla Vigo, who was residing in Toussaint. She fell into pensive mood, for the letter had troubled her. It bore some message between the lines which Assire sensed, but couldn't grasp. It was after midnight when Assire var Anahid, the Nilfgaardian sorceress, started up the megascope and established telecommunication with Montecalvo Castle in Redania.

Philippa Eilhart was in a skimpy nightdress with very thin straps, and had lipstick traces on her cheek and cleavage. Assire made an immense effort of will to suppress a grimace of distaste. *Never, ever, will I be capable of understanding it,* she thought. *And I don't want to understand it.*

'May we talk freely?'

Philippa made a sweeping hand movement, encircling herself in a sphere of discretion.

'We can now.'

'I have information,' Assire began dryly. 'It isn't sensational in and of itself, even old women at wells are talking about it. Nonetheless . . .'

*

'The whole of Redania,' said Esterad Thyssen, looking at his map, 'can at this moment field thirty-five thousand frontline troops, of whom four thousand are heavy armoured cavalry. Reckoning roughly, of course.'

Dijkstra nodded. The arithmetic was absolutely precise.

'Demawend and Meve had a similar army. Emhyr annihilated it in twenty-six days. The same thing will happen to the armies of Redania and Temeria if you don't reinforce them. I support your idea, Dijkstra, yours and Philippa Eilhart's. You're in need of troops. You require valorous, well-drilled and well-equipped cavalry. You need the kind of cavalry that costs around a million bizants.'

The spy nodded, confirming that this calculation couldn't be faulted either.

'As you no doubt know,' the king continued dryly, 'Kovir has always been, is, and will be neutral. We are bound by a treaty with the Nilfgaardian Empire, signed by my grandfather, Esteril Thyssen, and the imperator Fergus var Emreis. The letter of that treaty does not permit Kovir to support the enemies of Nilfgaard with military aid. Nor with money for troops.'

'When Emhyr var Emreis throttles Temeria and Redania,' coughed Dijkstra, 'he'll look to the North. Emhyr won't be satisfied. It may turn out that your treaty won't be worth a hill of beans. A moment ago the talk was of Foltest of Temeria, who managed – by negotiations – to buy himself a mere sixteen days of peace with Nilfgaard—'

'Oh, my dear,' Esterad snapped. 'One cannot argue like that. Treaties are like marriage: they aren't entered in to with the thought of betrayal, and once they're concluded one shouldn't be suspicious. And if that doesn't suit somebody, they shouldn't get married. Because you can't become a cuckold without being a husband, but you'll admit that fear of wearing the horns is a pitiful and quite ridiculous justification for enforced celibacy. And cuckolds aren't a subject for discussion in a marriage. As long as one doesn't wear horns, that subject isn't mentioned, and if one's already wearing them, then there's nothing to say. And since we're talking about horns, how is the husband of the fair Marie, the Marquess de Mercey, the Redanian Minister of Finances?'

'Your Majesty,' Dijkstra bowed stiffly, 'has enviable informants.'

'Indeed I do,' the king conceded. 'You'd be astonished how many and how enviable. But you, too, can't be ashamed of your own. Those you have at my courts, here and in Pont Vanis. Oh, I'll wager each of them deserves top marks.'

Dijkstra didn't even blink.

'Emhyr var Emreis,' Esterad continued, looking at the nymphs on the ceiling, 'also has a few good and well placed agents. Which is why I repeat: Kovir's raison d'état is neutrality and the principle of *pacta sunt servanda*. Kovir doesn't break treaties. Not even in anticipation of the other side breaking a contract.'

'May I observe,' Dijkstra said, 'that Redania isn't urging Kovir to break pacts. Redania is by no means seeking an alliance or military aid against Nilfgaard. Redania wishes . . . to borrow a small sum, which we shall return—'

'I can just see you returning it,' the king interrupted. 'But these are academic deliberations, for I shan't loan you a farthing. And don't ply me with duplicitous casuistry, Dijkstra, it suits you like a bib suits a wolf. Do you have any other, serious, intelligent and apposite arguments?'

'I do not.'

'You were lucky,' Esterad Thyssen said after moment's silence, 'that you became a spy. You'd never have made a career in commerce.'

*

The length and breadth of the world, all royal couples had separate bed chambers. The kings – with extremely varying frequency – visited the queens' bed chambers, and it also happened that queens paid unexpected visits to the kings' bed chambers. Afterwards the spouses returned to their own chambers and beds.

The royal couple of Kovir were an exception in this respect too. Esterad Thyssen and Zuleyka always slept together – in one bed chamber, on an immense bed with an immense canopy.

Before falling asleep, Zuleyka – after putting on her spectacles, in which she was ashamed to appear before her subjects – customarily read her Good Book. Esterad Thyssen usually talked.

That night was no different. Esterad put on his nightcap and picked up his sceptre. He liked to hold his sceptre and play with it; he didn't do it officially for he feared his subjects would accuse him of being pretentious.

'You know, Zuleyka,' he said, 'lately I've been having queer dreams. I've dreamed of that witch, my mother, I don't know how many times. She stands over me and repeats: "I have a wife for Tankred, I have a wife for Tankred". And she shows me a pretty, but very young girl. And do you know, Zuleyka, who that girl is? It's Ciri, Calanthe's granddaughter. Do you remember Calanthe, Zuleyka?'

'I do, my husband.'

'Ciri,' Esterad went on, playing with the sceptre, 'is the one Emhyr var Emreis reputedly wants to marry. A bizarre marriage, astonishing . . . How, damn it, ought she to be a wife for Tankred?'

'Tankred –' Zuleyka's voice faintly altered, as it did whenever she spoke of her son '– could do with a wife. Perhaps he would settle down . . . '

'Perhaps,' Esterad sighed. 'Though I doubt it, but perhaps. In any case, matrimony is some sort of chance. Hmmm . . . Ciri . . . Ha! Kovir and Cintra. The Yaruga estuary! Doesn't sound at all bad, not at all bad. An alliance would be fine . . . A nice little coalition . . . Well, but if Emhyr has his eye on the filly . . . But why is she appearing in my dreams? And why the hell am I dreaming that sort of nonsense? At the Equinox, do you recall, when I woke you. . . Brrr, what a nightmare that was, I'm glad I can't remember the details . . . Hmmm . . . Perhaps we ought to summon an astrologer? A soothsayer? A medium?'

'Madam Sheala de Tancarville is in Lan Exeter.'

'No.' The king grimaced. 'I don't want that witch. Too clever.

A second Philippa Eilhart is springing up under my nose! Power appeals too much to these clever women, one should not encourage them with favours and familiarity.'

'You're right, as ever, my husband.'

'Hmfff . . . But those dreams . . . '

'The Good Book –' Zuleyka turned over a few leaves '– says that when a man falls asleep, the gods open his ears and speak to him. Whereas the prophet Lebioda teaches that when gazing on a dream, one either sees great wisdom or great foolishness. The art is in recognising it.'

'A marriage of Tankred with Emhyr's betrothed is not exactly great wisdom,' Esterad sighed. 'But while we're on the subject of wisdom, I would be immensely pleased if it came to me during my slumbers. It concerns the case with which Dijkstra came. It concerns a most trying case. For you see, my dear beloved Zuleyka, good sense permits us not to rejoice with Nilfgaard pushing northwards hard and liable any day to seize Novigrad, for from Novigrad everything – including our neutrality – looks different than from the distant South. Thus it would be good if Redania and Temeria were to hold back Nilfgaard's advance, in order to push the invader back across the Yaruga. But would it be good, were it done using our money? Are you listening to me, my most beloved wife?'

'I am, husband.'

'And what do you think?'

'All wisdom is contained in the Good Book.'

'But does your Good Book say what to do if some Dijkstra shows up and demands a million from you?'

'The Book,' Zuleyka blinked from over her spectacles, 'says nothing about base mammon. But in one passage it says: "to give is a greater happiness than to receive, and supporting a pauper with alms is noble". It is said: "give away all, and it shall make your soul noble".'

'And makes the purse and breadbasket empty,' Esterad Thyssen muttered. 'Zuleyka, is any wisdom to be found in the Book concerning business apart from passages about noble free distribution and alms-giving? What does the Book, for instance, say about equivalent exchange?'

The queen straightened her spectacles and began to quickly turn over the pages of the incunabulum.

'Measure for measure,' she read.

Esterad was silent for a long while.

'And perhaps,' he finally drawled, 'something more?'

Zuleyka returned to turning the pages of the Book.

'I have found,' she suddenly announced, 'something amongst the wisdom of the prophet Lebioda. Should I read it?'

'If you would.'

'The prophet Lebioda: "in sooth, support the pauper with alms. But rather than give the pauper an entire watermelon, give him half a watermelon, for a pauper is liable to lose his wits from happiness".'

'Half a watermelon.' Esterad Thyssen bristled. 'You mean half a million bizants? And do you know, Zuleyka, that to have a half a million and not to have half a million is a whole million together?'

'You didn't let me finish,' Zuleyka scolded her husband with a harsh look over her spectacles. 'The prophet goes on: "better even is to give the pauper quarter of a watermelon. And it is even better to cause that some else give the pauper a watermelon. For in sooth, I tell you there will always be someone who has a watermelon and is inclined to share it with the pauper, if not out of nobleness, then out of calculation or on some other pretext".'

'Ha!' The King of Kovir thumped his sceptre down on the bedside table. 'In sooth, the prophet Lebioda was shrewd! Instead of giving, cause someone else to give? That appeals to me, those are in sooth flowing words! Study the wisdom of that prophet, my darling Zuleyka. I'm certain you will discover among it something that permits me to solve the problem of Redania and the army that Redania wishes to raise using my money.'

Zuleyka leafed through the book for a long time before she finally began to read.

'"A pupil of the prophet Lebioda once spake to him: 'teach me, master, how I am to act. For my neighbour is desirous of my favourite dog. If I give him my pet, my heart will break from sorrow. If, though, I do not give it, I shall be downhearted, for I shall pain my neighbour through my refusal. What to do?' 'Do you have,' asked the prophet, 'something you love less than your pet dog?'

292

'I have, master,' the pupil replied, 'an impish cat, a tiresome pest. And I love him not at all.' And thus spake the prophet Lebioda: 'Take that impish cat, that tiresome pest, and give it to your neighbour. Then you will know happiness. You will be rid of the cat, and will delight your neighbour. For most often it is so, that our neighbour does not desire a gift, but to be given'."'

Esterad was silent for some time and his brow was knitted.

'Zuleyka?' he finally asked. 'Was that really the same prophet?'

'"Take that impish cat—"'

'I heard it the first time!' the king yelled, but immediately restrained himself.

'Forgive me, most beloved. The point is I don't understand what cats have to do with . . .'

He fell silent. And pondered deeply.

*

After eighty-five years, when the situation had changed enough to allow talk about certain issues and persons, Guiscard Vermuellen, Duke of Creyden, grandson of Esterad Thyssen and son of his oldest daughter, Gaudemunda, spoke. Duke Guiscard was then a venerable old man, but he clearly remembered the events he had witnessed. It was Duke Guiscard who revealed where the million bizants came from, the million with which Redania equipped its cavalry for the war against Nilfgaard. That million didn't come – as had been thought – from Kovir's treasury, but from the hierarch of Novigrad. Esterad Thyssen, Guiscard disclosed, obtained the Novigradian money from his shares in the maritime trade companies being set up. The paradox was that those companies were set up with the active cooperation of Nilfgaardian merchants. Thus it appeared that Nilfgaard itself – to some degree – had financed the fielding of the Redanian army.

'Grandpappa,' Guiscard Vermuellen recalled, 'said something about watermelons, smiling roguishly. He said somebody always wants to give to a pauper, even if out of calculation. He also said that since Nilfgaard itself was contributing to increasing the strength and military capabilities of the Redanian Army, they couldn't blame others for doing the same.

293

'Later though,' the old man went on, 'grandpappa summoned my father, who was at that time the chief of intelligence, and the minister of internal affairs. When they learned what orders they were to execute, they fell into a panic. They were concerned about releasing more than three thousand people from prisons, internment camps and exile. House arrest was to be withdrawn from more than a hundred.

'No, it didn't only apply to bandits, common criminals and hired mercenaries. The pardons were mostly for dissidents. Among the pardoned were henchmen of the deposed King Rhyd and people of the usurper Idi, their virulent partisans. And not only those who had supported in word: most were in prison for sabotage, assassination attempts and armed revolts. The minister of internal affairs was horrified and papa extremely worried.

'While grandpappa,' the duke went on, 'was laughing as though it were a first-rate joke. And then he continued – I remember every word: "It's a great pity, gentlemen, that you don't read the Good Book before going to sleep. If you did, you would understand the ideas of your monarch. As it is, you'll be carrying out orders without understanding them. But don't worry, your monarch knows what he's doing. Now go and release all my impish cats, those tiresome pests."

'That's just what he said: impish cats, pests. And he meant – which no one then could have known – subsequent heroes, commanders covered in glory and fame. Those "cats" of grandpappa's became the celebrated condottieri: Adam "Adieu" Pangratt, Lorenzo Molla, Juan "Frontino" Guttierez . . . And Julia Abatemarco, who became famous in Redania as "Pretty Kitty" . . . You, youngsters, won't remember it, but when I was a boy, when we played at war, every lad wanted to be "Adieu" Pangratt, and every girl Julia "Pretty Kitty" . . . But to grandpappa they were mischievous cats.

'Later though,' mumbled Guiscard Vermuellen, 'grandpappa took me by the hand and led me out onto the terrace, where grandmamma Zuleyka was feeding the seagulls. Grandpappa said to her . . . Said . . .'

The old man slowly and with great effort tried to recall the words, which, eighty-five years ago, King Esterad Thyssen had said to his wife, Queen Zuleyka, on the terrace of Ensenada Palace, towering over the Great Canal.

'Do you know, my most beloved wife, that I have spotted one more piece of wisdom among the words of the prophet Lebioda? One that shows me yet another benefit of giving Redania those mischievous cats? Cats, my Zuleyka, come home. Cats always come home. Well, and when my cats return, when they bring their pay, their spoils, their riches . . . I shall tax them!'

*

When King Esterad Thyssen spoke to Dijkstra for the last time, it was in private, without even Zuleyka. Admittedly, a more or less ten-year-old boy was playing on the floor of the gigantic chamber, but he didn't count, and furthermore was so busy with his lead soldiers that he paid no attention to the two men talking.

'That is Guiscard,' Esterad explained, nodding towards the boy. 'My grandson, the son of Gaudemunda and that ne'er-do-well, Prince Vermuellen. But that little boy is Kovir's only hope, should Tankred Thyssen turn out to be . . . Should anything happen to Tankred . . . '

Dijkstra was aware of Kovir's problem. And Esterad's personal problem. He knew that something had already happened to Tankred. The lad, if he had any makings of a king, would only be a bad one.

'Your matter,' Esterad said, 'is already by and large sorted out. You may now start to ponder on the most effective way of using the million bizants which will soon end up in the Redanian coffers.'

He bent down and surreptitiously picked up one of Guiscard's brightly painted lead soldiers, a cavalryman with a raised broadsword.

'Take that and conceal it well. Whoever shows you another such identical soldier will be my emissary, even if he doesn't look like it, even though you have no faith that he is my man or is aware of the issue of our million. Anyone else will be an agent provocateur.'

'Redania,' Dijkstra bowed, 'will not forget this, Your Majesty. I, however, speaking for myself, would like to assure you of my personal gratitude.'

'Do not do so. Give me that thousand with which you hoped to gain my minister's favour. Why, isn't the king's favour deserving of a bribe?'

'Your Royal Highness is stooping . . .'

'We are, we are. Hand over the money, Dijkstra. To have a thousand and not to have a thousand—'

'. . . adds up to two thousand. I know.'

*

In a distant wing of Ensenada, in a chamber of much more modest size, the sorceress Sheala de Tancarville listened to the account of Queen Zuleyka with concentration and earnestness.

'Excellent,' she nodded. 'Excellent, Your Royal Highness.'

'I did everything as instructed, Lady Sheala.'

'Thank you for doing so. And I assure you one more time; we were acting in a good cause. For the good of the country. And dynasty.'

Queen Zuleyka coughed softly and her voice changed a little.

'And . . . And Tankred, Lady Sheala?'

'I gave my word,' Sheala de Tancarville said coldly. 'I gave my word that I would reciprocate for the help with help. Your Royal Highness may sleep serenely.'

'I desire that greatly,' Zuleyka sighed. 'Greatly. While we're on the subject of sleep . . . The king begins to suspect something. Those dreams are amazing him, and when something amazes him he grows suspicious.'

'I shall, then, stop sending the king dreams for some time,' the sorceress promised. 'Returning, however, to Your Majesty's dream, I repeat, he can be confident. Prince Tankred will bid farewell to that bad company. He will not linger at the Baron of Surcratasse's castle. Nor at Lady de Lisemore's residence. Nor at the Redanian ambassador's wife's.'

'He will no longer visit those personages? Never?'

'Those personages,' Sheala de Tancarville's dark eyes lit up with a strange glint, 'will no longer dare to trifle with Prince Tankred, for they shall be made aware of the consequences. I vouch for what I say. I vouch for the fact that Prince Tankred will take up his studies again and be a diligent scholar, a serious and level-headed young man. He shall also stop chasing skirts. He shall lose his ardour . . . until the moment we introduce to him Cirilla, Princess of Cintra.'

'Oh, if only I could believe that!' Zuleyka wrung her hands and raised her eyes. 'If only I could believe that!'

'It is sometimes difficult,' Sheala de Tancarville smiled, unexpectedly even for herself, 'to believe in the power of magic, Your Royal Highness. And actually, so should it be.'

*

Philippa Eilhart adjusted the gossamer-thin strap of her sheer nightdress and wiped the rest of the lipstick smudges from her cleavage. *Such a smart woman*, thought Sheala de Tancarville with slight distaste, *and she can't keep her hormones in check.*

'May we talk?'

Philippa surrounded herself with a sphere of discretion.

'We can now.'

'Everything has been sorted out in Kovir. Positively.'

'Thank you. Has Dijkstra set sail?'

'Not yet.'

'Why does he delay?'

'He conducts long conversations with Esterad Thyssen.' Sheala de Tancarville grimaced. 'They've taken an uncommon liking for each other, the king and the spy.'

*

'Do you know the jokes about our weather, Dijkstra? That there are only two seasons in Kovir—'

'Winter and August. I do.'

'And do you know how to tell if summer has reached Kovir?'

'No. How?'

'The rain becomes a little warmer.'

'Ha ha.'

'Joking aside,' Esterad Thyssen said gravely, 'it worries me somewhat that the winters come earlier and earlier and last longer

297

and longer. It was prophesied. You've read, I presume, Ithlinne's prophecy? It's said there that decades of unending winter will come. Some claim it's some kind of allegory, but I'm a little afraid. In Kovir we once had four summers of cold, rainy weather and poor harvests. Were it not for the tremendous import of food from Nilfgaard, people would have begun to die of starvation in droves. Can you imagine?'

'To be honest, I can't.'

'Well I can. The cooling climate may starve us all to death. Famine is a foe that is bloody hard to fight.'

The spy nodded, lost in thought.

'Dijkstra?'

'Your Majesty?'

'Is there peace inside the country now?'

'I wouldn't say so. But I'm doing my best.'

'I know, everyone's talking about it. Of the traitors on Thanedd, only Vilgefortz remains alive.'

'After the death of Yennefer, yes. Did you know, O king, that Yennefer met her death? She perished on the last day of August, in mysterious circumstances, over the infamous Sedna Trench, between the Isles of Skellige and Cape Peixe de Mar.'

'Yennefer of Vengerberg,' Esterad said slowly, 'was not a traitor. She was not an accomplice of Vilgefortz. If you wish I shall supply proof.'

'I do not,' Dijkstra responded after moment's silence. 'Or perhaps I will, but not right now. Now she's more convenient to me as a traitor.'

'I understand. Don't trust sorceresses, Dijkstra. Philippa in particular.'

'I've never trusted her. But we must co-operate. Without us Redania would plunge into chaos and perish.'

'That is true. But if I may advise you, loosen your grip a little. You know of what I speak. Scaffolds and torture chambers throughout the land, atrocities perpetrated against elves . . . And that dreadful fort, Drakenborg. I know you do it out of patriotism. But you are building yourself an evil legend. In it you're a werewolf, lapping up innocent blood.'

'Someone has to do it.'

'And someone has to bear the consequences. I know you endeavour to be just, but you can't avoid mistakes, can you, for they can't be avoided. Neither can you remain clean when you're slopping around in blood. I know you've never harmed anybody for self-interest, but who will believe that? Who'll want to believe that? The day that fate turns, they'll attribute the murder of innocent people to you, and worse, claim you profited from it. And lying sticks to a fellow like tar.'

'I know.'

'They won't give you a chance to defend yourself. People like you aren't given chances. They'll tar you . . . but later. After the fact. Beware, Dijkstra.'

'I shall. They won't get me.'

'They got your king, Vizimir. With a dagger plunged up to the guard in his flank, I heard . . . '

'It's easier to stab a king than a spy. They won't get me. They'll never get me.'

'And they ought not to. Do you know why, Dijkstra? For there ought to be some sort of fucking justice in this world.'

The day was to come when they would recall that conversation. Both of them. The king and the spy. Dijkstra recalled Esterad's words in Tretogor, as he listened closely to the steps of the assassins approaching from all directions, along all the corridors of the castle. Esterad recalled Dijkstra's words on the splendid marble staircase leading from Ensenada to the Great Canal.

*

'He could have fought back.' The misty, unseeing eyes of Guiscard Vermuellen gazed into the abyss of his recollections. 'There were only three assassins, and grandpappa was a powerful man. He could have fought, defended himself, until the guards arrived. He could have simply fled. But grandmama Zuleyka was there. Grandpappa shielded and protected Zuleyka. Only Zuleyka. He didn't care about himself. When help finally arrived, Zuleyka wasn't even grazed. Esterad had been stabbed more than twenty times. He died three hours later, without regaining consciousness.'

299

'Have you ever read the Good Book, Dijkstra?'

'No, Your Majesty. But I know what is written in it.'

'I, can you believe it, opened it at random yesterday. And I came across this sentence: "On the way to eternity everyone will tread their own stairway, shouldering their own burden". What do you think about that?'

'Time I went, King Esterad. Time to shoulder my burden.'

'Farewell, O Spy.'

'Farewell, O King.'

We trekked perhaps four hundred furlongs southwards from the ancient and far-famed city of Assengard, to a land called Centloch. When one looks on that land from the hills, one sees numerous lakes arranged, artificially, in manifold dispositions. Our guide, the elf Avallac'h, ordered us to seek among those dispositions one calling to mind a cloverleaf. And, in truth, we espied one such. Moreover, it came out that there were not three but four lakes, for one, somewhat elongated, stretching from south to north, is, as it were, the stem of the leaf. That lake, known as Tarn Mira, is ringed by a black forest. Meanwhile, the mysterious Tower of the Swallow, in the elven tongue Tor Zireael, was said to rise up at its northern margin. At first, nonetheless, we saw nothing save fog. I was readying myself to ask the elf Avallac'h about the tower, when he gestured me to be silent and spoke these words: 'Await and hope. Hope shall return with the light and a good omen. Gaze at the endless waters; there you shall discern the envoys of good tidings.'

Buyvid Backhuysen,
Peregrinations along Magic Trails and Places.

The book is humbug from beginning to end. The ruins by Tarn Mira Lake have been examined many and oft. They are not magical; contrary to the enunciations of B. Backhuysen they cannot thus be the remains of the legendary Tower of the Swallow.

Ars Magica, XIV edition

CHAPTER NINE

'They're coming! They're coming!'

Yennefer held her wet, windswept hair in both hands and stopped by the railing of the steps, getting out of the way of the women running to the wharf. Pushed by a west wind, a breaker crashed against the shore and white plumes of foam kept gushing from clefts in the rocks.

'They're coming! They're coming!'

Almost the entire archipelago could be seen from the upper terraces of Kaer Trolde citadel, Ard Skellig's main stronghold. Directly ahead, beyond the strait, lay An Skellig, its southern part low and flat, its hidden northern side precipitous and scored by fjords. Far away to the left, tall, green, mountainous Spikeroog, its peaks shrouded in cloud, broke up the waves with the sharp fangs of its reefs. To the right Undvik island's steep cliffs could be seen, teeming with gulls, petrels, cormorants and gannets. From behind Undvik emerged the forested cone of Hindarsfjall, the archipelago's smallest island. If, though, you were to climb to the very top of one of Kaer Trolde's towers and look southwards, you would see the solitary island of Faroe far from the others, jutting from the water like the back of a huge fish washed up at low tide.

Yennefer went down to the lower terrace, stopping by a group of women whose pride and social status prevented them from rushing pell-mell to the quayside to jostle with the excited rabble. Down below, beneath them, lay the harbour town, black and shapeless like some great marine crustacean spat out by the waves.

Longship after longship sailed out of the strait between An Skellig and Spikeroog. Their sails blazed white and red in the sun and brass bosses shone on the shields suspended from their sides.

'*Ringhorn* is coming first,' said one of the women. 'Followed by *Fenris* . . .'

'*Trigla*,' an excited speaker caught sight of another. '*Drac* follows . . . *Havfrue's* behind them. . . '

'*Anghira* . . . *Tamara* . . . *Daria* . . . No, it's *Scorpena* . . . *Daria's* not there. *Daria's* not there . . . '

A young, heavily pregnant woman with a thick, fair plait, cradling her belly, groaned softly, paled and fainted, collapsing on the flags of the terrace like a curtain torn from its rings. Yennefer leaped forward at once, dropping to one knee, placed her fingers on the woman's abdomen and shouted a spell to suppress the spasms and contractions, powerfully and securely binding the placenta – which was in danger of detaching – to the womb. Just to be certain, she cast another soothing and protective spell on the baby, whose kicks she could feel under her palm. She brought the woman around by slapping her face, in order not to waste magical energy.

'Take her away. Carefully.'

'Foolish girl . . .' said one of the older women. 'A close thing . . .'

'Hysterical . . . Her Nils may still be alive, he may be on another longship . . .'

'Thank you for your help, madam witch.'

'Take her away,' Yennefer repeated, getting to her feet. Then she stifled a curse on discovering her dress had burst at the seams when she'd knelt down.

She went down to an even lower terrace. The longships were pulling into the quay one after another and the warriors going ashore. Heavily-armed, bearded berserkers from Skellige. Bandages shone white on many of them and many had to be helped to walk by their comrades. Some had to be carried.

The women of Skellige, crowded on the quayside, were looking out for their men, whooping and crying for joy if they were fortunate. If not, they fainted. Or walked away, slowly, quietly, without a word of complaint. Occasionally they looked back, hoping that the white and red of *Daria's* sails would glint in the sound.

There was no sign of *Daria*.

Yennefer caught sight of the ruddy mane of Crach an Craite, the yarl of Skellige, one of the last to disembark from *Ringhorn's* deck, towering above the other heads. The yarl was yelling orders, giving instructions, checking, taking care of things. Two women with their eyes fixed on him – one fair and the other dark – were weeping. With joy. The yarl, finally certain he had seen to and made sure of everything, walked over to the women, embraced them both in a bear hug and kissed them. And then raised his head and saw Yennefer. His eyes blazed and his weather-beaten face hardened like the stone of a reef, like a brass shield boss.

He knows, thought the sorceress. *News spreads quickly. Even while still on board ship the yarl found out about my being caught in a net in the sound beyond Spikeroog. He knew he'd find me in Kaer Trolde.*

Magic or carrier pigeons?

He walked unhurriedly towards her. He smelled of the sea, of salt, tar and exhaustion. She looked into his bright eyes and immediately the war cries of the berserkers, the banging of shields and the clanging of swords and battle-axes resounded in her ears. The screaming of men being killed. The screaming of men jumping into the sea from the burning *Daria.*

'Yennefer of Vengerberg.'

'Crach an Craite, Yarl of Skellige.' She bowed slightly before him.

He didn't return the bow. *Not good,* she thought.

He immediately saw the bruise, a souvenir of a blow with an oar. His face hardened again and his lips twitched, revealing his teeth for a second.

'Whoever struck you will answer for it.'

'No one struck me. I tripped on the stairs.'

He considered her intently and then shrugged.

'If you don't want to tell tales that's your business. I have no time to launch an inquiry. Now listen. Carefully, because these will be the only words I shall utter to you.'

'Very well.'

'Tomorrow you will be put on a longship and shipped to Novigrad. You will be handed over to the town authorities there and afterwards to the Temerian or Redanian authorities; whichever comes forward first. And I know that both desire you just as ardently.'

'Is that everything?'

'Almost. Just one more clarification, which you, in truth, deserve.

305

Skellige has quite often given refuge to people being hunted by the law. There is no shortage of opportunities and occasions on the Isles to atone for one's guilt through hard work, fortitude, sacrifice and blood. But not in your case, Yennefer. I shall not give you refuge. If you counted on it, then you miscalculated. I detest people like you. I detest people who stir up trouble in order to gain power, who are driven by self-interest, who plot with the enemy and betray those to whom they owe not only obedience but also gratitude. I detest you, Yennefer. At the very moment you and your rebel comrades began inciting the rebellion on Thanedd at the instigation of Nilfgaard, my longships were fighting in Attre; my boys were coming to the aid of the insurrectionists there. Three hundred of my boys squared up to two thousand Black Cloaks! Valour and fidelity must rewarded, just as wickedness and treachery must be punished! How am I to reward those who fell? With cenotaphs? With inscriptions carved into obelisks? No! I shall reward and honour the fallen differently. Your blood, Yennefer, will trickle between the planks of the scaffold. In exchange for their blood, which soaked into the dunes of Attre.'

'I'm not guilty. I didn't participate in Vilgefortz's plot.'

'You will present proof of that to the judges. I will not judge you.'

'You already have. You've even pronounced sentence.'

'Enough talk! I've spoken: tomorrow at dawn you'll sail in manacles to Novigrad to stand before the royal court. To receive a just punishment. And now, give me your word you won't try to use magic.'

'And if I don't?'

'Marquard, our sorcerer, died on Thanedd; we no longer have a mage who could get you under control. But know this – you will be under the permanent observation of Skellige's finest bowmen. If you so much as move a hand suspiciously, you'll be shot.'

'Very well,' she nodded. 'Then I give my word.'

'Splendid. Thank you. Farewell, Yennefer. I shall not be escorting you tomorrow.'

'Crach.'

He turned on his heel.

'Yes.'

'I don't have the slightest intention of boarding a ship to Novigrad. I don't have the time to prove my innocence to Dijkstra. I can't risk discovering they've already fabricated proof of my guilt. I can't risk dying of a sudden cerebral haemorrhage or committing suicide in my cell in some spectacular way soon after my arrest. I can't waste time or take such a risk. Nor may I explain to you why it is so risky for me. I shan't sail to Novigrad.'

He gazed long at her.

'You won't sail,' he restated. 'What permits you to think like that? Is it that we once shared love's delights? Don't count on that, Yennefer. Let bygones be bygones.'

'I know, and I'm not counting on it. I shan't sail to Novigrad, yarl, because I must go and help someone I vowed never to leave alone and helpless. And you, Crach an Craite, Yarl of Skellige, will help me in my undertaking. Because you took a similar vow. Ten years ago. Right here on the wharf, where we stand. To the same person. To Ciri, the granddaughter of Calanthe. The lion cub of Cintra. I, Yennefer of Vengerberg, regard Ciri as my daughter. Which is why I demand on her behalf that you keep your vow. Keep it, Crach an Craite, Yarl of Skellige.'

*

'Really?' Crach an Craite made sure once again. 'You won't even try them? None of these dainties?'

'Really.'

The yarl did not insist, but took a lobster from the dish, laid it on a board and split it lengthwise with a powerful – though extremely accurate – blow with a cleaver. After sprinkling it liberally with lemon juice and garlic sauce, he began eating the flesh straight from the shell. With his fingers.

Yennefer ate in a dignified manner, using a silver knife and fork – but it was a mutton chop with spinach, specially prepared for her by the astonished and probably slightly offended cook. Because the sorceress didn't want oysters, or mussels, or salmon marinated in its own juice, or gurnard and cockle soup, or stewed monkfish tail, or roast swordfish, or fried moray eel, or octopus, or crab, or lobster, or sea urchin. Or – especially – fresh seaweed.

She associated everything that even faintly smelled of the sea with Fringilla Vigo and Philippa Eilhart, with the insanely dangerous teleportation, the fall into the sea, the sea water she had swallowed, and the net which had been thrown over her – to which, incidentally, had been stuck seaweed and algae identical to that on the dish. Seaweed and algae, smashed against her head and shoulders along with the excruciatingly painful blows from a pine oar.

'So then,' Crach resumed the conversation, sucking the flesh from the legs of the lobster after cracking open the joints, 'I've decided to put my faith in you, Yennefer. I'm not doing it for you, though, be aware of that. Bloedgeas, the blood oath I gave Calanthe, does indeed tie my hands. So if your intention to go to Ciri's aid is genuine and heartfelt, and I presume it is, I have no choice: I must help you with your scheme . . .'

'Thank you. But rid yourself of that pompous tone, please. I repeat: I didn't take part in the plot on Thanedd. Believe me.'

'Is it really so important what I believe?' he flared up. 'You ought rather to begin with the kings, with Dijkstra, whose agents are tracking you the length and breadth of the world. With Philippa Eilhart and the sorcerers loyal to the kings. From whom, as you yourself admitted, you fled here, to Skellige. You ought to present *them* with proof—'

'I have no proof,' she interrupted, angrily stabbing her fork into a Brussels sprout the offended cook had boiled to go with the mutton chop. 'But if I had, they wouldn't let me present it. I can't explain it to you; I'm forbidden from speaking. Take my word for it, Crach. Please.'

'I said—'

'I know,' she interrupted. 'You pledged your help. Thank you. But you still don't believe in my innocence. Believe me.'

Crach threw aside the sucked-out lobster's shell and drew a bowl of mussels closer. He rummaged around, rattling them, taking out the bigger ones.

'Very well,' he finally said, wiping his hands on the tablecloth. 'I believe you. Because I want to believe. But I shall not give you refuge or protection. I cannot. You may, though, leave Skellige whenever you wish and make for wherever you wish. I'd advise haste. You came here, so to speak, on the wings of magic. Others may follow you. They can also work magic.'

'I'm not looking for a refuge or a safe hideaway, yarl. I must go and rescue Ciri.'

'Ciri,' he repeated, lost in thought. 'The lion cub . . . She was a queer child.'

'Was?'

'Oh,' he flared up again. 'I expressed myself badly. Was – because she's no longer a child. That's all I meant. That's all. Cirilla, the Lion Cub of Cintra . . . she spent her summers and winters on Skellige. She was often mischievous! She was a Young Devil, not a Lion Cub . . . Damn it, I said "was" a second time . . . Yennefer, rumours find their way here from the mainland . . . Some say Ciri's in Nilfgaard—'

'She's not in Nilfgaard.'

'Others that the girl is dead.'

Yennefer said nothing, biting her lip.

'But I reject the second rumour,' the yarl said firmly. 'Ciri's alive. I'm certain. There've been no signs . . . She's alive!'

Yennefer raised her eyebrows, but didn't ask any questions. They were silent for a long time, listening intently to the roar of the waves crashing against the rocks of Ard Skellig.

'Yennefer,' Crach said after another moment's silence. 'Yet more tidings have reached us from the continent. I know that your Witcher – who hid in Brokilon after the affray on Thanedd – set off from there with the aim of reaching Nilfgaard and freeing Ciri.'

'I repeat, Ciri is not in Nilfgaard. I know not what *my* Witcher – as you chose to describe him – is planning. But he . . . Crach, it's no secret that I . . . am fond of him. But I know he won't rescue Ciri. He won't achieve anything. I know him. He'll become entangled in something, get lost, start philosophising and feeling sorrow for himself. Then he'll vent his rage, hacking whatever and whoever he can to pieces with his sword. Afterwards, to atone for it, he'll carry out some noble, but senseless feat. Then finally he'll be killed, foolishly, senselessly, probably by a stab in the back—'

'They say,' Crach quickly interjected, alarmed by the sorceress's ominously changing, strangely trembling voice. 'They say Ciri is bound to him by destiny. I saw it myself, back in Cintra, during Pavetta's betrothal—'

'Destiny,' Yennefer interrupted sharply, 'can be interpreted in many, many different ways. Anyway, let's not waste time on digressions. I repeat; I don't know what Geralt's plans are or even whether he has any. I mean to get down to work myself. Using my own methods. And actively, Crach, actively. I'm not accustomed to sitting and weeping, holding my head in both hands. I act!'

The yarl raised his eyebrows, but said nothing.

'I shall take action,' the sorceress repeated. 'I've already devised a plan. And you, Crach, will assist me with it, in accordance with your vow.'

'I'm ready,' he announced firmly. 'For anything. The longships are moored in the harbour. Give the order, Yennefer.'

She couldn't stifle a snort of laughter.

'Always the same. No, Crach, no demonstrations of bravery and manliness. It won't be necessary to sail to Nilfgaard and plunge a battle axe into the lock of the City of the Golden Towers. I need less spectacular, but more tangible help . . . What's the state of your treasury?'

'I beg your pardon?'

'Yarl Crach an Craite. The help I need is expressible in cash.'

*

It began the next day, at dawn. A frantic commotion broke out in the chambers put at Yennefer's disposal, which seneschal Guthlaf – who had been assigned to the sorceress – was having great difficulty controlling. Yennefer was sitting at a table, almost not raising her head from various papers. She was counting, totting up columns and doing calculations, which were immediately rushed to the treasury and the island branch of Cianfanellis' bank. She was making drawings and charts which immediately ended up in the hands of craftsmen: alchemists, goldsmiths, glaziers and jewellers.

Everything went smoothly for a while and then the problems began.

*

'I'm sorry, my lady,' seneschal Guthlaf said slowly. 'But if there isn't any, there isn't any. We gave you everything we had. We can't make magic or do miracles! And I'll take the liberty of observing that what's lying before you, madam, are diamonds with a combined value of—'

'What do I care about their combined value?' she snorted. 'I need one, but a suitably large one. How large, master jeweller?'

The lapidary looked again at the drawing.

'In order to make that cut and those facets? A minimum of thirty carats.'

'There's no such stone,' Guthlaf stated categorically, 'on the whole of Skellige.'

'That's not true,' the jeweller contradicted. 'There is.'

*

'How do you imagine this playing out, Yennefer?' Crach an Craite frowned. 'I'm to send armed men to storm and then plunder the temple? I'm to threaten the priestesses with my wrath if they won't give up the diamond? It's out of the question. I'm not especially religious, but a temple's a temple, and priestesses are priestesses. I can only ask politely. Hint at how much it matters to me and how great my gratitude will be. But it will still only be a request. A humble supplication.'

'That may be denied?'

'Indeed. But there's no harm in trying. What are we risking? Let's sail to Hindarsfjall together and present the supplication. I'll give the priestesses to understand what's needed. But then everything will be in your hands. Negotiate. Present your arguments. Try bribery. Pique their ambition. Appeal to higher reasons. Despair, weep, sob, beg for mercy . . . Call on all the sea devils. Must I teach you, Yennefer?'

'It'll all be for nothing, Crach. A sorceress will never reach agreement with priestesses. Certain differences of our . . . outlook are too marked. And when it comes to permitting a sorceress to use a "sacred" relict or artefact . . . No, we'd better forget it. There's no chance . . .'

'What do you actually need that diamond for?'

311

'To build a "window". I mean a telecommunicational megascope. I have to talk to several people.'

'Magically? At a distance?'

'If it was enough to climb to the top of Kaer Trolde and shout loudly, I wouldn't be bothering you.'

*

The gulls and petrels circling above the water clamoured. The red-beaked oystercatchers nesting on the steep rocks and reefs of Hindarsfjall squealed shrilly, and yellow-headed gannets screeched hoarsely and gaggled. The glistening green eyes of black-crested cormorants watched attentively as the launch sailed past.

'That large rock suspended above the water,' pointed out Crach an Craite, leaning on the rail, 'is Kaer Hemdall, Hemdall's Watchtower. Hemdall is our mythical hero. Legend has it that with the coming of Tedd Deireadh, the Time of the End, the Time of White Frost and the Wolfish Blizzard, Hemdall will face the evil powers from the land of Morhögg: the phantoms, demons and spectres of Chaos. He will stand on the Rainbow Bridge and blow his horn to signal that it is time to take up arms and fall in to battle array. For Ragh nar Roog, the Last Battle, which will decide if night is to fall, or dawn to break.'

The launch skipped nimbly over the waves, entering the calmer waters of the bay between Hemdall's Watchtower and another rock of similarly fantastic contours.

'That smaller rock is Kambi,' the yarl explained. 'In our myths the name Kambi is borne by a magical golden cock, whose crowing will warn Hemdall of the approach of Naglfar, the hellish longboat carrying the army of Darkness, the demons and phantoms of Morhögg. Naglfar is built from corpses' fingernails. You wouldn't believe it, Yennefer, but there are still people on Skellige who cut the nails of the dead before burial, so as not to supply the spectres of Morhögg with building materials.'

'I would. I know the power of legend.'

The fjord protected them a little from the wind and the sail fluttered.

'Sound the horn,' Crach ordered his crew. 'We're reaching the shore. We ought to inform the pious ladies that we're paying them a visit.'

*

The building – located at the head of a long, stone staircase – looked like a gigantic hedgehog, so overgrown was it by moss, ivy and bushes. Yennefer observed that not just bushes, but even small trees, were growing on the roof.

'This is the temple,' Crach confirmed. 'The grove surrounding it is called Hindar and is also a place of worship. It's here that people gather the sacred mistletoe, and on Skellige, as you know, people garnish and decorate everything with it, from a newborn's cradle to a grave . . . Have a care, the steps are slippery . . . The moss, ha-ha, is almost choking religion . . . Let me take your arm . . . As ever, that same perfume . . . Yenna . . .'

'Crach. Please. Let bygones be bygones.'

'I beg your pardon. Let's go on.'

Several silent young priestesses were waiting outside the temple. The yarl greeted them courteously and expressed a wish to talk to their superior, whom he called Modron Sigrdrifa. They went inside, to a space lit by shafts of light shining from stained-glass windows set high up. One of them was shining on the altar.

'By a hundred sea devils,' Crach an Craite muttered. 'I'd forgotten how large Brisingamen was. I haven't been here since I was a child . . . You could probably buy all the shipyards in Cidaris with it. Along with the labourers and the annual output.'

The yarl was exaggerating. But not by much.

A statue of Modron Freyja, the Great Mother, in her typical maternal aspect – a woman in flowing robes revealing her advanced state of pregnancy, which the sculptor had accented inordinately – towered above the modest marble altar, above figures of cats and falcons, above a stone basin for votive offerings. She stood with bowed head and facial features hidden by a scarf. Over the goddess' arms, which were folded on her chest, was a diamond, one element of a gold necklace. The diamond was tinged slightly blue, like the clearest water. It was large.

A hundred and fifty carats, or so.

'It wouldn't even need cutting,' Yennefer whispered. 'It's a rosette, exactly what I need. Facets perfect for diffracting light . . .'

'That means we're lucky.'

'I doubt it. The priestesses will soon appear, and I, being a heathen, will be sworn at and ejected.'

'Are you exaggerating?'

'Not in the slightest.'

'Welcome, yarl, to the temple of the Mother. And I welcome you too, O honourable Yennefer of Vengerberg.'

Crach an Craite bowed.

'Greetings, esteemed mother Sigrdrifa.'

The priestess was tall, almost as tall as Crach – which meant she was a head taller than Yennefer. She had fair hair and pale eyes, and an oval, none too pretty and none too feminine, face.

I've seen her somewhere before, thought Yennefer. *Not so long ago. Where?*

'On the steps of Kaer Trolde, leading to the harbour,' the priestess recalled with a smile. 'When the longboats were coming in from the sound. I stood over you as you helped a pregnant woman who was about to miscarry. On your knees, worrying not at all about your very costly camlet dress. I saw it. And I shall never more pay heed to tales of cold-hearted and calculated sorceresses.'

Yennefer coughed softly and lowered her head in a bow.

'You are standing before the altar of the Mother, Yennefer. May her grace fall on you.'

'Esteemed mother, I . . . I wish humbly to ask you . . .'

'Say nothing. Yarl, you are no doubt very busy. Leave us alone, here, on Hindarsfjall. We will manage to come to an agreement. We are women. It is unimportant what we are engaged in, or who we are: we always serve she who is the Virgin, the Mother and the Crone. Kneel beside me, Yennefer. Lower your head before the Mother.'

*

'Take Brisingamen from the goddess' neck?' Sigrdrifa repeated, and there was more disbelief than righteous indignation in her voice. 'No, Yennefer. It is quite impossible. The point is not even that I would not dare . . . Even if I did, Brisingamen cannot be removed. The necklace has no clasp. It is permanently bonded to the statue.'

Yennefer stayed silent for a long while, calmly eyeing up the priestess.

'Had I known,' she said coldly, 'I would have set sail at once for Ard Skellig with the yarl. No, no, by no means do I regard the time spent talking to you as wasted. But I have very little of it. Very little indeed. Your kindness and warmth beguiled me somewhat, I confess—'

'I am well-disposed towards you,' Sigrdrifa interrupted un-emotionally. 'I also support your plans, with all my heart. I knew Ciri, I liked the child, and her fate moves me. I admire you for the determination with which you hope to go to the girl's rescue. I shall grant your every wish. But not Brisingamen, Yennefer. Not Brisingamen. Do not ask for that.'

'Sigrdrifa, in order to go to Ciri's rescue, I urgently need some information. Without it I'll be helpless. I can only acquire the knowledge I need through telecommunication. In order to communicate at a distance, I must construct a magical artefact – a megascope – using magic.'

'A device something like your notorious crystal balls?'

'Considerably more complex. Crystal balls only permit telecommunication with another correlated crystal ball. Even the local dwarven bank has a crystal ball for talking to another at headquarters. A megascope has somewhat greater capabilities . . . But why theorise? Without the diamond nothing will come of it anyhow. Well, I shall say farewell . . .'

'Don't hurry so.'

Sigrdrifa stood up and passed through the nave, stopping before the altar and the statue of Modron Freyja.

'The goddess,' she said, 'is also the patron of soothsayers. Clairvoyants. Telepaths. As symbolised by her sacred animals: the cat, which sees and hears, itself unseen, and the falcon, which sees from above. And by the jewel of the goddess: Brisingamen, the necklace of clairvoyance. Why build some looking and listening device, Yennefer? Wouldn't it be simpler to ask the goddess for help?'

Yennefer stopped herself from swearing at the last moment. After all, it was a place of worship.

'The time for evening prayers is approaching,' Sigrdrifa continued. 'I shall devote myself to meditation along with the other priestesses. I shall ask the goddess for help for Ciri. For Ciri, who was here many times, in this temple, and looked at Brisingamen around the neck of the Great Mother many times. Sacrifice one more hour or two of your precious time, Yennefer. Stay here, with us, for the time of worship. Support me as I pray. With your thoughts and presence.'

'Sigrdrifa . . .'

'Please. Do it for me. And for Ciri.'

*

The jewel Brisingamen. On the goddess' neck.

She stifled a yawn. *Had there only been some singing*, she thought, *some incantations, some mystery . . . Some mystic folklore . . . It would have been less boring, she wouldn't be feeling so drowsy. But they were simply kneeling, with bowed heads. Motionless, soundless.*

But they're capable, when they want to, of using the Power, at times just as well as we sorceresses. It's still a mystery how they do it. Without any preparations, any learning, any studies . . . Just prayer and meditation. Divination? Some kind of autohypnosis? That's what Tissaia de Vries claims . . . They absorb energy unconsciously, in a trance, and they acquire the ability to transform it into something like our spells. They transform energy, treating it as a gift and favour of the godhead. Faith gives them strength.

Why have we sorceresses never succeeded with anything like that?

Ought I to try? Using the atmosphere and aura of this place? I could enter a trance myself, couldn't I? If only by gazing at the diamond . . . Brisingamen . . . Intensively thinking about how marvellously it would function in my megascope . . .

Brisingamen . . . shining like the morning star, there, in the gloom, in the smoke of incense and smouldering candles . . .

'Yennefer.'

She jerked her head up.

It was dark in the temple. It smelled strongly of smoke.

'Did I fall asleep? Forgive me . . .'

'There's nothing to forgive. Come with me.'

Outside, the night sky burned with a twinkling luminosity that changed like the colours in a kaleidoscope. The northern lights? Yennefer rubbed her eyes in amazement. The aurora borealis? In August?

'How much are you capable of sacrificing, Yennefer?'

'I beg your pardon?'

'Are you prepared to sacrifice yourself? Your priceless magic?'

'Sigrdrifa,' she said with anger, 'don't try your sublime tricks on me. I'm ninety-four years old. But treat that, please, as a confessional secret. I'm only confiding in you so you'll understand I can't be treated like a child.'

'You didn't answer my question.'

'And I don't mean to. For it's the mysticism I don't accept. I fell asleep during your worship. It wearied and bored me. Because I don't believe in your goddess.'

Sigrdrifa turned away and Yennefer took a very deep breath in spite of herself.

'Your disbelief is not very flattering to me,' said a woman with eyes filled with molten gold. 'But does your disbelief change anything?'

All Yennefer could do was to breathe out.

'The time will come,' said the golden-eyed woman, 'when absolutely no one, including children, will believe in sorceresses. I tell you that with deliberate spite. By way of revenge. Let us leave.'

'No . . .' Yennefer finally managed. 'No! I won't go anywhere. Enough of this! It's an enthrallment or hypnosis. An illusion! A trance! I have developed defence mechanisms . . . I can dispel all this with one charm, just like that! Dammit . . .'

The golden-eyed woman came closer. The diamond in her necklace burned like the morning star.

'Your speech is slowly ceasing to serve as communication,' she said. 'It is becoming art for art's sake. The more incomprehensible it is, the more profound and wise it is considered. In sooth, I preferred you when you could only say "Ugh" and "Ooh". Come.'

317

'This is an illusion, a trance . . . I won't go anywhere!'

'I don't want to force you. It would be a disgrace. For you're an intelligent and proud girl, you have character.'

A plain. A sea of grass. A moor. A boulder, jutting from the heather like the back of a crouching predator.

'You desired my jewel, Yennefer. I cannot give it to you without first making sure of a few things. I want to check what is deep inside you. Therefore I have brought you here, to this place of Power and Might from time immemorial. Your priceless magic is apparently everywhere. Apparently it's sufficient to merely hold out one's hand. Are you afraid to hold it out?'

Yennefer couldn't utter a sound from her tight throat.

'Are, then, Chaos, art and learning,' said the woman, whose name could not be uttered, 'according to you, the Powers capable of changing the world? A curse, a blessing and progress? And aren't they by any chance Faith? Love? Sacrifice?

'Do you hear? The cock Kambi is crowing. The waves are breaking against the shore, waves pushed by Naglfar's prow. The horn of Hemdall sounds as he stands facing his enemies on the rainbow-coloured arch of Bifrost. The White Frost is nigh, a gale and a blizzard are nigh . . . The earth trembles from the writhing movements of the Serpent . . .

'The wolf devours the sun. The moon turns black. There is only coldness and darkness. Hatred, vengeance and blood . . .

'Whose side will you be on, Yennefer? Will you be on the east or the west side of Bifrost? Will you be with Hemdall or against him?

'The cock Kambi is crowing.

'Decide, Yennefer. Choose. Only for this reason were you restored to life: that you might make a choice at the right moment.

'Light or Darkness?'

'Good and Evil, Light and Darkness, Order and Chaos? They are but symbols; in reality no such polarity exists! Brightness and Gloom are in each of us, a little of one and a little of the other. This conversation is pointless. Pointless. I will not come over to mysticism. To you and Sigrdrifa, the Wolf is devouring the Sun. To me it's an eclipse. And may it remain that way.'

Remain? What?

She felt her head spinning, felt some horrendous force twisting her arms, wrenching the joints in her shoulders and elbows, racking her vertebrae as though she were being tortured. She screamed in pain, thrashed around and opened her eyes. No, it wasn't a dream. It couldn't be a dream. She was on a tree, hanging arms akimbo from the boughs of a gigantic ash. High above her a falcon circled. Below her, on the ground, in the gloom, she heard the hiss of snakes, the rustling of scales rubbing against each other.

Something moved beside her. A squirrel ran across her tautened and aching shoulders.

'Are you ready?' asked the squirrel. 'Are you ready to offer your sacrifice? What are you prepared to sacrifice?'

'I have nothing!' The pain blinded and paralysed her. 'And even if I had, I don't believe in such a sacrifice! I don't want to suffer for millions! I don't want to suffer at all! For no one and in no one's stead!'

'No one wants to suffer. But yet it is our lot. And some suffer more. Not necessarily by choice. The point is not the bearing of suffering. The point is how it is borne.'

*

Janka! Dear Janka!

Take this hunchbacked monstrosity from me! I don't want to look at it!

She's your daughter as much as she is mine.

Indeed? The children I have sired are normal.

How dare you . . . How dare you suggest . . .

It was in your elven family that there were witches. It was you that aborted your first pregnancy. It was because of that. You have tainted elven blood and a tainted womb, woman. That's why you give birth to monsters.

It is an ill-fated child . . . Such was the will of the gods! She's your daughter as much as she is mine! What was I to do? Smother her? Not tie the birth cord? What am I to do now? Take her to the forest and leave her? What do you want from me, by the Gods?

Daddy! Mummy!

Get away, you freak.

How dare you! How dare you strike a child! Stop! Where are you going? Where? To her, are you? To her!

Yes, woman. I'm a man. I'm free to sate my lust where and when I want, as is my natural right. And I loathe you. You and the fruit of your degenerate womb. Don't wait with supper. I won't be back tonight.

Mummy . . .

Why are you weeping?

Why are you beating me and pushing me away? I was good, wasn't I?

*

Mummy! Dear Mummy!

*

'Are you capable of forgiveness?'

'I forgave long ago.'

'Having first satisfied your lust for vengeance.'

'Yes.'

'Do you regret it?'

'No.'

*

Pain, searing pain in her mutilated hands and fingers.

'Yes, I'm guilty. Is that what you want to hear? A confession and remorse? You want to hear Yennefer of Vengerberg grovel and abase herself? No, I won't give you that pleasure. I admit my guilt and await my punishment. But you will not hear my remorse!'

The pain reached the limits of what a person can withstand.

'You blame me for the betrayed, the deceived, the abused, you blame me for those who died – because of me – from their own hand, from my hand . . . For once having raised a hand against myself? You can see I had my reasons! And I regret nothing! Even if I could turn back time . . . I regret nothing!'

320

The falcon alighted on her shoulder.

The Tower of the Swallow. The Tower of the Swallow. Hurry to the Tower of the Swallow.

O Daughter.

*

The cock Kambi crows.

*

Ciri on a black mare, at a gallop, her ashen hair tousled by the wind. Blood sprays from her face, a vivid, intense red. The black mare soars like a bird, smoothly gliding over the top rail of a high gate. Ciri sways in the saddle, but doesn't fall off . . .

Ciri amidst the night, amidst a stony, sandy wilderness, with a raised arm. A glowing ball explodes from her hand . . . A unicorn churning up gravel with its hoof . . . Many unicorns . . . Fire . . . Fire . . .

Geralt on a bridge. In combat. Amidst fire. A flame reflected in his sword blade.

Fringilla Vigo, her green eyes wide open in sexual ecstasy, her close-cropped head on an open book, on the frontispiece . . . Part of the title is visible: *Remarks on Inevitable Death* . . .

Geralt's eyes reflected in Fringilla's.

A chasm. Smoke. Steps leading downwards. Steps that must be descended. Something is ending. Tedd Deireadh, the Time of the End, is nigh . . .

Darkness. Dampness. The dreadful cold of stone walls. The cold of iron on wrists, on ankles. Pain pulsing in mutilated hands, shooting down crushed fingers . . .

Ciri takes her by the hand. A long, dark corridor, stone columns, perhaps statues . . . Darkness. In it, whispers soft as the soughing of the wind.

A door. Endless doors with gigantic, heavy leaves open before them without a murmur. And finally, in the impenetrable darkness, a door which does not open by itself. Which it is forbidden to open.

321

If you are afraid, turn back.
It is forbidden to open this door. You know that.
I do.
But yet you are leading me there.
If you are afraid, turn back. There is still time to turn back. It is
not yet too late.
And you?
For me it is.
The cock Kambi is crowing.
Tedd Deireadh has come.
The aurora borealis.
Dawn.

*

'Yennefer. Wake up.'

She jerked her head up. She glanced down at her hands. She had both of them. Intact.

'Sigrdrifa? I fell asleep . . .'

'Come.'

'Where to?' she whispered. 'Where to this time?'

'I beg your pardon? I don't understand you. Come. You must see it. Something has happened . . . Something strange. None of us knows how to explain it. But I can guess. Grace . . . The goddess has bestowed her grace on you, Yennefer.'

'What do you mean, Sigrdrifa?'

'Look.'

She looked. And sighed aloud.

Brisingamen, the sacred jewel of Modron Freyja, was no longer hanging around the goddess's neck. It was lying at her feet.

*

'Did I hear that correctly?' Crach an Craite asked. 'You're moving to Hindarsfjall with your magical workshop? The priestesses will make the sacred diamond available to you? They'll let you use it in your infernal machine?'

'Yes.'

322

'Well, well. Yennefer, have you perhaps had a conversion? What happened on the island?'

'Never you mind. I'm returning to the temple and that's that.'

'And the financial resources you asked for? Will they still be necessary?'

'I'd say so.'

'Seneschal Guthlaf will carry out each of your relevant instructions. But Yennefer, issue them quickly. Make haste. I've received fresh tidings.'

'Dammit, I was afraid of that. Do they know where I am?'

'No, not yet. I was warned, though, that you may appear on Skellige and was ordered to imprison you immediately. I was also ordered to take prisoners on my expeditions and extract information from them, even if it was only scraps concerning you and your sojourn in Nilfgaard or in the provinces. Yennefer, hurry. If they tracked you and caught you here, on Skellige, I would find myself in a somewhat difficult situation.'

'I'll do everything in my power. Including whatever it takes to avoid compromising you. Don't worry.'

Crach grinned.

'I said *somewhat*. I'm not afraid of them. Not of kings, nor of sorcerers. They can't do anything to me, because they need me. And I was bound to help you by a feudal oath. Yes, yes, you heard right. I'm still formally a vassal of the Cintran crown. And Cirilla has formal rights to that crown. By representing Cirilla, by being her sole guardian, you have the formal right to give me orders, demand obedience and servitudes.'

'Casuistic sophistries.'

'Well certainly,' he snorted. 'I will shout as much myself, in a booming voice, if in spite of everything it turns out Emhyr var Emreis really has forced the girl to marry. Also if – by the help of some legal loopholes and flourishes – Ciri has been deprived of the right to the throne and someone else has been named as a substitute heir, including that lummox Vissegerd. Then I'll announce my obedience and declare my feudal oath forthwith.'

'But if,' Yennefer squinted, 'in spite of everything, it turns out that Ciri is dead?'

'She's alive,' Crach said firmly. 'I know that for certain.'

'How?'

'You won't want to give it credence.'

'Try me.'

'The blood of the queens of Cintra,' Crach began, 'is uncannily bound to the sea. When one of the women of that blood dies the sea falls into sheer madness. It's said that Ard Skellig bewails the daughters of Riannon. For the storm is so strong then that the waves striking from the west squeeze through crevices and caverns to the east side and suddenly salt brooks gush from the rock. And the entire island shudders. Simple folk say "See how Ard Skellig sobs. Someone has died again. Riannon's blood has died. The Elder Blood".'

Yennefer was silent.

'It's not a fairy tale,' Crach continued. 'I've seen it for myself, with my own eyes. Three times. Following the death of Adalia the Soothsayer, following the death of Calanthe . . . And following the death of Pavetta, Ciri's mother.'

'Pavetta,' Yennefer observed, 'actually perished during a storm, so it's hard to speak—'

'Pavetta,' Crach interrupted, still deep in thought, 'did not perish during a storm. The storm began after her death. The sea reacted as it always does to the death of one of the Cintran bloodline. I've investigated that matter long enough. And am certain of what I know.'

'Meaning what?'

'The ship Pavetta and Duny were sailing on vanished over the infamous Sedna Abyss. It wasn't the first ship to vanish there. You no doubt know that.'

'Fairy tales. Ships meet with disasters, it's a natural thing—'

'On Skellige,' he interrupted quite firmly, 'we know enough about ships and sailing to be able to distinguish between natural and unnatural disasters. Ships go down unnaturally over the Sedna Abyss. And not accidentally. That includes the ship Pavetta and Duny were sailing on.'

'I'm not arguing.' The sorceress sighed. 'Anyway, does that have any meaning to us? After almost fifteen years?'

'It does to me.' The yarl pursed his lips. 'I shall unravel the case. It's only a matter of time. I'll find out. . . I'll find an explanation.

I'll find an explanation to all the enigmas. Including the one from the slaughter of Cintra . . .'

'What enigma would that be?'

'When the Nilfgaardians invaded Cintra,' he muttered, looking her in the eyes, 'Calanthe ordered Ciri spirited out of the town. But the town was already aflame, Black Cloaks were everywhere, the chances of getting out of the siege were faint. The queen was advised against such a risky business, and it was suggested that Ciri formally capitulate before the hetmans of Nilfgaard, thus saving her life and the Cintran state. In the blazing streets she would surely and senselessly have died at the hands of the soldierly mob. But the Lioness . . . Do you know what, according to eye witnesses, she said?'

'No.'

'"It would be better for the girl's blood to flow over the cobbles of Cintra than for it to be defiled." Defiled by what?'

'Marriage to Emperor Emhyr. A filthy Nilfgaardian. Yarl, it's late. I begin tomorrow at dawn . . . I shall inform you of my progress.'

'I'm counting on it. Goodnight, Yenna . . . Hmmm . . .'

'What, Crach?'

'You wouldn't by any chance, hmmm, fancy . . .'

'No, yarl. Let bygones be bygones. Goodnight.'

*

'Well, well.' Crach an Craite received his guest with a tilt of his head. 'Triss Merigold in person. What a stunning dress. And the fur . . . chinchilla, isn't it? I would ask what brings you to Skellige . . . If I didn't know. But I do.'

'Wonderful,' Triss smiled seductively and neatened her gorgeous chestnut hair. 'It's wonderful that you know, yarl. It will save us the introduction and the preliminary explanations, and allow us to get to business right away.'

'What business?' Crach crossed his arms on his chest and glared at the sorceress. 'What ought to precede introductions, what explanations are you counting on? Who do you represent, Triss? In whose name have you come here? King Foltest, whom you served, released you from service with banishment. Although you weren't at fault, he banished you from Temeria. Philippa Eilhart, I've heard, who, along with Dijkstra, is presently ruling de facto in Redania, has taken you under her wing. I see that you're repaying for the asylum as well as you can. You don't even flinch at assuming the role of secret agent in order to track down your old friend.'

'You wrong me, yarl.'

'I humbly beg your pardon. If I'm in error. Am I?'

They were silent for a long while, eyeing each other up mistrustfully. Triss finally snorted, swore and stamped a high heel.

'Oh, to hell with it! Let's stop leading each other by the nose! What difference does it make now, who's serving whom, who's siding with whom, who's keeping faith with whom and with what motives? Yennefer's dead. It's still not known where or in whose grasp Ciri is . . . What's the point of playing at secrets? I didn't sail here as a spy, Crach. I came on my own initiative, as a private individual. Driven by concern for Ciri.'

'Everyone is concerned about Ciri. Lucky girl.'

Triss's eyes flashed.

'I wouldn't sneer at that. Particularly in your place.'

'I beg your pardon.'

They said nothing, looking out of the window at the red sun setting beyond the wooded peaks of Spikeroog.

'Triss Merigold.'

'Yes, O yarl.'

'I invite you to supper. Ah, the cook told me to ask if all sorceresses disdain finely cooked seafood?'

*

Triss did not disdain seafood. On the contrary, she ate twice as much as she had intended and now began to worry about her waistline – about the twenty-two inches she was so proud of. She decided to ease her digestion with some white wine, the celebrated Est Est of Toussaint. Like Crach, she drank from a horn.

'And so,' she took up the conversation, 'Yennefer showed up here on the nineteenth of August, falling spectacularly from the sky into some fishing nets. You, as a faithful vassal of Cintra,

326

granted her asylum. Helped her to build a megascope . . . With whom and about what she talked, you of course don't know.'

Crach an Craite drank deeply from the horn and suppressed a burp.

'I don't know,' he smiled craftily. 'Of course I don't know. How could I, a poor and simple sailor, know anything about the doings of mighty sorceresses?'

*

Sigrdrifa, the priestess of Modron Freyja, let her head drop low, as though Crach an Craite's question had burdened her with a thousand-pound weight.

'She trusted me, yarl,' she muttered barely audibly. 'She didn't demand of me the swearing of an oath of silence, but she naturally cared about discretion. I really don't know whether—'

'Modron Sigrdrifa,' Crach an Craite interrupted gravely, 'I'm not asking you to act as an informer. Like you, I support Yennefer, like you I desire to find and rescue Ciri. Why, I took Bloedgeas, a blood oath! Whereas regarding Yennefer, concern for her motivates me. She's an extremely proud woman. Even when taking a very great risk, she doesn't stoop to making requests. Therefore it will be necessary – I can't rule it out – to come to her aid unasked. In order to do that I need information.'

Sigrdrifa cleared her throat. She wore an uneasy expression. And when she began to speak, her voice slightly quavered.

'She built that machine of hers . . . In essence it's not a machine at all, because there's no mechanism, just two looking glasses, a black velvet curtain, a box, two lenses, four lamps, well and Brisingamen, of course . . . When she utters the spell, the light from the two lamps falls—'

'Let's leave out the details. Who did she communicate with?'

'She spoke to several persons. With sorcerers . . . Yarl, I didn't hear everything, but what I heard . . . Among them are truly wicked people. None wanted to help disinterestedly . . . They demanded money . . . They all demanded money . . .'

'I know,' Crach muttered. 'The bank informed me of the money orders she issued. A pretty, oh, a pretty penny my oath is costing

327

me! But money comes and goes. What I spent on Yennefer and Ciri, I shall make good in the Nilfgaardian provinces. But go on, O mother Sigrdrifa.'

'Yennefer,' the priestess lowered her head, 'blackmailed some of them. She gave them to understand she was in possession of compromising information and in the event of cooperation being declined she would reveal it to the whole world . . . Yarl . . . She's a clever and essentially good woman . . . But she doesn't have any scruples. She is ruthless. And merciless.'

'Indeed, as I know. But I don't want to know the details of the blackmail, and I advise you to forget about them as quickly as you can. It's dangerous knowledge. Outsiders shouldn't meddle with fire like that.'

'I know, yarl. I owe you obedience . . . And I believe that your ends justify your means. No one shall learn anything from me. Neither a friend in a convivial chat, nor a foe torturing me.'

'Good, Modron Sigrdrifa. Very good . . . What did Yennefer's questions concern, do you recall?'

'I didn't always overhear nor understand everything, yarl. They were using jargon that was difficult to grasp . . . There was often talk of a Vilgefortz . . .'

'Of course.' Crach audibly ground his teeth. The priestess glanced at him fearfully.

'They also spoke a lot about elves and about Knowing Ones,' she continued. 'And about magical portals. There was also mention of the Sedna Abyss . . . But mainly, it seems to me, it concerned towers.'

'Towers?'

'Yes. Two. The Tower of the Gull and the Tower of the Swallow.'

*

'As I supposed,' Triss said, 'Yennefer began by obtaining the secret report of Radcliffe's commission, which investigated the case of the events on Thanedd. I don't know what news of this affair has reached you here, on Skellige . . . Have you heard of the teleporter in the Tower of the Seagull? And about Radcliffe's commission?'

Crach an Craite glanced suspiciously at the sorceress.

'Neither politics nor culture reach the islands,' he grimaced. 'We're backward.'

'The Radcliffe commission –' Triss did not deign to pay attention either to his tone, nor his expression '– examined in detail teleportational trails leading from Thanedd. The portal on the island, Tor Lara, while it existed, negated all teleportational magic within a considerable radius. But, as you certainly know, the Tower of the Gull exploded and disintegrated, making teleportation possible. Most of the participants in the events on Thanedd got off the island using portals they opened.'

'As a matter of fact –' the yarl smiled '– you, for example, flew straight to Brokilon. With the Witcher on your back.'

'Well, I never.' Triss looked him in the eye. 'Politics don't reach here, culture doesn't reach here, but rumours do. But let's leave that for now, we'll return to the work of the Radcliffe commission. The commission's task was to determine precisely who teleported from Thanedd and whence. They used so-called synopses – spells capable of reconstructing an image of past events – and then collated the uncovered teleportational tracks with the directions they led to, as a result ascribing them to the specific individuals who had opened the portals. They were successful in practically all cases. Save one. One teleportational trail led nowhere. To be precise, into the sea. To the Sedna Abyss.'

'Someone,' the yarl guessed at once, 'teleported onto a ship waiting in a previously agreed location. I just wonder why they went so far . . . And to such a notorious place. Well, but if a battle axe is hovering over your neck . . .'

'Exactly. The commission also thought of that. And voiced the following conclusion: it was Vilgefortz, who having captured Ciri and having his other escape route cut off, took advantage of a reserve exit – he teleported with the girl to the Sedna Abyss, onto a Nilfgaardian ship waiting there. That, according to the commission, explains the fact that Ciri was presented at the imperial court in Loc Grim on the tenth of July, barely ten days after the events on Thanedd.'

'Well, yes.' the yarl squinted. 'That would explain a lot. On condition, naturally, that the commission wasn't mistaken.'

'Indeed.' The sorceress withstood his gaze and even afforded herself a mocking smirk. 'Naturally, a double – and not the real Ciri – could just as easily have been presented in Loc Grim. That may also explain a lot. It doesn't, though, explain one occurrence that the Radcliffe commission established. So bizarre that in the report's first version it was passed over as too improbable. In the report's second – and strictly confidential – version that occurrence was nonetheless presented. As a hypothesis.'

'I've been all ears for some time, Triss.'

'The commission's hypothesis reads: the teleporter in the Tower of the Gull was active, was functioning. Someone passed through it and the energy of the passage was so powerful the teleporter exploded and was destroyed.'

'Yennefer,' Triss continued a moment later, 'must have found out about it. What the Radcliffe commission uncovered. What was included in the confidential report. That is, there's a chance . . . the slightest chance . . . that Ciri managed to pass safely through the Tor Lara portal. That she eluded Nilfgaard and Vilgefortz . . .'

'Where is she then?'

'I'd like to know that too.'

*

It was dreadfully dark; the moon, hidden behind banks of cloud, gave no light at all. But in comparison to the previous nights there was almost no wind and for that reason it was not so cold. The dugout only rocked gently on the slightly rippling water. It smelled like a swamp. Of decaying weed. And eel slime.

Somewhere by the bank a beaver slapped its tail on the water, startling both of them. Ciri was certain that Vysogota had been dozing and the beaver had woken him.

'Go on with the story,' she said, wiping her nose with a clean part of her sleeve not yet covered in slime. 'Don't sleep. When you doze off my eyelids droop too. Then the current will take us and we'll wake up on the sea! Go on about those teleporters!'

'When you escaped from Thanedd,' the hermit continued, 'you passed through the portal of the Tower of the Gull, Tor Lara. And Geoffrey Monck, probably the greatest authority in the field of teleportation, the author of the work entitled *The Magic of the Elder Folk*, which is the opus magnum of knowledge about elven teleporters, writes that the Tor Lara portal leads to the Tower of the Swallow, Tor Zireael—'

'The teleport from Thanedd was warped,' Ciri interrupted. 'Perhaps, long ago, before it broke, it led to some swallow or other. But now it leads to a desert. That's what we call a chaotic portal. I learned about it.'

'I – just imagine – did too,' the old man snorted. 'I recall much of that wisdom. Which is why your story amazes me so much . . . Some parts of it. Particularly the ones that concern teleportation . . .'

'Could you speak more plainly?'

'I could, Ciri. I could. But now it's high time we hauled in the net. It sure to be full of eels. Ready?'

'Ready.' Ciri spat on her hands and took hold of the gaff. Vysogota grasped the cord speeding past in the water.

'Let's haul it in. One, two . . . three! And into the boat! Grab them, Ciri, grab them! Into the basket before they escape!'

*

It was the second night they had rowed the dugout to the river's boggy tributary, set nets and traps for the eels heading in great numbers towards the sea. They returned to the cottage well after midnight, smeared in slime from head to toe, wet and tired as hell.

But they didn't go to bed at once. The haul earmarked for barter had to be put in crates and sealed securely – should the eels find the smallest crack there wouldn't be a single one left the next morning. After the work was done Vysogota skinned two or three fat eels, chopped them into steaks, coated them in flour and fried them in a huge frying pan. Then they ate and talked.

'You see, Ciri, one thing still nags at me. I can't forget that right after your recovery we couldn't agree about the dates, even though the wound on your cheek constituted the most precise of possible calendars. The cut couldn't have been more than ten hours old, while you insisted that they'd wounded you four days earlier. Though I was certain it came down to a simple mistake, I couldn't

331

stop thinking about it. I kept asking myself the question: what happened to those four lost days?'

'So? What do you think happened to them?'

'I don't know.'

'That's marvellous.'

The cat made a long leap and the mouse it pinned with its claws squeaked shrilly. The tomcat unhurriedly bit through its neck, disembowelled it and began to eat it with relish. Ciri watched it impassively.

'The Tower of the Gull teleporter,' Vysogota began again, 'leads to the Tower of the Swallow. And the Tower of the Swallow—'

The cat ate the entire mouse, leaving the tail for dessert.

'The Tor Lara teleporter,' said Ciri, yawning widely, 'is warped and leads to a desert. I've probably told you that a hundred times.'

'That's not the point, I'm talking about something else. That there's a connection between the two teleporters. The Tar Lara portal was warped, I agree. But there is also the Tor Zireael teleporter. If you could reach the Tower of the Swallow, you could teleport back to the Isle of Thanedd. You would be far from the danger threatening you, out of reach of your enemies.'

'Ah! That would suit me. There's just one little snag. I have no idea where the Tower of the Swallow is.'

'Perhaps I'll find a remedy for that. Do you know, Ciri, what university studies give a person?'

'No. What?'

'The ability to make use of sources.'

*

'I knew I'd find it,' Vysogota said proudly. 'I searched and searched and . . . Oh, bugger . . .'

The armful of heavy tomes slipped through his fingers; grimoires tumbled onto the threshing floor, leaves fell from their decayed bindings and were strewn around haphazardly.

'What have you found?' Ciri kneeled beside him, and helped him gather up the scattered pages.

'The Tower of the Swallow!' The hermit drove away the tomcat, which had impudently settled on one of the leaves. 'Tor Zireael. Help me.'

'How dusty it is! And sticky! Vysogota? What's this? Here, in this picture? That man hanging from a tree?'

'This?' Vysogota examined the loose leaf. 'A scene from the legend of Hemdall. The hero Hemdall hung from the Ash of the Worlds for nine days and nights to gain knowledge and power through sacrifice and pain.'

'I've dreamed of something like that several times.' Ciri wiped her forehead. 'A man hanging from a tree . . .'

'The engraving fell out of this book, here. If you like, you can read more later. But now the more important thing is . . . Ah, I have it at last. *Peregrinations along Trails and Magical Places* by Buyvid Backhuysen, a book regarded by some as an apocryphal work . . .'

'You mean it's poppycock?'

'Something like that. But there were also those who valued the book . . . Here, listen . . . A pox on it, how dark it is . . .'

'There's enough light, you're going blind from old age,' said Ciri, with the detached cruelty befitting her age. 'Hand it over, *I'll* read it. Where from?'

'From here.' He pointed with a bony finger. 'Read it aloud.'

*

'That old Buyvid wrote in weird language. I think Assengard was some castle or other, if I'm not mistaken. But what's this land: Centloch? I've never heard of any such place. And what's trefoil?'

'Clover. And I'll tell you about Assengard and the Hundred Lakes when you finish reading.'

*

'For the life of me, barely had the elf Avallac'h uttered those words, than did hurry out from beneath the lake's waters those meagre black birds that had sheltered from the frost the whole winter at the bottom of the depths. For the swallow, as learned men know, does not fly south for the winter in the manner of other birds and return in the spring, but binds itself with its claws in great swarms and sinks to the bottom of the waters, there to spend the whole winter season, and only in the spring does it fly out *de profundis* from beneath the waters. Howbeit, that bird is not only the symbol of spring and hope, but also the model of unblemished purity, since it never alights on the ground nor with earthly dirt and filth have any commerce.

'Let us, though, return to our lake: you would have said that the circling avians dispersed the fog with their wings, for *tandem* a marvellous, occult tower unexpectedly emerged from the vapour, and we sighed in awe with one voice, because it seemed to be a tower woven from mist, having fog as its *fundamentum*, and its top was crowned with the gleam of the aurora, an enchanted *aurora borealis*. Indeed, that tower must have been erected using powerful occult arts, beyond human ken.

'The elf Avallac'h marked our awe and spake: "This is Tor Zireael, the Tower of the Swallow. This is the Gate of Worlds and the Threshold of Time. Feast your eyes on this sight, man, for not to everyone nor always is it given."

'But when asked if we might approach and from proximity gaze on the Tower or *propria manu* touch it, Avallac'h laughed. "Tor Zireael," he spake, "is for you a reverie, and reveries may not be touched. And a good thing it is," he added, "for the Tower serves only the few Chosen, for whom the Threshold of Time is a gate of hope and rebirth. But for the profane it is the portal of nightmare."

'Barely had he uttered those words than the fog fell once more and denied our eyes that enchanted prospect . . .'

*

'The land of a Hundred Lakes, once called Centloch,' Vysogota explained, 'is called Mil Tracta today. It's a very vast lake land bisected by the River Yelena in the northern part of Metinna, close to the border with Nazair and Mag Turga. Buyvid Backhuysen writes that they walked towards the lake from the North, from Assengard . . . Today Assengard is no more, only ruins remain and the nearest town is Neunreuth. Buyvid counted four hundred furlongs from Assengard. Various furlongs have been used, but we'll accept the most popular reckoning, according to which four hundred and twenty furlongs gives around fifty miles. South of Assengard, which is about three hundred and fifty miles from us here in Pereplut. In other words, there are more or less three hundred miles between you and the Tower of the Swallow. Ciri. That's some two weeks riding on your Kelpie. In the spring, of course. Not now, when the frosts may be upon us in a day or two.'

'Assengard – which I was reading about – is a ruin today,' Ciri murmured, wrinkling her nose pensively. 'But I've seen the elven town of Shaerrawedd in Kaedwen with my own eyes – I've been there. People prised out and pillaged everything, they only left bare stone. I bet only stones remain of your Tower of the Swallow. The larger ones, because the smaller ones have probably been stolen. If there was a portal there as well—'

'Tor Zireael was magical. Not visible to everybody. And teleporters are never visible.'

'True,' she admitted and pondered. 'The one on Thanedd wasn't. It suddenly appeared on a bare wall . . . Actually it appeared just in time, because that mage who was chasing me was close by . . . I could hear him . . . And then the portal materialised as though I'd summoned it.'

'I'm certain,' Vysogota said softly, 'that if you reached Tor Zireael, that teleporter would also appear to you. Even in the ruins, amidst the bare stones. I'm certain you'd manage to find and activate it. And it – I'm certain – would obey your order. For I think, Ciri, that you are the chosen one.'

*

'Your hair, Triss, is like fire in the candlelight. And your eyes are like lapis lazuli. Your lips are like coral—'

'Stop that, Crach. Are you drunk, or what? Pour me some more wine. And talk.'

'What about, exactly?'

'Come off it! About how Yennefer decided to sail to the Sedna Abyss.'

*

'How goes it? Tell me, Yennefer.'

'First of all, you answer my question: who are the two women I invariably encounter when I come to you? And who always give me looks usually reserved for cat shit on the carpet? Who are they?'

'Are you interested in their formal and legal – or actual – status?'

'The latter.'

'In that case, they're my wives.'

'I understand. Explain to them – when you get the chance – that bygones are bygones.'

'I have. But women are women. Never mind. Speak, Yennefer. I'm interested in how your work is progressing.'

'Unfortunately,' the sorceress bit her lip, 'there's scant progress. And time's running out.'

'It is,' the yarl nodded. 'And constantly supplying new sensations. I received news from the continent, it ought to interest you. It comes from Vissegerd's corps. You know, I hope, who Vissegerd is?'

'The general from Cintra?'

'The marshal. He commands a corps made up of Cintran emigrants and volunteers within the Temerian Army. Enough volunteers from the islands serve there for me to have first-hand news.'

'And what do you have?'

'You arrived here in Skellige on the nineteenth of August, two days after the full moon. The same day, the nineteenth, I mean, Vissegerd's corps picked up a group of fugitives during fighting by the Ina. Among them were Geralt and that troubadour friend of his—'

'Dandelion?'

'Quite. Vissegerd accused both of spying, imprisoned and perhaps meant to execute them, but the two prisoners ran away and sent some Nilfgaardians – with whom they were reputedly in league – after Vissegerd.'

'Nonsense.'

'I thought so too. But I can't get it out of my head that the Witcher, in spite of what you think, is perhaps carrying out some cunning plan. Wanting to rescue Ciri, he's worming his way into Nilfgaard's good graces . . .'

'Ciri's not in Nilfgaard. And Geralt isn't carrying out any plans. Planning isn't his strong point. Let's leave it. What's important is that it's already the twenty-sixth of August, and I still know too little. Too little to undertake anything . . . Unless I was to . . .'

She fell silent, staring out of the window, playing with the obsidian star fastened to a black velvet ribbon.

'Were to what?' Crach an Craite burst out.

'Rather than mocking Geralt, to try using his methods.'

'I don't understand.'

'One could try sacrifice, yarl. Apparently readiness to make sacrifices can pay off, produce favourable results . . . If only in the form of the grace of the goddess. Who likes and esteems people who sacrifice themselves and suffer for a cause.'

'I still don't understand,' he said, wrinkling his brow. 'But I don't like what you're saying, Yennefer.'

'I know. Neither do I. But still, I've gone too far . . . The tiger may already have heard the kid's bleating . . .'

*

'That's what I was afraid of,' Triss whispered. 'That's precisely what I was afraid of.'

'Which means I understood correctly.' The muscles of Crach an Craite's jaw worked vigorously. 'Yennefer knew someone would eavesdrop on the conversations she was conducting using that infernal machine. Or that one of her interlocutors would basely betray her . . .'

'Or the one and the other.'

'She knew.' Crach ground his teeth. 'But carried on regardless. Because it was meant to be bait? Did she intend to be bait herself? Did she pretend to know more than she did in order to provoke the enemy? And she sailed to the Sedna Abyss . . .'

'Throwing down the challenge. Provoking. She was taking an awful risk, Crach.'

'I know. She didn't want to expose any of us to danger . . . Apart from volunteers. So she asked for two longships . . .'

*

'I have the two longships you asked for. *Alkyone* and *Tamara*. And their crews, naturally. *Alkyone* will be commanded by Guthlaf, son of Sven. He asked for the honour, as he's taken a liking to you, Yennefer. *Tamara* will be commanded by Asa Thjazi, a captain in whom I have absolute faith. Aha, I almost forgot. My son, Hjalmar Wrymouth will also be in *Tamara*'s crew.'

'Your son? How old is he?'

'Nineteen.'

'You started early.'

'That's the pot calling the kettle black. Hjalmar asked to be added to the crew for personal reasons. I couldn't turn him down.'

'For personal reasons?'

'You really don't know that story?'

'No. Tell me.'

Crach an Craite drank from the horn and laughed at his recollections.

'Youngsters from Ard Skellig,' he began, 'love playing on skates during the winter, they can't wait for the icy weather. The first of them go out on the ice when the lake is barely ice-bound, so thin it wouldn't support adults. Races are the favourite sport, naturally. To gather speed and hurtle, as fast as they can, from one side of the lake to the other. Other boys compete at the so-called "salmon leap". They have to jump, in their skates, over lakeside rocks sticking up from the ice like sharks' teeth. Like salmon leaping up waterfalls. You choose a suitably long row of rocks like that, take a run-up . . . Ha, I jumped like that when I was a scrawny kid . . .'

Crach an Craite fell into a reverie and smiled slightly.

'Of course,' he continued, 'whoever jumps the longest row of rocks wins the competition and then struts around like a peacock. In my day, Yennefer, that honour often fell to your humble servant and present interlocutor, ha! During the time that interests us most, my son, Hjalmar, was the champion. He jumped over stones that none of the other boys dared to. And paraded around with his nose in the air, challenging anyone to try and defeat him. And the challenge was taken up. By Ciri, daughter of Pavetta of Cintra. Not even an islander, though she thought of herself as one, since she'd spent more time here than there.'

338

'Even after Pavetta's accident? I thought Calanthe had forbidden her from coming here?'

'You know about that?' He glanced at her keenly. 'Indeed, yes, you know a great deal, Yennefer . . . A great deal. Calanthe's rage and ban didn't last more than six months and then Ciri began to spend her summers and winters here again . . . She skated like a demon, but to compete at the salmon leap with the lads? And challenge Hjalmar? It was unbelievable!'

'She leaped,' the sorceress guessed.

'Yes, she did. The little Cintran half-devil leaped. A real Lion Cub from the Lioness's blood. And Hjalmar – so as not to expose himself to ridicule – had to risk a jump over an even longer row of stones. Which he did. He broke a leg, broke an arm, broke four ribs and smashed his face up. He'll have a scar for the rest of his life. Hjalmar Wrymouth! And his famous betrothed! Ha!'

'Betrothed?'

'Didn't you know about that? You know so much, but not that? She visited him when he was lying in bed recovering after his famous leap. She read to him, told him stories, held his little hand . . . And when someone entered the chamber, they both blushed like poppies. Well, finally Hjalmar informed me they were betrothed. I almost had an attack of apoplexy. I'll teach you, you rascal, I'll give you a betrothal, but with a rawhide whip! And I was a bit anxious, for I'd seen that the Lion Cub was hot-headed, that everything about her was reckless, for she was a daredevil, not to say a little maniac . . . Fortunately Hjalmar was covered in splints and bandages, so they couldn't do anything stupid . . .'

'How old were they then?'

'He was fifteen, she almost fifteen.'

'I think your fears were a little exaggerated.'

'Perhaps a little. But Calanthe, whom I had to inform about everything, by no means made light of the matter. I knew she had marriage plans regarding Ciri, I think it concerned the young Tankred Thyssen of Kovir, and perhaps the Redanian, Radovid. I can't be certain. But rumours might have harmed the marriage plans, even rumours about innocent kisses or half-innocent caresses. Calanthe took Ciri back to Cintra without a moment's delay. The girl kicked up a row, yelled and sobbed, but nothing

339

helped. There was no arguing with the Lioness of Cintra. After-wards, Hjalmar lay for two days with his face turned to the wall and didn't say a word to anyone . . . As soon as he had recovered, he planned to steal a skiff and sail to Cintra by himself. For that he was strapped, and he put it behind him. But later . . .'

Crach an Craite went silent, fell into a reverie.

'Later the summer came, then the autumn, and the entire Nilfgaardian might struck Cintra's southern wall, through the Marnadal Stairs. And Hjalmar found another opportunity to become a man. In Marnadal, at the Battle of Cintra and later at the Battle of Sodden, he faced the Black Cloaks valiantly. Later, too, when the longships sailed for the Nilfgaardian coasts, Hjal-mar avenged his make-believe betrothed with sword in hand, even though people thought she was dead by then. I didn't believe it, because those phenomena I told you about didn't occur . . . Well, and now, when Hjalmar learned of the possible rescue expedition, he volunteered.'

'Thanks for the story, Crach. It was restful for me to listen. I could forget about . . . my cares.'

'When do you set off, Yennefer?'

'In the coming days. Perhaps even tomorrow. It remains to me to perform one more, final telecommunication.'

*

Crach an Craite's eyes were like a hawk's. They bored deeply, to the very core.

'You don't by any chance know, Triss Merigold, who Yennefer spoke to that last time before disassembling the infernal machine? On the night of the twenty-seventh of August? With whom? Or about what?'

Triss hid her eyes behind her eyelashes.

*

The beam of light diffracted by the diamond animated the surface of the looking glass with a flash. Yennefer extended both hands and intoned a spell. The blinding reflection transformed into a swirl of

340

fog and an image quickly began to emerge from it. The image of a chamber whose walls were draped with a colourful tapestry.

A movement in the window. And an anxious voice.

'Who is it? Who's there?'

'It's me, Triss.'

'Yennefer? Is that you? O Gods! How . . . Where are you?'

'It isn't important where I am. Don't block, for the image is flickering. And take away the candlestick, it's blinding me.'

'I've done it. Of course.'

Though the hour was late, Triss Merigold was not in a negligee, or in working clothes. She was wearing an evening gown. As usual, buttoned all the way up to the neck.

'May we talk freely?'

'Of course.'

'Are you alone?'

'Yes.'

'You're lying.'

'Yennefer . . .'

'Don't trick me, girl. I know that expression, I've seen more than enough of it. You had one like that when you started sleeping with Geralt behind my back. You put on the identical innocent-whorish little mask then that I see on your face now. And it means the same now as it did then!'

Triss blushed. And beside her in the window appeared Philippa Eilhart, dressed in a dark-blue men's doublet with silver embroidery.

'Bravo,' she said. 'Sharp as usual, acute as usual. As usual difficult to comprehend and fathom. I'm glad to see you in good health, Yennefer. I'm glad that the crazy teleportation from Montecalvo didn't end tragically.'

'Let's assume you are indeed glad.' Yennefer grimaced. 'Although that's a most bold assumption. But we'll leave it. Who betrayed me?'

'Is it important?' Philippa shrugged. 'You've now been communicating for four days with traitors. With traitors to whom venality and treachery are second nature. And traitors whom you have forced to betray others in turn. One of them has betrayed you. That's the usual course of events. Don't tell me you didn't expect it.'

341

'Of course I did,' Yennefer snorted. 'I proved that by contacting you. I didn't have to, did I?'

'You didn't. Which means you stand to gain from it.'

'Bravo. Sharp as usual, acute as usual. I'm contacting you to assure you that the secret of your lodge is safe with me. I won't betray you.'

Philippa looked at her from beneath lowered eyelashes.

'If you expected,' she said finally, 'to buy yourself time, peace and safety with that declaration, you miscalculated. Let's not kid ourselves, Yennefer. By fleeing Montecalvo you made a choice, you threw in your lot with one side of the barricade. Whoever's not with the lodge is against it. Now you're trying to beat us to Ciri, and the motives driving you are counter to ours. You're acting against us. You don't want to allow us to use Ciri to serve our political ends. Know then, that we shall do everything to prevent you using the girl to serve your own sentimental ones.'

'So it's war, then?'

'Competition,' Philippa smiled venomously, 'Only competition, Yennefer.'

'Fair and honourable?'

'You must be joking.'

'Naturally. Nonetheless, I'd like to present one matter honestly and unambiguously. Banking, of course, on gaining something from it.'

'By all means.'

'In the course of the next few days – perhaps even tomorrow – events will occur whose outcome I'm unable to predict. It may turn out that our competition and rivalry will suddenly cease to have any meaning. For a simple reason. There won't be a rival any longer.'

Philippa Eilhart narrowed her eyes, which were accented with light blue eye shadow.

'I understand.'

'Ensure then, that I posthumously regain my reputation and good name. That I won't be thought of as a traitor and an accomplice of Vilgefortz. I ask that of the lodge. I ask you personally.'

Philippa was briefly silent.

'I decline your request,' she said finally. 'I'm sorry, but your rehabilitation is not in the interests of the lodge. Should you die, you die a traitor. To Ciri you shall be a traitor and a criminal, for then it will be easier to manipulate the maid.'

'Before you undertake anything that may prove fatal,' Triss suddenly said, 'leave us something . . .'

'A will?'

'Something that will allow us . . . to continue . . . to follow in your footsteps. And find Ciri. Surely it's in Ciri's interests, after all! It's about her life! Yennefer, Dijkstra has found . . . some tracks. If it's Vilgefortz who has Ciri, a terrible death awaits the girl.'

'Be quiet, Triss,' Philippa Eilhart barked sharply. 'There won't be any bargaining or horse-trading here.'

'I'll leave you directions,' Yennefer said slowly. 'I'll leave you information about what I've found out, and what I've undertaken. I'll leave a trail you'll be able to follow. But not for nothing. If you don't want to rehabilitate me in the world's eyes, then to hell with you and the world. But at least rehabilitate me in the eyes of one witcher—'

'No,' Philippa retorted almost immediately. 'That isn't in the interests of the lodge either. You shall remain a traitor and a dishonourable sorceress to your Witcher, too. It isn't in the lodge's interests to stir up trouble, looking for revenge, and if they have contempt for you, they won't want revenge. Besides, he's probably dead. Or will die any day.'

'Information,' Yennefer said hollowly, 'in exchange for his life. Save him, Philippa.'

'No, Yennefer.'

'For it isn't in the interests of the lodge.' Purple fire flashed in the sorceress's eyes. 'Did you hear, Triss? This is your lodge. This is its true countenance, these its true concerns. What do you say to that? You were the maid's mentor, almost an older sister, as you yourself said. And Geralt . . .'

'Don't beguile Triss with romance, Yennefer.' Now Philippa's eyes blazed in turn. 'We'll find the maid and rescue her without your help. And if you succeed, thanks a million, you'll help us, you'll save us the bother. You'll snatch her from Vilgefortz's hands, we'll snatch her from yours. And Geralt? Who is Geralt?'

'Did you hear, Triss?'

343

'Forgive me,' Triss Merigold said hollowly. 'Forgive me, Yennefer.'

'Oh, no, Triss. Never.'

*

Triss looked at the floor. Crach an Craite's eyes were like a hawk's.

'The day after the last secret communication,' the yarl of the Isles of Skellige said, 'one you, Triss Merigold, know nothing about, Yennefer left Skellige, setting a course for the Sedna Abyss. When asked why exactly she was heading there, she looked me in the eye and replied that she intended to find out how natural disasters differ from unnatural ones. She set off with two longships, *Tamara* and *Alkyone*, with crews made up entirely of volunteers. That was the twenty-eighth of August, two weeks ago. I haven't seen her since.'

'When did you find out—?'

'Five days later,' he interrupted quite bluntly. 'Three days after the September new moon.'

*

Captain Asa Thjazi, who was sitting behind the yarl, was anxious. He licked his lips, shifted around on the bench, and wrung his hands so hard the knuckles cracked.

The red sun, finally emerging from the clouds covering the sky, sank slowly over Spikeroog. 'Speak, Asa,' Crach an Craite ordered.

Asa Thjazi cleared his throat noisily.

'We were making good way,' he began, 'the wind behind us, we were doing a good twelve knots. Then on the night of the twenty-ninth we espied the lighthouse at Peixe de Mar. We struck out a little westwards, so as not to chance on any Nilfgaardians . . . And at dawn, one day before the September new moon, we reached the region of the Sedna Abyss. Then the sorceress summoned myself and Guthlaf . . .'

*

'I need volunteers,' Yennefer said. 'Only volunteers. No more than is necessary to steer a longship for a short time. I don't know how many men are needed for that, I'm not an expert. But please don't leave even one more man on *Alkyone* than is absolutely necessary. And I repeat – only volunteers. What I plan to do . . . is very dangerous. More so than a sea battle.'

'I understand,' the old seneschal nodded. 'And I volunteer first. I, Guthlaf, son of Sven, request that honour, madam.'

Yennefer looked him long in the eyes.

'Very well,' she said. 'And I, too, am honoured.'

*

'I also volunteered,' said Asa Thjazi. 'But Guthlaf disagreed. Someone, he said, must keep command on *Tamara*. Consequently, fifteen men volunteered. Including Hjalmar, yarl.'

Crach an Craite raised his eyebrows.

*

'How many are needed, Guthlaf?' the sorceress repeated. 'How many are essential? Please reckon it exactly.'

The seneschal was silent for some time as he added up.

'Eight of us can cope,' he said finally. 'If it's not for long . . . Why, but everyone here is a volunteer, no one's being forced—'

'Select eight from that fifteen,' she interrupted sharply. 'Choose them yourself. And order those selected to transfer to *Alkyone*. The rest are staying on *Tamara*. Aha, I shall choose one of those who stays. Hjalmar!'

'No, madam! You can't do that to me! I volunteered and will be at your side! I want to be—'

'Be silent! You're staying on *Tamara*! That's an order! One more word and I'll have you tied to the mast!'

*

'Go on, Asa.'

'The witch, Guthlaf and those eight volunteers boarded *Alkyone* and sailed for the Abyss. We, on *Tamara*, hung back according to our orders, but not too far away. But some devilry began with the weather, which had been wonderfully favourable till then. Aye, I speak truly that it was devilry, for the power was sinister, yarl . . . May I be keelhauled if I lie . . .'

'Go on.'

'Where we were, I mean *Tamara*, the sea was calm. Though the wind whistled some and clouds darkened the horizon so day almost became night. But where *Alkyone* was all hell suddenly broke loose. Hell indeed . . .'

*

Alkyone's sail suddenly fluttered so violently that they heard the flapping in spite of the distance separating the longships. The sky turned black and the clouds swirled. The sea, which seemed completely calm around *Tamara*, churned up and foamed white by *Alkyone's* sides. Someone suddenly yelled, someone chimed in, and a moment later everybody was yelling.

A cone of black clouds was striking *Alkyone*, making it bob on the waves like a cork. The ship twisted, spun, its bow and stern rising and falling into the waves. At times the longship almost completely vanished from sight. At times they could only see the striped sail.

'It's magic!' bawled someone behind Asa's back. 'It's devil magic!'

The whirlpool spun *Alkyone* around faster and faster. Shields torn from the sides by centrifugal force whirred in the air like discs, and splintered oars flew in all directions.

'Reef the sail!' yelled Asa Thjazi. 'To the oars! Row, boys! To the rescue!'

But it was already too late.

The sky above *Alkyone* turned black, and the blackness suddenly exploded in zigzags of lightning which entwined the longship like a medusa's tentacles. The clouds, swirling in fantastic shapes, writhed up into a horrendous funnel. The longship spun around with incredible speed. The mast snapped like a match, the torn sail dashed over the breakers like a huge albatross.

'Row, men!'

Over their own yells, over the all-deafening roar of the elements, they nonetheless heard the cries of the men from *Alkyone*. Cries so extraordinary they made their hair stand on end. And these were old sea dogs, bloodied berserkers, mariners who had seen and heard many things.

They dropped the oars, aware of their impotence. They were dumbfounded, they even stopped yelling.

Alkyone, still whirling, slowly rose above the waves. And rose higher and higher. They saw the keel, dripping water, covered in shellfish and algae. They saw a black shape, a figure falling into the sea. Then a second. And a third.

'They're jumping!' Asa Thjazi roared. 'Row, men, don't stop! With all your might! We must row to their aid!'

Alkyone was now a good hundred cubits above the boiling surface of the water. It continued to whirl, an immense spindle dripping with water, entwined in a cobweb of lightning, being dragged into the swirling clouds by an unseen force.

Suddenly an ear-splitting explosion rent the air. Although fifteen pairs of oars were pushing *Tamara* forwards, she suddenly leaped up and flew backwards, as if rammed. The deck flew from under Thjazi's feet. He fell over, banging his forehead on the side.

He couldn't stand up by himself, he had to be lifted to his feet. He was dazed; he twisted and shook his head, staggering and mumbling incoherently. The screams of the crew seemed muffled. He went over to the side, tottering like a drunkard and clung on to the rail.

The wind had dropped and the sea was calm. But the sky was still black from the billowing clouds.

There wasn't a single trace of *Alkyone*.

*

'Not even a trace was left, yarl. Well, tiny pieces of rigging, some rags . . . Nothing more.'

Asa Thjazi interrupted his tale, watching the sun vanishing beyond Spikeroog's wooded peaks. Crach an Craite, lost in thought, didn't hurry him.

347

'We know not,' Asa Thjazi finally continued, 'how many managed to jump before *Alkyone* was sucked into that devilish cloud. But no matter how many jumped, none survived. And we, though we spared neither time nor strength, fished out but two bodies. Two bodies, borne on the water. Only two.'

'Was the sorceress,' the yarl asked in an altered voice, 'not among them?'

'No.'

Crach an Craite was silent a long while. The sun was completely hidden behind Spikeroog.

'Old Guthlaf, son of Sven is lost,' Asa Thjazi spoke again. 'The crabs on the bottom of the Abyss have surely ate him till the last little bone . . . And the witch is certainly lost . . . Yarl, folk are beginning to talk . . . That it's all her fault. And punishment for her crimes . . .'

'Foolish nonsense!'

'She's perished,' Asa muttered, 'in the Sedna Abyss. In the same place as Pavetta and Duny did back then . . . It was an accident . . .'

'It was no accident,' Crach an Craite said with conviction. 'It was certainly no accident then. And nor was it now.'

It is proper for a hapless one to suffer. His pain and humiliation result from the laws of nature, and to carry out the aims of nature both the existence of the suffering one is necessary, as is that of those who, causing him suffering, enjoy their successes. That very truth ought to stifle the pang of conscience in the heart of a tyrant or malefactor. He must not bridle himself, he ought to commit all the deeds that arise in his imagination, since it is the voice of nature which suggests them. If the secret inspirations of nature lead us to evil it is evidently essential to nature.

Donatien Alphonse Francois de Sade

CHAPTER TEN

The clank and thud of the cell door first opening and then closing awoke the younger of the two Scarra sisters. The elder was sitting at a table, busy scraping dried porridge from the bottom of a tin bowl.

'Well, how was it in court, Kenna?'

Without a word Joanna Selborne, also known as Kenna, sat down on her plank bed with her elbows resting on her knees and her forehead on her hands.

The younger Scarra yawned, belched and farted loudly. Kohut, crouching on the opposite bed, muttered something indistinct and turned his head away. He was furious at Kenna, the sisters and the whole world.

In normal gaols the inmates were still traditionally separated according to sex. In military citadels it was different. Emperor Fergus var Emreis – confirming women's equality in the imperial army by special decree – had already ruled that if it was to be emancipation, then let it *be* emancipation. Equality ought to be complete and outright, without any exceptions or special privileges for either sex. Since then, inmates had been serving time in mixed cells in the strongholds and citadels.

'Well?' the older Scarra repeated. 'Are they letting you out?'

'Like hell they are,' said Kenna bitterly, head still resting on her hands. 'I'll be lucky if they don't hang me. Sod it! I told the truth, hid nothing, well, you know, almost nothing. But when those whoresons started grilling me, first they made a fool out of me in front of everyone, then it turned out I wasn't a credible person but a criminal element, and right at the end they brought out my complicity in a plot aimed at subversion with the aim of an insurrection.'

'Subversion,' the older Scarra nodded, as though she understood exactly what it was about. 'Aaah, if it's subversion . . . Then you're in the shit, Kenna.'

351

'As if I didn't know that.'

The younger Scarra stretched, yawned like a leopard, widely and noisily, jumped down from the upper bunk, vigorously kicked away Kohut's stool which was blocking her way and spat on the floor beside it. Kohut growled, but didn't dare do anything more.

Kohut was mortally offended by Kenna. But was afraid of the sisters.

When Kenna had been assigned to the cell three days earlier, it soon turned out that Kohut – if he tolerated the emancipation and equality of women at all – had his own views on the subject. He had thrown a blanket over Kenna's upper half in the middle of the night and intended to avail himself of the lower half, which he certainly would have done but for the fact that he had happened upon a tele-empathic. Kenna penetrated his brain so deeply that Kohut howled like a werewolf and cavorted around the cell as though bitten by a tarantula. Then, out of pure vindictiveness, Kenna telepathically forced him to go down on all fours and bang his head rhythmically against the metal-plated cell door. When the warders – alarmed by the dreadful thumping – opened the door, Kohut butted one of them, for which he received five lashes with a metal-tipped truncheon and as many kicks. Summing up, Kohut didn't get the gratification he'd been hoping for. And took offence at Kenna. He didn't even dare to take his revenge, because the next day the Scarra sisters joined them in the cell. The fair sex thus formed the majority, and furthermore it soon turned out that the sisters' views on equality were similar to Kohut's, if completely the other way around concerning the roles ascribed to the sexes. The younger Scarra looked at the man lasciviously and made explicit comments, while the older cackled and rubbed her hands together. As a result, Kohut slept with a stool with which he planned to defend his honour. Nonetheless, his chances and prospects were meagre; both Scarras had served on the front line and were veterans of numerous battles, so would not have been daunted by the stool. Had they'd wanted to rape him they would have, even if the man had been armed with a battle axe. Kenna, though, was certain the sisters were only joking. Well, almost certain.

The Scarra sisters were in the slammer for assaulting an officer, while in the case of Kohut – who had served as a quartermaster

– an investigation was ongoing into a notorious, major scandal regarding the theft of army bows, which was creating ever-widening ripples.

'In the shit, Kenna,' the older Scarra repeated. 'You've got yourself in a fine pickle. Or rather they got you into it. How come you never bloody caught on it was a political game?'

'Humph.'

Scarra glanced at her, not quite knowing how to interpret her monosyllabic response. Kenna looked away.

I'm not going to tell you something I kept quiet about in front of the judges, am I? she thought. *That I knew what kind of game I was getting tangled up in. Or when and how I found out.*

'You've landed yourself in a sorry mess,' said the younger Scarra solemnly. She was the much more dull-witted one, who – Kenna was certain – understood nothing of what it was about.

'And what finally happened with that Cintran princess?' The older Scarra kept probing. 'I mean you finally nabbed her, didn't you?'

'We did. If you could call it that. What's the date today?'

'September the twenty-second. It's the Equinox tomorrow.'

'Ah. Well, that's a queer coincidence. Tomorrow, it'll be a year to the day since those events . . . A year already . . .'

Kenna stretched out on her pallet, hands clasped behind her head. The sisters remained silent, hoping it had been an introduction to a story.

Nothing doing, sisters dear, thought Kenna, looking at the obscene drawings and even more obscene comments scrawled on the planks of the upper bunk. *There won't be any story. It's not even that that bastard Kohut smells like a bloody nark. I just don't feel like talking about it. I don't feel like remembering it.*

What happened a year ago. After Bonhart gave us the slip in Claremont.

We'd arrived there two days too late, she recalled, *the trail had already gone cold. No one knew where the bounty hunter had gone. No one apart from the merchant Houvenaghel, that is. But Houvenaghel didn't want to talk to Skellen, or even have him in the house. He communicated through his servants that he had no time and wouldn't grant them an audience. Tawny Owl was cross* and indignant, but what could he do? It was Ebbing, he didn't have the necessary jurisdiction. And we could do nothing about Houvenaghel any other way – I mean *our* way – for he had a private army down in Claremont, and we couldn't exactly declare war . . .

Boreas Mun sniffed around, Dacre Silifant and Ola Harsheim tried bribery, Til Echrade elven magic, I used telepathy and listened to his thoughts, but it wasn't much use. All we learned was that Bonhart had left the town through the southern gate. But before he left . . .

In Claremont there was a tiny little temple with larches, by the southern gate and the small market place. Before leaving Claremont, Bonhart had cruelly beaten Falka with a knout in the square in front of the temple. Before everybody's eyes, including the temple priests'. He yelled that he'd prove to her who her lord and master was. That he was flogging her with a knout as he wished, and if he so wished he'd flog her to death, because no one would stand up for her, no one would come to her aid. Neither people nor gods.

The younger Scarra was looking out of the window, hanging onto the grating. The older one was eating porridge from the bowl. Kohut took the stool, lay down and covered himself with a blanket.

The bell in the guardhouse tolled, the guards on the walls yelled out their presence . . .

Kenna turned her face to the wall.

We met several days later, she thought. Me and Bonhart. Face to face. I looked into his inhuman, fish-like eyes, thinking only of one thing – how he'd beaten the girl. And I looked into his thoughts . . . For a moment. And it was like sticking my head into a dug-up grave . . .

That was at the Equinox.

And the day before, the twenty-second of September, I'd realised that an invisible spy had wormed his way among us.

*

Stefan Skellen, the imperial coroner, listened without interrupting. But Kenna saw his face changing.

354

'Again, Selborne,' he drawled. 'Say it again, for I don't believe my own ears.'

'Cautiously, my lord coroner,' she murmured. 'Pretend to be angry . . . That I've come to you with a request and you won't grant it . . . For the sake of appearances, I mean. I'm not mistaken, I'm certain. An unseen guest has been hanging around us for two days. An invisible spy.'

Tawny Owl, to give him his due, was clever and understood at once.

'No, Selborne, I refuse,' he said loudly, but without over-dramatizing his tone or expression. 'Discipline applies to everyone. There are no exceptions.'

'Please, at least listen, lord coroner,' Kenna didn't have Tawny Owl's talent, failed to avoid awkwardness, but in the scene being played out awkwardness and embarrassment by the petitioner were permissible. 'Please at least see fit as to listen.'

'Speak, Selborne. But be brief and to the point!'

'He's been spying on us for two days,' she muttered, pretending she was humbly presenting her argument. 'Since Claremont. He has to ride behind us secretively, and when we're camped he approaches unseen, moves around among people, and listens.'

'He listens, the sodding spy.' Skellen didn't have to pretend to be stern and angry; the fury was trembling in his voice. 'How did you uncover him?'

'Yesterday, when you were giving Lord Silifant his orders outside the tavern, the tomcat sleeping on the bench hissed and flattened its ears. It seemed suspicious to me, because there wasn't anyone on that side . . . And then I picked up something, a thought, kind of, an unfamiliar thought and will. When there are familiar, ordinary thoughts all around, an unfamiliar thought like that, lord coroner, is as if someone were shouting . . . I started taking heed, intensely, I doubled my efforts and now I can sense him.'

'Can you always sense him?'

'No. Not always. He has some kind of magical protection. I only sense him from very close, and even then not every time. So I have to be vigilant, because I never know if he's not hiding nearby.'

'Just don't scare him away,' Tawny Owl muttered. 'Don't scare him away . . . I want him alive, Selborne. What do you suggest?'

'We'll give him the pancake treatment.'

'The pancake treatment?'

'Quiet, lord coroner.'

'But . . . Oh, never mind. Very well. I'm giving you a free hand.'

'Tomorrow, make sure we stop and billet in some village or other. I'll sort out the rest. And now for the sake of appearances give me a dressing-down and I'll go away.'

'I can't really.' He smiled at her with his eyes and winked slightly, immediately assuming the overbearing air of a stern commander. 'For I'm pleased with you, Miss Selborne.'

He said "miss". Miss Selborne. As though to an officer.

He winked again.

'No!' he said and brandished an arm, playing his role splendidly. 'Request denied! Dismissed!'

'Yes sir.'

*

The next day, in the late afternoon, Skellen ordered his soldiers to make camp in a village by the River Lete. The village was prosperous, ringed by a palisade, and they rode in through a fine gate of freshly cut pine palings. The name of the village was Unicorn and it took its name from its small stone temple, inside which there was a straw effigy of a unicorn.

I remember, Kenna recalled, how we laughed at that straw idol, and the village headman gravely explained that the sacred unicorn which looked after the village had many years before been made of gold, then silver, then copper; there were several versions in bone and several in hardwood. But all of them had been stolen. People came from far away to rob or steal it. Things had only been peaceful since the unicorn had been made of straw. We set up camp in the village. As agreed, Skellen occupied the headman's hall.

Less than an hour later we'd given the spy the pancake treatment. In classic, textbook fashion.

*

'Please come closer,' Tawny Owl ordered loudly. 'Please come closer and take a look at this document . . . Hold on? Is everybody here? So I won't have to explain twice.'

Ola Harsheim, who had just taken a sip of cream somewhat watered down with sour milk from a milking pail, licked the creamy moustache from his lips, put down the vessel, looked around and counted. Dacre Silifant, Bert Brigden, Neratin Ceka, Til Echrade, Joanna Selborne . . .

'Dufficey's not here.'

'Summon him.'

'Kriel! Duffi Kriel! To the commander for the briefing! To receive important orders! At the double!'

Dufficey Kriel ran into the hall, out of breath.

'Everybody's here, lord coroner,' Ola Harsheim reported.

'Leave the window open. We could expire from the smell of garlic in here. Open the door, too, make a draught.'

Brigden and Kriel obediently opened the window and the door. Kenna, meanwhile, thought once again that Tawny Owl would make a really splendid actor.

'Please step this way, gentlemen. I've received this document from the emperor, confidential and of extraordinary gravity. Your attention, please . . .'

'Now!' yelled Kenna, sending a powerful directional impulse, whose effect on the senses was similar to being struck by lightning.

Ola Harsheim and Dacre Silifant picked up the milk pail and simultaneously flung the cream in the direction Kenna was indicating. Til Echrade vigorously emptied a flour barrel which had been hidden under the table. A creamy, floury shape – amorphous at first – appeared on the floor of the chamber. But Bert Brigden was alert. Correctly judging where the pancake's head might be, he whacked it as hard as he could with a cast-iron frying pan.

Then everybody threw themselves at the spy who was plastered all over with cream and flour, tore the hat of invisibility from his head and seized his arms and legs. After upturning the table, they tied the captive's limbs to the legs. They pulled off his boots and footwraps and stuffed one of them into his mouth which was open and ready to shout.

In order to crown their work, Dufficey Kriel kicked the captive hard in the ribs, and the others took pleasure in watching the spy's eyes bulge out of their sockets.

'Magnificent work,' commented Tawny Owl, who hadn't moved during the entire, brief, incident but had stood with his arms crossed on his chest.

'Bravo. Congratulations. Above all to you, Miss Selborne.'

Bloody hell, thought Kenna. *If it carries on like this I really am liable to end up an officer.*

'Mr Brigden,' Stefan Skellen said coldly, standing over the prisoner spread out between the table legs, 'put the irons in the coals, please. Mr Echrade, please make sure no children are hanging around outside.'

He leaned over and looked into the bound man's eyes.

'You haven't shown your face for ages, Rience,' he said. 'I was beginning to think some misfortune had befallen you.'

*

The bell in the guardhouse – the signal for the changing of the guard – struck. The Scarra sisters snored euphoniously. Kohut, hugging the stool, smacked his lips in his sleep.

He played the hero, Kenna recalled, pretending to be brave, that foolhardy Rience. The sorcerer Rience, given the pancake treatment and tied to the legs of a table with his bare feet sticking up. He was playing the hero, but wasn't fooling anybody; least of all me. Tawny Owl warned us he was a sorcerer, so I scrambled his thoughts to stop him casting spells or sending for magical help. And read his thoughts while I was about it. He was blocking my way in, but when he caught a whiff of the smoke from the coal of the brazier where the irons were heating up, his magical protection and blockades burst along all their seams like old britches, and I was able to read him freely. His thoughts didn't differ from those of other people I've read in like situations. The thoughts of people who are about to be tortured. Chaotic, trembling thoughts; full of fear and despair. Cold, slimy, wet, foul-smelling thoughts. Like a corpse's entrails.

In spite of that, when the gag was removed, the sorcerer Rience tried to play the hero.

'Well, well, Skellen! You've caught me, you win! Congratulations. A deep bow to your technique, expertise and professionalism. Splendidly trained operatives; truly, it's enviable. And now please release me from this unseemly position.'

Tawny Owl drew up a chair and straddled it, resting his clasped fingers and chin on the backrest. He looked down at the captive. And said nothing.

'Have me released, Skellen,' Rience repeated. 'And then order your subordinates to leave. What I have to say is meant for your ears only.'

'Mr Brigden,' Tawny Owl said, without turning his head. 'What colour are the irons?'

'A bit longer, sir.'

'Miss Selborne?'

'I'm having difficulty reading him now,' Kenna shrugged. 'He's too afraid, the fear's drowning out all other thoughts. And there are lots of those thoughts. Including a few he's trying to hide. Behind magical screens. But it's not hard, I can—'

'That won't be necessary. We'll try the classic method: a red-hot iron.'

'Bloody hell!' the spy howled. 'Skellen! You surely don't mean—'

Tawny Owl leaned over, his face a little changed.

'First, it's *Mister* Skellen,' he hissed. 'Second, yes, absolutely, I plan to order your soles scorched, Rience. I shall do it with the utmost satisfaction. For I shall treat it as an expression of historical justice. I'll wager you don't understand.'

Rience remained silent, so Skellen continued.

'You see, Rience, I advised Vattier de Rideaux to scorch your heels back then, seven years ago, when you were fawning to the imperial intelligence service like a cur, begging for mercy and the privilege to be a traitor and a double agent. I repeated that advice four years ago, when you shamelessly kissed Emhyr's arse, mediating in contacts with Vilgefortz. When, during the hunt for the Cintran wench, you were promoted from a humble little turncoat to being virtually first resident spy. I wagered Vattier that when burned you'd say who you serve . . . No, I've got that wrong. That you'd name everyone you serve. And everyone you betray. And then, I said, you'll see, you'll be astonished, Vattier, how many points on the two lists correspond. But, well, Vattier de Rideaux didn't listen to me. And now surely regrets it. But nothing's lost. I'll only toast you a little, and when I know what I want to know, I shall leave you to Vattier's disposal. And he'll flay you, slowly, one piece at a time.'

Tawny Owl removed a handkerchief and a vial of perfume from his pocket. He sprinkled the perfume liberally on the handkerchief and pressed it to his nose. The perfume smelled pleasant, but nonetheless Kenna felt like vomiting.

'The iron, Mr Brigden.'

'I'm tracking you on Vilgefortz's orders!' Rience roared. 'It concerns the girl! By tracking your troop I hoped to get ahead of you, reach that bounty hunter before you did! I was going to try to negotiate the wench away from him! From him, not from you! Because you want to kill her, and Vilgefortz needs her alive! What else do you want to know? I'll tell you! I'll tell you everything!'

'Whoa, there!' Tawny Owl called. 'Not so fast! Why, a fellow's head could ache from such a racket and mass of information. Can you imagine, gentlemen, what will happen when we burn him? He'll scream us to death!'

Kriel and Silifant cackled raucously. Kenna and Neratin Ceka didn't join in the merriment. Neither did Bert Brigden, who had just then removed the iron from the coals and was examining it critically. The iron was so hot it seemed to be transparent, as though it wasn't iron, but a glass tube full of molten fire.

Rience saw it and shrieked.

'I know how to find the bounty hunter and the girl!' he yelled. 'I know! I'll tell you!'

'I'm certain of that.'

Kenna, still trying to read his thoughts, grimaced, picking up a wave of desperate, impotent fury. Something snapped in Rience's brain, yet another partition. He'll say something out of fear, thought Kenna, something he meant to keep until the end, as a trump card, an ace, which would have beaten all the other aces in a last, deciding hand for the highest stakes. Now he'll discard that ace, out of a banal, revolting fear of pain.

Suddenly something popped in her head, she felt heat in her temples and then sudden cold.

And she knew. She knew Rience's hidden thought.

By the Gods, she thought. What a pickle I'm in . . .

'I'll talk!' howled the sorcerer, reddening and staring goggle-eyed in the coroner's face. 'I'll tell you something genuinely important, Skellen! Vattier de Rideaux . . .'

Kenna suddenly heard another thought, belonging to someone else. She saw Neratin Ceka with a hand on his dagger moving towards the door.

Boots pounded and Boreas Mun rushed into the headman's hall. 'My lord coroner! Quickly, sir! You'll never believe who's here!'

Skellen gestured to Brigden, who was bending over towards the spy's heels with the iron, to stop.

'You ought to play the lottery, Rience,' he said, looking out of the window. 'I've never met anyone in my life with such luck.'

Through the window they could see a crowd and two people on horseback in the midst of it. Kenna knew at once who it was. She knew who the bony giant was, with the pale fishlike eyes, riding a powerful bay.

And who the ashen-haired girl on the splendid black mare was. With hands bound and a collar around her neck. And a bruise on her swollen cheek.

*

Vysogota returned to his cottage in a foul mood, dejected, taciturn – even angry. The reason was a conversation with a peasant, who had rowed over in a dugout canoe to collect some pelts. Perhaps for the last time before the spring, said the peasant. The weather's getting worse by the day. The rain and wind are so bad I'm afraid to venture onto the water. Ice on the puddles in the morning, blizzards are nigh, and after that frosts. The river will rise and flood at any time, then it's away with the dugout and out with the sleigh. But even a sleigh's no use on Pereplut, naught but bogs far as the eye can see . . .

The peasant was right. Towards the evening it became overcast and white flakes fell from the dark blue sky. A stiff, easterly wind flattened the dry reeds, whipping up white crests over the surface of the wetland. It had become piercingly, bitterly cold.

The day after tomorrow, thought Vysogota, is the feast of Samhain. According to the elven calendar it'll be the New Year in three days. According to the human calendar we'll have to wait another two months.

Kelpie, Ciri's black mare, stamped and snorted in the barn.

When he entered the cottage, he found Ciri rummaging around in his chests. He let her; even encouraged her. Firstly, it was quite a new activity – after riding Kelpie and leafing through books. Secondly, there were plenty of his daughters' things in the chests, and the girl needed warm clothing. Several changes of clothing, for in the cold and damp it took many days before the laundry finally dried.

Ciri was selecting, trying on, putting aside and discarding various items of clothing. Vysogota was sitting at the table. He ate two boiled potatoes and a chicken wing. In silence.

'Good workmanship.' She showed him some objects he hadn't seen in years and had even forgotten he had. 'Did these also belong to your daughter? Was it a hobby of hers?'

'Yes, she loved it. She couldn't wait for the winter.'

'Can I take them?'

'Take what you want,' he shrugged. 'They're of no use to me. If they'll come in handy and if the boots fit . . . But are you packing, Ciri? Are you preparing to go?'

She fixed her eyes on the pile of clothing.

'Yes, Vysogota,' she said after a brief silence. 'I've decided. Because you see . . . There's no time to lose.'

'Your dreams.'

'Yes,' she admitted, a moment later. 'I saw very unpleasant things in my dreams. I'm not certain if they've taken place, or are yet to happen. I have no idea if I can prevent it . . . But I must go. You see, once I felt aggrieved that the people closest to me didn't come to my aid. Left me at the mercy of fate . . . But now I think they're the ones that need my help. I have to go.'

'Winter's coming.'

'That's precisely why I must go. If I stay I'll be stuck here until spring . . . until the spring I'll be fretting in idleness and uncertainty, plagued by nightmares. I have to go, right now, to try to find the Tower of the Swallow. That teleporter. You worked out it'll take me a fortnight to reach the lake. I'd be there before the November full moon . . .'

'You can't leave your hideout now,' he said with effort. 'Not now. They'll capture you. Ciri . . . Your pursuers . . . they are very close. You cannot now—'

She threw a blouse down onto the floor and sprang up.

'You've learned something,' she said sharply. 'From the peasant who took the pelts. Tell me.'

'Ciri—'

'Tell me, please!'

He told her. He was later to regret it.

*

'The devil must have sent them, good sir hermit,' mumbled the peasant, breaking off from counting the pelts. 'Must of been the devil. They've been galloping through the forests since the Equinox, searching for some maid. Frightening folk, yelling and threatening, but always riding on, never tarrying long enough to do too much harm. But now they've thought up summat new: in some villages and settlements they've left some, what were it . . . Sent trees. They ain't no trees, good sir, sent or otherwise, just simply three or four good-for-nothing scoundrels, naught but trouble. They say they're going to lie in wait the whole winter, to see if the maid they're hunting doesn't creep out of some hidey-hole and venture into the village. Then that tree's s'pposed to nab 'er.'

'Are they in your village too?'

The peasant's face darkened and he ground his teeth.

'Not in our village. We was lucky. But in Dun Dare, half a day from us, there's four. They're quartered in the inn. Scoundrels, good sir hermit, damned scoundrels, rogues. They took their pleasure with the village wenches, and when the menfolk stood up to them, they killed them, good sir, without mercy. Killed them dead . . .'

'They killed people?'

'Two. The headman and one other. And is there a punishment

363

for such ne'er-do-wells, good sir? And is there a law? There's no punishment or law! A carter who came to Dun Dare with his wife and daughter, he said that years ago there used to be witchers in the world, so they say . . . They dealt with every kind of villainy. We ought to send a witcher to Dun Dare, he'd give those rascals short shrift . . .'

'Witchers killed monsters, not people.'

'They're knaves, good sir hermit, not people, naught but knaves from hell. A witcher's what needed for them, no more, no less . . . Well, time I were going, good sir hermit . . . Ooo, winter's coming! Soon it'll be away with the dugout and out with the sleigh . . . And what them knaves from Dun Dare need, good sir, is a witcher . . .'

*

'Oh, that's right,' Ciri repeated through clenched teeth. 'Oh, absolutely right. A witcher what's they need . . . Or a witcher girl. Four, is it? In Dun Dare, are they? And where is bloody Dun Dare? Upstream? Would I get there across the tussocks?'

'By the Gods, Ciri,' Vysogota said in terror. 'You can't seriously be thinking—'

'Don't swear by the gods, if you don't believe in them. And I know you don't.'

'Let's leave my views out of this! Ciri, what infernal ideas are you hatching? How can you even—'

'Now you leave *my* convictions alone, Vysogota. I know what I have to do! I'm a witcher!'

'You're an unstable young person!' he exploded. 'You're a child who's been through traumatic experiences; a damaged child on the verge of a nervous breakdown. And more than that, you're sick with a craving for revenge! Blinded by a lust for retribution! Don't you understand that?'

'I understand it better than you!' she yelled. 'Because you have no idea what it means to be hurt! You have no idea about revenge, for no one has ever truly wronged you!'

She rushed out of the cottage. A bitterly cold draught briefly blew through the hallway and the main room before she slammed the door shut. Soon after he heard neighing and the pounding of hooves.

Agitated, he banged the plate down onto the table. Let her go, he thought angrily, let her shake off the anger. It wasn't as if he was afraid for her, she'd ridden often enough among the bogs, by day and night; she knew the paths, causeways, tussocks and meadows. If, though, she did get lost, she'd only have to let go of the reins – her black Kelpie knew the way home to the goat's barn.

Some time after, when it was already very dark, he went out and hung the lantern on a post. He stood by the fence and listened out for the clatter of hooves or the splash of water. But the wind and the rustling of the reeds muffled all sound. The lantern on the post swayed crazily until it finally went out.

And then he heard it. From far away. No, not from the direction Ciri had ridden towards. But on the other side. From the bogs. A savage, inhuman, long-drawn-out, plaintive cry. A howl.

A moment of silence.

And again. A beann'shie.

An elven phantom. The harbinger of death.

Vysogota trembled, from cold and from fear. He quickly headed back towards the cottage, muttering and humming under his breath, so as not to hear it, not to hear it at all, because he must not hear it.

Kelpie emerged from the darkness before he managed to relight the lantern.

'Go into the cottage,' Ciri said, gently and softly. 'And don't leave. It's a foul night.'

*

They bickered again over supper.

'You seem to know a great deal about the problems of good and evil!'

'Because I do! And not from scholarly books, either!'

'No, of course. You know it all from experience. From practice. For you've acquired plenty of experience in your long sixteen years of life.'

'I've gained enough. Quite enough!'

'Congratulations. My learned friend.'

'You can sneer,' she clenched her teeth, 'without having any idea how much evil you've done to the world, you aged scholars, you theoreticians with your books, with your centuries-old experience of reading moral treatises so diligently you didn't even have time to look out of the window to see what the world was really like. You philosophers, artificially shoring up artificial philosophies in order to earn salaries at universities. And since not a soul would pay you for the ugly truth about the world, you invented ethics and morality; nice, optimistic sciences. Except they're fallacious and deceitful!'

'There's nothing more deceitful than a half-baked judgement, miss! Than a hasty and incautious conclusion!'

'You didn't find a remedy for evil! But I, a callow witcher, have! An infallible remedy!'

He didn't respond, but his face must have betrayed him, because Ciri leaped up from the table.

'Do you think I'm talking nonsense? Making wild claims?'

'I think,' he calmly replied, 'you're speaking in anger. I think you're planning your revenge in anger. And I strongly urge you to calm down.'

'I am calm. And revenge? Answer me: why not? Why should I eschew revenge? In the name of what? Higher reasons? And what's higher than an order of things where evil deeds are punished? To you, O philosopher and ethicist, revenge is an improper deed, reprehensible, unethical and ultimately unlawful. And I ask: where is the punishment for evil? Who should attest it, adjudge it and inflict it? The gods you don't believe in? The great demiurge-creator you've decided to replace the Gods with? Or perhaps the law? Perhaps Nilfgaardian justice, imperial judgements, prefects? You naive old man!'

'And so it's an eye for an eye, a tooth for a tooth? Blood for blood? And for that blood, more blood? A sea of blood? Do you want to drown the world in blood? O naive, damaged girl! Is that how you mean to fight evil, little witcher?'

'Yes. Just like that! For I know what Evil fears. Not your ethics, Vysogota, not sermons, not moral treatises about a worthy life. Evil fears pain, impairment, suffering, death, the end! When wounded,

Evil howls with pain like a dog! It rolls around on the floor and squeals, watching the blood spurt from its veins and arteries, seeing its bones stick out of stumps, seeing its guts crawl from its belly, sensing that with the cold, death is approaching. Then and only then does Evil's hair stand on end and Evil finally yell: "Mercy! I repent of my sins! I'll be good and decent now, I swear! Just save me, staunch the blood, don't let me perish ignominiously!"

'Yes, O hermit. That's how you fight Evil! If Evil wants to do you harm, inflict pain on you – anticipate it, ideally when Evil isn't expecting it. If, though, you didn't manage to anticipate Evil, if you were harmed by Evil, then pay it back! Catch it, ideally when it has forgotten, when it feels safe. Pay it back twofold. Threefold. An eye for an eye? No! Both eyes for an eye! A tooth for a tooth? No! All its teeth for a tooth! Pay Evil back! Make it howl with pain, so its eyeballs burst from its howling. And then, looking down at the floor, you may confidently say: what's lying there won't harm anybody any longer, it won't threaten anyone. For how can it threaten anyone without any eyes? If it has no hands? How can it do any harm when its guts are trailing over the sand, and the gore is soaking into it?'

'And you,' the hermit said slowly, 'stand with your bloodied sword in hand, and look at the blood soaking into the sand. And you have the audacity to think that the age-old dilemma has been solved, the philosophers' dream has been attained. You think the nature of Evil has been transformed?'

'I do,' she said defiantly. 'Because what's lying on the ground with blood gushing from it is no longer Evil. Perhaps it isn't yet Good, but it certainly isn't Evil anymore!'

'They say,' Vysogota said slowly, 'that nature abhors a vacuum. Whatever is lying on the ground, bleeding profusely, whatever died from your sword, is no longer Evil. What is it then? Have you ever thought about that?'

'No. I'm a witcher! When they were teaching me, I swore I would act against Evil. Always. And without thinking . . .

'Because when you start thinking,' she added hollowly, 'killing stops making sense. Revenge stops making sense. And you can't let that happen.'

He shook his head, but she gestured to him to stop arguing.

'It's time I finished my story, Vysogota. I've been unfolding it for you for thirty nights, from the Equinox to Samhain. But I haven't told you everything. Before I leave, you have to learn what happened on the day of the Equinox in the village called Unicorn.'

*

She groaned when he pulled her from the saddle. The hip he had kicked her in the day before was hurting.

He tugged on the chain attached to the collar and pulled her towards a light-coloured building.

Several armed men were standing in the doorway. And one tall woman.

'Bonhart,' said one of the men, slim and brown-haired, with a thin face, holding a brass-tipped knout. 'It has to be said that you're full of surprises.'

'Greetings, Skellen.'

The man addressed as Skellen looked her straight in the eye for some time. She trembled under his gaze.

'Well?' he addressed Bonhart again. 'Will you explain at once, or perhaps bit by bit?'

'I don't like explaining things in the courtyard, for you get a mouthful of flies. May we go inside?'

'By all means.'

Bonhart yanked the chain.

Another man was waiting in the main room. He was dishevelled and pale, and was probably the cook, because he was busy cleaning traces of flour and cream from his clothing. His eyes lit up at the sight of Ciri. He came closer.

He wasn't the cook.

She recognised him at once, remembered those hideous eyes and the ugly mark on his face. He was the one who had pursued her on Thanedd with the Squirrels. She'd escaped him by jumping out of a window, and he had ordered the elves to jump after her. What had that elf called him? Rence?

'Well, well!' he said mordantly, jabbing a finger hard and painfully into her breast. 'Miss Ciri! We haven't seen each other since

368

Thanedd. I've been looking for you a long, long time, miss. And I've finally found you!'

'I don't know, sir, who you are,' Bonhart said coldly. 'But what you've claimed to find is actually mine, so keep your mitts off, if you value your fingers.'

'My name's Rience.' The sorcerer's eyes flashed unpleasantly. 'Kindly condescend to commit that to memory, Mr Bounty Hunter, sir. And who I am will be soon be revealed. Whom the maid belongs to will also soon be revealed. But let's not get ahead of ourselves. For now I only want to give her my regards and make a pledge. You don't have anything against that, I trust?'

'You are free to trust.'

Rience approached Ciri and looked into her eyes from close up.

'Your guardian, the hag Yennefer,' he said slowly and scornfully, 'once fell into disfavour with me. And so when I got my hands on her, I, Rience, taught her pain. With these hands, with these fingers. And I promised her that should you fall into my hands, princess, I would also teach you pain. With these hands, with these fingers . . .'

'Risky,' Bonhart said softly. 'You're taking a great risk, Mr Rience, or whatever your name is, bothering my little girl and threatening her. She is vengeful, liable to hold it against you. I repeat: keep your hands, fingers and all other parts of your body well away from her.'

'Enough.' Skellen cut them off, without taking his curious eyes off Ciri. 'Stop it, Bonhart. And you too, Rience, calm yourself. I've shown you mercy, but I may change my mind and order you bound to the table legs again. Sit down, both of you. Let's talk like cultured people. Just the three of us and no one else. For we have, it seems to me, much to talk about. But for now we'll put the subject of our conversations under guard. Mr Silifant!'

'Just guard her well.' Bonhart handed Silifant the end of the chain. 'Guard her with your life.'

*

Kenna stayed on the sidelines. Granted, she wanted to observe the wench, whom everybody had recently been talking about, but she

369

felt a strange aversion to pushing in amongst the small crowd surrounding Harsheim and Silifant, who were taking the mysterious captive over to a post in the courtyard.

Everybody was crowding around, jostling, peering. They were even trying to touch her, shove her, pull her. The girl trod stiffly, limping slightly, but held her head high. He's beaten her, thought Kenna. But he didn't break her.

'So she must be Falka . . .'

'The maid's barely grown!'

'A maid, huh? A cut-throat!'

'I heard she slayed six men, the brute, in the arena in Claremont . . .'

'And before that? How many others? The she-devil . . .'

'She-wolf!'

'And the mare, what a mare, look. A horse of marvellous blood . . . And here, by Bonhart's saddle flap, what a sword . . . Ah . . . a marvel!'

'Leave it alone!' Dacre Silifant growled. 'Don't touch! Get your hands off other people's things. Don't touch the girl either; don't paw her, don't hinder or insult her! Show some charity. We know not if we shan't be executing her before dawn. May she at least know peace until that time.'

'If the wench is to go to her death,' grinned Cyprian Fripp the younger, 'perhaps we could sweeten the remainder of her life and satiate her well? Throw her on the hay and bed her?'

'Aye!' Kabernik Turent cackled, 'We could! Let's ask Tawny Owl if it's allowed—'

'I tell you it's not allowed!' Dacre cut them off. 'Naught else occupies your minds, you damned fornicators! I said leave the maid in peace. Andres, Stigward, stand here by her. Don't take your eyes off her, or move a foot away. And use the lash on any that come close!'

'Sod that!' said Fripp. 'Very well, makes no difference to us. Let's be off, fellows, to the hay barn, and join the villagers, they're roasting a ram and a porker for the banquet. For today is the Equinox, a feast, isn't it? While the masters are deliberating, we can make merry.'

'Let's go. Take a demijohn from the chest, Dede. We'll take a drink! May we, Mr Silifant? Mr Harsheim? It's the feast today, and we shan't be heading anywhere tonight.'

'Oh, what droll designs!' Silifant frowned. 'They think of naught but feasting and toping! And who will stay here to help guard the wench and wait on Sir Stefan's summons?'

'I shall stay,' said Neratin Ceka.

'And I,' said Kenna.

Dacre Silifant looked at them attentively. Finally, he gestured his assent. Fripp and company roared their thanks incoherently.

'But have a care down there, at that merrymaking!' Ola Harsheim warned. 'Don't molest any wenches, or you might get jabbed in the privates with a pitchfork!'

'Sod that! Coming with us, Chloe? And you, Kenna? Won't you think it over?'

'No. I'm staying.'

*

'They left me chained to the post, with my hands bound. Two of them were guarding me. And the two standing nearby kept glancing over, watching me. The tall, good-looking woman. And a man with slightly feminine looks and bearing. Odd in some way.'

The cat sitting in the middle of the room yawned broadly, bored, because the mouse it was tormenting had stopped providing amusement. Vysogota said nothing.

'Bonhart, Rience and that Skellen-Tawny Owl were still debating in the headman's hall. I didn't know what about. I might have expected the worst, but I was resigned. One more arena? Or would they simply kill me? Blow it, I thought, let it finally be over.'

Vysogota said nothing.

*

Bonhart sighed.

'Don't glower, Skellen,' he repeated. 'I simply wanted to make some money. It's time, you notice, I retired, to sit on the porch and watch pigeons. You gave me a hundred florins for the She-Rat, you badly wanted her dead. That puzzled me. How much

371

could the maid really be worth, I thought. And I worked out that if she were killed or handed over, she would certainly be worth less than if she were kept. An old principle of economics and commerce. Goods like her keep gaining in value. One can always haggle . . .'

Tawny Owl wrinkled his nose, as though there was a bad smell in the vicinity.

'You're painfully frank, Bonhart. But get to the point. To the explanations. You fled with the girl through the whole of Ebbing, and all of a sudden you show up and start explaining the laws of economics. Tell me what happened.'

'What is there to explain?' Rience smiled repellently. 'Mr Bonhart has simply finally grasped who the wench really is. And how much she's worth.'

Skellen didn't grace him with a glance. He was looking at Bonhart, into his fishlike, expressionless eyes.

'And he pushes this precious girl, this valuable acquisition, meant to guarantee his pension, out into the arena in Claremont,' he drawled, 'and makes her fight to the death. Risks her life, though she's allegedly worth so much alive. What's it about, Bonhart? Because something doesn't add up.'

'Had she perished in the arena,' Bonhart didn't lower his eyes, 'it would have meant she wasn't worth anything.'

'I see,' Tawny Owl frowned slightly. 'But rather than taking the wench to another arena you brought her to me. Why, if I might ask?'

'I repeat,' Rience grimaced. 'He twigged who she is.'

'You're shrewd, Lord Rience.' Bonhart stretched until his joints creaked. 'You've guessed right. Yes, it's true that there's one more riddle linked to the witcher girl trained in Kaer Morhen. In Geso, when the noblewoman was robbed, the wench's tongue wagged. That she was apparently so important and titled that the baron's daughter was such small beer and so low-ranking she ought to bow down before her. In that case, this Falka, I think to myself, must be at least the daughter of a count. Curious. Firstly: a witcher girl. Are there so many of them? Secondly: in the Rats' gang. Thirdly: the imperial coroner is chasing around after her, in person, from Korath to Ebbing and ordering her killed. And on top of all that

. . . she's a high-born noble woman. Ha, I think to myself, some-one ought to ask that wench who she really is.'

He was silent for a time.

'At first –' he wiped his nose with his cuff '– she wouldn't talk. Although I asked. I asked with hand, foot and whip. I didn't want to cut her . . . But as luck would have it, a barber surgeon turned up. With instruments for extracting teeth. I bound her to a chair . . .'

Skellen swallowed audibly. Rience smiled. Bonhart studied a cuff.

'She told me everything, before . . . As soon as she saw the instruments. Those toothed pliers and pincers. She became more forthcoming at once. It turns out she's a—'

'Cintran princess,' said Rience, looking at Tawny Owl. 'The heiress to the throne. A candidate for marriage to Emperor Emhyr.'

'Which Lord Skellen didn't deign to tell me,' the bounty hunter sneered. 'He ordered me simply to murder her, he stressed it sev-eral times. Kill her mercilessly, on the spot! Well, Lord Skellen? Kill a queen? Our emperor's future spouse? With whom, if one is to believe the rumours, the emperor will tie the knot any moment, after which there is to be a general amnesty?'

Bonhart glared at Skellen as he delivered his oration. But the imperial coroner didn't lower his eyes.

'And so,' the hunter continued, 'out it comes: a delicate situa-tion. Thus, though I regret it, I gave up my plans regarding the witcher girl-princess. I've brought the whole predicament here, to Lord Skellen. To talk, to sort things out . . . For I'd say that this predicament is a little too much for one Bonhart . . .'

'A very reasonable conclusion,' said a harsh voice from Rience's bosom. 'Very reasonable, Mr Bonhart. What you've caught, gen-tlemen, is a little too much for you both. Luckily, you still have me.'

'What's that?' Skellen leaped up from his chair. 'What the bloody hell is that?'

'My master, the sorcerer Vilgefortz.' Rience drew from his bosom a tiny silver casket. 'More precisely, my master's voice. Coming from this magical device; it's called a xenogloss.'

'Greetings to all you,' said the casket. 'Shame I can only hear you, but urgent business prevents me from using teleprojection or teleportation.'

'That's all we bloody need,' Tawny Owl snarled. 'But I might have guessed. Rience is too stupid to act alone and by himself. I might have guessed you were lurking somewhere in the gloom, Vilgefortz. You lurk in the dark like a fat old spider, waiting for your cobweb to quiver.'

'What a vivid comparison.'

Skellen snorted.

'And don't try to pull the wool over our eyes, Vilgefortz. You're using Rience and his casket not because of the amount of work you have, but from fear of the army of sorcerers, your former comrades in the Chapter, who are scanning the whole world in search of traces of magic with your algorithm. Were you to try teleportation, they would locate you in an instant.'

'What impressive knowledge.'

'We haven't been introduced.' Bonhart bowed quite theatrically before the silver box. 'But nevertheless, is the honourable Rience promising to torture the girl on your instructions and with your authorisation, master sorcerer? Am I not mistaken? Upon my word, the girl is becoming more and more important with every moment. It turns out she's necessary to everybody.'

'We haven't been introduced,' Vilgefortz said from the casket. 'But I know you, Leo Bonhart, you'd be astonished just how well. And the girl is, indeed, important. After all, she's the Lion Cub of Cintra, the Elder Blood. In keeping with Ithlinne's Prophecy, her descendants will rule over the world in the future.'

'Why do you need her so much?'

'I only need her placenta. Her womb. Once I've removed it, you can take the rest. What do I hear there, some kind of snorting? Some kind of disgusted sighing and puffing? Whose? Bonhart's – who physically and psychologically maltreats the girl every day in intricate ways? Or Stefan Skellen's – who intends to kill her on the orders of traitors and plotters? Eh?'

*

I eavesdropped on them, recalled Kenna, lying on her pallet with her hands behind her head. I stood around the corner and heard their thoughts. And my hair stood on end. Over my entire body. All of a sudden I understood the extent of the predicament I'd got myself into.

*

'Yes, yes,' said the voice from the xenogloss, 'you've betrayed your emperor, Skellen. Without hesitation, at the first opportunity.'

Tawny Owl snorted disdainfully.

'The charge of treachery from the lips of such an arch-traitor as you, Vilgefortz, is indeed a great matter. I'd feel honoured, if it didn't smack of a cheap, vulgar joke.'

'I'm not accusing you of treachery, Skellen, I'm mocking your naivety and inability to betray. Who are you betraying your emperor for? For Ardal aep Dahy and de Wett, princelings, their morbid pride piqued, insulted because the emperor rejected their young daughters by planning a marriage with the Cintran. Whereas they were hoping that a new dynasty would emerge from their families, that their families would become the first in the empire, that soon they'd rise even higher than the throne! Emhyr divested them of that hope at one stroke and then they decided to amend the course of history. They aren't yet ready with an armed rebellion, but they can at least eliminate the girl that Emhyr chose over their daughters. Of course, they don't feel like sullying their own delicate aristocratic hands; they found a hired thug, Stefan Skellen, suffering from an excess of ambition. Was it like that, Skellen? Don't you want to tell us?'

'What for?' Tawny Owl shouted. 'And tell whom? As usual you know everything, don't you, O great mage? Rience, as usual, doesn't know anything and that's as it should be, and Bonhart is unconcerned . . .'

'You, though, as I've already demonstrated, don't have anything to boast about. The princes bought you with promises, but you're too intelligent not to realise that you'll gain nothing with the lordlings. Today they need you as a tool to eliminate the Cintran, tomorrow they'll get rid of you, because you're a low-born

375

upstart. Did they offer you Vattier de Rideaux's position in the new empire? You surely don't believe that, Skellen. They need Vattier more, since secret services always stay the same – coups or not. They only want to murder using your hands, but they need Vattier to take over the security apparatus. Besides, Vattier is a viscount and you're a nobody.'

'Indeed,' Tawny Owl pouted. 'I'm too intelligent not to have noticed that. In that case, I ought in turn to betray Ardal aep Dahy and join you, Vilgefortz? Is that what you're driving at? But I am not a weathercock! If I support the idea of revolution, it's from conviction and principle. Autocratic tyranny ought to be finished, a constitutional monarchy introduced, and after that democracy . . .'

'What?'

'The power of the people. A system where the people will rule. The citizenry of all states, through the most worthy and honest representatives chosen in an honest election . . .'

Rience roared with laughter. Bonhart laughed wildly. The xenogloss of the mage Vilgefortz laughed heartily, if somewhat screechingly. All three of them laughed and guffawed, weeping great tears.

'Very well,' Bonhart interrupted the merriment. 'We haven't gathered here for diversion, but to trade. The girl, for now, doesn't belong to the population of honest citizens of all states, she belongs to me. But I can resell her. What does my lord sorcerer have to offer?'

'Does ruling the world interest you?'

'No.'

'Then I shall let you,' Vilgefortz said slowly, 'be present during what I do to the girl. You'll be able to watch. I know you prefer that kind of voyeurism to all other pleasures.'

Bonhart's eyes flashed with white flame. But he was composed.

'And more specifically?'

'And more specifically: I'm prepared to pay your fee twentyfold. Two thousand florins. Think, Bonhart; that's a sack of money you won't be able to lift. You're going to need a pack mule. It'll suffice you for your retirement, porch, pigeons, and even for vodka and harlots, if you do it in sensible moderation.'

'Agreed, mage, sir,' the hunter laughed, seemingly blithely. 'You've touched my heart with that vodka and those harlots. Let's strike a deal. But I'd also be interested in that observation you suggested, too. I'd prefer, admittedly, to watch her expire in the arena, but I'd also be glad to take a look at your knife work. Throw it in as a bonus.'

'Done.'

'That didn't take you long,' Tawny Owl observed sardonically. 'In sooth, Vilgefortz, you've struck up a partnership with Bonhart swiftly and smoothly. A partnership which indeed is and will be a *societas leonina*. But might you have forgotten something? The headman's hall where you're sitting and the Cintran you're trading are surrounded by two dozen armed soldiers. My soldiers.'

'My dear Skellen,' came Vilgefortz's voice from the box. 'You insult me by thinking I plan to disadvantage you in the exchange. On the contrary. I mean to be extremely generous. I can't guarantee you – as you deigned to call it – democracy. But I guarantee you material assistance, logistical support and access to information, owing to which you'll stop being a tool and a minion to the conspirators, and will become a partner. One whose person and opinion Prince Joachim de Wett, Duke Ardal aep Dahy, Count Broinne, Count d'Arvy and all the rest of the blue-blooded plotters will take into account. What if it's a *societas leonina*? Certainly, if Cirilla is the loot, then I shall take the lion's share, deservedly so, it seems to me. Does it pain you? After all, you will make a considerable profit. If you give me the Cintran, Vattier de Rideaux's position is yours for the taking. And as the head of the secret service, Stefan Skellen, one can enact all sorts of utopias, perhaps even democracy and honest elections. So as you see, I give you the fulfilment of your life's dreams and ambitions in exchange for one skinny fifteen-year-old. Do you see that?'

'No,' Tawny Owl shook his head. 'I only hear it.'

'Rience.'

'Yes, master.'

'Give Lord Skellen an example of the quality of our information. Tell him what you got out of Vattier.'

'There's a spy in your troop,' said Rience.

'What?'

377

'You heard. Vattier de Rideaux has planted someone here. They know about everything you're doing. Why you're doing it and for whom. Vattier has an agent amongst you.'

＊

He walked quietly over to her. She almost didn't hear him.

'Kenna.'

'Neratin.'

'You listened in to my thoughts. Over there, in the headman's hall. You know what I was thinking. So you know who I am.'

'Listen, Neratin—'

'No. You listen, Joanna Selborne. Stefan Skellen is betraying his country and his emperor. He's conspiring. Everyone who's with him will end up on the scaffold. Will be torn apart by horses in Millennium Square.'

'I don't know anything, Neratin. I carry out my orders . . . What do you want from me? I serve the coroner . . . And who do you serve?'

'The empire. Viscount de Rideaux.'

'What do you want from me?'

'To demonstrate good sense.'

'Go away. I won't betray you, I won't tell . . . But go away, please. I can't, Neratin. I'm a simple woman. It's too much for my head . . .'

＊

I don't know what to do. Skellen said 'Miss Selborne'. As though to an officer. Who am I serving? Him? The emperor? The empire? And how am I to know?

Kenna pushed herself away from the corner of the cottage, flourished a withy and growled menacingly to drive away some village children who were curiously watching Falka sitting at the foot of the post. Oh, I've got myself in a fine pickle.

Oh, there's a whiff of the noose in the air. And horse shit in Millennium Square.

I don't know how it will finish, thought Kenna. But I have to go inside her. Enter Falka. Sense her thoughts if only for a moment. Know what she knows.

Understand.

*

'She came close,' said Ciri, stroking the cat. 'She was tall, well-groomed, standing out very much from the rest of that pack . . . Even pretty, in her own way. And commanding respect. The two who were guarding me, vulgar oafs, stopped swearing when she approached.'

Vysogota said nothing.

'She,' Ciri went on, 'leaned over and looked me in the eyes. I felt something at once . . . Something strange . . . It was as though something had crunched at the back of my head. It hurt. There was a rushing sound in my ears. For a moment everything went very bright . . . Something entered me, something repulsive and slimy . . . I recognised it. Yennefer had shown it to me in the temple . . . But I didn't want to allow that woman do it . . . So I simply pushed away the thing she'd put into me, pushed it away and expelled it from myself, with all the strength I could muster. And the tall woman bent backwards and staggered, as though she'd been punched, took two steps backwards . . . And blood rushed from her nose. From both nostrils.'

Vysogota said nothing.

'But I,' Ciri raised her head, 'understood what had happened. I suddenly felt the Power in me. I'd lost it in Korath desert, I'd renounced it. Later I couldn't draw on it, couldn't make use of it. But she, that woman, had given me the Power, had literally shoved the weapon into my hand. It was my chance.'

*

Kenna staggered and sat down heavily on the sand, swaying and feeling for the ground as though drunk. Blood was pouring from her nose and down her mouth and chin.

'What's . . .' Andres Vierny leaped up, but all of a sudden seized his head in both hands, opened his mouth and uttered a croak.

379

He stared at Stigward with eyes wide open, but blood was already dripping from the pirate's nose and ears and his eyes had clouded over. Andres dropped to his knees, looking at Neratin Ceka, who was standing to one side and watching impassively.

'Nera . . . tin . . . Help . . .'

Ceka didn't move. He was looking at the girl. She turned her eyes on him and he tottered.

'It's not necessary,' he quickly forestalled. 'I'm on your side. I want to help you. Here, I'll cut through your bonds . . . Take the knife, cut through the collar yourself. I'll fetch the horses.'

'Ceka . . .' Andres Vierny stammered out, choking. 'You trai—'

The girl struck him with a gaze and he fell onto Stigward, who was lying motionless and curled up in a foetal position. Kenna still couldn't stand up. Sticky drops of blood dripped onto her chest and stomach.

'Alarm!' yelled Chloe Stitz, suddenly appearing from behind the cottages and dropping a mutton rib. 'Alaaaaarm! Silifant! Skellen! The girl's getting away!'

Ciri was already mounted. She was holding a sword.

'Yaaaaaa, Kelpie!'

'Alaaaaaaarm!'

Kenna was clawing the sand. She couldn't get up. Her legs were totally unresponsive, as though made of wood. A psionic, she thought. I've encountered a super-psionic. The girl is about ten times stronger than me . . . I'm lucky she didn't kill me . . . How come I'm still conscious?

A group was now running from the cottages, led by Ola Harsheim, Bert Brigden and Til Echrade, and the guards from the gate – Dacre Silifant and Boreas Mun – hurried into the courtyard. Ciri wheeled her horse around, yelled and galloped towards the river. But armed men were already running from there.

Skellen and Bonhart dashed out of the hall. Bonhart holding his sword. Neratin Ceka yelled, rode his horse at them and knocked them both down. Then he hurled himself, straight from the saddle, at Bonhart and pinned him to the ground. Rience dashed out onto the threshold and looked on, dumbfounded.

'Seize her!' Skellen roared, springing up from the ground. 'Seize her or kill her!'

'Alive!' Rience howled. 'Aliiiive!'

Kenna saw Ciri driven away from the riverside palisade, rein her mare around and speed towards the gate. She saw Kabernik Turent leap forward and try to drag her from the saddle, saw a sword flash and a crimson outpouring gush from Turent's neck. Dede Vargas and Fripp the younger also saw it. They decided not to bar the girl's way, but bolted between the shacks.

Bonhart jumped to his feet, pushed Neratin Ceka away with a blow of his sword pommel and smote him terribly, diagonally across his breast, and then raced after Ciri. Neratin, slit open and spurting blood, managed to catch him by the legs, and only released him when he was skewered to the sand with the point of a sword. But those few seconds of delay were sufficient. The girl spurred her mare, fleeing from Silifant and Mun. Skellen came up stealthily and wolf-like from the left, and swung an arm. Kenna saw something sparkle in flight, saw the girl writhe and sway in the saddle and a fountain of blood erupt from her face. She leaned back so far that for a moment she was lying on the mare's croup. She didn't fall but straightened up and remained in the saddle, then pressed herself to the horse's neck. The black mare jostled the armed men and raced straight for the gate. Behind her ran Mun, Silifant and Chloe Stitz with a crossbow.

'She won't jump it! She's ours!' Mun yelled triumphantly. 'No horse can clear seven feet!'

'Don't shoot, Chloe!'

Chloe Stitz didn't hear in the general uproar. She stopped. Put the crossbow to her cheek. It was widely known that Chloe never missed.

'She's dead meat!' she cried. 'Dead meat!'

Kenna saw a man whose name she didn't know run forward, raise a crossbow and shoot Chloe point-blank in the back. The bolt passed right through her in an explosion of blood. Chloe dropped without a sound.

The mare reached the gate and drew back its head a little. And jumped. It soared and quite simply scaled the gate, gracefully gathered up its fore hooves and streamed over it like a black silk ribbon. Its curled hind hooves didn't even brush the upper bar.

'Ye Gods!' screamed Dacre Silifant. 'Ye Gods, what a horse! Worth its weight in gold!'

'The mare goes to whoever catches her!' Skellen screamed. 'To horse! Mount up and after her!'

The search party galloped through the finally open gate, kicking up dust. Bonhart and Boreas Mun galloped ahead of everyone.

Kenna stood up with effort. And immediately staggered and sat down heavily on the sand. Her legs were tingling painfully.

Kabernik Turent wasn't moving, but lay in a red puddle with arms and feet splayed apart. Andres Vierny tried hard to lift the still-unconscious Stigward.

Chloe Stitz, huddled up on the sand, seemed as tiny as a child.

Ola Harsheim and Bert Brigden dragged the short man, the one who'd killed Chloe, before Skellen. Tawny Owl was panting and trembling with fury. From the bandolier slung across his chest he took out another orion, the same kind of steel star he had wounded the girl's face with a moment earlier.

'May you rot in hell, Skellen,' said the short man. Kenna recalled his name. Mekesser. Jediah Mekesser. A Gemmerian. She had first met him in Rocayne.

Tawny Owl stooped and swung his arm vigorously. The six-toothed star whined in the air and plunged deeply into Mekesser's face, between his eye and nose. He didn't even cry out when hit, but simply began shaking violently and spasmodically in Harsheim and Brigden's grip. He shook for a long time and bared his teeth so ghoulishly that everybody turned their heads away. Everybody except Tawny Owl.

'Pull my orion from him, Ola,' said Stefan Skellen, when at last the corpse was hanging inertly in the two men's arms. 'And bury that scum in the muck, with that other scum, the hermaphrodite. Not a trace shall remain of those two execrable traitors.'

The wind suddenly howled and clouds massed. It suddenly became dark.

*

The guards on the citadel walls shouted. The Scarra sisters were snoring a duet. Kohut pissed noisily into the empty bucket. Kenna

382

pulled the blanket up under her chin. She was thinking back.

They didn't catch the girl. She vanished. Simply vanished. Boreas Mun – unprecedentedly – lost the black mare's trail after about three miles. Suddenly, without warning, it became dark, the wind flattening trees almost to the ground. The rain lashed down, nay, even thunder rumbled and lightning flashed.

Bonhart didn't give up. They returned to Unicorn. They all yelled at one another, interrupting and shouting each other down: Bonhart, Tawny Owl, Rience and the fourth, mysterious, inhuman, croaking voice. Then they ordered the entire hanza to mount up, unlike those – like me – who were unable to ride. They banded together peasants with torches and drove them into the forests. They returned just before dawn.

With nothing. If you didn't count the horror in their eyes.

The tales, Kenna recalled, only began a few days later. In the beginning everyone was too afraid of Tawny Owl and Bonhart. They were so furious it was better to get out of their way. Even Bert Brigden, an officer, was hit across the head with the handle of a knout for some imprudent word.

But later people talked about what had happened during the chase. About the tiny straw unicorn from the little chapel that suddenly grew to the size of a dragon and scared the horses so much the riders fell from them, only miraculously avoiding breaking their necks. About the cavalcade of fiery-eyed apparitions galloping across the sky on skeleton horses led by a terrible skeleton king ordering his phantom servants to wipe out the black mare's hoof prints with their ragged cloaks. About the macabre choir of goatsucker nightjars, calling: "Liiiquorrrr of blood, liiiquorrrr of blood!" About the horrific wailing of the ghastly beann'shie, the harbinger of death . . .

The wind, rain, clouds, bushes and fantastically-shaped trees, and fear, which turns everything into nightmares, commented Boreas Mun, who had been there, after all. That's the whole explanation. But the nightjars? The nightjars were screaming, as nightjars always do, he added.

And the trail, the hoof prints, which suddenly vanish, as though the horse had flown up into the heavens?

The face of Boreas Mun, a tracker able to track down a fish

in water, stiffened at the question. The wind, he answered, the wind covered the tracks with sand and foliage. There's no other explanation.

Some people even believed, Kenna recalled. Some people even believed that they were all natural or predictable phenomena. And even laughed at them.

But they stopped laughing. After Dun Dare. No one laughed after Dun Dare.

*

He stepped back involuntarily and sucked in air on seeing her.

She had mixed goose lard with soot from the chimney and with the greasepaint thus created had blackened her eye sockets and eyelids, extending them with long lines to her ears and temples.

She looked like a demon.

'From the fourth tussock up to the high forest, keeping to the very edge,' he repeated the directions. 'Then along the river until you get to three dead trees, and then due west through a hornbeam woodland. When you see the pines, ride along the edge and count the tracks. Turn into the ninth and don't turn off after that. Then it'll be the Dun Dare settlement, there's a hamlet on the north side. A few cottages. And beyond them, at the crossroads, a tavern.'

'I remember. I'll make it, don't worry.'

'Be most vigilant at the bends in the river. Beware of places where the reeds thin out. And places covered in knotgrass. And should darkness overtake you before the pine forest, stop and wait until morning. Under no circumstances ride across the bogs at night. It's almost a new moon now, and the clouds—'

'I know.'

'As far as the Lake Land goes . . . Head north, across the hills. Avoid main roads, the main roads are heaving with soldiers. When you get to a river, a large river, which is called the Sylte, you're over halfway.'

'I know. I have the map you drew.'

'Oh, yes. Indeed.'

Ciri checked her harness and saddlebags yet again. Mechanically. Not knowing what to say. Putting off what had to be said.

'It was agreeable to have you to stay,' he forestalled her. 'Truly. Farewell, O witcher girl.'

'Farewell, O hermit. Thank you for everything.'

She was already in the saddle, already prepared to click her tongue at Kelpie, when he came over and took her arm.

'Ciri. Stay. See out the winter . . .'

'I'll reach the lake before the frosts. But later, if it's as you said, nothing will matter any longer. I'll teleport back to Thanedd. To the school in Aretuza. To Madam Rita . . . Vysogota . . . Like it used to be . . .'

'The Tower of the Swallow is a legend. Remember, it's just a legend.'

'I'm just a legend,' she said bitterly. 'Have been since my birth. Zireael, the Swallow, the Unexpected Child. The Chosen One. The Child of Destiny. The Child of the Elder Blood. I'm going, Vysogota. Farewell.'

'Farewell, Ciri.'

*

The tavern by the crossroads past the hamlet was empty. Cyprian Fripp the younger and his three companions had forbidden the local people from entering and drove away travellers. They, however, spent their time eating and drinking, never leaving the smoky, gloomy tavern, which smelled as a tavern usually does in winter when the doors and windows are kept shut – of sweat, cats, mice, footwraps, pinewood, farts, fat, burnt food and wet, steaming clothing.

'Sod this rotten place,' centurion Yuz Jannowitz, a Gemmerian, said for probably the hundredth time, gesturing towards the serving wenches to bring him vodka. 'Damn that Tawny Owl. Ordering us to hunker down in this mangy hole! I'd sooner be riding through forests with the patrols!'

'Then you must be stupid,' replied Dede Vargas. 'It's bloody freezing outside! I'd druther be here in the warm. With the maid close at hand!'

He slapped the wench hard on the bottom. She squealed, not very convincingly and with evident apathy. She was slow-witted, to tell the truth. Working in a tavern had only taught her that when they slap or pinch you, you should squeal.

Cyprian Fripp and his company had already begun to take advantage of the two serving wenches the day after arriving. The innkeeper was afraid to complain and the wenches too dim-witted to think about protesting . . . Life had taught them that if a wench protested she got hit. It was more judicious, usually, to wait till they get bored.

'That there Falka,' Rispat La Pointe, bored, took up another stock topic of their bored evening conversations, 'croaked somewhere in the forests, I tell you. I saw Skellen slice her face open with the orion and the blood shooting out in a fountain! She can't have come through that, I tell you!'

'Tawny Owl missed her,' Yuz Jannowitz stated. 'He barely scratched her with the orion. Granted he carved her face up good and proper, saw it for myself. But did it stop the wench jumping the gate? Did she fall from her horse? Not a chance! And we measured the gate afterwards: seven foot effing two. And? She jumped it! And then what! You couldn't have stuck a knife blade between the saddle and her little arse.'

'Blood was pouring from her,' protested Rispat La Pointe. 'She rode away, I'm telling you, rode off and then fell and croaked in a hollow somewhere. Wolves and birds ate the carcass, martens finished it off, and ants. That's the end, *deireadh*. So we're sitting here in vain, drinking our money away. Our money, it is, for I don't seem to see any pay!'

'It can't be that no traces or signs of a corpse are left,' said Dede Vargas with conviction. 'Something's always left: the skull, pelvis or one of the bigger bones. Rience, that sorcerer, will eventually find Falka's remains. Then the matter will be over.'

'And perhaps then they'll drive us so hard we'll recall with delight this idleness and this lousy pigsty.' Cyprian Fripp the younger threw a bored glance at the tavern's walls, on which he already knew every nail and every damp patch. 'And that poxy booze. And those two, what smell of onions, and when you rut them they lie like calves, staring at the ceiling and picking their teeth.'

'Everything's better than this tedium,' Yuz Jannowitz stated. 'I feel like howling! Let's fucking do something! Anything! Shall we torch the village or what?'

The door creaked. The sound was so unexpected that all four of them leaped up from their seats.

'Scram!' Dede Vargas roared. 'Get out, old man! Beggar! Filthy bastard! Get back outside!'

'Leave him.' Fripp, bored, waved an arm. 'See, he's lugging some pipes. He's just a beggar, probably an old soldier who earns a crust by playing and singing in taverns. It's cold and rainy outside. Let him stay . . .'

'Just well away from us.' Yuz Jannowitz showed the beggar where to sit. 'Or we'll be crawling with lice. I can see from here what specimens are crawling over him. You'd think they were tortoises, not lice.'

'Give him some victuals, landlord!' Fripp the younger beckoned imperiously, 'And us some hooch!'

The beggar took off his bulky fur hat and solemnly gave off a stench that filled the room.

'Thanks be to you, m'lord,' he said. 'For today is Samhain's Eve, a holy day. It doesn't befit to drive anyone away on a holy day, to be soaked and frozen in the rain. It befits to regale a body on a holy day . . .'

'In truth!' Rispat La Pointe slapped himself in the forehead. 'Today is Samhain's Eve! The end of October!'

'A night of witchcraft.' The beggar slurped the watery broth he was brought. 'A night of ghosts and horrors!'

'Oho!' said Yuz Jannowitz. 'The old gimmer, heed you, is about to divert us with beggarly tales!'

'Let him divert us,' Dede Vargas yawned. 'Anything's better than this boredom!'

'Samhain,' repeated Cyprian Fripp the younger. 'It's already five weeks since Unicorn. And two weeks that we've been here. Two whole weeks! Samhain, ha!'

'A night of portents.' The beggar licked the spoon, fished something out of the bowl with a finger and ate it. 'A night of dread and witchcraft!'

'What did I say?' Yuz Jannowitz grinned. 'We'll have a beggar's tale!'

The beggar sat up straight, scratched himself and hiccoughed.

'Samhain Eve,' he began with emphasis, 'the last night before the November new moon, is the last night of the old year to the elves and when the new day dawns it'll be their New Year. Thus there is among the elves a custom that on the night of Samhain every fire in the homestead and yard should be lit with a single pitch taper, and the rest of the taper stowed well away until May, when Beltane is kindled with the same flame. Then, they say, there will be prosperity. Not only elves do thus; some of our folk do likewise. To protect themselves from evil spirits . . .'

'Ghosts!' Yuz snorted. 'Just listen to the old fart!'

'It's Samhain night!' the beggar said in an excited voice. 'On this night spirits walk the earth! The spirits of the dead knock on the windows. "Let us in," they moan, "let us in". Then they should be given honey and groats, all sprinkled with vodka . . .'

'I'd sooner sprinkle my own throat with vodka,' Rispat La Pointe chortled. 'And your ghosts, old man, can kiss me right here.'

'Oh, m'lord, don't make fun of ghosts, they're liable to hear, and they're vengeful! Today it's Samhain Eve, a night of dread and witchcraft! Prick up your eyes, do you hear something rustling and tapping all about? It's the dead coming from the beyond, they want to steal into homesteads, to warm themselves by the fire and eat their fill. There, over the bare stubble fields and leafless forests rages a gale and a frost, the poor ghosts are chilled, so they head towards homesteads where there's fire and warmth. Then one mustn't forget to put out food for them in a bowl on the step, or on the threshing floor, for if the phantoms find nothing there, they go into cottages themselves after midnight, to search for—'

'Oh my!' one of the serving wenches whispered loudly, and immediately squealed, as Fripp pinched her behind.

'Not a bad tale!' he said. 'But a long way off being a good one! Pour the old man a mug of mulled wine, landlord, and perhaps he'll tell a good one! The test of a good ghost story, boys, is when you goose the wenches and they're so engrossed they don't even notice!'

The men cackled and the two girls, whose degree of attentiveness was being tested, squealed. The beggar quaffed the mulled wine, slurping loudly and burping.

'Just don't get drunk or fall asleep here!' Dede Vargas warned menacingly. 'We aren't giving you drink for nothing! Tell a tale, sing, play the pipes! We want merriment!'

The beggar opened his mouth, where a single tooth stood like a white milepost in a dark steppe.

'It, it's Samhain, m'lord! What music? What playing? 'Tis not allowed! Samhain's music is the gale outside! It's the howling of werewolves and vampires, the wailing and moaning of vengeful ghosts, and ghouls grinding their teeth! The beann'shie howls and cries and whoever hears her cry is destined to die soon. Every evil spirit leaves its hideaway, witches fly to their last coven before winter! Samhain is a night of frights, of marvels and visions! Don't venture into the forest or a leshy will maul you to death! Don't pass through the boneyard or a corpse will seize you! Better not to leave your house at all, and to be on the safe side stick a new iron knife into the threshold. No evil will dare to pass over it. Whereas womenfolk must closely guard their children, for on Samhain night a rusalka or weeper may steal her child and replace it with a loathsome changeling. And if any woman is with child she better not go outside, for a night spirit may enchant the foetus in her womb! Instead of a babe a striga with iron teeth will be born—'

'Lawks!'

'With iron teeth. First it bites its mother's breast. Then her hands. It bites her face . . . Ooh, but now I have a hunger . . .'

'Have a bone, there's still meat on it. Bain't be healthy for old people to eat too much, they might choke and peg it, ha, ha! Oh, all right, bring him more wine, wench. Well, old man, go on about those ghosts!'

'Samhain, m'lord, is the last night for spectres to make merry. Later the frost takes their strength away, so they sink into the Chasm, beneath the earth, from where they don't stick their noses out the whole winter. For that reason from Samhain right until February, to the holy day of Imbaelk, is the best time for an expedition to haunted places, to search for treasure. If when it's warm someone pokes around by a wight's barrow, for example, the wight will awake as sure as eggs is eggs, jump out annoyed and devour the rummager. But from Samhain to Imbaelk poke and dig around, as much as you're able: the wight sleeps soundly like an old bear.'

389

'What has he dreamed up, the old bugger!'

'But I speaks the truth, m'lord. Yes, yes. Samhain is a magical, awful night, but also at once the best for all kinds of prophecies and predictions. On such a night it's worth telling fortunes and prophesying from bones and palms and from a white cock, from an onion, from cheese, from a cony's innards, from a rotting flitter-mouse . . .'

Fripp spat on the ground.

'The night of Samhain, a night of frights and phantoms . . . Better to sit tight at home. With all the family . . . By the fire . . .'

'With all the family,' Cyprian Fripp repeated, suddenly grinning voraciously at his comrades. 'All the family, see? Along with her, what's been slyly hiding away from us in the bushes!'

'The blacksmith's daughter!' Yuz Jannowitz guessed at once. 'That golden-haired peach! You're cute, Fripp. Perhaps we'll catch her at home today! Well, boys? Shall we dart over to the blacksmith's shack?'

'Ooh, why not now.' Dede Vargas stretched vigorously. 'I can see that blacksmith's daughter in front of me now, I tell you, those titties bouncing, that little bottom wiggling . . . We ought to have taken her then, not wait, but Dacre Silifant, that stupid stickler. . . Well, but now Silifant ain't here, and the blacksmith's daughter's at home! Waiting!'

'We've already hacked down the village headman with a battle axe.' Rispat grimaced. 'We butchered the churl who came to help him. Do we need more corpses? The blacksmith and his son are built like oak trees. We won't take them with fear. We need to—'

'Cut them up,' Fripp completed the sentence calmly. 'Just cut them a little, nothing more. Drink up, we'll get set and ride to the village. We'll have ourselves a Samhain! We'll don our sheepskins with the fur on the outside, we'll bellow and clamour, the boors will think it's devils or wights!'

'Shall we fetch the blacksmith's daughter here, to our quarters, or make merry our way, in the Gemmerian style, in front of her family?'

'The one doesn't rule out the other.' Fripp the younger looked out into the night through the window's oiled parchment. 'What

390

a blizzard's whipped up, dammit! The poplars are bending right over!'

'Oh, ho, ho,' said the beggar from over his mug. 'That isn't the wind, m'lord, that's not a blizzard! It's witches dashing astride their brooms, though some are in stone mortars, sweeping over their tracks with their brooms. Who knows when one of them may cross a fellow's path in the forest or steal up from behind? Who knows when she may attack! And she has teeth like these!'

'It's children you should be frightening with witches, beggar!'

'Don't speak, my liege, at the wrong time. For I'll tell you more, that the most menacing hags, the countesses and duchesses of the witchly state, oh, ho, ho, they don't ride on brooms, or on peels or in mortars, no! Those ones gallop on their black cats!'

'He, he, he, he!'

'It be the truth! For on Samhain Eve, on that one and only night of the year, hags' cats turn into mares as black as pitch. And woe betide he who on a night as black as a pall hears the clatter of hooves and sees a hag on a black mare. He who meets such a witch will not shun death. The witch will twist him around like a leaf blown in the wind and carry him off to the beyond!'

'You can finish when we return! And come up with a good tale, you bloody beggar, and make ready your pipes! When we return, there'll be revels here! There'll be dancing and the blacksmith's maid will be dandled . . . What is it, Rispat?'

Rispat La Pointe, who had gone out onto the porch to relieve himself, returned at a run with a face as white as snow. He was gesticulating frantically, pointing at the door. He didn't manage to utter a word. And there was no need. A horse neighed loudly from the courtyard.

'The black mare,' said Fripp, his face almost stuck to the parchment. 'The same black mare. It's her.'

'A witch?'

'It's Falka, you dolt.'

'It's her ghost!' Rispat sucked in air. 'A phantom! She *can't* have survived! She died and is returned as a spectre! On the night of Samhain . . .'

'She will come at night like a black pall,' muttered the beggar, pressing the empty mug to his belly. 'And who shall meet her will not avoid death . . .'

'Weapons, get your weapons,' Fripp said excitedly. 'Quickly! Cover the door from both sides! Don't you understand? We've struck lucky! Falka doesn't know about us, she's come here to get warm, cold and hunger have driven her out of her hideout! Straight into our arms! Tawny Owl and Rience will shower us with gold! Get your weapons . . .'

The door creaked.

The beggar hunched over the table and squinted. His sight was poor. His eyes were old and ruined, fogged and chronically sore. On top of that it was gloomy and smoky in the tavern. So the beggar could barely see the slender figure that had entered the main chamber from the hallway, dressed in a jerkin of muskrat pelts, wearing a hood and shawl which covered her face. The beggar had good hearing, though. He heard the soft cry of one of the serving wenches, the clatter of the other's clogs and the innkeeper's hushed curse. He heard the scraping of swords in scabbards. And Cyprian Fripp's quiet, scornful voice:

'We have you, Falka! Didn't expect us here, did you?'

'Oh, yes I did,' the beggar heard. And he trembled at the sound of her voice.

He saw the slender figure move and heard a sigh of terror. The muffled scream of one of the wenches. He couldn't see that the girl named Falka had removed her hood and shawl. He couldn't see her hideously disfigured face. Or her eyes painted all around with a paste of soot and grease, like a demon's.

'I am not Falka,' said the girl. The beggar saw again her fast, blurred movement, saw something shine fierily in the light of the cressets.

'I'm Ciri of Kaer Morhen. I'm a witcher! I've come here to kill you.'

The beggar, who had seen many a tavern brawl in his life, had a practiced method for avoiding injury: he ducked under the table, curled up and grabbed the table legs tightly. From that position, naturally, he couldn't see anything. And didn't want to. He was clutching the table tightly, and it was sliding around the room with the other furniture, amidst clattering, banging and crunching, the thudding of heavily booted feet, curses, shouts, grunts and the clanging of steel.

One of the serving wenches was yelling shrilly, unremittingly.

Someone tumbled onto the table, shifting it along with the beggar, and fell onto the floor alongside him. The beggar yelled, feeling hot blood splash onto him. Dede Vargas, the one who had at first wanted to drive him away – the beggar recognised him by the brass buttons on his jerkin – croaked horribly and thrashed about, spurting blood and flailing his arms around. One of his wild movements caught the beggar right in the eye. He could no longer see anything. The screaming serving wench choked, fell silent, took a breath and began to yell again, at a somewhat higher pitch.

Someone sprawled on the floor with a thud and blood splashed the freshly cleaned pine floorboards. The beggar couldn't tell that the dying man was Rispat La Pointe, slashed in the side of the neck by Ciri. He didn't see her turn a pirouette right in front of Fripp and Jannowitz's noses, and pass through their guards like a shade, like grey smoke. Jannowitz slipped behind her with a swift, soft, feline turn. He was an expert swordsman. Standing firmly on his right foot he struck out with a long, extended thrust, aiming at the girl's face, straight at her hideous scar. He couldn't miss.

But he did.

He was too slow to shield himself. She lunged from close up, two-handed, cutting him across his chest and stomach. And at once sprang back, whirled around, evading Fripp's blow, and slashing the crouching Jannowitz across the neck. Jannowitz pitched over headfirst against a bench. Fripp leaped over the bench and the corpse and struck powerfully. Ciri parried obliquely, made a half-turn and jabbed him in the side above his hip. Fripp staggered, sprawled onto the table and instinctively extended his arms in front of himself to keep his balance. The moment he rested his hand on the table Ciri hacked it off in a swift slash.

Fripp raised the stump spurting blood, examined it intently and then looked at the hand lying on the table. And suddenly dropped – sitting down heavily on the floor with a thud, just as though he had slipped on some soap. He sat, yelling, and then began to

393

bay, with a savage, high-pitched, long-drawn-out wolf-like howl. Crouching under the table, the blood-drenched beggar heard the ghastly duet continue for a moment – the monotonously yelling serving wench and the spasmodically howling Fripp.

The wench was the first to fall silent, her screaming ending in an inhuman, choking croak. Fripp simply fell silent. 'Mamma . . .' he suddenly said, utterly distinctly and lucidly. 'Dear mamma . . . What is this . . . ? How did . . . ? What has . . . happened to me? What's . . . the matter with me?'

'You're dying,' said the disfigured girl.

What was left of the beggar's hair stood up on his head. He clenched his teeth on the sleeve of his coat in order to stop them chattering.

Cyprian Fripp the younger made a sound as though he was having difficulty swallowing. After that he uttered no more sounds. None at all.

It was completely silent.

'What have you done . . . ?' the innkeeper groaned in the silence. 'What have you done, girl . . . ?'

'I'm a witcher. I kill monsters.'

'They'll hang us . . . They'll burn down the tavern and the village!'

'I kill monsters,' she repeated, but in her voice suddenly appeared something like surprise. Something like hesitancy. Uncertainty.

The innkeeper moaned and groaned. And sobbed.

The beggar slowly emerged from under the table, moving away from Dede Vargas's body, and his hideously mutilated face.

'You ride a black mare . . .' he mumbled. 'On a night as black as a pall . . . You sweep away the tracks behind you . . .'

The girl turned around and looked at him. She had already wrapped the shawl around her face and the black-ringed spectral eyes looked out from over it.

'Whoever meets you,' the beggar mumbled, 'will not avoid death . . . For you yourself are death.'

The girl looked long at him. Long. And rather dispassionately.

'You're right,' she said finally.

*

394

Somewhere in the swamps, far away, but much closer than before, a beann'shie's plaintive wailing sounded a second time.

Vysogota lay on the floor, where he had collapsed as he was getting out of bed. He found to his horror that he couldn't stand up. His heart pounded in his throat, choking him.

Now he knew whose death the elven apparition's nocturnal cry was auguring. Life was beautiful, he thought. In spite of everything.

'O Gods . . .' he whispered. 'I don't believe in you . . . But if you do exist . . .'

A dreadful pain suddenly exploded in his chest, behind his breastbone. Somewhere in the swamps, far away, but much nearer than before, the beann'shie howled savagely for the third time.

'If you do exist, protect the witcher girl on the road!'

'I have enormous eyes, all the better to see you with!' shrieked the great, iron wolf. 'I have enormous paws, all the better to seize and hug you with! Everything about me is enormous, everything, and soon you will discover it for yourself. Why are you looking at me so strangely, little girl? Why do you not answer?

The witcher girl smiled.

'I have a surprise for you.'

Flourens Delannoy,
The Surprise, from the book *Fairy Tales and Stories*

CHAPTER ELEVEN

The novices stood before the high priestess as straight as ramrods, tense, mute, slightly pale. They were ready to set off, prepared down to the minutest detail. Men's grey travelling clothes, warm, loose-fitting sheepskin coats and comfortable elven boots. Haircuts which could easily be kept clean and tidy on camps and marches, so as not to interfere with work. Very small bundles, containing only provisions and essential equipment. The army was to provide them with the rest. The army they were enlisting in.

The faces of the two girls were composed. Seemingly. Triss Merigold could see that the hands and lips of the two girls were quivering faintly.

The wind tugged at the bare branches of the trees in the temple grounds, swept dead leaves across the flagstones of the courtyard. The sky was a deep blue. A blizzard was in the air. You could feel it.

Nenneke broke the silence.

'Do you have your postings?'

'I don't,' Eurneid mumbled. 'For the moment I'll be in winter quarters in a camp outside Vizima. The recruiting officer said that in the spring mercenary units from the North will be stopping there . . . I'm to be a nurse in one of them.'

'But I,' said Iola the Second, 'already have my posting. To Mr Milo Vanderbeck, field surgeon.'

'Mind you don't disgrace me.' Nenneke gave the novices a menacing look. 'Mind you dishonour neither myself, nor the temple, nor the name of Great Melitele.'

'Certainly not, O mother.'

'And look after yourselves.'

'Yes, O mother.'

'You'll be dead tired attending the wounded, you will not know sleep. You'll be frightened and have doubts as you gaze on pain and death. And then it's easy to misuse narcotics or stimulants. Be careful of that.'

'We know, O mother.'

'War, fear, slaughter and blood,' the high priestess' eyes drilled into the two girls, 'mean a slackening of morals, and for some are also a powerful aphrodisiac. How they will act on you, my girls, you do not and cannot know at present. Please be careful about that too. If, though, it comes to it, take preventative measures. Should one of you get into trouble, in spite of that, stay well away from shady quacksalvers and village wise-women! Search for a temple, or better yet a sorceress.'

'We know, O mother.'

'That's everything. Now come closer to receive my blessing.'

She placed her hands on their heads in turn, embraced and kissed them in turn. Eurneid sniffed, Iola the Second simply burst into tears. Nenneke, although her eyes were shining a little more than usual, snorted.

'Don't make a scene,' she said, seemingly crossly and sharply. 'You're going to a normal war. People return from them. Take your things and I bid you goodbye.'

'Goodbye, O mother.'

They walked briskly towards the temple gate, without looking back. The high priestess Nenneke, the sorceress Triss Merigold and the scribe Jarre watched them go.

Jarre drew attention to himself by grunting intrusively.

'What's the matter?' Nenneke glared at him.

'You let them!' the boy exploded bitterly. 'You allowed them, girls, to sign up! And me? Why am I not allowed? Am I to continue leafing through dusty parchments, here, behind these walls? I'm neither a cripple nor a coward! It's a disgrace for me to stay in the temple, when even girls—'

'Those girls,' the high priestess interrupted, 'have spent their whole young lives learning to treat and heal illnesses and to care for the sick and wounded. They are going to war not out of patriotism or a hankering after adventure, but because there are countless wounded and sick people there. Piles of work, day and night! Eurneid and Iola, Myrrha, Katje, Prine, Debora and the other girls are the temple's contribution to this war. The temple, as part of society, is repaying its debt to society. It's giving the army and the war its contribution: experts and specialists. Do you understand that, Jarre? Specialists! Not arrow fodder!'

'Everybody's joining the army! Only cowards are staying at home!'

'You're talking nonsense, Jarre,' Triss said sharply. 'You don't understand anything.'

'I want to go to war . . .' the boy's voice broke. 'I want to rescue . . . Ciri . . .'

'My, my,' Nenneke said mockingly. 'The knight errant wants to ride out to rescue his sweetheart. On a white horse . . .'

She fell silent under the sorceress's gaze.

'In any case; enough of this, Jarre.' She shot the boy a black look. 'I said I'm not letting you! Return to your books! Study. Your future is scholarship. Come, Triss. Let's not waste time.'

*

A bone comb, a cheap ring, a book with a tattered binding, and a faded light blue sash lay spread out on a cloth before the altar. Iola the First, a priestess with prophetic powers, was kneeling over the objects.

'Don't hurry, Iola,' Nenneke, standing beside her, warned. 'Start concentrating slowly. We don't want a dazzling prophecy, we don't want an enigma with a thousand solutions. We want an image. A distinct image. Take the aura from these objects; they belonged to Ciri, Ciri touched them. Take the aura. Slowly. There's no hurry.'

Outside, a strong wind howled and a snowstorm whirled. Snow quickly covered the temple's roofs and courtyard. It was the nineteenth day of November. A full moon.

'I'm ready, O mother,' Iola the First said in her melodious voice. 'Begin.'

'One moment.' Triss sprang up from the bench and threw the chinchilla fur from her shoulders. 'One moment, Nenneke. I want to enter the trance with her.'

'That isn't safe.'

'I know. But I want to see. With my own eyes. I owe her that. I owe it to Ciri . . . I love that girl like a sister. She saved my life in Kaedwen, risking her own life to do it . . .'

The sorceress's voice suddenly broke.

'Just like Jarre.' The high priestess shook her head. 'Run to the rescue, blindly, recklessly, not knowing where or why. But Jarre is a naive young boy, and you're supposedly a mature, wise sorceress. You ought to know that you won't be helping Ciri by entering a trance. But you may harm yourself.'

'I want to enter the trance with Iola,' Triss repeated, biting her lip. 'Let me, Nenneke. As a matter of fact, what am I risking? An epileptic fit? Even if I am, you'd pull me out of it, wouldn't you?'

'You risk,' Nenneke said slowly, 'seeing things you ought not to see.'

The hill, Triss thought in horror, *Sodden Hill. Where I died. Where I was buried and my name was carved into the obelisk over the grave. The hill and the grave that will one day call for me.*

I know it. It was prophesied.

'I've already made my decision,' she said coldly, haughtily standing up and throwing her luxuriant hair back with both hands onto her shoulders.

'Let us begin.'

Nenneke kneeled down and rested her forehead on her folded hands.

'Let us begin,' she said softly. 'Make ready, Iola. Kneel beside me, Triss. Take Iola's hand.'

It was dark outside. The snowstorm moaned. Snow was falling.

*

In the South, far beyond the Amell mountains, in Metinna, in a land called Hundred Lakes, in a place far from the town of Ellander and the Temple of Melitele, five hundred miles away as the crow flies, a nightmare jolted the fisherman Gosta awake. After waking, Gosta could remember nothing of the dream, but an eerie anxiety kept him awake for a long time.

*

Every experienced angler knows you must wait for the first ice to land a perch.

That year, the winter – although unexpectedly early – played tricks and was as fickle as a pretty, popular girl. The first frost and snowstorm came as an unpleasant surprise, like a brigand from an ambush, at the beginning of November, right after Samhain, when no one had been expecting snow or frost and there was still plenty of work to do. By the middle of November the lake was already glazed over with a very thin layer of ice, which seemed just about able to bear the weight of a man, when the fickle winter suddenly subsided. Autumn returned, torrents of rain shattered the ice and a warm, southerly wind pushed it against the bank and melted it. What the devil? the peasants wondered. Is this winter or is it not?

Not even three days passed before winter returned. This time it came with no snow, with no wind; instead, the frost gripped like a pair of blacksmith's tongs until everything creaked. Over the course of a night the eaves dripping with water now grinned with sharp-fanged icicles, and astonished waterfowl almost froze to their duck ponds.

And the lakes of Centloch heaved a sigh and turned to ice.

Gosta waited one more day, just to be sure, then took the chest with a shoulder strap where he kept his fishing tackle down from the loft. He stuffed his boots well with straw, donned a sheepskin coat, took his chisel and a sack and hurried to the lake.

It's common knowledge that it's best to fish for perch with the first ice.

The ice was thick. It sagged a little beneath the man, groaned a little, but held firm. Gosta reached the broad water, cut an ice-hole with the chisel, sat down on the chest, unwound a horsehair line fastened to a short larch rod, attached a little tin fish with a hook, and cast it into the water. The first perch, measuring half a cubit, snatched the bait before it had sunk or the line become taut.

Before an hour was up more than four dozen striped green fish with blood-red fins lay all around the ice hole. Gosta had more perch than he needed, but his angler's euphoria wouldn't let him stop fishing. After all, he could always give the fish away to his neighbours.

He heard a long-drawn-out snort.

He lifted his head up from the ice hole. A splendid black horse was standing on the lake shore, steam belching from its nostrils. The face of the rider, who was dressed in a muskrat coat, was covered.

Gosta swallowed. It was too late to run. In his heart of hearts he hoped the rider wouldn't dare to venture out onto the thin ice.

He was still mechanically moving his rod as another perch jerked the line. The angler hauled it out, removed the hook and tossed it down on the ice. Out of the corner of his eye he saw the rider dismount, toss the reins onto a leafless bush and walk towards him, treading gingerly on the slippery surface. The perch flapped about on the ice, flexing its spined dorsal fin and moving its gills. Gosta stood up and reached for his chisel, which as a last resort might serve as a weapon.

'Fear not.'

It was a girl. Now, the scarf was removed he could see her face, disfigured by a hideous scar. On her back was a sword. He saw a hilt of exquisite workmanship, sticking up above her shoulder.

'I won't do you any harm,' she said quietly. 'I only want to ask the way.'

Course you do, thought Gosta. *Pull the other one. Now, in winter. In the frost. Who treks or travels? Only a brigand. Or an outcast.*

'This land, is it Mil Trachta?'

'It is . . .' he mumbled, staring into the ice hole, into the black water. 'Mil Trachta. But we says: Hundred Lakes.'

'And Tarn Mira lake? Do you know of such a place?'

'Everyone does.' He glanced at the girl, frightened. 'We calls it Bottomless Lake, mind. It's enchanted. Awfully deep . . . Rusalkas live there, drown folk, they do. And phantoms live in the ancient, enchanted ruins.'

He saw her green eyes light up.

'There are ruins there? A tower, perhaps?'

'What tower?' He couldn't suppress a snort. 'Stone upon stone, covered over with stone, overgrown with weeds. A heap of rubble . . .'

The perch had stopped flopping, and was lying, moving its gills, amidst its colourful, striped brothers. The girl stared at it, lost in thought.

'Death on the ice,' she said, 'has something bewitching about it.'

'Eh?'

'How far is it to the lake with the ruins? Which way should I ride?'

He told her. He showed her. He even scratched it on the ice with the sharp end of the chisel. She nodded, trying to remember. The mare at the lakeside struck its hooves on the frozen ground and snorted, belching steam from its nostrils.

*

He watched her move away along the western edge of the lake, gallop along the edge of the cliff against a background of leafless alders and birches, through a breathtaking, fairy-tale forest, adorned with a white icing of hoarfrost. The black mare ran with unutterable grace, swiftly, but at the same time lightly, the beat of its hooves barely audible on the frozen ground, a faint silver powder of snow dropping from the branches it knocked against. As though it were not an ordinary horse but one from a fairy-tale, as if a spectral horse was running through a mythical forest, the trees bound in hoarfrost like icing.

And perhaps it *was* an apparition?

A demon on a ghostly horse, a demon that assumed the form of a girl with huge green eyes and a disfigured face?

Who, if not a demon, travels in winter? Or asks the way to enchanted ruins?

After she had ridden away, Gosta quickly packed away his fishing tackle. He walked home through the forest. He was going out of his way, but his good sense and instincts warned him not to take the forest tracks, to stay out of sight. The girl, his good sense told him, had not – contrary to all appearances – been a phantom. She was a human being. The black mare hadn't been an apparition, it was a horse. And people who gallop through the wilds – in winter, to boot – are very often being hunted.

An hour later a search party galloped along the forest track. Fourteen horses.

*

Rience shook the silver box once again, swore and smacked his saddle pommel in fury. But the xenogloss was silent. As the grave.

'Magic shit,' commented Bonhart coldly. 'It's broken, the cheap gewgaw.'

'Or Vilgefortz is showing what he thinks of us,' Stefan Skellen added.

Rience raised his head and glared at the two of them.

'Thanks to this cheap gewgaw,' he stated caustically, 'we're on the trail and won't lose it now. Thanks to Lord Vilgefortz we know which way the girl is headed. We know where we're going and what we have to do. I'd call that plenty. Compared to your efforts of a month ago.'

'Don't talk so much. Hey, Boreas? What does the trail say?'

Boreas Mun straightened up and cleared his throat.

'She was here an hour before us. She's riding hard where she can. But it's difficult terrain. Even on that exceptional mare she's not more than five, six miles ahead of us.'

'And so she's still pushing on among those lakes,' Skellen muttered. 'Vilgefortz was right. And I didn't believe him . . .'

'Neither did I,' Bonhart admitted. 'Until yesterday, when those peasants confirmed there really is some kind of magical structure by Tarn Mira.'

The horses snorted, steam billowing from their nostrils. Tawny Owl glanced over his left shoulder at Joanna Selborne. For several days he had been none too pleased by the telepath's expression. I'm getting edgy, he thought. This chase has exhausted all of us, physically and mentally. It's time to be done with it. High time.

A cold shudder ran down his back. He recalled the dream that had visited him the night before.

'Very well!' he said, coming back to his senses. 'That's enough meditation. To horse!'

*

Boreas Mun hung from his saddle, looking for tracks. It wasn't easy. The earth had frozen solid, hard as iron, and the loose

406

snow, quickly blown away by the wind, only lingered in furrows and clefts. It was in them that Boreas was searching for the black mare's hoof prints. He had to pay close attention in order not to lose the trail, especially now, when the magical voice coming from the silver box had fallen silent, stopped giving advice and instructions.

He was unbelievably weary. And anxious. They'd been tracking the girl for almost three weeks, since Samhain and the massacre in Dun Dare. Almost three weeks in the saddle, constantly on the hunt. And still neither the black mare nor the girl riding it had weakened or slowed their pace.

Boreas Mun looked for tracks.

He couldn't stop thinking about a dream from the night before. In it he had been drowning. The black water had closed over his head and he sank to the bottom, the icy water gushing into his throat and lungs. He awoke hot and sweaty, wet through, although a truly bitter winter was raging around them.

That's enough, he thought, hanging from his saddle, looking for tracks. It's high time we were done with it.

*

'Master? Do you hear me? Master?'

The xenogloss was silent as the grave.

Rience moved his arms vigorously and breathed on his numb hands. The cold nipped his neck and shoulders, his lower back and loins hurt; each jolt of the horse reminded him of the pain. He didn't even feel like swearing. Almost three weeks in the saddle, in an unending pursuit. In the bitter cold and for several days in severe frost.

And Vilgefortz was silent.

We are too. And we're scowling at each other.

Rience rubbed his hands and pulled down his sleeves.

Skellen, he thought, looks at me strangely. Might he be plotting a betrayal? He came to an agreement with Vilgefortz too quickly and too easily back then . . . And that troop, those thugs, it's him they're loyal to, it's his orders they carry out. When we seize the maid, he's liable – heedless of the agreement – to kill or carry her away to those conspirators of his, in order to enact his insane ideas about democracy and civil government.

But perhaps Skellen's got over his conspiracies by now? Perhaps that born conformist and opportunist is now thinking about delivering the maid to Emperor Emhyr?

He looks at me strangely. That Tawny Owl. And that whole mob of his . . . That Kenna Selborne . . .

And Bonhart? Bonhart is an unpredictable sadist. When he speaks of Ciri, his voice trembles with fury. Depending on his whims, if we capture the girl he's liable to beat her to death or kidnap her and make her fight in the arena. The agreement with Vilgefortz? He won't care about it. Particularly now, when Vilgefortz . . .

He removed the xenogloss from his bosom.

'Master? Do you hear me? It's Rience . . .'

The device was silent. Rience didn't even feel like swearing.

Vilgefortz remains silent. Skellen and Bonhart made a pact with him. Only in a day or two, when we catch up with the girl, it may turn out that there is no pact. And then I might have my throat cut. Or ride in fetters to Nilfgaard, as proof of and as ransom against Tawny Owl's loyalty . . .

Sod it!

Vilgefortz remains silent. He isn't giving us any advice. He's not giving us directions. He isn't dispelling our doubts with his calm, logical voice, which touches the depths of your soul. He's silent.

The xenogloss has broken down. Perhaps because of the cold? Or maybe . . .

Maybe Skellen was right? Perhaps Vilgefortz really has turned his attention to something else and doesn't care about us or our fate?

By all the devils, I never thought it would turn out like this. Had I, I wouldn't have been so enthusiastic about this mission . . . I would have gone and killed the Witcher instead of Schirrú . . . Damn it! I'm freezing out here and Schirrú is probably nice and warm . . .

To think that I insisted on going after Ciri, and Schirrú after the Witcher. I asked for it myself . . . Back at the beginning of September when Yennefer fell into our hands.

The world, a moment ago still an unreal, soft and muddily sticky blackness, abruptly took on hard surfaces and contours. It became brighter. And materialised.

Yennefer opened her eyes, rocked by convulsive shivers. She lay on the stones, among dead bodies and tarred planks, littered with the remains of the rigging of the longship *Alkyone*. She could see feet all around her. Feet in heavy boots. One of the boots had just kicked her, to bring her around.

'Get up, witch!'

Another kick, sending pain shooting right into the roots of her teeth. She saw a face bending over her. 'Get up, I said! On your feet! Recognise me?'

She blinked. Yes, she did. It was the man she had burned, when he was fleeing from her using a teleporter. Rience.

'We'll square accounts,' he promised her. 'We'll square accounts for everything, you slut. I'll teach you what pain is. I'll teach you what pain is with these fingers and these hands.'

She tensed up, clenched and spread her fingers, ready to cast a spell. And immediately curled up in a ball, choking, wheezing and trembling. Rience guffawed.

'Nothing doing, eh?' she heard. 'You haven't even got a scrap of power! You're no match for Vilgefortz when it comes to sorcery! He's squeezed the very last drop out of you, like whey from curds. You can't even—'

He didn't complete the sentence. Yennefer pulled out a dagger from a sheath fastened to her inner thigh, sprang like a cat and thrust blindly. She missed. The blade merely brushed her target, tearing his trousers. Rience leaped aside and fell over.

Immediately, a hail of blows and kicks rained down on her. She howled as a heavy boot dropped on her hand, squeezing the dagger from her crushed fist. Another boot kicked her in the belly. The sorceress curled up, rasping. She was picked up from the ground, her arms jerked behind her. She saw a fist flying towards her, the world suddenly flashed brightly, and her face exploded with pain. A wave of pain passed downwards, to her stomach and crotch, transforming her knees into a thin jelly. She drooped in the arms holding her up. Someone seized her from behind by the hair, lifting up her head. She was struck once more, in the eye socket, and again everything vanished in a blinding flash.

She didn't faint. She could still feel. They beat her. They beat her hard, cruelly, as a man is beaten. With blows that aren't just meant to hurt, but meant to fracture, meant to crush all energy and the will to resist from the victim. She was beaten, jerking in the steely grip of many hands.

She wanted to faint but couldn't. She could feel it.

'Enough,' she suddenly heard from far away, from behind the curtain of pain. 'Have you gone mad, Rience? Do you mean to kill her? I need her alive.'

'I vowed to her, master,' snarled the shadow looming in front of her, which gradually took on Rience's form and face. 'I promised I'd pay her back . . . With these hands . . .'

'I care little for what you promised her. I repeat, I need her alive and capable of articulated speech.'

'It's not so easy,' laughed the one holding her by the hair, 'to knock the life out of a cat or a witch.'

'Don't be clever, Schirrú. I said she's been sufficiently beaten. Pick her up. How do you do, Yennefer?' The sorceress spat red and lifted her puffy face. At first she didn't recognise him. He was wearing a kind of mask, covering the entire left side of his head. But she knew who it was.

'Go to hell, Vilgefortz,' she mumbled, gingerly touching her front teeth and cut lips with her tongue.

'What did you make of my spell? Did you like it when I lifted you and that boat up from the sea? Did you enjoy the flight? What charms did you protect yourself with to survive the fall?'

'Go to hell.'

'Tear that star from her neck. And to the laboratory with her. Let's not waste time.'

She was dragged, pulled, occasionally carried. A stony plain, with *Alkyone* lying smashed on it amid numerous other wrecks with protruding ribs, like the skeletons of sea monsters. Crach was right, she thought. The ships that disappeared without trace on the Sedna Abyss weren't victims of natural disasters. Ye Gods . . . Pavetta and Duny . . .

Above the plain, in the distance, mountain peaks thrust up into the overcast sky.

Then there were walls, gates, cloisters, floors, staircases. Everything somehow odd, unnaturally large ... Still too few details to let her work out where she was, where she'd come to, where the spell had carried her. Her face was swelling up, making observations all the more difficult. Smell became the one sense supplying her with information – she smelled formalin, ether and spirits. And magic. The smells of a laboratory. She was brutally shoved down into a steel armchair. Cold, painfully tight clamps slammed shut on her wrists and ankles. Before the steel jaws of a vice tightened on her temples and immobilised her head, she managed to glance around the large and glaringly lit room. She saw one more armchair and a strange steel construction on the stone floor.

'Yes indeed,' she heard the voice of Vilgefortz from behind her. 'That little chair is for your Ciri. It's been here for ages; it can't wait. Neither can I.'

She heard him up close, literally felt his breath. He stuck some needles into her head, attached something to her ears. Then he stood before her and removed the mask. Yennefer sucked in air involuntarily.

'That's the work of your Ciri,' he said, indicating his once classically beautiful, now hideously mutilated face, criss-crossed with golden clasps and fastenings securing a multifaceted crystal in his left eye socket.

'I tried to catch her when she entered the Tower of the Gull,' the sorcerer calmly explained. 'I meant to save her life, certain that the teleporter would kill her. How naive of me! She passed through smoothly, with such force that the portal exploded, blew up right in my face. I lost an eye and my left cheek, as well as a lot of skin from my face, neck and chest. A very disagreeable, very bothersome, very complicated accident. And very ugly, isn't it? Ha, you ought to have seen me before I began to regenerate magically.

'If I believed in such things,' he continued, pushing a bent copper tube into her nose, 'I'd have thought it was Lydia van Bredevoort's revenge. From beyond the grave. I'm regenerating, but it's slow, time-consuming and heavy going. It's particularly difficult with the regeneration of the eyeball ... The crystal in my eye socket

411

plays its role splendidly; I can see in three dimensions, but yet it's a foreign body, and the lack of a natural eyeball occasionally makes me absolutely furious. Then, seized by – let's face it – irrational anger, I vow to myself that when I catch Ciri – immediately after catching her – I'll order Rience to pluck out one of those huge, green eyes. With his fingers. With these fingers, as he likes to say. You're saying nothing, Yennefer? Perhaps because you know I'd also like to rip out one of your eyes? Or both?'

He stuck thick needles into the veins on the back of her hands. Sometimes he missed and jabbed to the very bone. Yennefer gritted her teeth.

'You've caused me problems. You've made me interrupt my work. You've exposed me to risk. Forcing your way over the Sedna Abyss in that boat, towards my Maelstrom . . . The echo of our brief duel was powerful and travelled far, it may have reached the wrong ears, prying ears. But I couldn't stop myself. The thought that I would have you here, that I'd be able to connect you up to my scanner, was too appealing.

'For you can't possibly imagine –' he stuck in another needle '– that I was taken in by your provocation? That I swallowed the bait? No, Yennefer. If you think so, you're mistaking stars reflected in the surface of a pond at night for the sky. You thought you were tracking me, whereas in fact I was tracking you. You made my job easier by sailing over the Abyss. For I cannot find Ciri, you see, even with the help of my peerless scanning device. The girl has powerful, innate defence mechanisms, her own powerful anti-magical and suppressive aura: it's the Elder Blood, after all. But my super-scanners ought to detect her anyhow. Yet they don't.'

Yennefer was now completely entwined in a network of silver and copper wires and encased in a scaffolding of silver and porcelain tubes. Glass vessels containing colourless liquids wobbled on racks placed by the chair.

'And so I thought –' Vilgefortz thrust another tube into her nose, this time a glass one '– that the only way of tracking Ciri was an empathic probe. For that I needed someone who had a sufficiently strong emotional bond with the girl and had developed an empathic matrix, a kind of algorithm – to coin a phrase – of feelings and mutual affection. I thought about the Witcher, but he had disappeared, and besides, witchers are poor mediums. I planned to order the kidnapping of Triss Merigold, our Fourteenth from the Hill. I pondered over abducting Nenneke of Ellander . . . But when it turned out that you, Yennefer of Vengerberg, were literally forcing yourself into my hands . . . Truly I couldn't have hoped for anything better . . . Once connected to the scanner you will track down Ciri for me. Admittedly, the operation requires your cooperation . . . But there are, as you know, ways of making people cooperate.

'Of course,' he went on, rubbing his hands, 'you deserve a few explanations. For example – how did I find out about the Elder Blood? About Lara Dorren's legacy? What that gene actually is? How Ciri ended up having it? Who passed it on to her? How will I take it from her and what will I use it for? How does the Sedna Maelstrom work, who have I sucked into it, what did I do with them and why? Plenty of questions, aren't there? It's such a pity there's no time to tell you everything, explain everything. Nay, even astonish you, for I'm certain several of the facts would astonish you, Yennefer . . . But, as has been said before, there's no time. The elixirs are beginning to take effect, so it's time you started concentrating.'

The sorceress clenched her teeth, stifling the deep groan shooting from her guts.

'I know,' Vilgefortz nodded, drawing closer a professional looking megascope; a screen and a great crystal ball on a tripod, wrapped around by a web of silver wires. 'I know it's most disagreeable. And very painful. The sooner you set about scanning, the sooner it'll be over. Well, Yennefer. I want to see Ciri, here, on this screen. Where she is, who she's with, what she's doing, what she eats, where and with whom she sleeps.'

Yennefer screamed shrilly and wildly, in despair.

'It hurts,' Vilgefortz guessed, staring at her with his living eye and his dead crystal. 'Well, of course it hurts. Start scanning, Yennefer. Don't resist. Don't play the hero. You know full well it's impossible to endure this. The result of resistance may be pitiful; a stroke will follow, you'll suffer paraplegia or simply turn into a vegetable. Start scanning!'

413

She clenched her jaw so hard her teeth creaked.

'Why not, Yennefer?' the mage said kindly. 'If only out of curiosity! You're surely curious about how your darling's coping. Perhaps danger is hanging over her? Perhaps she's in need? You know, after all, how many people wish Ciri ill and desire her death. Start scanning. When I find out where the girl is, I'll bring her here. She'll be safe . . . No one will find her here. Ever.'

His voice was warm and velvety.

'Start scanning, Yennefer. Start scanning. I implore you. I give you my word: I'll only take what I need from Ciri. And then I'll give both of you your freedom. I swear.'

Yennefer gritted her teeth even harder. Blood trickled down her chin. Vilgefortz suddenly stood up and beckoned.

'Rience!'

Yennefer felt some kind of device tightening over her hands and fingers.

'At times,' said Vilgefortz, bending over her, 'where magic, elixirs and narcotics fail, what works on the stubborn is good old-fashioned pain. Don't make me do it. Start scanning.'

'Go to hell, Vilgefoooortz!'

'Tighten the screws, Rience. Slowly.'

*

Vilgefortz glanced at the torpid body being dragged across the floor towards the stairs to the cellar. Then he lifted his eye towards Rience and Schirrú.

'There's always the risk,' he said, 'that one of you will fall into the hands of my enemies and be interrogated. I'd like to think that you'll demonstrate as much fortitude. Yes, I'd like to think so. But I don't.'

Rience and Schirrú said nothing. Vilgefortz started up the megascope again and projected the image generated by the huge crystal onto the screen.

'That's all she could produce,' he said, pointing. 'I wanted Cirilla, she gave me the Witcher. Fascinating. She didn't allow the girl's empathic matrix to be wrested from her, but she cracked when it came to Geralt. And I didn't suspect her of harbouring

414

any feelings for Geralt at all . . . Well, for now let's settle for what we have. Witcher, Cahir aep Ceallach, the bard Dandelion, some woman? Hmmm . . . Who'll undertake this task? The final solution to the witcher problem?'

*

Schirrú volunteered, recalled Rience, raising himself up in the stirrups to give his saddle-sore buttocks at least some relief. Schirrú volunteered to kill the Witcher. He recognised the countryside Yennefer had traced Geralt and his company to; he had friends or family there. Vilgefortz sent me, meanwhile, to negotiate with Vattier de Rideaux, and then to tail Skellen and Bonhart . . .

And I – stupidly – was glad at the time, certain that the easier and more pleasant task had fallen to me. One I would make short, easy, pleasant work of . . .

*

'If the peasants weren't lying –' Stefan Skellen stood up in his stirrups '– the lake must be over that hill, in the valley.'

'The trail leads there,' Boreas Mun confirmed.

'Why have we stopped here?' Rience rubbed a frozen ear. 'Spur on the horses and let's go!'

'Not so fast.' Bonhart held him back. 'Let's split up. We'll encircle the valley. We don't know which of the lake's shores she took. If we choose the wrong way, we may put the lake between us.'

'How very true,' Boreas nodded.

'The lake's frozen over.'

'It may be too thin for the horses. Bonhart's right, we must split up.'

Skellen quickly issued orders. The group led by Bonhart, Rience and Ola Harsheim, numbering seven horses in total, galloped along the eastern shore, quickly disappearing into the black forest.

'Very well,' Tawny Owl ordered. 'Let's go, Silifant . . .'

He realised at once that something wasn't right.

He reined his horse around, slapped it with his knout and rode

415

directly for Joanna Selborne. Kenna backed up her mount, and her face seemed to be made of stone.

'It's no use, sir,' she said hoarsely. 'Don't even try. We're not going with you. We're turning back. We've had enough.'

'We?' Dacre Silifant yelled. 'Who's "we"? What is this, a mutiny?'

Skellen leaned over in the saddle and spat on the frozen earth. Andres Vierny and Til Echrade, the fair-haired elf, had stopped behind Kenna.

'Miss Selborne,' said Tawny Owl scathingly, in a slow, drawling voice, 'It isn't the point that you are squandering a very promising career, that you're permanently throwing away the chance of a lifetime. You'll be handed over to the hangman. Along with these fools who've listened to you.'

'Whoever's meant to hang won't drown,' Kenna replied philosophically. 'And don't threaten us with the hangman, sir. For who knows who's closer to the scaffold; you or us.'

'Is that what you think?' Tawny Owl's eyes flashed. 'You're convinced of that after slyly eavesdropping on somebody's thoughts? I thought you were cleverer than that. But you're stupid, woman. Whoever's with me wins, whoever's against me always loses! Remember that, girl. Even though you think I'm incriminated now, I'll still manage to send you to hang. Do you hear, you mutineers? I'll have your flesh torn from your bones with red hooks.'

'We have but one life, sir,' Til Echrade said softly. 'You've chosen your way, and we've chosen ours. Both are uncertain and risky. And no one knows what fate will befall any of us.'

'You won't set us on the girl like dogs, Mr Skellen, sir.' Kenna raised her head proudly. 'And we won't let ourselves be killed like dogs, like Neratin Ceka. Oh, enough talking. We're turning back! Boreas! Come with us.'

'No.' The tracker shook his head, wiping his forehead with his fur hat. 'Farewell. I don't wish you ill. But I'm staying. It's my service. I took the oath.'

'To whom?' Kenna frowned. 'The Emperor or Tawny Owl? Or a sorcerer talking from a box?'

'I'm a soldier. I serve.'

'Wait,' called Dufficey Kriel, riding out from behind Dacre Silifant. 'I'm with you. I've had enough of this too! Last night I dreamed of my own death. I don't want to croak for this lousy, suspicious affair!'

'Traitors!' yelled Dacre, flushing like a cherry. It seemed as though dark blood would spurt from his face. 'Turncoats! Miserable curs!'

'Shut your trap.' Tawny Owl was still looking at Kenna, and his eyes were just as hideous as the bird from which he took his name. 'They've chosen their way; you heard. There's no point shouting or wasting spit. But we'll meet again one day. I promise you.'

'Perhaps even on the same scaffold,' Kenna said without spitefulness. 'For they won't put you to death alongside noble princes, will they Skellen? But with us churls. But you're right, there's no point wasting spit. Let's be going. Farewell, Boreas. Farewell, Mr Silifant.'

Dacre spat over his horse's ears.

*

'And beyond what I've said here –' Joanna Selborne proudly raised her head, brushing a dark lock from her forehead '– I have nothing to add, Illustrious Tribunal.'

The convenor of the tribunal looked down on her. His face was inscrutable. His eyes grey. And decent.

Anyway, what do I care? thought Kenna. *I'll try. You can only die once; sink or swim. I'm not going to rot in the citadel and wait for death. Tawny Owl didn't make wild promises, he's liable to take revenge even from beyond the grave . . .*

What do I care? Perhaps they won't notice. Sink or swim!

She pressed her hand to her nose, seemingly wiping it. She looked straight into the grey eyes of the tribunal convener.

'Guard!' said the convener. 'Please take the witness Joanna Selborne back to . . .'

He broke off and started coughing. Sweat suddenly broke out on his forehead.

'To the tribunal chancellery,' he finished, sniffing loudly. 'Write

out the appropriate documents. And release her. The witness Selborne is of no further use to the court.'

Kenna surreptitiously wiped away the drop of blood that was
trickling from her nose. She smiled charmingly and thanked him
with a delicate bow.

*

'They've deserted?' Bonhart repeated in disbelief. 'More of them
have deserted? And just rode away, like that? Skellen? You permitted it?'

'If they inform on us . . .' Rience began, but Tawny Owl interrupted him at once.

'They won't inform, because they don't want to lose their own
heads! And besides, what could I have done? When Kriel joined
them, only Bert and Mun were left with me and there were four of
them . . .'

'Four,' said Bonhart malevolently, 'isn't many at all. As soon as
we've caught up with the girl I'll go after them. And I'll feed them
to the crows. In the name of—'

'Let's catch her up first,' Tawny Owl cut him off, urging on his
grey with his knout. 'Boreas! Keep your eyes on the trail!'

The valley was filling up with a dense blanket of fog, but they
knew that down below was a lake, because there was a lake in every
valley in Mil Trachta. The one, meanwhile, to which the black
mare's hoof prints were leading, was undoubtedly the one they
were looking for, the one Vilgefortz had ordered them to look for.
Which he had described to them precisely. And whose name he
had given them.

Tarn Mira.

The lake was narrow, no wider than an arrow shot, crowded
into a slightly bent crescent between high, steep hillsides covered
in black spruce, beautifully sprinkled with a white, snowy powder.
The hillsides were swathed in such a silence that there was a ringing in their ears. Even the crows – whose portentous cawing had
accompanied them on the trail for the last fortnight or so – had
fallen silent.

'This is the southern end,' stated Bonhart. 'If the mage hasn't made a hash of everything and landed us in it, the magical tower is on the northern shore. Keep your eyes on the trail, Boreas! If we pick up the wrong one, the lake will separate us from her!'

'The trail is clear!' Boreas Mun called from below. 'And fresh! It's leading towards the lake!'

'Ride!' Skellen brought his grey, skittering on the steep slope, under control. 'Downhill!'

They rode down the slope, cautiously, reining back the snorting horses. They struggled through the bare, black, ice-covered thicket blocking the way to the bank.

Bonhart's horse stepped gingerly onto the ice, crunching through the dry reeds sticking up from the glazed surface. The ice creaked and long arrows of cracks diverged like a star from under the horse's hooves.

'About face!' Bonhart pulled in the reins and turned his snorting horse back towards the bank. 'Dismount! The ice is thin.'

'Only by the bank, in the reeds,' Dacre Silifant judged, striking a heel onto the icy crust. 'But even here it's at least an inch and a half. It'll hold a horse sure as anything, no need to wo—'

His words were drowned out by cursing and neighing. Skellen's grey slipped, sat down on its haunches, and its legs spread apart under it. Skellen struck it with his spurs, swore again, and this time the curse was accompanied by the harsh crunch of ice breaking. The grey pounded with its fore hooves. Its hind ones, imprisoned, thrashed about in the tangle, breaking up the ice and churning the dark water spurting from under it. Tawny Owl dismounted, tugged on the reins, but slipped and went sprawling, miraculously not falling under the hooves of his own horse. The two Gemmerians, now also on their feet, helped him up. Ola Harsheim and Bert Brigden hauled the whinnying grey out onto the bank.

'Dismount,' Bonhart repeated, his eyes fixed on the fog covering the lake. 'There's no sense risking it. We'll catch up with the maid on foot. She also dismounted, she's also moving on foot.'

'How very true,' confirmed Boreas Mun, pointing at the lake. 'It's plain to see.'

Only at the very edge, beneath overhanging branches, was the crust of ice smooth and translucent, like the dark glass of a bottle. Under it reeds and water plants turned brown were visible.

Further from the bank, the ice was covered in a very thin layer of wet snow. And on it, as far as the fog permitted them to see, were dark footprints.

'We have her!' Rience cried heatedly, throwing his reins on a broken bough. 'So she's not as cunning as she seems! She set off on the ice, straight across the middle of the lake. Had she chosen one of the banks or the forest, it wouldn't have been easy to pursue her!'

'Straight across the middle of the lake . . .' Bonhart repeated, giving the impression of being lost in thought. 'The shortest and straightest way to the alleged magical tower Vilgefortz talked about leads across the middle of the lake. She knows that. Mun? How far ahead of us is she?'

Boreas Mun, who was already on the lake, knelt down over a boot print, leaned over low and examined it.

'A half-hour,' he estimated. 'Not more. It's getting warmer, but the print isn't fuzzy, you can see every hobnail in the sole.'

'The lake,' mumbled Bonhart, vainly trying to look through the fog, 'stretches north for more than five miles. So said Vilgefortz. If the maid has half an hour's start, she's about a mile ahead of us.'

'On slippery ice?' Mun shook his head. 'Not even that. Six, seven furlongs, at most.'

'Even better! March!'

'March,' Tawny Owl repeated. 'Onto the ice and quick march!'

They walked swiftly, puffing. The quarry's closeness excited them, filled them with euphoria like a narcotic.

'She won't escape us!'

'As long as we don't lose the trail . . .'

'And as long as she isn't leading us up the garden path in this fog . . . It's white as milk . . . You can't see twenty paces ahead, dammit . . .'

'Move your arses,' Rience snarled. 'Quick, quick! As long as there's snow on the ice, we're following her trail . . .'

'The trail is fresh,' Boreas Mun suddenly muttered, stopping and stooping down. 'Very fresh . . . You can see the print of every hobnail . . . She's just in front of us . . . Just in front of us . . . Why can't we see her?'

'And why can't we hear her?' Ola Harsheim wondered. 'Our

420

footsteps boom on the ice, the snow creaks. So why don't we hear her?'

'Because you're yakking!' Rience cut them off abruptly. 'Keep marching!'

Boreas Mun took off his hat to wipe his sweat-covered forehead. 'She's there, in the fog,' he said softly. 'Somewhere there, in the fog . . . But the devil knows where. The devil knows whence she'll strike . . . Like back there . . . In Dun Dare . . . On Samhain Eve . . .'

He began to draw his sword from its scabbard with a trembling hand. Tawny Owl leaped at him, seized him by the arm and tugged him forcefully.

'Shut your trap, you old fool,' he hissed.

But it was too late. The terror had spread to the others. They also drew their swords, involuntarily positioning themselves to have one of their companions behind them.

'She's not a spectre!' Rience snapped loudly. 'She isn't even a witch! And there are ten of us! In Dun Dare there were only four and they were all drunk!'

'Spread out,' said Bonhart suddenly, 'to the left and right, in a line. And move forward together! Don't lose sight of each other.'

'You too?' Rience grimaced. 'Has it infected you too, Bonhart? I thought you were less superstitious than that.' The bounty hunter looked at him with eyes that were colder than ice.

'Spread out into a line,' he repeated, ignoring the sorcerer. 'Keep your distance. I'm going back for my horse.'

'What?'

Bonhart didn't grace Rience with an answer again. Rience swore, but Tawny Owl quickly placed a hand on his shoulder.

'Leave it,' he snapped, 'let him go. And let's not waste time! In a line! Bert and Stigward, left! Ola, right . . .'

'What for, Skellen?'

'The ice will break more easily under men walking in a group,' Boreas Mun muttered, 'than spread out in a line. Furthermore, if we walk in a line abreast, there's less of a risk the wench will outflank us.'

'Outflank us?' Rience snorted. 'How could she? The tracks in front of us are as plain as a pikestaff. The maid is going straight ahead. Were she to try to turn, the trail would betray it—'

'Enough chatter.' Tawny Owl cut them off, looking back into the fog into which Bonhart had vanished as he left them. 'Forward!' They went on.

'It's getting warmer,' Boreas Mun panted. 'The ice on top is melting, it'll form overflow ice . . .'

'The fog's getting thicker . . .'

'But the footprints can still be seen,' said Dacre Silifant. 'Moreover, it seems the girl has slowed down. Her strength is waning.'

'As is ours,' Rience tore off his hat and fanned himself with it.

'Quiet,' Silifant suddenly stopped. 'Did you hear that? What was it?'

'I didn't hear anything.'

'But I did . . . Like a scraping . . . A scraping on the ice . . . But not from there,' Boreas Mun pointed at the fog, into which the trail was fading. 'It seems to be over on the left, to the side . . .'

'I heard it too,' Tawny Owl confirmed, looking anxiously around. 'But now it's gone quiet. Dammit, I don't like it. I don't like it!'

'The footprints!' Rience said with wearied emphasis. 'We can still see her footprints! Don't you have eyes? She's walking straight ahead! If she took even a single step to one side we'd know it from the trail! Quick march, we'll have her soon! I give my word, we'll see her in a moment—'

He broke off. Boreas Mun sighed so hard his lungs groaned. Tawny Owl cursed.

Ten paces in front of them, just before the limit of visibility bordered by the dense fog, the tracks ended. They vanished.

'A pox on it!'

'What is it?'

'Has she taken flight or what?'

'No.' Boreas Mun shook his head. 'She hasn't. It's worse.'

Rience swore crudely, pointing at scratches in the icy crust.

'Skates,' he growled, involuntarily clenching his fists. 'She has skates . . . Now she's darting across the ice like the wind . . . We won't catch her! What, damn his eyes, has become of Bonhart? We won't catch the maid without horses!'

Boreas Mun hawked loudly and sighed. Skellen slowly

unbuttoned his sheepskin coat, uncovering a bandolier with a row of orions slung across his chest.

'We won't have to hunt her,' he said coldly. 'She'll be the one hunting us. I'm afraid we won't have long to wait.'

'Have you gone mad?'

'Bonhart anticipated this. That's why he went back for his horse. He knew the girl would lure us into a trap. Beware! Listen for the grating of skates on ice!'

Dacre Silifant paled visibly despite his cheeks being flushed from the cold.

'Fellows!' he yelled. 'Beware! Take heed! And gather together! Don't get lost in the fog!'

'Shut up!' Tawny Owl roared. 'Keep quiet! Absolute silence or we won't hear . . .'

They heard. A short, strangled cry reached their ears from the fog to the left, from the furthest end of the line. And the sharp, rough grating of skates, making the hair stand on end like iron scoring glass. 'Bert!' Tawny Owl yelled. 'Bert! What's happening over there?'

They heard an unintelligible cry, and a moment later Bert Brigden emerged from the fog, fleeing pell-mell. As soon as he was near he slipped, fell over and slid across the ice on his stomach.

'She got . . . Stigward,' he panted out, struggling to get up. 'She cut him down . . . as she flashed past . . . So swiftly . . . I barely saw her . . . She's a witch . . .'

Skellen swore. Silifant and Mun, both with swords in hand, whirled around, staring goggle-eyed into the fog. Grating. Grating. Grating. Quick. Rhythmic. And more and more clearly. More and more clearly.

'Where's it coming from?' roared Boreas Mun, spinning around, flourishing the blade of his sword two-handed. 'Where's it coming from?'

'Quiet!' screamed Tawny Owl with an orion in his raised hand. 'I think it's from the right! Yes! From the right! She's coming up on the right! Look out!'

The Gemmerian walking on the right wing suddenly cursed, turned around and ran blindly into the fog, sloshing through the melting layer of ice. He didn't get far, not even out of sight. They heard the sharp grating of skates gliding and made out a blurred, flickering shadow. And the flash of a sword. The Gemmerian howled. They saw him fall, saw a broad spray of blood on the ice. The wounded man thrashed about, curled up, screamed and moaned. Then he fell silent and stopped moving.

But while he was still moaning he drowned out the sound of the skates. They didn't expect the girl to be able to turn back so swiftly.

She fell among them, right in their midst. She cleaved Ola Harsheim as she flashed past, low, beneath the knee, folding him up like a penknife. She spun in a pirouette, covering Boreas Mun in a stinging hail of icy shards. Skellen leaped aside, slipped and caught Rience by a sleeve. They both fell over. The skates grated just beside them and cold, sharp fragments stung their faces. One of the Gemmerians yelled and his cry broke off in a savage croak. Tawny Owl knew what had happened. He'd heard many people having their throats cut.

Ola Harsheim shouted, rolling around on the ice.

Grating. Grating. Grating.

Silence.

'Mr Stefan,' Dacre Silifant gibbered. 'Mr Stefan . . . You're my only hope . . . Save me . . . Don't let me—'

'She's fucking crippled meeeee!' Ola Harsheim bellowed. 'Help me, for fuck's sake! Help me get up!'

'Bonhart!' Skellen yelled into the fog. 'Bonhaaaart! Heeeelp us! Where are you, you whoreson? Bonhaaaart!'

'She's got us surrounded,' Boreas Mun gasped, spinning around and straining to hear. 'She's skating around us in the fog . . . She'll strike at will . . . Death! That wench is death! We'll breathe our last here! It'll be a massacre, like it was on Samhain Eve in Dun Dare . . .'

'Stick together,' Skellen groaned. 'Stick together, she's picking us off one by one . . . When you see her looming up, don't lose your heads . . . Trip her up with swords, saddlebags, belts . . . Use anything to stop her—'

He broke off. This time, they didn't even hear the scraping of skates. Dacre Silifant and Rience saved their lives by dropping flat onto the ice. Boreas Mun managed to jump aside, slipped, fell over

424

and upended Bert Brigden. As the girl flashed by, Skellen swung and threw an orion. It found a target. But not the right one. Ola Harsheim, who had managed to get up, tumbled over in convulsions onto the blood-spattered ice; his staring eyes seemed to cross on the steel star sticking out of the bridge of his nose.

The last of the Gemmerians threw down his sword and began to sob in short, choking spasms. Skellen sprang at him and struck him hard in the face.

'Pull yourself together!' he roared. 'Get a grip on yourself! It's just one girl! Just one girl!'

'Like in Dun Dare on Samhain Eve,' said Boreas Mun softly. 'We shall never get off this ice, off this lake. Listen out, listen out! And you'll hear death gliding towards you.'

Skellen picked up the Gemmerian's sword and tried to shove it into the sobbing man's hand, but unsuccessfully. The Gemmerian, racked by spasms, turned his dull gaze onto him. Tawny Owl threw down the sword and jumped at Rience.

'Do something, sorcerer!' he roared, tugging at his arm. Terror redoubled his strength, and although Rience was taller, heavier and more powerful, he flopped around in Tawny Owl's grasp like a rag doll. 'Do something! Summon that high and mighty Vilgefortz of yours! Work some magic yourself! Work magic, perform witchcraft, invoke spirits, conjure up demons! Do something – anything – you little turd! Do something, before that she-phantom kills us all!'

The echo of his cry boomed across the forested hillsides. Before it died away, the skates grated again. The sobbing Gemmerian fell to his knees and covered his face in his hands. Bert Brigden howled, flung his sword away and bolted. He slipped, fell over and scampered for a few paces on all fours, like a dog.

'Rience!'

The sorcerer swore and raised a hand. As he chanted the spell, his hand was trembling, his voice too. But he was successful. Though not, admittedly, completely successful.

The threadlike, fiery lightning bolt spurting from his fingers carved up the ice, fracturing the surface. But not crossways, as it should have, to bar the way of the approaching girl. It broke lengthways. The crust of ice cleaved open with a loud cracking sound, black water gushed and rumbled, and the rapidly widening rift shot towards Dacre Silifant, who was looking on in stupefaction.

'Jump aside!' Skellen yelled. 'Ruuuuuun!'

It was too late. The crack sped between Silifant's legs and split open, the ice shattering like glass and breaking into huge slabs. Dacre lost his balance, and the water stifled his howl. Boreas Mun fell into the breach, the kneeling Gemmerian vanished under the water, and Ola Harsheim's body disappeared. Rience plopped after them into the black depths, followed by Skellen, who managed to catch hold of the edge at the last moment. Meanwhile, the girl pushed off powerfully and flew over the breach, landing so hard the melting ice splashed, and darted after the fleeing Brigden. A moment later a hair-raising scream reached the ears of Tawny Owl, who was hanging onto the edge of the ice floe.

She'd caught up with him.

'Sir . . .' moaned Boreas Mun, who by some miracle had managed to crawl out onto the ice. 'Give me your hand . . . My lord coroner . . .'

After being hauled out, Skellen turned blue and began to shiver violently. The edge of the ice was breaking under Silifant, who was struggling to drag himself out. Dacre vanished beneath the water again. But he surfaced at once, choking and spitting, and dragged himself onto the ice with superhuman effort. He crawled out and collapsed, exhausted to the limits. A puddle spread out beside him. Boreas moaned and closed his eyes. Skellen was trembling.

'Save me . . . Mun . . . Help . . .'

Rience hung onto the edge of the ice, submerged up to his armpits. His wet hair was plastered smoothly to his skull. His teeth were chattering like castanets, sounding like a ghoulish overture to some infernal *danse macabre*. The skates grated. Boreas didn't move. He waited. Skellen was trembling.

She approached. Slowly. Blood trickled from her sword, marking the ice with a trail of drops. Boreas swallowed. Although he was soaked to the skin with icy water, he suddenly felt unbearably hot.

But the girl wasn't looking at him. She was looking at Rience, who was vainly struggling to get out onto the ice.

'Help me . . .' Rience overcame the chattering of his teeth. 'Save me . . .'

The girl braked, whirling on the skates with the grace of a dancer. She stood with legs slightly apart, holding her sword in both hands, low, across her thighs.

'Help me . . .' Rience howled, digging his numbing fingers into the ice. 'Save me . . . And I'll tell you . . . where Yennefer is . . . I swear . . .'

The girl slowly pulled the scarf from her face and smiled. Boreas Mun saw the hideous scar and fought to stifle a shout.

'Rience,' said Ciri, still smiling. 'You were going to teach me pain, weren't you? Do you remember? With those hands. With those fingers. Those ones? Those, the ones you're holding the ice with?'

Rience answered, but Boreas didn't understand what he said, for the sorcerer's teeth were chattering and rattling so much they made articulated speech impossible. Ciri spun around on her skates and lifted the sword. Boreas clenched his teeth, convinced she would slash Rience, but the girl was picking up momentum to set off. To the tracker's astonishment she skated away, quickly, gathering speed with powerful thrusts. She vanished into the fog, and a moment later the rhythmic scraping of the skates also died away.

'Mun . . . Puuull . . . me . . . out . . .' Rience barked out, chin on the edge of the ice floe. He flung both hands on the ice, trying to hang on with his fingernails, which had largely been torn away. He spread his fingers, trying to cling to the blood-stained ice with his hands and wrists. Boreas Mun looked at him and was certain, terrifyingly certain . . .

They heard the grinding of the skates at the last moment. The girl approached at extraordinary speed, literally a blur. She skated up at the very edge of the floe, speeding along right beside the brink.

Rience screamed. And choked on the viscous, leaden water. And vanished.

There was blood on the ice, on the perfectly even tracks left by the skates. And fingers. Eight fingers.

Boreas Mun vomited on the ice.

*

427

Bonhart galloped along the edge of the lake, hurtling along, heedless that any moment the horse might break its legs on the snow-covered clefts. Frosted over spruce branches lashed his face, and whipped his arms, and icy powder poured down his collar.

He couldn't see the lake. The entire valley was filled with fog, like a bubbling witch's cauldron.

But Bonhart knew the girl was there.

He sensed it.

*

Deep under the ice, a school of striped perch curiously followed the silver, fascinatingly glimmering casket which had slipped out of the pocket of a corpse floating in the water. Before the casket had sunk to the bottom, raising a cloud of silt, the boldest of the perch even tried to nudge it with their snouts. But they suddenly took flight in terror.

The casket was emitting strange, alarming vibrations.

'Rience? Can you hear me? What's been going on? Why haven't you responded for two days? Give me your report! What about the maid? You can't let her enter the tower! Do you hear? You can't let her enter the Tower of the Swallow . . . Rience! Answer, dammit! Rience!'

Rience, naturally, could not answer.

*

The embankment came to an end, the shore flattened out. *It's the end of the lake,* thought Bonhart, *I've done it. I've trapped the maid. Where is she? And where's that sodding tower?*

The curtain of fog suddenly ruptured and lifted. And then he saw her. She was right in front of him, sitting on her black mare. *She's a witch,* he thought, *she communicates with that beast. She sent it to the end of the lake and ordered it to wait for her.*

But that won't help her.

I have to kill her. The devil take Vilgefortz. I have to kill her. First I'll make her beg for her life . . . And then I'll kill her.

428

He yelled, pricked his horse with his spurs and launched into a breakneck gallop.

And suddenly realised he had lost. That she'd deceived him.

Not more than a furlong separated him from her – but over thin ice. She was on the other side of the lake. What's more, the crescent of open water now curved around the opposite way – the girl, riding along the 'bowstring', was much closer to the end of the lake than he was.

Bonhart swore, tugged on the reins and steered his horse onto the ice.

*

'Ride, Kelpie!'

Frozen earth shot from under the black mare's hooves.

Ciri clung to the horse's neck. The sight of Bonhart pursuing her filled her with dread . . . She was afraid of him. An invisible fist tightened on her stomach at the thought of facing him in combat.

No, she couldn't fight him. Not yet.

The Tower. Only the tower could save her. And the portal. As on Thanedd, when the sorcerer Vilgefortz was upon her, was already reaching for her . . .

The only hope was the Tower of the Swallow.

The fog lifted.

Ciri reined in her horse, suddenly feeling a dreadful heat. Unable to believe what she saw. What was in front of her.

*

Bonhart saw it too. And yelled triumphantly.

There was no tower at the end of the lake. There weren't even the ruins of a tower; there was nothing. Just a barely visible, barely outlined hillock, just a mound of boulders covered in frozen, leafless stalks.

'That's your tower!' he roared. 'That's your magical tower! That's your salvation! A heap of stones!'

The girl seemed not to hear or see. She urged the mare nearer the hillock, onto the stony mound. She raised both hands towards

429

the sky, as though cursing the heavens for what had befallen her.

'I told you that you were mine!' roared Bonhart, spurring on his bay. 'That I'll do what I want with you! That no one will stop me from doing it! Not people, not gods, not devils, nor demons! Or enchanted towers! You're mine, witcher girl!'

The bay's shoes jangled on the icy surface of the lake.

The fog suddenly swirled, boiled under the impact of a strong wind appearing as if from nowhere. The bay whinnied and danced, baring its teeth on the bit. Bonhart leaned back in the saddle, and tugged on the reins with all his might, because the horse was frantic, tossing its head, stamping and slipping on the ice.

In front of him – between him and the shore where Ciri was standing – a snowy-white unicorn was dancing on the ice, rearing up, as if on a heraldic shield.

'Don't try tricks like that on me!' roared the bounty hunter, fighting to get control of his horse. 'You won't frighten me with sorcery! I'll catch you, Ciri! I'll kill you this time, witcher girl! You're mine!'

The fog swirled again, and seethed, forming bizarre shapes. The shapes became clearer and clearer. They were horsemen. Nightmarish silhouettes of eerie horsemen.

Bonhart stared goggle-eyed.

Skeleton riders rode skeleton horses, dressed in rust-riddled armour and chainmail, ragged cloaks, dented and corroded helmets decorated with buffalo horns and the remains of ostrich and peacock plumes. The spectres' eyes shined with a bluish light from under their visors. Ragged pennants swished.

An armed man with a crown on his helmet and a necklace bumping against the rusty cuirass on his chest, galloped at the head of the demonic cavalcade.

Begone, rumbled a voice in Bonhart's head. *Begone, mortal. She is not yours. She is ours. Begone!* There was no denying Bonhart had one thing: courage. He did not take fright at the apparitions. He overcame his terror, and did not give in to panic.

But his horse turned out to be less resolute.

The bay reared, danced ballet-like on its hind legs, whinnied frantically, kicked and pranced. The ice broke with a horrifying crunching sound under the impact of its hooves, the sheets of ice stood up vertically and water gushed out. The horse squealed and struck the edge with its forehooves, fracturing it. Bonhart yanked his feet from the stirrups and jumped. Too late.

The water closed over his head. There was a drumming and a ringing as though in a belfry. His lungs were full to bursting.

He was lucky. His feet – kicking out in the water – struck something, probably his horse as it sank to the bottom. He pushed off, bursting from the water, spitting and gasping. He seized hold of the edge of the ice hole. Without yielding to panic, he drew a knife, drove it into the ice and hauled himself out. He lay, panting heavily, the water trickling from him and splashing down.

The lake, the ice, the snowbound hillsides, the black and frost-encrusted spruce forest – all of a sudden everything was flooded with an unnatural, pallid light.

Bonhart struggled to his knees with immense effort.

Above the horizon, the deep blue was lit by a crown of brightness, a luminous dome, from which fiery pillars and spirals suddenly rose and scintillating columns and vortices of light burst forth. Shimmering, flickering, rapidly-changing shapes, ribbons and curtains hung on the horizon.

Bonhart croaked. It was as though he had an iron garrotte around his throat.

A tower had risen up where a moment before had been only a barren hillock and a pile of stones. Majestic, soaring and slender, black, glassy and gleaming, as though carved from a single piece of basalt. Fire flickered in the few windows and the aurora borealis glowed in the serrated battlements.

He saw the girl, looking towards him from the saddle. He saw her bright eyes and the cheek slashed by the line of an ugly scar. He saw the girl spur her black mare and unhurriedly ride into the black gloom, under the arched stone entrance.

And disappear.

The aurora borealis exploded in dazzling swirls of fire.

When Bonhart regained his sight, the tower was gone. There was the snow-topped hillock, the pile of stones, the withered black stalks.

Kneeling on the ice, in the puddle of water trickling from him, the bounty hunter screamed savagely, horribly. On his knees, arms raised towards the sky, he screamed, howled, swore and railed against people, gods and demons.

The echo of his cries rolled over the spruce-forested hillsides, drifted over the frozen surface of Tarn Mira lake.

*

At first, the inside of the tower reminded her of Kaer Morhen – the same long, black corridor behind a colonnade, the same unending abyss in the perspective of columns or statues. It was beyond comprehension how that abyss could fit into the slender obelisk of the tower. But she knew, of course, that there was no point analysing it – not in the case of a tower that had risen up from nothingness, appearing where it had not been before. There could be anything in such a tower and one ought not to be surprised by anything.

She looked back. She didn't believe Bonhart had dared – or managed – to enter after her. But she wanted to make certain. The colonnade she had ridden into blazed with an unnatural brilliance.

Kelpie's hooves rang on the floor; something crunched under them. Bones. Skulls, shinbones, ribcages, thighbones, hipbones. She was riding through a gigantic ossuarium. *Kaer Morhen*, she thought, recalling. *The dead should be buried in the ground . . . How long ago that was . . . I still believed in something like that then . . . In the majesty of death, in respect for the dead . . . But death is simply death. And a dead person is just a cold corpse. It's not important where it's lying, where its bones decay.*

She rode into the gloom, under the colonnade, among the columns and statues. The darkness undulated like smoke. Her ears were filled with intrusive whispers, sighs, and soft incantations. Suddenly brightness flamed before her, as a gigantic door opened. One door opened after another. Doors. An infinite number of heavy doors opened before her without a murmur.

Kelpie went on, horseshoes resounding on the floor.

The geometry of the walls, arcades and columns surrounding her was suddenly disrupted; so confusingly that Ciri felt dizzy. She felt as though she were inside an impossible, multifaceted solid, some gigantic polyhedron.

The doors kept opening. But now they weren't delineating a

single direction. They were pointing to infinite directions and possibilities.

And Ciri began to see.

A black-haired woman leading an ashen-haired girl by the hand. The girl is afraid, afraid of the dark, fears the whispers growing in the gloom, is terrified by the ringing of horseshoes. The black-haired woman with a star sparkling with diamonds around her neck is also afraid. But does not let it show. She leads the girl on. Towards her destiny.

Kelpie walks on. More doors.

Iola the Second and Eurneid, in sheepskin coats, with their bundles, marching along a frozen, snowy road. The sky is deep blue.

More doors.

Iola the First kneeling before an altar. Beside her is Mother Nenneke. They are both looking at something, their faces contorted in a grimace of dread. What do they see? The past or the future? Truth or untruth?

Above Nenneke and Iola – hands. The hands of a woman with golden eyes held out in a gesture of blessing. In the woman's necklace – a diamond, shining like the morning star. On the woman's shoulder – a cat. Over her head – a falcon.

More doors.

Triss Merigold holds back her glorious chestnut hair, buffeted and tugged by gusts of wind. There is no escape from the wind, nothing can shelter from the wind.

Not here. Not on the brow of the hill.

A long, unending row of shadows encroaches on the hill. Forms. They are walking slowly. Some turn their faces towards her. Familiar faces. Vesemir. Eskel. Lambert. Coen. Yarpen Zigrin and Paulie Dahlberg. Fabio Sachs . . . Jarre . . . Tissaia de Vries.

Mistle . . .

Geralt?

More doors.

Yennefer, in chains, fastened to a dungeon wall dripping with water. Her hands are a single mass of clotted blood. Her black hair is tousled and dishevelled . . . Her mouth is cut and swollen . . . But her will to fight and resistance are undamped in her violet eyes.

'Mummy! Hold on! Don't give up! I'm coming to help you!'

More doors. Ciri turns her head away in distress. And embarrassment.

Geralt. And a green-eyed woman with black, close-cropped hair. Both naked. Engrossed by and consumed with each other. With giving each other sensual pleasure.

Ciri fights to overcome the adrenaline tightening her throat and spurs Kelpie on. Hooves clatter. Whispers pulsate in the darkness.

More doors.

Welcome, Ciri.

'Vysogota?'

I knew you would succeed, O courageous maiden. My brave Swallow. Did you emerge unharmed?

'I defeated them. On the ice. I had a surprise for them. Your daughter's skates . . .'

'I meant psychological harm.'

'I held back from vengeance . . . I didn't kill them all . . . I didn't kill Tawny Owl . . . Even though he hurt and disfigured me. I controlled myself.'

'I knew you'd prevail, Zireael. And that you'd enter the tower. Why, I've read about it. Because it has already been described . . . It has all been written about. Do you know what learning gives you? The ability to make use of sources.

'How's it possible that we're talking . . . O Vysogota . . . are you . . .'

Yes, Ciri. I'm dead. Oh, never mind! What I have learned is more important, what I have worked out . . . Now I know what became of the lost days, what happened in Korath desert, how you vanished from the sight of your pursuers . . .

'And how I entered here, entered this tower, right?'

The Elder Blood that flows in your veins gives you power over time. And over space. Over the dimensions and the spheres. You are now Master of the Worlds, Ciri. You have a mighty Power. Do not let criminals or rogues take it from you and use it to their own ends . . .

'I won't.'

Farewell, Ciri. Farewell, Swallow.

'Farewell, Old Raven.'

More doors. Brightness, dazzling brightness.

And the heady scent of flowers.

*

A mist lay on the lake, a haze as light as down, which the wind quickly blew away. The surface of the water was as smooth as a mirror, flowers shone white on green carpets of flat lily pads.

The banks drowned in leaves and flowers.

It was warm.

It was spring.

Ciri was not surprised. How could she be? After all, now everything was possible. November, ice, snow, frozen ground, the mound of stones on the hillock bristling with dried stalks – that was there. But here is here; here a soaring basalt tower crowned with serrated battlements, reflected in the green water of the lake, dotted with the white of waterlilies. Here it's May, for wild roses and bird cherry bloom in May, don't they?

Nearby, somebody was playing on a whistle or a pan flute; they were playing a jolly, lively tune.

On the lakeside, two snow-white horses were drinking, fore hooves in the water. Kelpie snorted and banged a hoof against a rock. Then the horses lifted their heads and nostrils, dripping water, and Ciri sighed.

Because they weren't horses, but unicorns.

Ciri was not surprised. She was sighing in awe, not in astonishment.

She could hear the tune more and more clearly. It was coming from behind the shrubs of bird cherry festooned with white blossom. Kelpie moved towards the sound by herself, without any urging. Ciri swallowed. The two unicorns, as still as statues, reflected in the surface of the water as smooth as a mirror, looked at her.

A fair-haired elf with a triangular face and huge, almond-shaped eyes was sitting on a round stone beyond the bird cherry shrub. He played on, nimbly running his lips over the pipes. Although he could see Ciri and Kelpie – although he was looking at them – he didn't stop playing.

The small flowers gave off a scent; Ciri had never before encountered bird cherry with such an intense fragrance. *No wonder*, she thought quite soberly. *Bird cherry blossom simply smells different in the world I've lived in until this moment.*

435

Because everything is different in that world.

The elf finished his tune with a long-drawn-out, high-pitched trill, took the instrument from his mouth and stood up.

'What took you so long?' he asked with a smile. 'What kept you?'

The story continues in . . .

LADY OF THE LAKE

A novel of the Witcher
Coming in Summer 2017

extras

orbit

meet the author

ANDRZEJ SAPKOWSKI was born in 1948 in Poland. He studied economy and business, but the success of his fantasy cycle about the sorcerer Geralt of Rivia turned him into a bestselling writer. He is now one of Poland's most famous and successful authors.

introducing

If you enjoyed
THE TOWER OF SWALLOWS,
look out for

BATTLEMAGE

by Stephen Aryan

*"I can command storms, summon fire, and unmake stone,"
Balfruss growled. "It's dangerous to meddle with things you
don't understand."*

Balfruss *is a Battlemage, sworn to fight and die for a country
that fears and despises his kind.*

Vargus *is a common soldier—while mages shoot lightning from
the walls of the city, he's down in the front lines getting blood on
his blade.*

Talandra *is a princess and spymaster, but the war may force her
to risk everything and make the greatest sacrifice of all.*

**Magic and mayhem collide in this explosive epic fantasy
from a major new talent.**

CHAPTER 1

Another light snow shower fell from the bleak grey sky. Winter should have been over, yet ice crunched underfoot and the mud was hard as stone. Frost clung to almost everything, and a thick, choking fog lay low on the ground. Only those desperate or greedy travelled in such conditions.

Two nights of sleeping outdoors had leached all the warmth from Vargus's bones. The tips of his fingers were numb and he couldn't feel his toes any more. He hoped they were still attached when he took off his boots; he'd seen it happen to others in the cold. Whole toes had come off and turned black without them noticing, rolling around like marbles in the bottom of their boots.

Vargus led his horse by the reins. It would be suicide for them both to ride in this fog.

Up ahead something orange flickered amid the grey and white. The promise of a fire gave Vargus a boost of energy and he stamped his feet harder than necessary. Although the fog muffled the sound, it would carry to the sentry up ahead on his left.

The bowman must have been sitting in the same position for hours as the grey blanket over his head was almost completely white.

As Vargus drew closer his horse snorted, picking up the

scent of other animals, men and cooking meat. Vargus pretended he hadn't seen the man and tried very hard not to stare at his longbow. After stringing the bow with one quick flex the sentry readied an arrow, but in order to loose it he would have to stand up.

"That's far enough."

That came from another sentry on Vargus's right who stepped out from between the skeletons of two shattered trees. He was a burly man dressed in dirty furs and mismatched leathers. Although chipped and worn the long sword he carried looked sharp.

"You a King's man?"

Vargus snorted. "No, not me."

"What do you want?"

He shrugged. "A spot by your fire is all I'm after."

Despite the fog the sound of their voices must have carried as two others came towards them from the camp. The newcomers were much like the others, desperate men with scarred faces and mean eyes.

"You got any coin?" asked one of the newcomers, a bald and bearded man in old-fashioned leather armour.

Vargus shook his head. "Not much, but I got this." Moving slowly he pulled two wine skins down from his saddle. "Shael rice wine."

The first sentry approached. Vargus could still feel the other pointing an arrow at his back. With almost military precision the man went through his saddlebags, but his eyes nervously flicked towards Vargus from time to time. A deserter then, afraid someone had been sent after him.

"What we got, Lin?" called Baldy.

"A bit of food. Some silver. Not much else," the sentry answered.

"Let him pass."

Lin didn't step back. "Are you sure, boss?"

The others were still on edge. They were right to be nervous
if they were who Vargus suspected. The boss came forward and
keenly looked Vargus up and down. He knew what the boss
was seeing. A man past fifty summers, battle scarred and grizzled with liver spots on the back of his big hands. A man with
plenty of grey mixed in with the black stubble on his face and
head.

"You going to give us any trouble with that?" asked Baldy,
pointing at the bastard sword jutting up from Vargus's right
shoulder.

"I don't want no trouble. Just a spot by the fire and I'll share
the wine."

"Good enough for me. I'm Korr. These are my boys."

"Vargus."

He gestured for Vargus to follow him and the others eased
hands away from weapons. "Cold enough for you?"

"Reminds me of a winter, must be twenty years ago, up
north. Can't remember where."

"Travelled much?"

Vargus grunted. "All over. Too much."

"So, where's home?" asked Korr. The questions were
asked casually, but Vargus had no doubt about it being an
interrogation.

"Right now, here."

They passed through a line of trees where seven horses were
tethered. Vargus tied his horse up with the others and walked
into camp. It was a good sheltered spot, surrounded by trees on
three sides and a hill with a wide cave mouth on the other. A
large roaring fire crackled in the middle of camp and two men
were busy cooking beside it. One was cutting up a hare and

dropping pieces into a bubbling pot, while the other prodded some blackened potatoes next to the blaze. All of the men were armed and they carried an assortment of weapons that looked well used.

As Vargus approached the fire a massive figure stood up and came around from the other side. It was over six and a half feet tall, dressed in a bear skin and wide as two normal men. The man's face was severely deformed with a protruding forehead, small brown eyes that were almost black, and a jutting bottom jaw with jagged teeth.

"Easy Rak," said Korr. The giant relaxed the grip on his sword and Vargus let out a sigh of relief. "He brought us something to drink."

Rak's mouth widened, revealing a whole row of crooked yellow teeth. It took Vargus a few seconds to realise the big man was smiling. Rak moved back to the far side of the fire and sat down again. Only then did Vargus move his hand away from the dagger on his belt.

He settled close to the fire next to Korr and for a time no one spoke, which suited him fine. He closed his eyes and soaked up some of the warmth, wiggling his toes inside his boots. The heat began to take the chill from his hands and his fingers started to tingle.

"Bit dangerous to be travelling alone," said Korr, trying to sound friendly.

"Suppose so. But I can take care of myself."

"Where you headed?"

Vargus took a moment before answering. "Somewhere I'll get paid and fed. Times are hard and I've only got what I'm carrying."

Since he'd mentioned his belongings he opened the first skin and took a short pull. The rice wine burned the back of his throat, leaving a pleasant aftertaste. After a few seconds the warmth in his stomach began to spread.

Korr took the offered wineskin but passed it to the next man, who snatched it from his hand.

"Rak. It's your turn on lookout," said Lin. The giant ignored him and watched as the wine moved around the fire. When it reached him he took a long gulp and then another before walking into the trees. The archer came back and another took his place as sentry. Two men standing watch for a group of seven in such extreme weather was unusual. They weren't just being careful, they were scared.

"You ever been in the King's army?" asked Lin.

Vargus met his gaze then looked elsewhere. "Maybe."

"I reckon that's why you travelled all over, dragged from place to place. One bloody battlefield after another. Home was just a tent and a fire. Different sky, different enemy."

"Sounds like you know the life. Are you a King's man?"

"Not any more," Lin said with a hint of bitterness.

It didn't take them long to drain the first wineskin so Vargus opened the second and passed it around the fire. Everyone took a drink again except Korr.

"Bad gut," he said when Vargus raised an eyebrow. "Even a drop would give me the shits."

"More for us," said one man with a gap-toothed grin.

When the stew was ready one of the men broke up the potatoes and added them to the pot. The first two portions went to the sentries and Vargus was served last. His bowl was smaller than the others, but he didn't complain. He saw a few chunks of potato and even one bit of meat. Apart from a couple of wild onions and garlic the stew was pretty bland, but it was hot and filling. The food, combined with the wine and the fire, helped warm him all the way through. An itchy tingling starting to creep back into his toes. It felt as if they were all still attached.

When they'd all finished mopping up the stew with some flat bread, and the second wineskin was empty, a comfortable silence settled on the camp. It seemed a shame to spoil it.

"So why're you out here?" asked Vargus.

"Just travelling. Looking for work, like you," said Korr.

"You heard any news from the villages around here?"

One of the men shifted as if getting comfortable, but Vargus saw his hand move to the hilt of his axe. Their fear was palpable.

Korr shook his head. "Not been in any villages. We keep to ourselves." The lie would have been obvious to a blind and deaf man.

"I heard about a group of bandits causing trouble in some of the villages around here. First it was just a bit of thieving and starting a couple of fights. Then it got worse when they saw a bit of gold." Vargus shook his head sadly. "Last week one of them lost control. Killed four men, including the innkeeper."

"I wouldn't know," said Korr. He was sweating now and it had nothing to do with the blaze. On the other side of the fire a snoozing man was elbowed awake and he sat up with a snort. The others were gripping their weapons with sweaty hands, waiting for the signal.

"One of them beat the innkeeper's wife half to death when she wouldn't give him the money."

"What's it matter to you?" someone asked.

Vargus shrugged. "Doesn't matter to me. But the woman has two children and they saw who done it. Told the village Elder all about it."

"We're far from the cities out here. Something like that isn't big enough to bring the King's men. They only come around these parts to collect taxes twice a year," said Lin with confidence.

"Then why do you all look like you're about to shit yourselves?" asked Vargus.

An uncomfortable silence settled around the camp, broken only by the sound of Vargus scratching his stubbly cheek.

"Is the King sending men after us?" asked Korr, forgoing any pretence of their involvement.

"It isn't the King you should worry about. I heard the village Elders banded together, decided to do something themselves. They hired the Gath."

"Oh shit."

"He ain't real! He's just a myth."

"Lord of Light shelter me," one of the men prayed. "Lady of Light protect me."

"Those are just stories," scoffed Lin. "My father told me about him when I was a boy, more than thirty years ago."

"Then you've got nothing to worry about," Vargus grinned.

But it was clear they were still scared, more than before now that he'd stirred things up. Their belief in the Gath was so strong he could almost taste it in the air. For a while he said nothing and each man was lost in his own thoughts. Fear of dying gripped them all, tight as iron shackles.

Silence covered the camp like a fresh layer of snow and he let it sit a while, soaking up the atmosphere, enjoying the calm before it was shattered.

One of the men reached for a wineskin then remembered they were empty.

"What do we do, Korr?" asked one of the men. The others

were scanning the trees as if they expected someone to rush into camp.

"Shut up, I'm thinking."

Before Korr came up with a plan Vargus stabbed him in the ribs. It took everyone a few seconds to realise what had happened. It was only when he pulled the dagger free with a shower of gore that they reacted.

Vargus stood up and drew the bastard sword from over his shoulder. The others tried to stand, but none of them could manage it. One man fell backwards, another tripped over his feet, landing on his face. Lin managed to make it upright, but then stumbled around as if drunk.

Vargus kicked Lin out of the way, switched to a two-handed grip and stabbed the first man on the ground through the back of the neck. He didn't have time to scream. The archer was trying to draw his short sword, but couldn't manage it. He looked up as Vargus approached and a dark patch spread across the front of his breeches. The edge of Vargus's sword opened the archer's throat and a quick stab put two feet of steel into Lin's gut. He fell back, squealing like a pig being slaughtered. Vargus knew his cries would bring the others.

The second cook was on his feet, but Vargus sliced off the man's right arm before he could throw his axe. Warm arterial blood jetted across Vargus's face. He grinned and wiped it away as the man fell back, howling in agony. Vargus let him thrash about for a while before putting his sword through the man's face, pinning his head to the ground. The snow around the corpse turned red, then it began to steam and melt.

The greasy-haired sentry stumbled into camp with a dagger held low. He swayed a few steps one way and then the other; the tamweed Vargus had added to the wine was taking effect.

Bypassing Vargus he tripped over his own feet and landed face first on the fire. The sentry was screaming and the muscles in his arms and legs lacked the strength to lift him up. His cries turned into a gurgle and then trailed off as the smoke turned greasy and black. Vargus heard fat bubbling in the blaze and the smell reminded him of roast pork.

As he anticipated, Rak wasn't as badly affected as the others. His bulk didn't make him immune to the tamweed in the wine, but the side effects would take longer to show. Vargus was just glad that Rak had drunk quite a lot before going on duty. The giant managed to walk into camp in a straight line, but his eyes were slightly unfocused. Down at one side he carried a six-foot pitted blade.

Instead of waiting for the big man to go on the offensive, Vargus charged. Raising his sword above his head he screamed a challenge, but dropped to his knees at the last second and swept it in a downward arc. The Seveldrom steel cut through the flesh of Rak's left thigh, but the big man stumbled back before Vargus could follow up. With a bellow of rage Rak lashed out, his massive boot catching Vargus on the hip. It spun him around, his sword went flying and he landed on hands and knees in the snow.

Vargus scrambled around on all fours until his fingers found the hilt of his sword. He could hear Rak's blade whistling through the air towards him and barely managed to roll away before it came down where his head had been. Back on his feet he needed both hands to deflect a lethal cut which jarred his arms. Before he could riposte something crunched into his face. Vargus stumbled back, spitting blood and swinging his sword wildly to keep Rak at bay.

The big man came on. With the others already dead and his senses impaired, part of him must have known he was on borrowed time. Vargus ducked and dodged, turned the long blade aside and made use of the space around him. When Rak overreached he lashed out quickly, scoring a deep gash along the giant's ribs, but it didn't slow him down. Vargus inflicted a dozen wounds before Rak finally noticed that the red stuff splashed on the snow belonged to him.

With a grunt of pain he fell back and stumbled to one knee. His laboured breathing was very loud in the still air. It seemed to be the only sound for miles in every direction.

"Korr was right," he said in a voice that was surprisingly soft. "He said you'd come for us."

Vargus nodded. Taking no chances he rushed forward. Rak tried to raise his sword but even his prodigious strength was finally at an end. His arm twitched and that was all. No mercy was asked for and none was given. Using both hands Vargus thrust the point of his sword deep into Rak's throat. He pulled it clear and stepped back as blood spurted from the gaping wound. The giant fell onto his face and was dead.

By the fire Lin was still alive, gasping and coughing up blood. The wound in his stomach was bad and likely to make him suffer for days before it eventually killed him. Just as Vargus intended.

He ignored Lin's pleas as he retrieved the gold and stolen goods from the cave. Hardly a fortune, but it was a lot of money to the villagers.

He tied the horses' reins together and even collected up all the weapons, bundling them together in an old blanket. The bodies he left to the scavengers.

It seemed a shame to waste the stew. Nevertheless Vargus stuck two fingers down his throat and vomited into the snow until his stomach was empty. Using fresh snow he cleaned off the bezoar and stored it in his saddlebags. It had turned slightly brown from absorbing the poison in the wine Vargus had drunk, but he didn't want to take any chances so made himself sick again. He filled his waterskin with melting snow and sipped it to ease his raw throat.

Vargus's bottom lip had finally stopped bleeding, but when he spat a lump of tooth landed on the snow in a clot of blood. He took a moment to check his teeth and found one of his upper canines was broken in half.

"Shit."

With both hands he scooped more snow onto the fire until it was extinguished. He left the blackened corpse of the man where it had fallen amid wet logs and soggy ash. A partly cooked meal for the carrion eaters.

"Kill me. Just kill me!" screamed Lin. "Why am I still alive?" He gasped and coughed up a wadge of blood onto the snow.

With nothing left to do in camp Vargus finally addressed him. "Because you're not just a killer, Torlin Ke Tarro. You were a King's man. You came home because you were sick of war. Nothing wrong with that, plenty of men turn a corner and go on in a different way. But you became what you used to hunt."

Vargus squatted down beside the dying man, holding him in place with his stare.

Lin's pain was momentarily forgotten. "How do you know me? Not even Korr knew my name is Tarro."

Vargus ignored the question. "You know the land around here, the villages and towns, and you know the law. You knew how to cause just enough trouble without it bringing the King's men. You killed and stole from your own people."

"They ain't my people."

Vargus smacked his hands together and stood. "Time for arguing is over, boy. Beg your ancestors for kindness on the Long Road to Nor."

"My ancestors? What road?"

Vargus spat into the snow with contempt. "Pray to your Lantern God and his fucking whore then, or whatever you say these days. The next person you speak to won't be on this side of the Veil."

Ignoring Lin's pleas he led the horses away from camp and didn't look back. Soon afterwards the chill crept back in his fingers but he wasn't too worried. The aches and pains from sleeping outdoors were already starting to recede. The fight had given him a small boost, although it wouldn't sustain him for very long. The legend of the Gath was dead, which meant time for a change. He'd been delaying the inevitable for too long.